Molly Sparkes

Molly Sparkes

Sheila Newberry

Copyright © 2001 by Sheila Newberry

First published in Great Britain in 2001 by
Inner Circle, an imprint of
Judy Piatkus (Publishers) Ltd of
5 Windmill Street, London W1T 2JA
email: info@piatkus.co.uk

The moral right of the author has been asserted

A catalogue record for this book is available from the British Library

ISBN 1 85018 120 9

Set in Times by
Action Publishing Technology Ltd, Gloucester

Printed and bound in Great Britain by
MPG Books Ltd, Bodmin, Cornwall

For Helen Pedersen of Brisbane, my lifelong friend, with grateful thanks for all her encouragement in my exploration of life in Australia around a century ago when her forebears journeyed there from Great Britain and Scandinavia. Also, for the 'spark' generated by Helen's youngest son Henning, a talented clown acrobat . . .

Bibliography

Circus – a World History by Rupert Croft-Cooke and Peter Cotes.
Published by Elek, 1976

Circus by Rodney N. Manser.
Published by Richford Enterprises Ltd, 1987

I Saw A Strange Land by Arthur Groom.
Published by Angus and Robertson, 1950

The Sunburnt Country edited by Gilbert Murray, O.M.
Published by Collins, 1953

I wish to also acknowledge the generous assistance with my research of the late Miss D Gamble, a stewardess with P & O between the wars.

Prologue

England – April 1906

Molly pointed out the blossom on the gnarled apple trees to the chuckling baby riding on her back. Pudgy arms clung tightly round her neck, and small jigging feet in soft kid boots urged her on through the old orchard. 'Look, Fay, *snow in April . . .*'

She set the baby down, and Fay, who at eleven months was still uncertain on her feet, swayed and clutched at her new friend's long skirt. Then Molly unbuckled her belt, lifted Fay up and settled her on her lap on the old plank swing. The belt secured them together at the waist: Molly covered Fay's clinging hands with her own, and began the momentum.

The jerking of the bough from which the ropes were suspended sent petals floating down, softly brushing their upturned faces. *'Snow!'* Fay shouted in excitement. 'Snow!' Molly echoed. What fun she had had out here with the youngest convent girls making tracks in the real stuff, she thought, not so long ago. But there was the gentle warmth of spring in the air today, the sweet scent of blossom, wild flowers in the long grass. This was always an enchanted place for children to explore and play in, the very heart of the Weald of Kent.

Molly's eyes were suddenly bright with tears at the realisation that she would shortly be leaving this place where

1

she had always felt secure and happy. Don't be silly, she reproved herself. Haven't you been looking forward to finding a job – being independent – travelling the world and seeing the sights, as a governess perhaps or a lady's companion? It was just, she thought, that this opportunity had come completely out of the blue . . .

Although tact was hardly Molly's strong point, she had obediently gone out with Fay this afternoon, at Sister Margaret Mary's suggestion, soon after her prospective employer's arrival with her late daughter's child. They were having a serious discussion, she guessed, about her suitability for caring for Fay on a long sea voyage. Molly knew that much, no more, but it was all very exciting. She airily dismissed the thought that such a lowly employee was rarely given time off for sightseeing.

At almost eighteen years old Molly was a determined girl even though she was naive in the ways of the world – too impulsive, as she had been throughout her sheltered childhood. How the nuns sighed over her exuberance at times! Her dramatic utterances would cause the younger girls to squeal, but in delight, not terror. They particularly enjoyed: *Here comes the ghost of Benjamin Barrett – stabbed in the back with a rusty carrot!* However, most of them had a soft spot for young Molly Sparkes because she was invariably cheerful. 'Sparkle, that should have been her name,' remarked Sister Margaret Mary with a wry smile. 'Comes of having an actress for a mother, I suppose, even though Molly hardly knew her. Blood will out.'

Now, Molly steadied the swing and said: 'That's enough for this afternoon, Fay, or you might be sick on your best dress – and somehow I don't think your granny would approve of *that*.' Mrs Nagel appeared rather forbidding, she thought. She unfastened the belt, hoisted the protesting Fay in her arms and scrambled to her feet.

'Oh, *don't* you?' a cool voice observed, from behind them.

Startled, Molly swung round. A tall woman stood there.

2

She was in her late-forties, still in mourning clothes, with tiny lozenge-shaped jet beads gleaming on the pin-tucked bodice of her black watered silk dress. She had piercing blue eyes under frowning brows, a creamy complexion, and thick, dark hair swept up into an elaborate arrangement of curls.

'Mrs Nagel.' Molly bit her lip. 'I'm sorry, I didn't mean to be rude—'

Alexandra Nagel accepted her apology with a brief nod, regarding Molly frankly in her turn. The scrutiny embarrassed her, made her aware of her lack of height which she often sighed over for she must have finished growing, she supposed. Besides a slight figure she had a childish snub nose which made her look younger than she was, hazel eyes which she liked to imagine were green, and long, straight, fine brown hair which in sunlight glinted red. The nuns had considered curling rags an indulgence and Molly had been only too glad to escape their discomfort. She was aware that her fringe needed trimming, that she should have ironed her white muslin blouse instead of shaking it out hopefully, and that Fay was burrowing her face against her neck and demanding another swing.

'The child has taken to you, that's obvious,' Mrs Nagel stated, looking as if she could not imagine why this should be. 'We have clearly made the right decision. I have already been in touch with your father in India through my son-in-law who is in his regiment. I understand that Colonel Sparkes has no objections to your working for me. He has recently remarried, I believe, but will not be returning to this country for some time yet. And, of course, you were due to leave school this summer anyway. Come back to the house with me now, I should like to make the necessary arrangements today, and no doubt you must return to your studies.'

They sat in the austere dining room, Mrs Nagel, Sister Margaret Mary and Molly, while Fay crawled energetically away to hide under the big table – expecting someone to cry '*Boo!*' Molly thought, but she restrained herself and listened to Mrs Nagel.

'For some time I have considered going away to have a complete break for a year or so from my business in London. I am not going to prevaricate, Molly: my daughter and I were estranged when she tragically died within a month of Fay's birth. I considered her too young to marry at just twenty-one – I had married in haste myself and it ended unhappily. I did not go to Lucy's wedding, have not yet even met her husband, and Fay was cared for by foster parents until I decided that a reconciliation with her father was in the child's best interests. He knows how much I regret the past ... He is a generous and forgiving chap and has agreed that, for now, Fay should be with me, and that I may take her abroad on an extended holiday. I shall devote myself to her during this time. I owe it to my daughter.

'A cousin visited me recently and mentioned that her brother Frank in Australia was urging her to join him, but that she felt apprehensive about travelling all that way on her own. On impulse, I wrote to Frank and suggested that we might accompany her. The upshot is that we are welcome to stay for a time on his sheep farm in a place called Bodenflower, but naturally this could not be a permanent arrangement. I would then look for a place to rent, in a more civilised part of the country.

'Once we have arrived in New South Wales I would expect to engage a local nursemaid. In return for your caring for the baby while we are aboard ship, I would like you to regard yourself as more of a travelling companion to us thereafter. I am prepared to pay all your expenses and to make you an allowance. Well, what d'you say?'

Even while she was aware that this was a generous offer indeed, and that, in an unexpected way, her dreams of travelling were about to come true, Molly thought: I do hope we won't clash – she's very formidable! And I can't help speaking out, at times ...

4

'I say, yes – thank you!' She was aware that Sister Margaret Mary was smiling approvingly. 'If it's only for a year,' Molly added firmly. 'When would we leave?'

'In June. We should arrive in Australia in the cooler weather, giving us time to adjust to the change in the climate.'

'*Boo!*' Fay declaimed plaintively. Molly scooped her up and hugged her unselfconsciously. 'We've got a lot in common, you and me, Fay – we're *both* motherless girls, you see . . . Would you like me to take her out in the garden again and amuse her, Mrs Nagel?' she asked.

After a long pause, Mrs Nagel said coolly: 'Better not. We really must go, we have a train to catch.' However, she made no attempt to take the child from Molly's arms.

Fay will need me, Molly thought. She'll need cuddling and loving because it may take quite a while for her to win her grandmother over.

Part One

Chapter One

To Australia

They left Tilbury on a dazzling morning in June, having embarked the previous afternoon. Mrs Nagel, who had been in business importing and selling leather goods following the breakup of her marriage, had negotiated shrewdly with the shipping company for a large shared cabin.

Noting the six narrow bunks, Molly commented breezily: 'It's fortunate there are only four of us – Fay will take up most of the space with her paraphernalia!'

The baby's collapsible canvas travelling cot was secured to Molly's lower bunk for safety. 'Now, we can't have the little lass bowling back and forth when the ship starts rolling,' remarked the rotund, cheerful purser, who would be responsible for their comfort and well-being during the six-week-long journey. 'Sorry, ma'am,' he added, catching a glimpse of a flaring match as Mrs Nagel took a cigarette from a shagreen box, 'not allowed in the cabins. Fire risk, you know. However smoking is allowed in the drawing room, naturally, ma'am. The gentlemen usually retire to the smoking room after dinner.'

'You suggest I join them, then?' she queried sharply, and closed the box with a snap.

The purser thought it wise to assume that ma'am was joking. He changed the subject swiftly. 'The stewardess will be only too happy to see to the baby's bottles for you.

9

She will contact you shortly,' he told Molly, swiftly concealing his surprise at her saucy wink.

She had privately nicknamed their travelling companion, Miss Elfie Wills, 'Will o' the Wisp', for straying strands of her own mousy hair gave away the fact that she wore an auburn hairpiece. Miss Wills, she noted with a grin, was soon ensconced on the bunk furthest from the baby. She had obviously had little to do with children and obviously had no intention of being called upon to act as substitute nurse. Her precious possessions were placed in an orderly fashion on the upper bunk, including religious books and a bulging knitting reticule. Molly had already glimpsed a hank of harsh puce wool. She hoped it was not to be knitted up into a garment for Fay. Concealed under Elfie's pillow, closer to hand, in case the ship sank in a hurry, was her family bible, potent smelling salts, a leather wallet containing documents and photographs, and a discreet small bottle of brandy which she told the others was for warding off sea-sickness. Molly saw her taking a nip or two even before the first throbbing of the ship's engines. Mind you, she had a treasure or two secreted under her own pillow.

Elfie had already told the kindly purser about her brother who, two years earlier, had taken a free passage to New South Wales, having lodged the required deposit with the State Government as a guarantee that he would settle. He had built a homestead fit for a wife, but (or so her captive audience deduced) believing family to be cheaper, had sent for his unmarried sister to act as his housekeeper. His frugality was confirmed when Mrs Nagel interrupted this saga with the dry comment that they, of course, would be *paying* guests.

Alexandra Nagel unclasped her heavy dressing case and seated herself by the handbasin and mirror to apply powder to her nose, which was shining following all the recent exertion, and to tidy her luxuriant hair. She regarded her pale face critically. More lines, she saw to her chagrin, had recently been etched around her mouth and under her eyes. Yet the black dress suited her colouring, she thought vainly. She had actually favoured black for many years, believing it gave her the appearance and status of a wealthy widow rather than a divorcee.

She tested the pin of the oval brooch, set around with milky pearls like tears, to ensure that Fay's tugging fingers had not disturbed the safety catch. She had carried her aboard earlier while Molly managed their hand baggage. She glanced down at the curl of hair behind the glass facing of the brooch. Did one ever fully recover from the devastating loss of a child? she wondered, biting at her lower lip to stem the rush of forbidden tears – especially when mother and daughter had been at odds with one another . . . Why had she never been able to tell Lucy that she loved her? Now, it was too late.

Fay rocked impatiently in her cot, she hated being restrained. It was a nuisance, Alexandra thought, that although she was now walking, she was not proficient enough to be let loose in the cabin. She had forgotten how demanding children of this age were. Yes, it was a good thing Molly was with them, even though she anticipated that the girl would try her patience at times . . . She, like Lucy, was not averse to answering back.

Molly intercepted her look, interpreted her sigh. 'You won't be able to keep Fay down for long,' she murmured.

Alexandra was forced to admit to herself that flighty young Molly was surprisingly competent with the baby. Sister Margaret Mary had been right: Molly certainly had a rapport with young children. The small fry at the convent would miss her.

'I think it would be – easier,' Alexandra said now to Molly, 'if you were to address us by our first names. Perhaps you would care to call me Alexa, as Elfie does. D'you agree, Elfie?'

There was a faint moan from her bunk where she lay limply, with a guest towel soaked in eau de cologne pressed firmly to her closed eyes.

11

Elfie, Molly mused, obviously did not care for her. She didn't realise it was because she was too vibrant, too outspoken, too young – too *much* . . .

'We haven't even steamed through the Channel yet, Elfie,' Molly informed her cheerfully. 'I think she agrees to the informal touch, Alexa. I certainly do!'

'Oh, I guessed you would,' her employer returned, and actually smiled at herself in the mirror.

Sea sickness took its toll of Molly, Alexa and Elfie between Gibraltar and Naples. After dinner, which she had been determined to attend even though she could only manage to eat a bread roll and had to wave away the lobster salad, Molly was obliged to lean over the rail while she heaved her heart out. She wasn't up to deck games in the day, or dancing at night, but she carried out her duties determinedly.

Elfie was confined to bed, groaning each time the ship lurched and rolled, sending the loathsome receptacles hurtling back and forth across the cabin boards, invariably spilling some of the contents. Then Alexa would summon help: an elderly woman would arrive with a clanking bucket and mop, and then there was a strong odour of carbolic everywhere which was also intolerable . . .

When the cleaner departed, with a cheerful 'See you soon, ladies!' Alexa, whey-faced, downed a large tooth glass brimming with brandy and sprinkled eau de cologne all over her pillow, before lying down and attempting to sleep.

Fortunately, Fay seemed unaffected, sleeping soundly each night despite the turbulence. Molly, naturally, had to keep going, for her sake.

When they reached Naples, Molly and Alexa, on wobbly legs, went on deck to marvel at the views. They were glad to leave Elfie, still languishing on her sickbed, wafting the smelling salts under her quivering nostrils, who had reluctantly agreed to keep an eye on Fay while she had her after-lunch nap.

Alexa, clutching her well-thumbed guide book, informed Molly that nowadays all large sea-going vessels used the modern landing stage opposite Via Duomo. 'Naples was completely transformed when the tumbledown, over-crowded buildings were razed some years ago in an effort to combat cholera: it's no longer so picturesque, those narrow alleys gone forever,' she added with regret. 'I explored them all when my parents brought me here on a cruise. I was about your age, Molly.'

'It's a shame we can't go ashore, and that we're only here for the coaling,' she said.

'At least we're getting a glimpse,' Alexa replied. They could hear the voluble, excited chattering of the Italian dock workers, far below their lofty platform. 'It's only two months since Vesuvius erupted, they can't take any risks, Molly.'

'It's strange, isn't it, that the volcano blew up just twelve days before that terrible earthquake in San Francisco?'

'You rarely get a single disaster.'

'I read all about it in the paper – apparently there was a glowing, searing circle around the volcano which completely cut off many villages and towns.' Molly could picture it vividly. 'My parents spent their honeymoon in Naples. It must then have been more as you remember it.'

'You don't often mention your father,' Alexa observed.

'I wrote to him every month while I was at the convent, but I suppose you could say I hardly know him. He only comes home on leave every two years or so, and then we stay in a hotel together, usually in London, so we can go to the theatre, but sometimes in Bath – he has relatives there. He sold the family home after my mother died, you see.'

'D'you remember her at all?'

'Just. I think I was three when she died. It was peritonitis, I believe. I don't know if I really remember this, or whether I was told it, but on summer evenings my mother

13

would wind up the gramophone, open the french doors and dance out into the garden with me in her arms ... I can't *imagine* how my father ever married her – he's so stiff and – and military – and she was an actress. I wonder how they met?'

'You have her picture, don't you? Forgive me, but I have seen you looking at it, at nights.'

'She'll never grow old, Alexa – in her photograph she's always young and beautiful. Florence Almond, that was her name.'

The Suez Canal (Molly wrote in her diary) is chock-a-block with boats. The banks are swarming with traders, with laden donkeys – ribs all showing, poor things. They all scream at each other, and us, incessantly it seems ... Elfie flatly refuses to show her face on deck until we are safely through!

So much perspiring, makes us feel like expiring – I didn't know it could be so hot – the sun is relentless. Have to make sure Fay drinks plenty. None of us feels like eating much, but at least we've stopped being sick ...

Finally, *Australia!* They'd arrived in Melbourne – not journey's end, it was true – for a few days' break before rejoining the ship to sail on to Sydney.

'Shades of dear old England!' Molly exclaimed as they journeyed by cab to their modest hotel, warmly recommended by the purser. 'All this could have been transported here and set in place.' The streets of Victorian-style houses, with primly railed gardens, did indeed seem strangely familiar, resembling the outskirts of any town or city in Great Britain. And it was raining; not the dispiriting, lashing rain of winter at home, but a solid downpour which left the roads well and truly wet, and then abruptly ceased. Melbourne was a solid town, like that solid citizen of Great Britain it had been named for.

'Look – the cathedral!' Alexa said. They craned their necks to glimpse its grey bulk through the steamy cab windows. But they were not in the mood for sightseeing in such weather.

They were welcomed by their landlady, Mrs Serena Kelly, who asked eagerly: 'And how is London? It's thirty years since I sang and danced in the chorus at the Alhambra . . . I was born in Islington, y'know, not far from The Angel. My parents and grandparents trod the boards before us: my sisters, my brother and me. Music halls – end of the pier – that was us. We travelled around!

'I married dear Paddy Kelly when I was twenty. He was one for travelling even further afield, so he brought me here. Six children we have, all doing well, but only one in the business, you could say. My youngest, Rory, is with the circus . . . Their father died four years ago. Left me enough to invest in this place and, oh, I do love to have folk from the old country come to stay . . .'

She led the way upstairs. 'Two nice rooms I've made ready. Wally never fails to send me guests when his ship docks – folk he's got to like while he's been at sea.' She was a heavy woman but walked lightly, elegantly, like the dancer she once was. She opened the doors and the gemstones in her many rings flashed. She saw Molly's admiring gaze. 'My Sam mines the gems in a small way. He sends me a ring every birthday – each one unique, he says. This is my favourite, this opal, see . . . In here for you, Miss Wills.'

Molly thought: *Rings on her fingers, bells on her toes. I wonder if my mother was larger than life like Mrs Kelly? If so, however did my father unbend enough to marry her? Maybe I remind him too much of her: maybe that's why he seems relieved when it's time for us to part . . .*

'Thank goodness Elfie has her own room! I've had just about as much as I can stand, of watching her sniffing those salts until she has a paroxysm, or licking her finger to turn

15

the pages of her nightly dose of scripture,' Alexa remarked tartly as Molly laid a drowsy Fay in the centre of their double bed. 'I didn't reckon on us all sharing – don't anticipate much sleep,' she sighed.

The furniture was lighter than the heavy mahogany Molly was used to in England, of polished pine with brass handles. The chair seats were of woven cane, an Indian rug barely covered the stained floor boards, and the bedclothes were, naturally, lightweight for despite the rain it certainly wasn't cold. Molly investigated the roll-up window blind. 'This is nice, eh, Alexa?'

She was still complaining about Elfie. 'I'm not sure if I'll be able to tolerate her once we arrive at the farm. They say you never know a person until you live with them, don't they? Perhaps we'll move on quickly, maybe to Queensland. I have an old schoolfriend there with whom I have always kept in touch. Let's give it a month or so . . .

'As you will have gathered by now, Molly, I'm not a woman given to over-sentimentality. I'm sure we will clash now and again over this next year because it's obvious you are strong-willed, but then so am I.' She paused, cleared her throat. 'Nevertheless I'm glad you are with me just now. It's been difficult, you see since . . .'

She was touched by Molly's swift rejoinder. 'And I'm glad to be here, too, Alexa.'

As Molly tided her hair, Fay stirred, sat up and rubbed her eyes. 'Boo!' Molly cried, scooping her up and kissing her. 'Are you wondering where on earth you are, darling? Let's all go down for that cup of tea which our friendly Mrs Kelly is even now brewing, eh?'

Serena's pastry was short and crumbly, the meat tender, the gravy rich and dark brown. They all ate well, even Elfie, who was obviously greatly relieved to be on terra firma once more. Fay bounced about on a little chair with curved wooden arms, piled high with cushions, and smiled at nice Mrs Kelly, who sat down to eat with them. 'No objection,

16

my dears? Just us ladies here, tonight. What a lovely child, so good.'

'Not always,' Molly said ruefully, 'but *you* seem to know the secret of sitting her down and expecting her to clean her plate!'

'Practice, Molly – years of practice! You don't get time for worrying who'll eat this and who won't when you've six of 'em around the table, you see. You put good food before them and you expect it to vanish. Simple!'

'Did you . . . did you ever hear of an actress named Florence Almond?' Molly wondered, hoping that Alexa wouldn't think she was being too familiar with their landlady.

Serena was dishing out ginger steamed pudding. 'About my age, is she? Forty and a bit?'

'I suppose she would be – if she'd lived. She was my mother. I don't really know much about her. I don't imagine she was famous or anything, or you'd have recognised the name, wouldn't you?'

'Sorry, dear, but I can't say I do. She probably moved in higher circles than us. I reckon you're like her, though – just a feeling I got. Ever thought of going on stage yourself?'

Molly didn't dare look at Alexa or Elfie as she said simply: '*Oh, yes!*'

Chapter Two

Flocks of sea birds scolded and circled endlessly overhead as they travelled through cobalt blue water in the wake of the famous Captain Cook into Sydney harbour.

From Sydney they travelled by train, a jolting, thoroughly uncomfortable journey. A delay was caused at one point by a 'scale a rattler', a young man who had jumped on – and then off – the train, hotly pursued by the guard and some irate male passengers. As they crowded to the carriage window to watch the chase they were excited to glimpse another train lurching in the distance. 'Take your thumb out and look!' Molly, holding a sleepy Fay against her shoulder, turned her so that she was facing in the right direction. 'A *camel* train!'

After a long, enervating day they finally descended on decidedly wobbly legs to wait at a station halt which looked, as Molly remarked to her silent, dispirited companions, 'like the end of the world'. They were dusty, crumpled, hungry, and above all thirsty. Only Fay, who had finally ceased whimpering barely half an hour since, was able to give way to the deep sleep of sheer exhaustion in her by now somewhat battered pushchair.

Just as they were giving up hope of ever being met, Elfie's brother Frank arrived, greeted them laconically, and they were hoisted aboard his cart. Their luggage was roughly thrown on to a following cart, driven by Frank's stockman.

They drank great gulps of cold tea from the corked bottles he had brought: fell upon the uncouth sandwiches he had made from tough dry bread filled with thick slices of succulent lamb, lavishly spread with pickle. They were scarcely aware of the discomfort as they stretched their legs out at last and rested their backs against the unyielding sides of their conveyance.

The rough road soon gave way to an iron-hard track along which they bowled in hair-raising fashion, seemingly just missing the gum trees but inhaling their overpowering smell. They were showered with muddy water as the horses blundered through a shallow creek.

Molly was dozing uneasily when they arrived at the homestead paddock, startling a brumby or wild horse which skittered away with flaring nostrils and a flash of the whites of its eyes in the gathering gloom.

They passed flocks of sheep. 'If you hear the howling of a dingo, you'll know the devils are busy slashing the lambs' bellies,' Frank informed them gloomily. 'Don't start yelling, if you hear shooting, that'll be the lookout doing his job ...'

Molly was perking up. 'Dingoes are nocturnal, like foxes at home, aren't they, Frank?' she asked curiously.

'That's right, Moll. Nights can be noisy hereabouts,' he said.

Elfie sniffed at her salts until the tears rolled down her cheeks. Life out here had definitely coarsened her brother!

The welcoming lights of the homestead heartened them all, and the interior was not nearly as bad as they had imagined. There were reasonably comfortable beds, serviceable pieces of furniture, even a bath-house, Molly was pleased to see, thinking of the grubby little girl they had brought so far from home – and blessed hot water boiled for their use by a sweetly smiling Aboriginal girl with unexpected tow-coloured hair.

Cleansed, but aching all over, Molly crawled thankfully at last into the single iron bedstead she was to share with

Fay, past caring about the coarse linen and lumpy pillows. Alexa had a similar bed to herself, at a distance across the spacious room. Elfie had been shown to her own permanent quarters on the other side of the house. Maybe they wouldn't have to see as much of her, Molly hoped – then felt guilty.

She didn't always say her prayers but she did that night, hoping the Almighty would excuse her not going down on her knees. She gave the pillow a thump and lay down. 'Thank you, dear God, for bringing us safely to our journey's end . . .' she murmured drowsily. 'Amen.' Then she, Alexa and Fay slept for many hours.

Molly and Alexa took the new life in their stride, literally. Molly had ridden an old donkey and occasionally driven it, too, while she was at school; Alexa had not been in the saddle since she was in her teens. When Molly said: 'I always rode astride – usually bareback when the Sisters weren't looking – what else can you do on a donkey?' Alexa replied: 'I've never ridden side-saddle either . . .'

Molly was surprised to learn that her employer had been brought up in the country. 'We were poor but honest, as they say – but I always wanted more from life. My father and his brother, Elfie and Frank's father, took over the family farm from our grandfather. Gradually, they sold off the land and Frank came out here to make a fresh start. I had the same idea when I left my husband – all I wanted for Lucy was for her to be an independent young woman.' She looked very stern as she said that.

They were waiting by the stables for the stockman to saddle a horse, at Alexa's behest. Behind them was the timber-built homestead, raised on piles, with a long ver-andah all round, where Molly hoped to sleep out in the heat to come, and windows blank with blinds. The single-storey house was flanked by outbuildings, one of which was used by the resident workers as a bunkhouse. All the buildings had corrugated-iron roofs, and the timber used in their construction was of varying widths, like the original trees. The young girl who had seen to their bath tubs that first evening pegged Fay's nappies on a line strung between two trees, and smiled widely as she caught Molly's friendly glance. She wore what looked like a faded school dress, once checked in blue and white, with a ragged sailor collar, and nothing on her feet. Toby was her name, and somehow it didn't sound incongruous. She presumably went home each night, but so far they had not seen her come or go. 'She's here right now, but if the fancy takes her she might not be tomorrow,' Frank grunted laconically at breakfast-time when Elfie said how helpful and willing the girl was, though it was going to take time to understand her pidgin English.

Now, Alexa sat on a bony, knobby-kneed mare and announced her intention of circling the boundary with the stockman, as soon as he said the word. Molly grinned, because the horse hardly looked capable of circling the paddock, but she admired Alexa's spirit. Elfie, coming out to shake her mop, because she had been horrified at all the cobwebs festooning the rafters, overheard this and looked shocked. 'Oh, Alexa, at your age, do you think you ought to?'

'Your turn will come, Molly. Soon, I hope,' Alexa said, 'when we find that competent nursemaid for Fay. But meanwhile . . .'

'Meanwhile,' Molly supplied, 'I don't mind a bit carrying on as before . . .' But secretly she wished that she could be the first one to ride out with Henning Rasmussen, the Danish stockman. 'Call me Henny,' he'd offered shyly when they'd introduced themselves earlier. He was lean and tanned with a shock of sun-bleached hair and a shy smile which revealed uneven but good, white teeth – unlike Frank, who had a mouthful of gaps and whose breath was offensively sour. Henny's eyes, narrowed against the bright light as he gazed into the distance, were surprisingly blue. Sydney blue, Molly fancied. He didn't speak unless he was

21

directly addressed, but she liked his accent and deep voice. She didn't know anything about him, of course, and no doubt, she thought wryly, he wouldn't be the slightest bit interested in her, but ... Molly was growing up fast.

That evening, while they were waiting for supper to be served up, Alexa repeated to Frank her intention of riding regularly. 'You'll want some breeches then, you can't ride in that silly skirt,' he stated baldly. He was obviously wondering just what he had taken on. Elfie was already proving tiresome with her 'vapours' and was not the competent housekeeper he remembered: he didn't realise that she had been content with things as they had always been, back at home, and the differences here were difficult for her to grasp. The visiting relatives, too, wished to be involved in areas where he would much rather not have been bothered. He was certainly not going to offer the use of his own powerful rangy horse to Alexa or Molly. He rummaged in a cupboard and extracted a dog-eared catalogue, minus its cover.

'Here, you can order from this. You won't find a lot in the local stores, though the men get their stuff there.'

Molly and Alexa pored over the pages of *Lassetter's, The Universal Providers*. The clothes, on the whole, were simpler but less modern than the fashions back home. They were cheaper too.

'Two shillings!' Molly exclaimed, pointing out an illustration. The model wore a wide-brimmed chip hat, trimmed with full-blown roses. 'Imagine wearing that here! Just right for a garden party in England. No, it's topees for us from now on, eh?'

'Ah, this is what I want. Look, Molly, "riding breeches to order",' Alexa said, pleased.

'Um, Alexa – they're for *men*!'

She ignored this. 'How ridiculous! They actually charge extra for knee strappings ... and buckskin ones are, wait for it, ten-and-six more!' Having worked hard for her money, she was careful with it, though she could be

22

surprisingly generous as Molly already knew. She had a trunkful of pretty dresses bought for her in London by Alexa: an older woman's choice, it was true, but in light, airy materials suitable for a warmer clime. Molly had no intention of ever wearing the bust bodices and firm corsets also provided. What was the point, she asked herself, when she was so lacking in voluptuous curves? And anyway, garters held up her stockings perfectly well.

'I do like the striped shirt and the bush hat, though,' Molly said. 'And what about these boots – though I imagine they'd be the very devil to get on!'

'Got a self-measurement form if you're set on them,' Frank observed, easing his feet out of his own cracked boots and revealing great potatoes in the toes of his felted socks. He added, rubbing his feet, which made his guests turn their faces away, 'You can send orders post-free.'

'I'm sure Elfie's got a tape-measure in that bag of hers. We'll measure each other tonight – in the bedroom.' Alexa had noted Frank's sly glances at young Molly. 'Anything else you fancy?' she asked the girl. 'A camera, perhaps, to record life in this – place?'

'Would I? Please, Alexa!' Molly agreed enthusiastically.

It would soon be supper time. She didn't feel so enthusiastic about the prospect of eating the first meal cooked by Elfie, on the help's evening off, she thought.

'You've come at a good time,' Frank informed them. 'The old-timers say there was a plague of darned rabbits in the eighties. Then there was a drought round about seven years ago which was disastrous for the sheep – Australia is only now recovering from that. Still, the wool market revived last season,' he added. 'Over a million bales were recorded in the auction sheds.' He didn't enlarge on this, not wanting them to know that he had doubled his initial investment already. He was a cautious chap, Frank, always on the lookout for trouble or setbacks. Molly had already guessed that he and Elfie were alike in that respect.

'I'd better go and make sure that Fay is asleep,' she

23

said, rising. 'And if I'm likely to be able to eat my food in peace ...'

Fay slumbered peacefully, right in the middle of their bed, under the net canopy which kept the flies at bay. Molly took up her diary and licked the pencil, thoughtfully. Nothing much exciting had happened today, unless you counted Henny awkwardly patting her back – well, swatting a creepy-crawly which was about to insinuate itself under her collar ... She wrote in capital letters: OLD FRANK IS A PROPHET OF GLOOM & DOOM!

Gloomy Frank drove them on their first visit to the indispensable stores at the settlement in Bodenflower. 'You can find your own way in future – think yourselves lucky it don't take us more'n fifteen minutes to get here. That you haven't landed up on one of them huge spreads in the outback hundreds of miles from anywhere ...'

It was nice, Molly thought, to meet up with other friendly females, mostly Scots and Irish, who really seemed to thrive out here, but there were a few Europeans, too. The women wore sensible holland dresses, with no concessions to fashion; plain, wide-brimmed hats; and what looked like men's boots. Their hair was combed back and either plaited round the head or fastened in a tight knot at the nape of the neck. They didn't buy by the pound but by the sack or drum, and meanwhile they chattered happily, obviously enjoying the company. There was an all-too-pervasive smell of oil, sawdust underfoot, the long counters were scarred and the heavy brass scales looked to be antique.

'I'm paying,' Alexa said through her teeth when Frank displayed anxiety as the goods were piled up high. 'I'm not going to be deprived of best butter and cheese.'

He obviously considered beer and tobacco to be of higher priority.

'Here you are, Miss Sparkes,' said the soft-voiced Scotswoman who presided over the post-office counter. 'Some letters for you – one from Melbourne, one from abroad and one from back home. There'll be cold weather on the way there, I guess. How d'you think you'll do in the heat when it's summer here? You'll need to wear long sleeves and boots still, because of all those stinging insets and snakes.'

'I haven't seen a single snake yet, thank goodness,' Molly told her, with a shiver. She tucked the letters in her bag to read later. The one from Melbourne puzzled her; the handwriting on the other letters was familiar, both sent to await their arrival: one from her father and the other from dear Sister Margaret Mary.

Near the store was the Lutheran mission and school. Their friendly postmistress invited them to attend a service there the following Sunday. 'It's a regular meeting place, you'll make friends there, I'm sure. Your lubra, Toby, came from the mission. Sunny, loveable girls they all are, but don't be surprised if she goes walking now and then.'

'Oh, we've already been warned of that,' Molly said.

'It's hard to believe sometimes,' Mrs Mac continued, blithely ignoring the queue for mail and stamps, 'that not so long ago, families like hers lived on kangaroo, wild cat and ant's eggs. They used water bags made from 'roo skin and made fire by rubbing two sticks . . .'

'Save the history lesson, Missis, willyer?' a gruff voice interrupted from behind Molly.

'See you Sunday, then,' Mrs Mac said, unabashed.

The Melbourne letter was from Serena Kelly, hoping that they had arrived safely, that they would enjoy living on the farm, and ending:

Well, keep in touch, Molly dear. You never know, I might be able to help you in your ambition – I've still got a lot of contacts back home and my Rory is touring just now in Queensland. Look out for the circus, if you go there as Mrs Nagel said you might . . .

Molly didn't show that one to Alexa – she wasn't sure if her employer would approve. Besides, she thought, she was committed to her year with Fay in Australia.

Alexa had collected a letter from her son-in-law, Matthew Dunn. They read their mail sitting under the canopy of the verandah, drinking tea.

Alexa's lips were working as she turned to the second page of the letter. She looked up and caught Molly's concerned glance.

'Matthew has decided to resign his commission at the end of the year – he believes he should have done this earlier, but the shock of losing Lucy – well . . .' She cleared her throat. 'He should be settled back in England, he says, before we return with Fay. Of course, he has to seek suitable employment and proper care for his daughter – that will be his first priority. My letters, apparently, about Fay's progress since the two of us came together, have prompted this decision. Oh, Molly, my dear, it's ridiculous when I know this is the best thing for Fay but I'm not sure where this leaves *me*. I suppose I was secretly hoping he would allow me to continue looking after her when we were home again. How *should* I feel?'

'Just be happy for them,' Molly said simply. 'I only wish my father had done the same for me.'

Chapter Three

Frank grudgingly agreed to drive them to the mission, but
said he would call back for them later. Once they had gone
inside the church, he drove on down the street to the small
hotel and its public bar.

The elderly German pastor spoke in English and there
was a fascinating variety of accents when the congregation
responded: Norwegian, Dutch, and the true Australian
twang.

The mission hut had a tin roof, reminding Elfie of one
she had attended as a child, uneven limed walls and hard
wooden benches, but it was packed to capacity. The harmonium, suffering from the climate, wheezed and coughed
through the familiar hymns, but Elfie was heartened to
realise that the mission girls, wearing simple cotton shifts
and bonnets, knew every word, although as Alexa
observed, 'I wonder if they understand what they are
singing?' To Elfie this was irrelevant because they
responded so stirringly to the music and atmosphere.
Fortunately, it had this effect on Fay, too: she sat on
Molly's lap, playing with her grandmother's fan, taking it
all in.

Elfie's usual tight expression was quite transformed. She
had been thinking before today that she had made a dreadful
mistake. Frank was even more taciturn and unappreciative
than he had been back home, and she was too hidebound to

discard her stuffy clothes and rigid corsetry. All her life, looking after first elderly, ailing parents, then her brother, she had followed a strict regime. She thought nostalgically now of her childhood home: its cool dairy where she churned butter; then feeding the hens and collecting the eggs, or sitting mending thick socks, rocking in the old, creaking chair which had belonged to her grandmother. Here she could not summon the energy to cook meals at unearthly hours when Frank and his men returned, tired, dirty and grumbling, sitting down at the table still wearing their boots and with their hands unwashed. Her brother had let his standards slip badly, in Elfie's opinion. And as for Alexa and Molly, well, she could guess how *they* felt about her ... She was already sick and tired of roasting mutton, she thought inconsequentially. But here, in the cooler atmosphere of the little chapel, she turned the familiar pages of her prayer book and felt sheer relief. Here was a haven from what she might, if she had been so impolite, have termed hell.

After the service, they stood outside, wilting in direct sunlight, while the rest of the congregation eagerly asked them how things were back at home.

'All those invitations to visit their homesteads!' Molly whispered. 'I've never felt so popular in my life before!'

The pastor, shaking Elfie's damp, limp hand, seemed to sense how she was feeling. He was a kindly man, a childless widower of many years' standing, who regarded his motley congregation as his family. He was stooped, his once ruddy complexion thickened and tanned like leather, contrasting with the soft white fringe of hair round his otherwise bald head. 'Miss Elfrida,' he said, 'I wonder – the ladies, they have the sewing party, you know? They meet at the next homestead to you, for the mission. Each Tuesday afternoon.'

Elfie, to her companions' delight, answered quickly that she would be delighted to attend. Then they could tell by her expression that she had belatedly remembered Frank. What would he say to this?

'Leave him to me, Elfie,' Alexa murmured. 'I'll persuade him to take you, just as long as you don't expect me to join . . .'

'Or me!' Molly added quickly. 'Anything I sew falls apart!'

'By the way,' the pastor said to Alexa, 'I understand that you are looking for a girl to help with the little one? Well, I know someone highly suitable for this post. She has made the most of her education at the mission, although her circumstances did not permit her to continue beyond this. She is called Nancy Atkins, and has only casual work at present – may I tell her to come to see you?' For some reason he seemed rather anxious.

'If you wish, certainly,' Alexa replied. 'You would be prepared to write a reference for this girl, I presume? Fay's father naturally holds me responsible for her wellbeing.'

'I should indeed,' the pastor assured her. 'She shall bring the letter with her.'

Fay was becoming restless, but here was Frank, even redder in the face than usual, with their transport, cracking his whip to let them know it was high time they stopped jabbering and climbed aboard. So they said goodbye to their new acquaintances and were waved away by a veritable sea of arms.

Nancy had been running – now, she slowed down and gulped in some deep breaths. She looked at her shoes which she had buffed up earlier, and saw to her dismay that they were covered in dust from the track. When she bent to wipe them clean with a handful of scrubby grass, the scuffs were revealed once more. They were second-hand, of course – she had picked them from the mission box this morning, and been grateful they actually fitted. 'You will look nice for the meeting with Mrs Nagel, Nancy,' the pastor told her as he handed her a discreetly wrapped parcel. 'Mrs Mac sent this for you to wear. No hurry to return it, my dear . . .' It was the dress Mrs Mac had worn to Sunday service;

not that Nancy was aware of that, for she had been up to the elbows in greasy washing-up water in the hotel kitchen on the sabbath.

The sober grey frock constricted her youthful round bosoms but hung in folds round her narrow hips. The style was too old for her, but Nancy appreciated the thought, and the dress was brightened by a deep lace collar in snowy white. She had buttoned up the introductory letter within her bodice, for safety, not possessing a bag.

Now she rubbed her sleeve across her damp forehead and thought ruefully that the bright sunlight would add to the many freckles on her fair-skinned face. Because she so seldom bothered with a hat, her hair was bleached like straw the year round. Ma had rubbed it vigorously with rough hands smeared with lard and then yanked back her mane and divided it, so that it hung down her back in a long bellrope. 'You don't want to look too pretty,' she'd advised. 'No mistress likes that. But try not to show that chipped tooth when you talk . . .' Nancy gave an involuntary shudder, remembering how this had happened. Worse things had gone on in the past which she could not talk about, even to her ma who had enough troubles of her own, with a drunken husband who couldn't keep a job and four great wayward sons.

Calm down, Nancy Atkins, she told herself sternly. Pastor says they're nice folks – they won't bite . . . Pity it's not a live-in job and might not last long. Young lady's about my age, he says. Depended, though, if she was above mixing with one born the wrong side of the tracks.

She was approaching the paddock gates now and saw someone waving energetically. It was a girl with long, light hair, dressed in a white muslin frock and hanging on to an energetic toddler who was climbing up the bars of the gate. Nancy felt a flicker of disappointment. The girl looked very friendly, but at first sight she appeared to be not much more than a child herself.

'You must be Nancy.' The girl smiled, swinging the gate

open but retaining a firm grip on her charge as the baby chortled and enjoyed the ride. 'Welcome to Wills' Spread. I'm Molly and this is Fay – Fay, this is Nancy who's going to help us look after you ... Mrs Nagel's waiting for you on the verandah. She sent me down here to see if I could spot you coming. Oh, I'm glad you're young, I've been missing company of my own age!' She beamed.

'I'm seventeen,' Nancy told her. She forgot her mother's warning, and smiled back.

'And I was eighteen in May and Fay was one. Come on! Mrs Nagel's already looking at her watch.'

'Had to finish my morning's work before I come,' Nancy said. 'Hope that'll be my last time at the hotel – if I get this position, of course. Here, why don't you hold my hand, too?' she invited Fay and they walked with the little girl between them, lifting her off her feet every now and then and swinging her along, to quicken the pace. Fay was a happy little soul, rosy-faced and beaming, with a new crop of dark curls just showing under her firmly tied sun bonnet. She wasn't shy with strangers.

'Oh, you'll get the job – I'll make sure of that!' Molly said firmly. 'And don't be taken in by this dress: Mrs Nagel's choice – not exactly *my* style. I'm only wearing it to please her. I hope she doesn't see the hedge tear in the skirt ... Now you're here, I might be allowed to do a bit of exploring, eh? Old Frank ... that's Mr Wills, but don't worry, I don't suppose you'll encounter *him* much ... puts such a damper on things. D'you know, he says it's unwise for me to go out alone further than the paddock because I wouldn't know a venomous snake from a harmless one. That's rubbish because Alexa – Mrs Nagel – showed me some pictures and said to watch out for the black ones with the blue bellies ... He rubbed it in, he really did, about huge poisonous spiders—'

'Frighten Miss Muffet away!' Fay put in with relish.

'Mr Wills is right, I'm afraid. And so are you, Fay,' Nancy remarked. 'You can easily get lost in the bush. A young lady who was visiting the mission vanished into thin air 'bout two years ago. She'd gone out by herself to do some sketching. They never found her, just her pencils and paper all scattered ... And when the old sun is burning down like it will be soon, well, you have to watch out for bush fires. You'll hear a fierce cracking sound when the bark splits on the gum trees.' Molly needed holding back, for her own sake; Nancy had realised that right away.

'Old Frank went on about that, too – but I'd really love to see it,' she said.

'Did Mr Wills warn you about the anthills?'

''Course he did. But he doesn't talk about all the beautiful things in this amazing continent, like silver-tailed lyre and bower birds. And the native animals – well, some of them – are beyond belief.'

'It's a great country, for some. I've lived here since I was three and I haven't been further than Bodenflower yet ...' Maybe, Nancy prayed, she would get the chance at last.

They had reached the verandah, and Alexa, who had probably heard most of this as they approached, rose from her chair and said to Molly: 'Take Fay with you – I'm sure Nancy already feels she knows you both. Also, Fay should be having her nap. Come back in fifteen minutes or so with refreshments, will you, please? Oh, and ask Elfie if you can borrow her tape-measure – we can add Nancy's uniform to our Lassetter's order. Sit down, Nancy, and relax – you look overheated. Now, tell me all about yourself? But don't worry, the job is yours, Fay has taken to you just as she did to Molly, that's obvious.'

'Collected this at the stores,' Alexa said, straight-faced, displaying the large, cardboard package addressed to *Mr Alexander Nagel*: the clerk at Lassetter's in Sydney having obviously decided there must be some mistake. Molly, Nancy and Fay crowded round while she opened the box.

Molly couldn't resist it: 'They must have wondered what

32

sort of men possessed such feminine measurements, Alexa. Large bottoms and barrel chests, eh?'

'I shall ignore that, Molly.' But Alexa was not riled, Molly having generously included herself in this description, although of course she could easily fit into boys' breeks. Anyway, as the one paying for the goods, Alexa had the privilege of unpacking them. She had not forgotten Elfie – the chip hat, lavishly decorated with roses, was for her.

Her cousin, hovering in the background, was pink and pleased when this was handed over. 'Oh, I never thought – just the hat for Sundays. Thank you very much, Alexa.'

'For you, Nancy.' She passed her the impeccably folded garments, not the uniform Nancy had envisaged, but a good quality navy blue skirt and crisp cotton blouse striped in blue and white. There were cotton stockings too, and leather house shoes. Nancy was too surprised and pleased to murmur more than: 'Thank you very much, Mrs Nagel.'

'Here you are, Fay. A pretty parasol and a Sunday bonnet, now Elfie's made a regular church goer of you, eh?'

'Don't like hats,' Fay said cheerfully, and tossed the bonnet in the air.

'Oh – thanks!' Molly exclaimed, in turn, as she received a bullseye box camera and several rolls of film. 'Let's gather all this up and get changed quick, Alexa – then I can take your photograph outside, and you can take mine with Fay and Nancy, if she'll delay doing her ironing for a few minutes. Put on your hat, Elfie, so I can snap you, too. Oh, and don't forget to take off your pinny . . .'

Alexa was grateful when Molly said not a word about the tight fit of her breeches, only: 'You look a real pioneer!'

'I shall probably have to enlist your aid,' Alexa said ruefully, 'in pulling them off later.'

Molly executed a couple of high kicks – what freedom, she thought exultantly, from tiresome, bulky skirts – and determined to wear the breeches whenever she could, whether she was going riding or not. Now that Nancy was here to take care of Fay, she'd wear down Alexa's resistance to her going out on horseback with Henny one day.

Little Fay, excited by all the laughter, endeavoured to copy her, and landed on her bottom. She looked more surprised than hurt.

'Darling!' Molly cried, picking her up. 'We'll wheedle round your Aunt Elfie to make you some cool and comfy cotton trousers, eh? At one of her sewing bees.'

Alexa clamped her hat on her head, looked critically in the mirror. 'I believe I look like an Alexander now. Elfie's sewing is intended for the mission children, Molly—'

'Well, she can sew trousers for them, too! Charity begins at home, don't they say? Right, outside – sit on the fence and I'll take my very first photograph! Nancy, where are you?'

'Better read the instructions first,' Alexa reminded her.

Chapter Four

Molly tried, in her diary, to describe the smell of greasy wool from the Merino sheep: the endless meals of mutton; the sweat which trickled continually from them and stained and rotted their underclothes; the bliss of cold water pouring over her head from a bucket obligingly tipped by young Toby. She was reticent on paper about her growing infatuation with Henny but she resolved to remember every detail of this strange place, to the end of her life. In time, she thought, she might confide in Nancy: she was unaware that Nancy *knew*.

Unfortunately, Alexa's first experience of riding out with Henny had been a disaster – she had not worn her breeches since, and spoke darkly of blisters in unmentionable places. She told Molly that it would be much better to confine her contact with horses to driving down to the stores with Nancy and Fay in the sulky, a two-wheeled carriage with a hood and a most useful box for carrying goods on the back. Frank hadn't complained when the pastor offered to loan them this, together with a willing pony which proved to be a good ride as well as safe to drive. Alexa had given a generous donation to the mission, and even Elfie had taken up the reins with enthusiasm; it didn't take much guessing why – she could now drive herself to the mission whenever Frank grudgingly allowed her time off.

Molly intended to badger Alexa again tonight. Time was

passing, and she did so want the chance to get to know Henny better, before Alexa arranged the visit to Queensland. Her friend actually seemed in no hurry regarding this, which was strange, considering her earlier comments. The good thing was that Nancy would be going with them too.

They set off early one morning, Molly, Henny, four of the fellas, as Frank termed them, and Toby, as convention decreed Molly must have a female companion overnight camping out in the vast forest of tall pines. The men would be marking trees to be felled shortly for wood to be used on the homestead.

Henny handed Molly up on the pony's broad and dusty back. Rusty stood patiently while he adjusted the stirrups. Toby grinned at all the palaver. She rode without a saddle, without breeches, without boots: her only concession to the sun overhead a battered straw hat. Her gleaming dark skin was impervious to burning. A pack horse carried the minimum for such a short stay – rolled blankets, mosquito nets, tucker – as Molly had learned to call food, and water bottles. They would sleep fully clothed. Behind them skittered the homestead dogs, long-limbed yellow-coated creatures with sharp, intelligent faces, twitching pricked ears and tightly curled tails. Rather like their arch enemies the dingoes themselves, Molly fancied.

They inspected stock, maize, fencing, water holes on the circuitous journey; they replenished the water bottles several times. The billy-can boiled at each stopping place; they drank milkless tea with plenty of sugar from chipped enamel mugs.

At nightfall they chose their resting place among the trees, improvised little tents from protective netting and sticks to keep the insects at bay, and the fellas coaxed a bright, crackling fire to life to cook supper and to spread warmth and a circle of light as the atmosphere cooled and darkness set in.

Molly and Toby stretched out on heaped leaves spread over with one of the blankets, and Molly watched Henny as he busied himself mixing damper dough from flour and water which he suspended from a stick to be baked in the fire's glow. They would dunk this bread substitute later into a pot of delicious, bubbling stew, prepared from strips of dried meat. It was a very satisfying meal, and Molly realised just how hungry she was after all that riding.

Toby whispered: 'Hear all the rustlin', Missee? Maybe we hear bullroarer – but us no *see* . . .'

Molly looked to Henny for reassurance. He said: 'Only in the still of the forest will you hear such an extraordinary sound: it is forbidden for women and children to see it. Always secret – but a powerful instrument.'

'Your hand over ears,' Toby demonstrated.

Molly had read about the Aboriginal bullroarer. It sounded so simple, she thought, just a flat piece of wood attached to one end of a piece of string and whirled at great speed so that it vibrated. The noise rose and fell, having an eerie effect on all who heard it. She was not too sure she wanted such an experience tonight . . .

'The dogs,' Henny told her, seeing her apprehension, 'will keep the wild things at bay, I will sleep close by.'

Surprisingly, when they crawled under their nets, Molly found it very easy to drift off into sleep. She did not stir when Toby crept away to join the fellas, who were keeping a respectful distance, lying by the horses. There was muffled giggling and mock sparring by the two younger ones, until Toby warned them, tongue in cheek: 'You be still now. I shut eyes.'

At some time during a night scented with pine and woodsmoke Molly stretched out her hand uncertainly and it was instantly clasped by a large hand calloused from rough work but still warm and comforting.

'Sleep on, little Molly,' Henny mouthed. He remained awake himself for some considerable time. He must take care not to betray his attraction to this young and innocent girl. He had come to this place, like many others, to lose himself. To forget.

At first light, the fire was rekindled, the billy boiled, and Toby gently shook Molly's shoulder to wake her. The space next to her was empty, the blanket neatly rolled. 'Wakee, Missee, you want wash? We go crick when men come back?'

'We go crick,' Molly agreed, still bemused. She needed the shock of cold water to dispel the magic, she thought.

Molly was decidedly saddle-sore on the journey home. She and Toby brought up the rear, but now and again Toby, with one of her disarming grins, slapped her pony on the rump, encouraging it to gallop gamely in order to catch up with the fellas. After a while, she would drop back to ride with Molly once more. Rusty, being well-schooled, blinked at all the to'ing and fro'ing but kept to a steady trot. The intention was to be back at Wills' Spread by mid-morning.

Henny had exchanged a few words with Molly while they ate their simple breakfast, two eggs apiece from the dozen Elfie had carefully wrapped and packed, which they boiled in the water for the tea. There was leftover damper from supper. 'Sleep well, Miss Sparkes? No bullroarer?'

'Molly – please,' she'd insisted, blushing. She was aware that her hair was hanging in damp rat's tails down her back, that her clothes were crumpled and grubby. She had merely removed her shirt at the creek, leaning over the rim of the water, taking a deep breath and dipping in her face and hands. Toby had had no such inhibitions, divesting herself of her dress in an instant, while a startled Molly became aware that that was all she wore, and splashing happily about. 'Come! Nice!' she called out. The shining water and rose-ribboned sky made Molly feel good. She realised why she had felt apprehensive in the dark place where they had settled for the night: it was because the tall trees obscured sight of the starry heavens above.

Henny rode back now, to see how she was doing. 'We'll

rest soon, the next waterhole is near, Molly. Toby has deserted you again, I see.'

'I don't mind, really,' she said. 'She'll be back.'

'You are used to the countryside?' he asked. 'You have taken well to the life here.'

'Country, yes – but in a very small way – just an English village ... Of course, I am only visiting here, that makes a big difference. I don't have to work from dawn to dusk and longer, as you do, Henny,' she said frankly.

'Oh, I like it. It suits me. I, too, come from a small place, a farming community in Denmark.'

'Did you come here for the adventure?'

'Adventure?' His hearty laughter took her by surprise. 'That is how you see it, Molly? Danger, sometimes, certainly – but work is work the world over. It is good for the soul, they say ...'

'Will you stay here for good?'

'I cannot know that. For now, it is right. Maybe I will settle down—'

'If you can find the right woman to settle with!' she finished for him daringly.

He put out a hand to restrain her pony. 'We are here ... See, the others have stopped. I shall not marry, Molly. I am thirty-six years old: twice your age. Ten years ago would have been the time for me – that time is not yet come for you. Don't look to *me*, Molly, please.' He shaded his eyes, looked directly at her.

'Oh, whatever gave you that idea?' she flashed. '*You* may not want an adventurous life but I assure you, I do!' She dismounted, disregarding his move to help, and went to join Toby in the boiling of the billy can.

'Enjoyed yourself?' Nancy asked later, out on the verandah.

Molly was lying face down on a line of cushions. She had been only too glad to discard her breeches and slip on a cool dress. Alexa had passed the arnica with a quizzical lift of her eyebrows, and left Nancy to her anointing of all the sore places.

'I did, but I'm paying for it now . . .' she murmured ruefully.

Nancy glanced round. Mrs Nagel and Fay were sleeping off lunch in their room. Elfie likewise. Frank and the men were nowhere to be seen. Only Toby was nearby: squatting outside on a patch of grass, singing cheerfully and sending up a cloud of feathers as she plucked a chicken for supper. 'Git!' she told the dogs as they sniffed around. It was all right to talk more intimately.

'Find out anything – you *know* – 'bout Henny, Molly?'

'What d'you mean?' Molly's voice was muffled, wary.

'You can tell me! I've seen the way you look out for him. He's a real handsome fella . . . all the ladies hereabouts got excited when he first come, but he don't have the eye for none of 'em, it seems.'

'Well, you can add *me* to your list,' Molly told her ruefully.

'I ain't too sure 'bout that. I guess he likes you all right. Maybe he needs you to show you like him first.'

Molly rolled over and sat up, wincing. 'Oh, he's aware of that, Nancy – d'you know, he had the cheek to tell me this morning that he's not the marrying kind. And he's twice my age, anyway!' She sounded as indignant as she felt.

'He wouldn't say that 'less he was interested,' Nancy said confidently.

'Well, I won't be pleading to go riding with him again!' Molly said. 'I'm not giving him that satisfaction. You'd better go and collect Fay, she's burbling away. Alexa won't be pleased if she wakes her up.'

I'm obviously not lucky in love, she thought. Much better to plan a sparkling career. When I'm famous, the only man I've met so far will see what he has missed. Think I'll write to Serena again, and ask her advice on that!

*

40

It was mutton again for their Christmas dinner, which they ate in the evening, out on the front verandah because, being midsummer, it was stifling indoors. Elfie triumphantly produced a Christmas pudding she had prudently made before their departure. 'There was only a little mould on the top,' she said proudly to Alexa. Frank even set the traditional brandy alight, while Molly held on tight to the excited Fay. 'A toast: to absent family and friends!' Alexa announced, and they raised their glasses. There were no sad reminders of Christmases past, of her daughter, in Australia. It was an entirely different way of life.

Alexa noticed that even Elfie was content and smiling, and obviously delighted that the pastor had come to join them at their celebration meal. Alexa had enjoyed arranging that surprise. She felt much less irritation with Elfie nowadays, for she fully understood the reason why her cousin had become what she was: Frank. No wonder, Alexa thought, he'd never found a wife! She took delight in slyly pointing out his sister's achievements since her arrival here: how she shone in the Ladies' Circle, how she was teaching the mission girls to knit and sew. She had even put Elfie up to telling her brother Frank: 'I am entitled to adequate time off, Frank. You drink and smoke with your pals; my interest lies with the mission.'

'With that pastor, more like,' he had grumbled. Alexa thought this much nearer the truth than he imagined, the old curmudgeon.

She had actually delayed moving on because she felt that she was helping her cousin in her quest for a truly new way of life, by championing her cause. Also, Fay, and Molly had settled so well, particularly since the advent of Nancy.

She'd give Frank more food for thought today, Alexa decided. The workers, including Nancy, had been given the day off; Henny, being far from home, had eaten with them, but made vague excuses and retired to the bunkhouse after the meal. 'You and I, Frank, will tackle the washing up,' she'd said, 'while Molly takes Fay off to bed. Why don't you entertain Ernst, Elfie, while we're busy?'

Only Molly rightly interpreted the innocent expression on Alexa's face.

Nancy certainly had no reason to want to be at home on Christmas Day; not that she could tell Mrs Nagel that. She chose instead to go to the hotel and to help there. Ma agreed. 'You'll get a better meal there, gal,' she said. 'With any luck, they'll all be stupefied with the drink when you get back . . .'

Maybe I'll be out of all this soon, Nancy thought, trying to boost her spirits. Dear Ma, well, there's no escape for her. I only hope she buys something for herself with the money Mrs Nagel gave me . . .

But washing up, despite the mountain of dirty dishes, came to an end eventually. Nancy walked slowly home afterwards, thinking how different to hers Molly's day would have been.

Molly felt strangely restless when she had settled Fay down. She didn't want to go and play gooseberry to Elfie and Ernst in the parlour. Elfie, she thought, bemused, was obviously not too old at all to have romantic feelings. Alexa and Frank were already arguing, she could hear them, over who should scour the saucepans. She wished Nancy was here so that they could play a traditional board game or two. Suddenly, she felt very homesick. This wasn't like Christmas in England at all.

On impulse, she went quietly on to the back verandah which opened off her room. She had humped and arranged a spare mattress there earlier, declaring her intention to sleep out. Startled, she realised that she was not alone. Someone was leaning on the verandah rail. She almost screamed, but of course, despite its being late, it wasn't yet dark, and it was only Henny.

'I guessed you would come out here sometime,' he said calmly. 'You are not going to bed yet, surely?'

'At ten o'clock on Christmas evening?' she asked, quickly recovering her composure.

'Will you sit and talk with me for a little while, Molly?' He pulled forward a verandah chair. 'I have something for you – nothing at all, really. I like to carve wood with my knife sometimes.'

'Whittling,' Molly said, 'that's what we call it, Henny. Well, aren't you going to give it to me, then?'

He gravely handed her a little wooden horse, smoothed and polished. She fingered the pale wood, the tiny hooves, the curve of the head and neck. This was carving she thought, not idle whittling. She cleared her throat. 'Thank you, Henny, it's lovely, I didn't expect—'

'I know you didn't,' he said.

'I'll keep it always.' She really meant it.

'I hope you will. Molly, did I upset you when we rode together that morning? You hardly speak to me since.'

She looked up from the little horse, unsure what to say.

His hand covered both of hers, still holding his gift in her lap. She was instantly reminded of the night in the forest. 'You held my hand before . . .' she whispered.

'I didn't know you realised,' he said slowly. 'It was impertinent, I think.'

'I didn't mind at all. I fact, I liked it. You spoiled it all,' she added childishly, 'when you said what you did, you know . . .'

'Shall I say I am sorry? Is that what you want?'

'I think,' Molly said softly, 'I would like you to kiss me, Henning Rasmussen.'

'Not here,' he said. 'Come. A walk, and you may change your mind, Molly.'

'No, I won't,' she said. She was sure of that.

He put an arm casually and lightly round her shoulders.

'You shiver,' he exclaimed, concerned, feeling the slight tremor through the thin stuff of the pretty muslin dress which Elfie had painstakingly mended for her.

How could she tell him that she was shaky with

excitement? They were at the bunkhouse. 'Wait a moment,' he said, 'I fetch a coat for you, Molly.'

She followed him just inside the door, and waited as he took a jacket from a hook. There were four bunks, covered in drab blankets, all empty tonight, and a strong smell of rank tobacco, and of kerosene from the lamp.

Molly closed the door behind her. He looked at her, startled, offering the coat. 'You can kiss me here,' she said. 'Just to wish me a happy Christmas, you understand.'

'I understand, I think,' he said slowly.

'This will be my first real kiss.' She was being painfully honest. 'Just think, Henny, I'm eighteen . . .'

'That's all,' he told her, 'one kiss. No more. Then we go walking, or you go back to your verandah . . .'

She made the first move to close the gap between them. He put his hands lightly on her shoulders, ensuring that they were still a little apart, then bent his head. It was a brief kiss, certainly not passionate, she admitted to herself later, but warm and nice, all the same. A proper kiss: on the lips.

'Now, just down to the stables, to see that all is well,' he told her, wrapping the jacket round her, and pushing open the door. 'Or we may expect a search party, eh?'

Rusty whinnied and came toward them, poking her head over the stable door, nosing at the familiar jacket, which sure enough had a few lumps of sugar in the pocket.

'Shall I tell you something?' Henny asked. 'I left my home country because I was unhappy . . . My brother and I were very close. Just a year between us. He married the girl I was in love with, too. I tried to keep it from him, but she knew, yes, she knew . . . She played us off, one against the other. Maybe it amused her to do so. We had a dreadful quarrel, my brother and I. He asked her to choose between us. She chose *me*.'

'But?'

'I made a choice, too. For his sake. You understand, Molly?'

'I think so.'

'Well, then, I want to go back home but I do not know if my brother will welcome that, if he has forgiven me or if I can forgive myself.'

'Surely it was the girl who was in the wrong?' she exclaimed.

He fastened the half-door of the stable. 'Goodnight, my friend. See the lamp moving outside the homestead, Molly? The pastor makes ready to return. Let's go quietly, eh, and hope we are not seen . . .'

Molly tucked her diary under her pillow. How did one describe a kiss? She couldn't. She had written instead: *Today, I was given a very special Christmas present.* And she closed her fingers round the little carved horse, protectively, under the covers, and waited for the dreaming to begin.

Chapter Five

The shearing was the highlight of the year. A large work-force was recruited and had to be fed and watered. Molly enjoyed hugely her role in all this, taking out tucker to the lean, brown men, bare to the waist and glistening with sweat. Elfie flatly refused to do this chore. 'They are almost *naked*, Molly,' she squeaked, 'and their language – my dear mother would have fainted if she could have heard them.'

'I don't think they intend to blaspheme, Elfie,' Molly returned, 'it's just their normal way of talking. And your mother's not here, is she?'

'Little Fay came out with a dreadful word the other day—'

'Alexa says it's best to ignore it, and she'll soon forget it,' Molly said cheerfully.

As the horse teams moved off with their great loads of pressed wool bales, a rumbling cheer rose from the men. The barrels of beer were rolled out from the barn, and far into the night the roistering went on. Even Frank unbent, and Molly danced her way on tireless feet, almost thrown from partner to partner, with steely arms clapped round her waist. The accordions, soaring fiddles and penny whistles played the wildest, jolliest tunes, and Elfie blushed fiercely again when she caught the words of some of the songs. She retired indoors in haste.

'But she's listening, I reckon, through her open window!' Molly reported with glee to Nancy. Alexa had told Nancy to go off and enjoy herself with Molly, but the girl seemed to prefer to watch her friend dancing; she shook her head when prospective partners approached. 'Do be careful, Molly,' she had warned earlier. 'Drink makes men – *eager*, and they're all much bigger and stronger than you. Stay in sight of the house.'

Alexa sat on a rug spread on the ground with the baby asleep in her lap. As she leaned against the rough bark of a tree, her hair, loose for once on her shoulders, gleamed in the flaring lights. Many an admiring, speculative glance was cast in her direction. She rather enjoyed the compliment it seemed. 'At my age, too!' as she drily remarked to Molly when she plumped down breathlessly beside her. 'They obviously haven't noticed the wrinkles!'

Molly gulped down a tall glass of warm ginger beer – never mind the odd fly floating in it, she thought. She wondered where Henny had got to, she hadn't seen him all evening. Not that she'd had time to feel disappointed, with so many merry admirers.

'Nonsense, Alexa, you might get a proposal – I've had four so far tonight!'

'What kind of proposals, Molly?' Alexa asked keenly.

'Well, one or two were the sort I can't repeat! But don't worry, I haven't accepted a single one. Nancy saw to that. She's appointed herself my moral protector!'

There was a piercing shriek: Toby was being pursued, and perhaps hoping to be caught, by a gangly youth with his intentions written all over his face. 'She's obviously used to the shearing boys,' Molly observed. Did Alexa know what Nancy had told her earlier, emphasising her words of caution, that Toby had had a baby as a result of a shearing party the year before last? Her mother had obligingly added the little boy to her own extended family. She also wondered fleetingly if that was why Nancy had declined to join the celebrations: she certainly hadn't dressed up like Molly. It didn't occur to her that Nancy hadn't any decent clothes other than the ones Alexa had bought her for every day.

Molly smiled, reached down and tousled Fay's curls. 'Lovely, her hair, isn't it? Just the same as—' She was going to add: 'yours'.

'Lucy's,' Alexa finished for her. 'Don't worry, Molly, I can say that now. I love this little one dearly, so it's going to be a real wrench when I have to part with her. I probably shouldn't have taken her on – should have left things as they were. Though I'm grateful to have found such an excellent nursemaid in Nancy, and, of course, you more than pull your weight on that score. You remind me very much of my daughter – not in looks, but in spirit. I hope we won't lose touch with each other, Molly, when we return to England?'

'I feel the same. Don't worry, I won't disappear,' she said with a grin.

'Thank you. I must admit, I wondered at the start if we would actually get on – like each other – when I asked you to travel here with me. If later you need a job, and would like to move to London, well, don't be afraid to apply to me.'

'Oh, I won't! But there *is* something else I'd like to try, first.'

'Would you care to dance, Molly?' Henny was standing there. Unlike some of the other men, he had obviously bathed and changed his clothes. He wore a new shirt, with a neat cravat, drill trousers and shoes, instead of the usual boots.

Molly was glad that she was wearing her light, full skirt and flame-coloured silk blouse with puffed sleeves.

Alexa gave her a little nudge. 'Yes, go along, Molly, enjoy yourself! Here's Nancy – oh, good, with more ginger beer. She can keep me company. We'll put Fay to bed later . . .'

Henny helped Molly to her feet, smiled at the others,

then led her away. Nancy's warnings went unheeded. They went past the crowd to a patch of scrubby grass ringed by eucalypts where they danced by themselves in their own private space. Her face was pressed to his broad chest, against the smooth cotton of his shirt; she was vibrantly aware of their closeness, of his fast-beating heart. His hands were firm round her slender back. They seemed to burn her skin through the thin stuff of her blouse and petticoat. She stretched up, resting her own hands on his shoulders. 'I thought you'd never come,' she murmured. 'I was so hoping you would, though ...'

'I wasn't sure I could trust myself.'

'Can you?' she asked daringly. His hands slipped to her waist, holding her even more tightly.

'I must,' he told her, his voice muffled by her hair. 'But you are not making it easy ... Anyway, I really brought you here because I have something to tell you, Molly. I am leaving tomorrow, joining up with the shearing team.'

She pushed him away, folding her arms. '*Why?*' she cried.

'The pay is good, I can soon earn enough to return home. I heard from my brother at last. His wife left him two years ago. He wants me back, to run the farm together; for us to be good friends once more.'

'And that will make you happy, Henny?' she asked, blinking rapidly to stop the treacherous tears from falling.

'Yes, I think it will. I am sorry, Molly, if you—' He paused, trying to put it tactfully.

'If I imagined I was falling in love with you? That's all it was, just imagining ...'

'You wish me well, then?'

'Yes, I wish you well, Henny.' She turned. 'Let's go back or people will be imagining there is something between us.' She tried to say this lightly, as if she really didn't care. 'Have you told Frank?'

'Not yet. He will be displeased, I know that, but I know of one seeking a post like mine. I will give his name to Mr

49

Wills.' He caught at her arm, restraining her. 'Will you say goodbye to me now, Molly? I can kiss you here, but not in front of the others at the house, eh?'

Then she was back in his arms, hugging him convulsively, and the kissing was bitter-sweet this time, because it was just how she wanted it to be, except it was the end, not the beginning of what might have been a love affair . . .

Nancy, hurrying towards them, saw it all. Her voice rang out hoarsely: '*Molly!* Mrs Nagel was worried – we couldn't see you. Will you come back now please?'

Alexa, still holding the baby, looked at Molly searchingly but said only: 'I didn't think you would be back so soon. Uh-oh! here comes Frank. D'you know, I believe he's had one too many . . .'

He lurched uncertainly towards them, almost falling down beside Alexa, who recoiled from his proximity. It was the first time she had seen Frank merry, if you could call it that, and it was no improvement as far as she was concerned, she thought.

'Want to know what the old girl just let slip when I caught up with her, lurking indoors?' he roared.

'If you are referring to your sister,' Alexa told him disdainfully, passing the drowsy Fay to Nancy on her other side. She didn't want him breathing all over her granddaughter.

'Who else?' Frank mocked her. 'She reckons she's going to leave me in the lurch – says she's going to keep house for old Ernst!' He gave a great, belching laugh.

'Good for her. I didn't think she had it in her, eh, Molly?' Alexa removed Frank's damp hand very firmly from where it had slipped on to her knee.

'I shall have to get myself a wife after all.'

'If you're implying that you have me in mind, Frank, you can forget it.' She rose, dusting her skirt down. 'We shan't be here much longer in any case. I promised to visit a friend in Queensland, and this seems the right timing.

50

Come on, girls, let's take Fay indoors, shall we? *Goodnight*, Frank.'

'Can I – can I go home now, Mrs Nagel? Ma'll be wondering why I'm so late.' Nancy didn't want to discuss with Molly what had happened tonight.

'Of course. You heard what I said to Mr Wills? You can warn your mother we'll be leaving for Brisbane shortly.'

'Drunk as a lord,' Alexa said crossly to Molly as they weaved round the dancers towards the house. 'I suppose he has made us at home here, in his funny way, so I won't ask him for any money back – I fear I was much too generous – but I intend to telegraph Cicely tomorrow. We'll start packing in the morning. She and her husband have done splendidly in Australia, it seems.'

'We'll all be deserting him,' Molly said, clearing her throat. She opened the nets, turned down the sheet which was the only covering on the bed, and laid Fay down. 'It'll wake her, if we undress her, I think . . .' She crossed to the window, to pull the blinds. With her back to Alexa, she went on: 'Frank doesn't know it yet, but Henny is leaving tomorrow. He's going off with the shearers.'

Unexpectedly, Alexa's arm went round her shoulders. 'Oh, my dear, I'm so sorry,' she said, and hugged the girl, feeling pain at the thought that she should have hugged Lucy this way but now it was too late . . .

'I do hope Nancy's ma will let her come with us to Queensland,' Molly said.

'I'll make sure she does. You can't lose both your new friends in one fell swoop, can you? That would be too much. I'll leave you for a bit, if you don't mind. I want to ask Elfie what's what while Frank's not around.'

'Thank you, Alexa.'

'Whatever for?'

'For not asking *me* what's what.'

In Cicely's house in Brisbane Molly was pleased to find that she had a big, airy bedroom all to herself – although

51

the communal sleeping arrangements both on the boat and at Frank's had not worried her as much as her companions, because, after all, it was not so long since she had slept in a dormitory at the convent.

Alexa expressed satisfaction with her own room. It had fine furniture and, at the tug of a bell-pull, servants ready to scurry about at her every whim. 'I shall at last get a decent night's sleep,' she stated confidently.

'It's parry-dise, Molly!' Nancy breathed rapturously in her turn. She obviously felt equal, in her smart new powder-blue 'Universally Provided' frock, to those below-stairs in this grand colonial house, with its sweep of broad steps under white columns to the massive front door. 'I never thought I'd have a bedroom to meself, and a nursery off for Fay. Eh – and what about all that lovely hot water gushing from real gold taps in a proper bathroom . . .'

'Wonderful!' Molly agreed. She was pleased to hear later from Alexa that Nancy was to be allowed to accompany them on most of their daytime excursions, for Cicely, childless herself, was eager to show off the pretty baby to her circle. They smiled at Nancy's bemused face, her artless exclamations at each new discovery, but then, they didn't realise just how glad she was to be away from her own home.

An icehouse in the terraced garden, with its exotic jacaranda and flame trees, ensured that food was always fresh.

'How nice to taste roast beef once more,' Alexa remarked appreciatively the first evening. Cicely, who had been rather in awe of her at school, for Alexa had been a dominant personality even then, was delighted to show her old friend just how much she had improved her status in the new country. The many courses were all served on gold-rimmed dishes and the table setting was perfect. Nancy watched anxiously over her charge as she banged her spoon on her plate.

No wonder, Molly thought, smiling to herself because she had really taken to Alexa's bubbly, kind friend, Cicely was like a small, round butterball, if she ate like this every day!

Cicely's excited pink face was topped with a plaited false crown, the severity of which failed to repress her own fluffy golden hair. 'She hasn't changed a bit,' Alexa confided in Molly, when Cicely excused herself to answer the telephone in the hall: 'She's just as sweet as ever she was! We nicknamed her Cherub at school ... She was married for the first time when she was very young, an older man who had already made his pile, but it was a happy marriage, I believe, though cut short by her husband's death. She remarried rather on the rebound, so I thought, but I suppose she was looking for someone younger and more—'

'Virile?' Molly suggested cheerfully.

'Shush!' Alexa reproved, as Cicely returned, beaming.

'That was my husband ... I'm so glad to have you with me just now,' she confided: 'Ran – that's what I call Randolph – has already been away over a month on business. I do get lonely at times, despite the social whirl ...'

This was an enchanting place, they all decided, with its elegant, fresh-coloured painted wooden houses standing on piles – to avoid the invasion of ants Cicely said, with a shudder; the way the long streets climbed upwards seemingly to disappear in the misty hills and the cargo boats smartly navigated the great river which curved around the city terraces. The shopping parades contrasted sharply with the unsophisticated general stores back in Bodenflower. This was very obviously the domicile of wealthy and advantaged people, like Cicely and her husband.

The Gold Coast was even more beautiful. Cicely sent them out very early in her carriage, with a picnic basket, on the day she expected her husband home. 'I didn't get time to tell him, when I spoke to him the other night, that we have company. I must break it to him gently!' she said. For some reason, she sounded rather agitated, not her usual cheerful self. Both Molly and Alexa experienced a feeling of disquiet at this, but neither spoke of it to the other. But Molly thought: I hope he won't turn out to be another Frank ... Still, he looked very handsome in all the photographs Cicely had placed adoringly in every room.

On the Coast they walked for the first time across great stretches of pale sand – almost like hot, powdered snow, Molly imagined – towards the rolling, sparkling sea. Fay paddled and splashed in the water with enormous delight, and got her drawers well and truly soaked, as did Molly and Nancy, larking about like two year olds themselves. Alexa said not a word about that.

'I admire Australian women very much. They were awarded the vote in 1902, you know,' she told Molly. 'They are way ahead of the women at home: it's disgraceful that we are still waiting.' She put up her parasol, leaning back under its shade in her deck chair. The sun was really hot today, even though summer was almost over, but the sea air was intoxicating. However, Alexa was covered from top to toe. She wasn't going to risk her complexion turning to the texture of an old boot, she said.

'You'll be the perfect candidate if women ever get into Parliament back home,' Molly said, and meant it. She removed Fay's wet underwear, spreading it out to dry. 'Here, darling, you must cover up or you'll soon burn. Put on these funny trousers Elfie made you.'

'Funny's the word,' Alexa sniffed. 'With those ruffles round the ankles, and that rather perished elastic holding them up under her armpits ...'

'I think she looks like a dear little clown in her baggy pants, Mrs Nagel,' Nancy said proudly. 'And what lovely bright material.' She was trying to coax Fay into the matching, floppy sun hat with the fluted curtain at the back to screen her neck against harmful rays.

Fay struggled out of Nancy's restraining hands. 'Don't like Elfie hat,' she insisted, but Alexa caught hold of her and tied the ribbon very firmly under her chin.

54

'They seem to go in for bold colours at those sewing parties; I'd call this bilious green, not emerald as Elfie fancied it was.'

Alexa gave Fay a reproving tap on her bottom. 'Take that off, at your peril, child!' But she didn't look cross.

'You should be glad Elfie hasn't found time to finish off her knitting anyway!' Molly grinned.

Alexa shuddered. 'I thought I might be unwrapping that at Christmas ... But you've reminded me of something, Nancy, with your allusion to clowns. Mrs Colton mentioned that the circus is in town. She thought you girls might like to take Fay along one afternoon this week. You needn't stay for the whole performance if she becomes restless. What d'you think?'

Nancy waited for Molly to speak first. 'Believe it or not, I've never been to a circus,' she said. 'Fancy, who would have thought that the first time would be in Australia? Yes, please, Alexa, I'd love to go.' Wouldn't it be a coincidence, she thought, if it was the circus Serena Kelly had mentioned in her letter? She must endeavour to find out! Rory – that was the name of Serena's son.

'So would I!' Nancy echoed happily.

'So'd I!' Fay shouted, and she rolled over and over on the sand, just like a little green roly-poly clown as Nancy had said, but failed to dislodge the hated hat.

One look at Mr Randolph Colton's face as they divested themselves of gritty shoes and parasols in the hall was enough for Nancy. She knew right away that he didn't care for children for he ignored Fay's beaming, 'Hello, man!' However, she caught his speculative glance at Molly when Cicely introduced them.

Nancy picked Fay up. 'I'll take her up to the nursery, Mrs Nagel, time for her tea. Then I'll bath her and get her off to bed. Will you pop up and say goodnight?'

Alexa was obviously relieved not to have to ask Nancy to keep Fay tactfully out of the main reception rooms while the master of the house was at home. 'Yes, of course I will, Nancy, thank you.'

'I'll come up with you, I must get changed,' Molly said quickly, following Nancy and Fay upstairs.

'Wear your new dinner dress tonight, Molly,' Alexa called after her. The elegant Ran would surely expect them to dress in all their finery.

'Your arrival has obviously been just the tonic Cissy needs. Unfortunately, she is subject to irrational worries and depression at times,' her husband observed as they relaxed in the conservatory among the cool leafy plants after a lengthy dinner. He patted his pocket. 'Would you object if I lit a cigar, ladies? A small indulgence with my brandy.' They murmured politely.

Molly, shifting her chair a little so that she could see the garden through the glass, was dismayed when Randolph moved alongside her. 'And how do you like it here?' he asked. 'Not too dull, I hope, without a companion of your own age?'

She answered smartly: 'I am having a most enjoyable time, thank you, Mr Colton. And I do have Nancy to giggle with, if that's what you mean?'

'Nancy? Ah, the child's nurse,' he said dismissively.

'We share responsibility for Fay's care,' Molly told him. She knew that Alexa was giving her little warning glances, and that she probably sounded curt and rude, but she couldn't help it. She had taken an instant dislike to the smooth, good-looking Ran, with his pomaded hair, the drooping moustache accentuating moist red lips, and his expensive clothes. She had noted the signs of distress, quickly concealed, on Cicely's face when her husband had commented on her health: that was uncalled for, Molly thought. She wrapped the shawl closer round her exposed shoulders, acutely aware that this defensive gesture amused her host. It was going to be a long evening.

*

Sometime during the night Molly awoke, feeling uneasy. The knob on her door clicked: she held her breath, thankful that she had turned the key in the lock. Then she silently chided herself. Was it Nancy, coming to fetch her because Fay was unwell?

She called out, feeling rather foolish. 'Who's there?'

There was no reply, only the sound of softly retreating footsteps.

Just as Molly began to relax again, turning her pillow and shaking it, to induce sleep, she thought she heard a muffled cry. But she must have imagined it because then there was silence, and eventually sleep did claim her, and the next thing she knew it was morning, and the maid was knocking on her door because it was time for early-morning tea.

Randolph did not appear at the breakfast table. Cicely poured tea with a bright smile seemingly fixed on her face, but Molly, and Alexa, too, noted the slight trembling of her hands. The floaty scarf round her neck did not quite conceal the red marks on her throat.

Chapter Six

Huge posters appeared, boldly illustrated, all around and out of town: obscuring shop windows, slapped up on blank walls, hammered on barn doors, creased on sandwich boards: WINGER'S NEW CIRCUS – MAGNIFICENT! THRILLS, THRILLS, THRILLS! CRAZY CLOWNS! KELLY'S ACROBATS! EQUESTRIAN FEATS! FELIPE'S FLYING TRAPEZE! AND MUCH MORE! Pictures of all these, at odd angles, crowded every inch of space, jostling the smaller print but having the desired effect for the posters required much studying and head-turning from side to side.

Then came the ear-splitting ringing as the giant King poles were struck with military precision, followed by the Queens, the quarters and the side poles. There was an outbreak of cheering as the Big Top finally followed and became taut. Naptha lights were secured. Seating was carried in and arranged before the side canvas was added; the performers were responsible for the erection and safety of their own apparatus. Soon rehearsing would begin on the freshly strewn sawdust.

A settlement of smaller tents and wagons mushroomed at a discreet distance from the Big Top on the ground which was the circus's temporary home, the tober. The travelling blacksmith was already busy with repairs, the sideshows were set up, the noise and bustle was deafening, the anticipation almost unbearable to the small-fry watching at a respectful distance.

Then there was the grand parade through the streets, crowded on either side by eager spectators, to drum up customers for the first performance. It certainly did not seem like a small circus though it was, having just one performing ring. The Wirths and the Colleanos were the great names of the Australian circus scene. None of them featured here – but this show had the Kellys, acrobats who juggled, walked and bounced on the slack wire.

The bandwagon, drawn by a team of beautifully turned out liberty horses, almost took Molly's breath away. She, Nancy and Fay had been lured away from their shopping by the music – literally swept along by the crowd. The decorations on the wagon were in white and gilt bas-relief, depicting nubile maidens in scanty Grecian dress pursued by muscular young men in chariots. The wheels were painted crimson, with the spokes picked out in gold.

The musicians – brass buttons and instruments polished and gleaming in the sun – played with panache. They were followed by a white-faced clown with a chattering chimpanzee on his shoulder, arms clutched around his neck. A statuesque woman, robed like the pictures on the wagon panels, with her hair in a topknot to complement the brace of black French poodles posing on their hind legs, marched behind. The leading horses were ridden by girls in spangled costumes, with plumed headbands like their steeds. Alongside the parade, clowns towered on stilts, waving cheerily to the excited masses. The ringmaster doffed his top hat and cracked his whip. He was accompanied by a little fellow, a miniature version of himself, identically dressed, running to keep up, but pausing now and then to bow to the onlookers in appreciation of their applause. The enduring legend of tiny General Tom Thumb, a protégé of the great Barnum and a firm favourite of Queen Victoria, assured his popularity.

'*First performance at two o'clock!*' was the spiel, loud

59

and clear, as the bandwagon passed. Then there were the cage-wagons with their glimpses of exotic animals which sent a shiver down the spine . . . just suppose one escaped! Finally, the dust settled, and the crowd slowly dispersed.

'Oh, I'd give anything to be part of all that!' Molly said aloud.

Nancy grinned at her, hoisting Fay higher on her sturdy young shoulders. 'You'd fit in all right, I reckon – if you had them spangles!'

They arrived early, so that they could wander round the sideshows before they settled in their seats. Alexa needn't have worried that Fay would become restless. She sat, thumb in mouth, absorbed in all that was going on. She took her cue from Molly and Nancy, laughing when they did at the rumbustious clowns and their fooling – pointing dramatically upwards whenever they gasped at seemingly impossible feats on the trapeze or high wire.

The Kelly troupe of acrobats had them holding their breath, too, with their juggling on the bouncing rope, their pliable limbs bending, somersaulting, flip-flapping with incredible speed. They were dressed identically in white tights and sequinned cropped jackets, flashing silver, when the four men discarded their capes after their entrance, and the two women tossed aside their tulle skirts. Long, braided black hair was the females' only concession to femininity.

Which of the three younger men was Rory Kelly? Molly wondered. Two were tall and dark like the women; the other was shorter, stockier, with sandy hair which gleamed gold under the spotlights. He was obviously related to the older man, the muscular foundation of the act, who caught and held steady the others – the one on whom they relied at all times.

The girls skipped off to return with the rosin-backs, palomino ponies that wheeled and turned, two abreast, with their riders performing fearless feats on the leading pair. One by one, as the ponies passed them in the ring, the other acrobats leapt on their pre-selected mount and, gripping with their feet, stood perfectly balanced, waving to the audience.

Molly was quite carried away with all the cheering. After the Kellys swept off she was soon wiping her eyes as the tiny clown they had seen in the parade made them laugh with his tricks on the unicycle, hindered by the antics of the poodles and their woman trainer who indignantly insisted that the clown was encroaching on her act. It was a put-up job, they all knew that.

All too soon it was over and they walked reluctantly from the Big Top, blinking in the bright afternoon light.

'I wish we could go again tonight,' Nancy breathed.

'Nancy, let's hang about here a bit – I want to find out if Mrs Kelly's son is one of the acrobats,' Molly suggested impulsively.

'We oughter get back, I reckon, or Mrs Nagel will be worrying where we are. Besides, the chauffeur will be at the gate, waiting – we told him four o'clock,' Nancy reminded her.

'Please! Not longer than half an hour, I promise! Jackson will wait,' Molly pleaded.

'Oh, all right. But if Fay starts grizzling, well—'

'I know you know your duty! Thanks, Nancy.'

They struck lucky with their first enquiry at one of the booths. 'Rory Kelly?' A woman was taking the money from those wishing to enter a tent to marvel at the freaks, even if they hadn't yet recovered from fearfully watching the Big Cats. She smiled at Molly. 'Friend, are you? Over there – behind the Big Top, the dressing tent. Don't you just barge in, mind. Call out first. If he's there, he'll answer.'

One of the dark-haired acrobats invited them to step just inside the tent flap, which made the girls blush when they realised they were in the half reserved for the males to change. 'All decent, I believe,' he said cheerfully. 'That's Rory over there, with the leader of our troupe, his uncle – you're a friend of his mother, you say?'

61

Molly felt a little pang of disappointment that this was not Rory himself, for the tall young man was very dashing. 'My brother, Alfredo – Alfie!' he introduced them. 'I am Carlos, but out of the ring plain Charlie. We have joined the Kellys for this tour, with our wives, but in Europe we are with our own family. You may have heard of us – the Orlas? Ah, Rory Kelly. You have some admirers, it seems!'

Molly blushed again as Rory turned, startled, then walked towards them, followed by the older man.

'You're Molly Sparkes? Yes, my mother did mention you, but I didn't somehow think we would meet like this. Australia is a such a big country!'

'I know,' she managed. 'I just thought – well, it might be you . . . This is my friend Nancy, and this is Fay.'

'Good to meet you all! We're busy for a while, I am afraid, but if you can stay around for an hour or so, it would be nice to talk.'

Nancy nudged Molly in the ribs. She said airily: 'I'll see you to the gate, Nancy, to be sure that Jackson is there – then you can explain to Mrs Nagel and Mrs Colton that I will return later on by cab, and not to send out a search party, eh?'

She could tell that Nancy was not too sure she should leave her on her own with such new acquaintances. 'I promise to be back before six. It's still broad daylight, after all. Mrs Nagel met Mrs Kelly in Melbourne, too, so I'm sure she won't be alarmed.'

'I will ask my wife to act as chaperone,' Rory's uncle assured Nancy.

She sat in the Kelly family wagon, with Rory and his uncle and aunt, drinking tea and eating soda bread dotted with currants and spread thickly with butter. To Molly's surprise, Mrs Cora Kelly turned out to be the tall willowy trainer of the poodles, who were much in evidence, begging for titbits at the table. Mrs Kelly was not aloof at all, but full of fun. The men let her do most of the talking, but now and again Molly was aware that Rory was looking at her and smiling. She told herself firmly: I'm not going to succumb to physical attraction this time – I mustn't fall in love with every handsome chap I meet. I've had one brief excursion in romance which came to nothing, after all . . . She should be happy just to relax in good company and feel that she had made new friends, she promised herself.

'Come and see us rehearse something for the evening performance. Wouldn't you like a glimpse of what goes on behind the scenes?' Rory invited her.

Despite her good intentions Molly was glad she was wearing her striking scarlet blouse because she was very aware that heads turned admiringly as they made their way back to the Big Top.

The strong man, in leopardskin leotard and wide buckled belt ornamented with medallions, grunted a greeting as he lifted a great iron bar, the sweat running in rivulets down his neck.

'Hello,' Molly breathed in awe.

Rory's uncle lay in the *trinka*, or cradle, to steady him, while he juggled globes with his feet; Rory helped Molly, when she had shed her shoes and donned borrowed slippers, to balance on the low wire. She managed a few steps to her own delight, before she swayed and was caught in his arms. Oh, dear, she thought, here I go again. He's so strong, and the way his hair flops almost into his eyes is very appealing . . .

'You could soon learn, Molly,' he encouraged her, releasing her with a grin.

'Not in that skirt,' one of the watching girl acrobats said, with a touch of spite. 'Finished with my slippers?'

'Could I really?' Molly asked Rory, ignoring the girl.

'With me to teach you, yes. You have a very slender supple body.' His hands were unselfconsciously expressive.

'*Oh!*' Molly breathed. 'I should go, I think.'

'But you will come back tomorrow?'

'If I can.' She knew she would.

Alexa was displeased. 'You really are far too impulsive, Molly. We met his mother, yes, but you could hardly say we know her well, and you are still very young.'

'I'm getting on for nineteen, Alexa!' They were talking in Molly's room while she changed quickly for dinner, having arrived well after tea had been taken. 'You allowed me to go out that time with Henny, and sleep next to him in the forest.'

'I didn't know *that*!' Alexa exclaimed. She looked quite horrified. 'I do hope—'

'Allow me to finish! All perfectly innocent, nothing I can't tell you about. The same as today. Alexa, don't you see? I can't go back to England, to my old way of life.'

'Are you trying to tell me you've decided to stay on here? Don't forget I made your father a promise that I would act as your guardian, Molly. Bring you home safely, with Fay, after the year was up.'

'Actually, I hadn't thought of staying in Australia until you just put the idea into my head! I'd been wondering whether to take you up on your offer of a job in London.' Molly twisted her hair into a knot in the nape of her neck. 'Could you hook me up, please?' she asked. She felt Alexa's fingers tremble at their task, and was sorry she had upset someone she now thought of as a real friend. 'Thank you,' she said. 'I'm not going to do anything rash, I promise you.'

But she already knew that good intentions were not always enough.

'Just we two at breakfast today,' Alexa observed, already seated at the table and tackling poached egg on toast when Molly appeared at last. 'Fay was sick in the night apparently, and Nancy felt it better to let her sleep in this morning – I sent up a tray for her. She assures me there's no need to call out a doctor. I presume the child is suffering the after-effects of too much excitement – or too many sweets? – at the circus yesterday.'

'It was your idea that we should go,' Molly said mildly, helping herself to bacon and mushrooms. She had no wish to argue with Alexa, but was determined to go along to the Big Top to watch the Kellys rehearsing this morning as Rory had suggested. She hoped she would be allowed another try on the rope. 'Where are the others?' she asked.

Alexa waited until the maid had poured coffee for them both and then departed to fetch stewed prunes for her. 'Old habits die hard,' she said. 'That bowl of exotic fruit looks tempting, but my mother believed in the humble prune . . . The maid told me that Cicely is not too well, either, with one of her migraines – and Randolph, our reluctant host, breakfasted early and has taken off again.'

'What does he *do*, exactly?' Molly asked.

'He sells real estate. He's the top man, so Cicely says, in his company . . . I shouldn't say this to you Molly, but I do feel theirs is not the happiest of marriages.'

'Cicely obviously misses him when he is away, though.'

'Well, you know what they say?'

'Mmm. Absence makes the heart grow fonder! Then *you* won't need *me* around this morning, will you, Alexa?'

'I suppose not,' she replied drily. 'I may go to the local agents myself, to see if we can rent a house for our last three months in Australia. It's becoming rather obvious to me that we can't stay on here without Randolph's approval and I should hate to make things worse for dear Cicely. Oh, don't worry, it will take a while to find the right place, I imagine, and the circus is only here this week, eh?'

Molly side-stepped that one. 'Are you thinking of staying in Brisbane?'

'Perhaps. Who knows?'

Rory greeted Molly with a hug, just as if they had been friends for ages. Then he spun her round, with her feet off the ground, laughing as he did so.

65

'What's so funny?' she asked, when she got her breath back and her feet on the sawdust.

'*You*, Molly. In those breeches, you look like a little *boy!*'

She felt rather put out. 'I thought they were the best thing to wear!' she retorted, aware that they had a grinning audience of performers practising nearby. 'Having been told that a skirt was unsuitable . . .'

'You really want to try again on the rope?'

'Yes, I do. I won't cry if I fall off.'

'I'll be here to catch you,' Rory assured her. And he was.

'I ought to go back to lunch, really,' she told Aunt Cora Kelly later. Molly took in all the details of the wagon, marvelling at the way so much was packed into so small a space. Yesterday, she thought, I was too busy looking at Rory and hoping he wouldn't notice! Today, I feel comfortable with him.

'A light lunch, before the afternoon performance,' Cora said. 'Don't want stomachs of lead.'

So Molly spooned up her bowl of broth, and dipped in her bread, just as the others did.

'You did well today,' Rory's uncle told her. 'A natural, I should say. Mother in the business once, eh?'

'She was an actress. I asked Serena if she'd heard of her – her name was Florence Almond – but—'

'Music hall?' asked Thomas.

'Oh, I don't think so, but I don't really know.'

'Knew a girl of that name once. In the chorus she was.' Thomas smiled at the memory, which caused his wife to look at him sharply. 'Back in the old country, before I joined the circus. Before I met you, old girl! In one of the provincial halls . . . A bright spark, that Florence. Ambitious in the marriage stakes.'

'If it's the same Florence, then she married my father!' Molly said. I don't care if she wasn't really an actress, just a chorus girl, she thought. I expect my father thought it sounded, well, better. I really can't picture him at a music hall! But if Thomas's Florence was my mother, then that's *why* I'm *me*!

Echoing her thoughts, he said: 'That would explain it . . .'

'I've got an idea. Move your elbows, Thom, let me brush the crumbs off the cloth,' Cora admonished him. 'Molly'd make a nippy lad in the act. When the Orlas leave us, well, there could be an opening then.'

'Here, in Australia?' she exclaimed.

'No, my dear, you're going home, aren't you? So are we, hopefully to do a bit in Europe before we tack down for the winter in the eastern corner of England where my folks come from. Travelling's in our blood, Thom and me, we got no youngsters to tie us down. You're coming with us, too, aren't you Rory?'

'I'm thinking about it, particularly if Molly is!'

'When are you intending to go?' she asked, feeling flattered.

'End of the season. May, maybe June.'

'Then we could all be sailing together.'

'Doubt we'd be in the same class – but we'd make sure we all met up the other end,' Cora said.

Molly wisely said nothing about her meal in the caravan but ate another, more substantial, lunch with Alexa and Cicely when she arrived back at the house.

Alexa waved a letter at her: 'Elfie's getting married, Molly, and she wants me to be there, to keep Frank in line. The wedding's the day after tomorrow which means leaving this afternoon. She suggests that we – she means you, Nancy and Fay, of course, only Fay is still under the weather – should stay at Ernst's house—'

'Why don't you take Cicely?' Molly suggested. 'We'll be all right here, if she doesn't object? It wouldn't do Fay any good to go on the train if she's still feeling sick, would it?'

'It could well be beneficial, Cicely, for you to get away for a few days,' Alexa considered. 'What d'you think?' she asked her.

'Well,' their hostess was already brightening up, 'it would certainly take my mind off – things – with Ran away, and the girls would have the staff here to take care of them. Could I get packed in time, though?'

'I'll help you!' Molly offered.

'Just one thing, my girl,' Alexa told her. 'I don't want you to be dashing off all the time to your new friends in the circus. We'll be back by Friday, and as they don't move on until after the Saturday performances, you'll be able to see them then.'

'I promise I'll stay here with Nancy and Fay,' Molly assured her. Now she'd have to write a letter to Rory! But she hugged the secret of what might come to be to herself, because now was definitely not the moment to divulge that . . .

Chapter Seven

It was rather nice, Molly thought, to play house on their own when the servants retired to their quarters downstairs. She made Nancy laugh as they sat that night in her room after Fay was asleep, gossiping over the last cup of tea of the day.

'Wish I'd been with you this mornin' – watching you bouncing about on that rope,' the other girl said wistfully.

'Don't you miss your family, Nancy, when you're away from them like now?' Molly asked, a little later. She was curious about Nancy's family, but her friend was strangely reticent on the subject. 'There are a lot of you, aren't there?' she prompted.

Nancy's face clouded. 'There are. It's not a life I want to talk about, though. I'm glad to be away from it. It suits me fine, livin' in, like I am at the moment. I'll miss you when you leave, though. Well, I'm ready for some shut-eye now in case I get another disturbed night. How about you?' Molly wasn't really prying, but her questioning clearly made Nancy uneasy.

She took the hint. 'Goodnight, Nancy, sweet dreams,' she said. 'Remember, I'm only next door . . .'

'Night, Molly dear.'

The stairs creaked as Randolph Colton made his way upstairs well after midnight. He was exceedingly drunk.

This was not a regular thing with him but some incident would trigger him off and then he would drink steadily, always spirits, for hours. This time the cause had been an abortive invitation to the theatre he had issued to a client. It was out of town, necessitating a long drive, just the two of them in close proximity. He had considered her to be a woman who needed a man, and he was definitely a man who desired a woman, but she had firmly shut her hotel door in his face. 'Go away! You disgust me, slobbering over me like that!'

Stumbling back to the waiting cab, he had inadvertently given his home address, instead of the hotel where he himself was staying. It had been a long drive back, and he'd slept until the fare was rudely demanded, his pockets emptied, and he was abandoned on his front steps. His servants affected not to hear his arrival, deeming it wiser.

He looked into his wife's room, but she was obviously not there. He moved on, surprised, to pause, swaying, outside Molly's door. He tried the handle, finding it unlocked for once.

Molly was lying on top of the covers on her bed, turning the pages of a book. She was finding it difficult to get to sleep tonight, after all the excitement at the circus. When the door swung open, and she recognised who was there, she sat bolt upright only to be pushed roughly down again. Strong arms pinioned her. She could feel the heat of his sweaty hands through the flimsy cotton shift she wore; could smell the strong liquor on his breath. In the flickering candlelight, he loomed over her. She opened her mouth to scream as his face came nearer, then he fell upon her, trapping her with the weight of his body, and she knew instinctively what he intended to do, although such things had never been mentioned at the convent school.

Even as she struggled, but could make no sound, Nancy came rushing in and pounded her attacker furiously on the back. He released his grip on Molly, turning to curse the other girl and shake her off, to push her outside and lock the door. Nancy's fist came up smartly and smacked him on the point of his jaw. Randolph lurched, then fell backwards across Molly's legs on the bed. Frantically, she pulled herself free and scrambled to the floor.

'Oh, Nancy, thank you!' she sobbed hysterically. 'Is – is he *dead*?'

She was answered by moaning as Randolph came to his senses, sitting up groggily and rubbing his jaw. He looked puzzled. 'What did you do that for?' he muttered.

Nancy actually put her arm round him, not unkindly. 'Come on, Mr Colton, I'll put you to bed. He didn't mean to frighten you, Molly, I'm sure . . . It's the drink, you see. Will you help me steady him along the corridor? I don't want him to crash down again and wake Fay up.'

Molly could hardly bring herself to touch him, but she forced herself somehow to propel him along on the other side. He seemed semi-conscious.

'You go back to my room, Molly, and lock the door,' Nancy said quietly. 'I'll keep watch on him, you listen out for the little one. I'll knock for you to open up when he's asleep.'

'You were marvellous, Nancy,' Molly whispered shakily. 'Wherever did you learn to punch like that?'

'Don't I have a father and big brothers as gets drunk?' she asked simply. Together they rolled Randolph on to his bed.

Poor Nancy would not tell Molly that she had, far too often, submitted to the violation she had just prevented her friend from enduring. She added now: 'It was easy, really. There's only *one* of him.'

Molly lay awake for what she imagined to be hours but Nancy did not return and eventually she fell asleep. Fay, thank goodness, slept through it all.

Nancy crept along the corridor to the bathroom where she was wretchedly sick. It always had that effect on her. She washed her face in the basin and fought to compose herself.

71

She had taken in silence the payment exacted for that punch, for Molly's sake. Colton had all too soon revived.

It was almost dawn when she knocked on the door. Molly opened it cautiously. 'Are you all right, Nancy?' she asked apprehensively. She had drifted in and out of sleep herself. Now she wondered why it had taken so long before her friend returned.

'Quite all right, Molly. But I might as well stay up now, I think. I'll get dressed. You go back to bed for a while . . .' Somehow she managed to keep her voice steady.

'Randolph . . .?' Molly asked fearfully.

'He's sleeping it off. Don't worry, Molly, I don't think he's really a drinking man.' Mentally she crossed herself at this lie. 'It was just that he took advantage of his wife and Mrs Nagel being away . . . They'll keep him in check in future. It won't happen again.' Nancy hoped fervently that this was true.

'D'you think we ought to tell Alexa about this, Nancy?'

'No. Nothing happened to you, did it?' She didn't want an inquisition. The girl was always blamed in cases like this, or so she thought, not yet knowing Alexa as Molly did. Nancy liked her job so much she didn't want to leave, be told to go home. Surely Mr Colton would keep his mouth shut if he didn't want his wife to find out? And there were no bruises that showed, one tiny consolation for her ordeal.

Molly, inexperienced as she was, accepted this advice.

Later, when Nancy carried in the breakfast tray, Molly had already washed and dressed Fay who was full of beans and obviously feeling better this morning.

'He's gone off again already,' Nancy said. 'Jackson took him to the station, the housekeeper said. I don't suppose he will remember any of it. Thank you for seeing to Fay.'

'Oh, I enjoyed it – you're so quick and efficient, Nancy, I don't often get the chance nowadays!' Molly looked covertly at her friend. Thank goodness, she looked and sounded quite normal. Perhaps she was making more of this incident than it warranted, thought Molly. She'd put it out of her mind, as Nancy insisted.

Alexa and Cicely returned, a day early, full of the wedding. 'We didn't want to play gooseberry to the newly weds!' Alexa smiled.

'Excuse me,' Cicely said, 'I really must go and change my shoes and put on something more comfortable. I can slouch around while Ran's not here.'

Fay toddled over to her grandmother. 'Did you miss me?' Alexa asked fondly.

'Did Elfie look blooming?' Molly asked.

'She wore a most becoming costume. Frank was complaining, of course. He said Elfie had made a fool of him, let him down, and that I had quite a lot to do with it, too. His sister, marrying like that – and at *her* age! I hissed in his ear when I got the chance that it was a pity he was such an old grump, and that age had nothing to do with it . . . You girls obviously coped all right without us, I can see. Yes, Fay, Granny *has* got something for you in her bag. Just wait a moment while I take off my hat—'

The telephone shrilled and the maid answered it. The call was for Alexa.

While she was gone, Nancy whispered to Molly, giving her hand a little, comforting pat: 'Now remember what I said, please, Molly . . .'

'That was the agent, how fortunate we were back.' Alexa sounded excited. 'He thinks he has found us just the right property, on a short let – what are you two looking guilty about? I wonder what you *really* got up to while we were away, eh?'

When Cicely heard the news, she exclaimed, 'I shall miss you – I've been so happy to have you here,' and dabbed at her eyes.

Nancy thought: I wonder if she realised, when she went into her room, that her husband has been and gone . . .

*

The rented house was not large or sumptuous like the one they had left; it was further downtown but as Alexa observed: 'Quite adequate, and we can please ourselves with regard to outings now. Not that Cicely wasn't kindness itself.' They cooked for themselves, but a capable daily woman saw to the cleaning and laundry.

Alexa could stay up late when she chose, she thought – as she was tonight, relaxing in the square sitting room with its rather impersonal feel because it was full of the unknown owner's things. She was catching up on news from home as she re-read the morning post and smoked one of her increasingly rare cigarettes. She wished suddenly that the journeying was behind them, and that she had already handed Fay over, for she knew that it would be a cruel wrench to part with her granddaughter. Her life and priorities, she recognised, had changed unbelievably over this past year.

She glanced up, startled, when the door opened and Nancy ventured into the room. The girl's face was very pale, which made the splattering of freckles look very prominent, especially as she had combed her blonde hair back off her forehead and wound it into curling rags. Her eyes were shadowed, as if she had lately had little sleep, and she wore a crumpled old gown over a skimpy night-dress. I didn't think to 'universally provide' night attire, Alexa thought with compunction. Nancy's been very subdued ever since we moved from Cicely's. I don't like to pry, but maybe there is something wrong ... She said now: 'Is Fay all right, Nancy?'

'Oh, yes, Mrs Nagel. I just – I just wondered if you could spare me a pill?'

'Of course.' Alexa unclasped her handbag and brought out the small box of tablets. 'Headache?' she queried.

Nancy sat down suddenly and put her head in her hands, her thin shoulders shaking. Her breath was expelled in little, gasping sobs.

It was obvious to Alexa that she was deeply distressed.

Immediately, she was reminded of Lucy sobbing like that after the stupid quarrel which had led to her daughter packing and leaving home. 'Mummy, you don't understand, I *love* Matthew! I want to be with him *now*, because soon he'll be going away – we don't have much time ...' How prophetic those words had been. 'Go, then,' she'd cried. 'But don't expect me to come to your wedding! You've only known this chap a couple of months – oh, *why* did you have to be in the salesroom that day he came to select a new saddle? He's a soldier, Lucy, his career will always come first ...'

'My dear, it's not as bad as all that, surely?' Alexa took a deep breath, determined to put the memories from her. She wondered briefly why Nancy had come to her, rather than to Molly, who no doubt was sitting up in bed writing replies to the letters she had received this morning: one from Serena Kelly's son with news of the circus, she had volunteered, plus one re-addressed by Frank. It didn't take much to deduce that this crumpled letter, which Molly had tucked in her pocket, unopened, was from one who was unaware they had moved on: Henning, Alexa conjectured.

'No.' Nancy's voice sounded strangled. 'It ain't, Mrs Nagel ... I was late you see, and scared stiff, but—'

'*Late?*' Alexa stubbed out her cigarette, cleared her throat. Should she go over to the girl, put an arm round her, comfort her? She added: 'Ah ...' Then she fetched a tumbler of water from the kitchen, passed it to Nancy and shook two tablets into her hand. 'Here you are. If that's all it is, these'll soon put you right.' But she guessed there was more to come.

'I ain't been a bad girl, you know that, Mrs Nagel. I've never even had a young man – not been out on me own since I started work with you.'

'I do know that, Nancy. Is – is there anything you would like to know, my dear?' Alexa couldn't really credit that, coming from a large family, Nancy was unaware of the facts of life.

75

'I just got to tell someone . . .' she wept.

'Then why not me?' Alexa asked.

'We must confront him with this,' she raged a few moments later. 'He mustn't be allowed to get away with it! You poor child, suffering such abuse – what kind of man is he? You could well have been pregnant, as you feared . . . Whatever possessed me to leave you girls by yourselves at Cicely's?'

'You weren't to know he'd come back, Mrs Nagel, and we weren't alone in the house. There was them downstairs.'

'Why didn't you call out for help, my dear?'

'I didn't want Molly to know, she'd been frightened enough, as it was . . .'

'You are a brave girl, Nancy. Thank you for what you endured for her sake.' Alexa put out one hand awkwardly and touched the girl's wrist.

'Please, Mrs Nagel, I don't want no fuss. There ain't going to be a baby, after all, and poor Mrs Colton has enough to bear, I reckon, don't you? He'd only deny it, that sort always does. Anyway . . .' Nancy hesitated, then went on, in a whisper: 'It's happened to me before, only not – always all of it. More black eyes and that . . . I daren't say too much or I'll have to pay for telling when I have to go back home.'

'You mean,' Alexa exclaimed, sickened, 'your own family?'

Nancy nodded. She covered her face again with shaking hands at the shame of it.

Then Alexa was hugging her close and saying vehemently: 'You shan't go back there, Nancy, if I have anything to do with it. You must come to England with us – not as nursemaid, Fay's father is making his own arrangements, but I will take you to my own home and guarantee you a new life and steady work. I agree, it would destroy Cicely if we divulged all this, but I will try and restore your faith in human nature, I promise you.' And in men, she

76

thought, even though my own experience was unhappy. But although we were incompatible, at least my husband was never violent . . .

'What about Molly?' Nancy asked. 'Will she be living with you, too? Oh, Mrs Nagel, I don't deserve all this kindness.'

'Nancy, believe me, you do! As for Molly, you are probably right, we will say nothing of all this to her at the moment. I don't know if she will take me up on my offer of employment: her head is full of dreams of the circus just now it seems.' She managed a wry smile.

'We mustn't spoil her dreams!' Nancy said, in her old-fashioned way as she clung to one she had been in awe of until now. Loyalty was all she had to give, but both Alexa and Molly would be grateful for that in the years ahead.

Molly put her pen down. Blow! She'd made a big blot on the turned back sheet, she thought. She was too comfortable in bed to go down for a drop of milk to try and shift the stain; anyway, she had other things on her mind.

Rory's friendly note had told her of further circus triumphs, minor mishaps (one of Cora's poodles had bitten the ringmaster, but been forgiven, being old), and reminded her that the family hoped she really would join them, and 'learn the ropes' when they were all in England. Thom was convinced she could be a dancer like Florence – he'd recalled that she had changed her name from Nutt to Almond, by the way! Florence's high kicks were much envied by the other girls at the time. She was amazingly supple, apparently. Yes, their passage was booked – they would be travelling together, but not together, she'd know what he meant! Maybe they would meet up first at his mother's in Melbourne. Rory hoped so. Cora and Thom sent their best.

With strange reluctance, she tore open the second envelope.

My dear Molly,

I thought I could forget you, let you go out of my life, but I cannot. I know I hurt you. I also was sad in myself.

I must go back to Denmark, yes, and make my peace there. Dare I ask that you will come with me? I cannot offer marriage, indeed I should not, until I am established once more, but Molly, I know I love you – is that enough for now?

It will be difficult for you, but you have a strong heart. If you wish to come, I am sure you will, I will be at this address in Sydney, waiting. I sail on . . .

The date had come and gone, and so had Henny, more than a month ago. Molly put her head under the covers to stifle her weeping. She would have gone like a shot, even if it had meant leaving Alexa in the lurch and abandoning her plans for joining the circus. That was how being hopelessly in love affected you. She hadn't got over him after all. Now he must feel he had been a fool, writing like that, and that she didn't care. She had no idea of his address in Denmark. It was too late! It would have been better if she had never received his letter.

It was the morning of their departure for Sydney. Molly, Alexa, Nancy and Fay waved goodbye to Cicely, who had come to see them off on the train.

What was she calling out now as the train moved off and she blew them a last kiss? 'Will I ever see you again, Alexa?' Molly realised. She felt a pang of distress. Poor Cicely, left with that rotten husband, she thought. Wealth meant nothing if you didn't have happiness. She glanced at Nancy. Her friend looked happy and excited. It was really nice of Alexa to have asked her to come with them. Nancy had written to her ma, enclosing the confirmation from her employer.

Now Alexa was rubbing at a smut on Fay's face. 'Keep still, child, will you, please?' She didn't want her companions to see the tears welling in her own eyes at her old friend's final farewell words.

It won't be too long before I see the Kellys again, Molly thought. I must accept that any relationship with Henning is just not meant to be . . . but I'm going to make it clear to Rory that only friendship is on the cards for us.

'You've got a loose button on that cuff, Molly,' Nancy reproved her, giving it a little tug. The button came off in her hand. 'There you are! Can't you sew?'

'Certainly can't,' Molly admitted cheerfully.

Nancy rummaged in her bag, full of Fay's requirements and a packed lunch for them all. 'Here, I've got my mending things. Hold your arm steady,' she ordered, 'and I'll sew the button back on.'

'Mind you don't connect me to it, then! Who taught you to sew like that?' she asked curiously.

'Not Ma, I can tell you that. I learned at the mission. There you are, all done.' Nancy snipped the thread with nail scissors, not biting it off as Molly would have done.

'Sewing,' Alexa murmured. 'Now, there's an idea . . .' But she did not enlighten them further.

Serena greeted them like old friends. Rory, who had been there to meet them from the boat after the second stage of their journey, helped the cab driver carry in their luggage. 'Oh, my,' the landlady marvelled, 'young Fay's not a baby any more.'

'I'm a big girl. Old enough to know better,' she agreed.

'I can guess who told you that!' Serena said. 'Upstairs, to freshen up, eh, and then . . .'

'A nice cup of tea,' Molly finished for her. 'Elfie's changed, don't you think?' she joked. 'This is Nancy from Bodenflower, Serena. She's coming home with us.'

'Mrs Nagel advised me, in her letter. Miss Wills married, eh? The air must have perked *her* up no end! You've got the rooms you had before. I'll leave it up to you who you share with.'

*

79

'I'm glad to catch you on your own, young man,' Alexa told Rory, on entering the dining room.

He looked up with a smile from laying out cutlery on the table. 'Yes, Mrs Nagel?' He pulled out a chair, inviting her to sit down. 'Dinner won't be long, Mother's just dishing up.'

'I'm in no hurry to eat. I just wanted to warn you not to fill Molly's head with romantic tales of your way of life – before she makes her mind up to join the circus.'

'She already has,' he said mildly.

'Maybe. But she's not yet of age, and her father must give his permission. Until he does, Molly is in my charge.'

'I understand that, Mrs Nagel. But Molly will, I am very sure, do exactly as she pleases. However, I assure you I will not put pressure on her in any way. Will that do?'

'I suppose it will have to,' Alexa sighed.

He said unexpectedly: 'And please don't worry that I will take advantage of her. She is very attractive, yes, but not quite a woman yet. If we are to work together it is probably best that we have a purely friendly relationship based on trust, because that is the nature of the job. We should keep other feelings in check ... Anyway, she doesn't see me in a romantic light.'

'You are a perceptive fellow. You spoke of trust? Well, I believe I can trust you now, to do the right thing.'

'Shall we drink to that, Mrs Nagel?' He poured sherry into glasses.

He's hardly the type to bowl a maiden over, he has some maturing to do himself, Alexa thought, raising her glass to him. He's not – oh dear! – our class, but he has integrity. Despite his profession, he might even be a steadying influence on dear Molly Sparkes ...

She came rushing into the room. 'Oh, here you are! Look, Alexa, Serena gave me this ring. For good luck in the future, she says, and to remember her by!'

She flashed her hand at Alexa who couldn't help an involuntary shiver. She wouldn't say, of course, but the opal was rumoured to be an unlucky stone ...

Part Two

Chapter One

London – 1907

Alexa's house in Whitechapel was in a terrace of impeccably maintained residences, each of three storeys with heavily curtained sash windows and a railed front area opening directly on to the street. A town house, convenient for tram and train, for the city and business affairs. A place where privacy was paramount and the return of Mrs Nagel that summer to number 84, with two young ladies and a small girl, was considered none of their business by the neighbours.

The next day there was an unexpected visitor. They were all upstairs, still in the process of unpacking, tired and somewhat disorientated after their lengthy travels.

Molly volunteered to answer the shout of the daily, Mrs Moore: 'Gentleman to see you, Mrs Nagel!' when Alexa exclaimed: 'Oh, I can't face anyone until I've tidied myself – will one of you go, please?' So Molly, with Fay in tow, intent on not missing out, descended the stairs to see who waited in the square hall. It was someone so tall he partially blocked the light spilling from the stained glass window over the front door.

'Hello, man!' Fay said cheerfully, but she pulled at Molly's sleeve to let her know that she should lift her up.

Molly was aware that she was grubby from her forays under her bed, shoving a soft-topped case out of sight, for

83

attention later. She couldn't live up to Alexa and Nancy, she told herself, putting garments to one side to press before hanging them in the wardrobe, and she didn't feel guilty about it in the least. She had tied a checked duster over her hair, at Alexa's insistence, and was padding about bare-foot because it was hot. The house was carpeted from top to bottom, so she wouldn't get splinters in her feet from wooden floors which had been one of Sister Margaret Mary's dire warnings in the past. 'Slippers, Molly Sparkes – *slippers!*'

'Good morning,' she said, regarding the caller curiously. He was not only tall, he stood very straight and for a moment she was puzzled because he vaguely reminded her of her father: then she realised that it was the military bearing and that this solemn-faced stranger with short dark hair and a fierce moustache must be Fay's father.

'Good morning, I'm Matthew Dunn. I believe Mrs Nagel is expecting me?' He had a pleasant, resonant voice.

'Not *today* . . . Well, you didn't say *when* in your letter – we only got back yesterday,' Molly floundered. She couldn't pull the covering from her hair because she was holding on to Fay. She was also conscious that Matthew Dunn had glanced at her bare feet and then looked tactfully away; he seemed even loftier because the heels on her shoes would have given her the illusion of extra height.

'This is my daughter, of course.' He did not attempt to take Fay, regarding him curiously. 'And you are?'

'Molly Sparkes.'

He was smiling now, and it quite transformed his face. He was younger than Molly had imagined him to be: perhaps not yet thirty. 'Oh, I've heard all about *you!*'

She smiled back. 'Nice things, I hope?'

'Naturally! Fay, let me introduce myself. I'm your daddy.'

'You're *Matthew*,' Fay retorted, looking up at him. 'Granny said so.'

'And Granny is right. I don't mind what you call me as

84

long as we get on famously. Well, Fay, will you please fetch your granny – tell her who's here?'

Fay slid to the ground from Molly's arms and made for the stairs. 'Granny, Granny – come and see! Matthew's here!'

He wasn't smiling now. He looked at Molly and said quietly: 'She's Lucy all over again. It's amazing, *wonderful*, but it hurts . . .'

I didn't think men were as emotional as women, but poor Matthew Dunn looks so utterly bereft at this moment, Molly thought. She put out one grubby hand and lightly touched his arm. 'Come and wait in the drawing room,' she suggested.

'Your dress is all rucked up at the back, please forgive me for mentioning it,' he murmured apologetically, as he walked after her into the room.

'Well, that cheered you up, didn't it?' she said brightly, smartly tweaking her skirt. 'Even though you've made me blush!'

'You aren't expecting to take her with you today?' Alexa appealed to Matthew.

Mrs Moore had rustled up coffee and the girls had opened the french windows in the drawing room and taken Fay outside into the garden, to give the two of them a chance to talk.

'Oh, no, Mrs Nagel,' he hastened to reassure her. 'It's just that your homecoming fortunately coincided with the start of the summer holidays at school—'

'School?'

'I have recently obtained a post at a boys' preparatory school in Sevenoaks. I commence my teaching duties, mathematics, geography and games, in the autumn. I understand from Colonel Sparkes that, by a coincidence, the school is in the vicinity of the convent where his daughter was educated. He warmly recommends the education there so I shall consider it for Fay in the future.

'I am renting a house in the area, with a view to buying later on; my new address is on the note I sent you. The journey between London and Sevenoaks doesn't take long, as you know. We will come to you, or you can come to us – it's very important, I'm sure you'll agree, that you and Fay should see each other often.'

'How will you manage? Will you employ a nanny?' Alexa asked.

'I intend to devote myself to Fay, care for her myself for the next few weeks. I owe her that. Anyway, it's something I very much want to do.

'A cleaner comes in twice a week. She also deals with the laundry. From September, a kindly local lady will look after Fay at home during the day while her own older children are at school. How does that sound to you?' Matthew obviously wanted her approval of his plans.

'It – all sounds very satisfactory,' she agreed.

'I thought I might stay around here for a short while; see Fay as much as possible, so that she gets to know me properly, if that is agreeable to you? Then, when I feel she's ready, we'll go home.'

'You seem to have thought things over very well,' Alexa said. 'Of course I agree to your suggestion. Particularly as you are allowing me a little time to get used to the fact that I have to part with Fay ... But I also have a proposition to put to you. I haven't mentioned this to her yet because I wanted your opinion first. Why not invite Molly to accompany you when you return to Kent? Stay a few days to ease Fay in? I'm sure it would help.'

'Molly and Nancy will be working, shortly, in my business here in London. In Molly's case this will be purely a temporary arrangement. She has plans for a more exotic career which may, or may not, come to fruition in a few months' time,' Alexa added drily.

'I am suggesting Molly because Nancy has enough adjusting to do here at present. She has to come to terms with a very different environment ... Molly, on the other hand, takes most things happily in her stride.' She doesn't let disappointment get her down, thought Alexa.

'I can see that,' Matthew observed. 'I think it is an excellent idea, and I hope Molly will, too.' He paused, looked thoughtfully at his mother-in-law. 'We're going to be friends, aren't we? I'm really grateful for the way you have looked after Fay this past year – glad you have become so close. I won't do anything to spoil that, I promise you.'

Molly was soon enjoying a stay at Wren's Nest, Matthew and Fay's new home, a typical weatherboarded Kentish house with a big garden, in a quiet lane on the outskirts of a village. It was nice, she thought, to be at ease with a man who obviously had no romantic interest in her at all. She liked Matthew Dunn very much; she could understand how Lucy, not much older than she was now, had fallen for him. He was so good-looking, so charming, so well-mannered – and young Fay had taken to him in a big way.

Molly knew a picnic spot, an ideal outing for her final day with Fay and Matthew. 'We always came here, the convent girls, on the last days of term each July . . . The air is so good on the crest of the knoll, but if the wind is strong, it can nearly blow your head off. Once we flew a kite, but I got the string all tangled in a bush and Sister said, "Trust Molly Sparkes."'

'I can imagine,' Matthew commented, walking with loping strides, his daughter riding on his shoulders, supported by the canvas picnic bag on his back. Molly almost had to skip to keep up.

They had travelled here by bus, but there was a winding path to traverse before they began the steeper climb up the springy grass, dotted all over with what Fay called 'rabbit currants'. Near the top, under a rather stunted tree, Matthew gallantly spread his jacket for the girls to sit down on.

'You've squashed the sandwiches, sitting on them like that, Fay,' Molly observed, unwrapping the greaseproof paper packages. 'Still you've done a good job of cracking the hard-boiled eggs ...'

'You're worse than she is,' Matthew told her, amused. He lightly flicked some tomato pips from the yoke of her pale green summer dress, then moved a little further away. Molly obviously had no idea how attractive she was, with her light hair feathering in the promised breeze; how young and unexpectedly disturbing she was at that moment to one who had not looked at another woman since his brief marriage and cruel loss. 'But I wish I could persuade you to stay on with us, you know. Fay will miss you so much.'

Molly couldn't help betraying her surprise. 'Oh, I love Fay dearly and I'm going to miss her terribly, too, and one day I hope I have a little girl of my own just like her. But didn't Alexa tell you my plans? I'm going to work at her business, the House of Leather, until the autumn, to earn some money to finance my future – in case my father doesn't approve and cuts me off without a penny.'

'Oh, I'm sure he'd never do that, Molly.'

'Well, he might, because I'm going to join some friends from Australia. They're circus performers travelling in Europe right now, but they'll be wintering here in England and then they'll train me to join them in their act – they're acrobats. I don't know if my father ever mentioned it – I don't suppose he did – but I'll be following in my mother's footsteps because she was a dancer once.' Molly paused for breath.

'Steady on,' Matthew said mildly. 'Well, my offer can't compete with that ... More lemonade, Fay? Wipe your sticky hands on the grass, eh, not on your dress.'

'*Rory Kelly!*' Fay grinned. '*Whoops-a-daisy!*' And she performed a perfect somersault, landing with her feet in her father's lap.

'You don't need me,' Molly told him. 'You're a natural father, Matthew. Fay's a very lucky little girl.'

'Then I hope you'll give a favourable report to Mrs Nagel! But thank you for saying that. I do want to be a good parent to Fay more than anything. My own father also worked abroad – he still does – and my mother stayed with him. That was her choice, and I believe it was right for if things had been different Lucy would eventually have joined me in India ... When I was young I travelled with my parents, of course, until I was sent back to school here when I was twelve. They considered they were doing their best for me, but I don't want all those goodbyes for Fay. I don't want to miss out on any more of her childhood, especially as she only has me.' He cleared his throat. 'I wish you the very best of luck, and you know you're always welcome to visit us here at any time.'

'Don't worry, I will,' Molly said. Then she scrambled to her feet. 'Come on, Fay, I'm going to show you how to roll downhill – it's the greatest fun! Don't worry, Matthew, I know what I'm doing – I'll stop her going all the way!'

Matthew was surprisingly competent in the kitchen. He insisted on cooking dinner for the two of them once Fay was in bed that evening.

'Can we eat out on the terrace?' Molly asked. 'It's too nice to be cooped up indoors. We'll leave the door open so we can hear Fay if she wakes and calls.'

Matthew carried out a collapsible card table and covered the green baize with a doubled-up tablecloth. There were garden chairs already out there, and he lit a candle and stuck a single full-blown pink rose in a little vase. Molly brought cutlery and a basket of bread rolls.

Fillet steak, mushrooms cooked in butter, and mashed potato; raspberries picked from the garden, dusted with sugar and served with cream; a glass of red wine; finally, tiny cups of coffee.

'There – my clean plate speaks for itself, doesn't it? And, look, I didn't get a single thing down my front,' Molly said ingenuously. She leaned towards him across the table so that he could see the dinner dress, which Alexa had insisted she pack 'just in case', was unmarked. Her bare throat gleamed white in the candle light. 'Thank you, Matthew, I enjoyed every mouthful.'

'You're so like Lucy,' he said, almost to himself.

'Alexa said that once – not in looks, of course.' She took it as a compliment, but wondered what was coming next.

'No. Lucy was tall, like her mother, with black, curly hair – a beautiful face. She was lively like you, though, with a great sense of fun – and, like you, she had no artifice. When I saw you playing with Fay, I couldn't help thinking that Lucy would have been the same. So Alexa sees that quality in you, too? It's such a pity that she did not understand at the time, was jealous because it had been just the two of them for so long. When Lucy and I met and fell so passionately in love, she was compelled to follow her feelings and it hurt her mother dreadfully. I must guard against that myself ...'

'Oh, you'll get married again, surely?' Molly blurted out.

He shook his head. 'At the moment, I can't see that happening. She'd need to be a very special lady.'

It was getting towards dusk; the midges were becoming a nuisance. It was an excuse for Matthew to blow the candle out, pile the tray with dishes. 'Time to go in, I think. Thank you for those kind words and the good company, Molly.' He added casually, unexpectedly: 'Who is Rory Kelly?'

'He's one of my circus friends.'

'Maybe rather more than that?' he hazarded a guess.

'What has Fay been telling you! He might think – *hope* – so but —'

'But?'

'I don't have to tell you, you know!'

'Of course not. It's just that, well, over the last few days I feel we've become good friends, and I sense you're not entirely happy, despite your smiling face. I wonder: am I right?'

'You've been honest with me, so if you really want to

90

know, I fell hopelessly in love with another chap when we were on the farm. He said he was too old for me – that he was going back to his home country. I knew he had *feelings* for me because he gave himself away before he left. I told myself it was just infatuation and that I would forget him, would find someone else. It *could* have been Rory if I hadn't received a letter from the other one, saying he'd made a mistake, that he wanted us to be together. But by then it was too late. I only learned this after he had left Australia ...'

Matthew put the tray down on the table and gave her a brief brotherly hug. 'I understand how you feel, Molly, I really do,' he said softly. 'You can always talk to me.'

Rory was touring in France with Cora and Thom. He believed he had a great idea for a new double act but decided not to mention this in the letter he sat writing over afternoon tea in the caravan.

Dear Molly,

How is life treating you, now you are back at home once more? You must excuse smears of butter and crumbs from Cora's soda bread ... We live the life of Riley – well, Kelly! – as you know. Our present tour is going well, but we miss our circus 'family' in Australia, and, of course, Mum in Melbourne and the rest of 'em, scattered around Down Under.

Cora has decided to work behind the scenes in the future – she misses her dogs now they are retired and living with my mother. She and Thom send their best, and like me, look forward to seeing you when you join us in October.

We will be spending the winter in the farmhouse where Cora was born. It belongs to her cousin now. The land was sold long ago, but there are a couple of useful barns, one where we can store the caravan and things – the other we will use for rehearsing ... So you won't have to worry about proprieties in a caravan just yet!

I will advise date and address nearer the time. Cora estimates that you will need around £25 to cover your lodging and food until spring.

Meanwhile, I hope you enjoy your proposed stay with Mrs Nagel and Nancy in London. I will send this to that address.

Your friend,
Rory Kelly

Cora was busy, too, among the teacups and plates: darning the toes of a pair of pink tights. She squinted her eyes as she read the letter. 'Is it all right, Cora?' Rory asked.

'I shall have to get myself some spectacles ... Strange, I can still see plain enough to thread a needle, but print is difficult these days,' she sighed.

'I suffer from the same problem,' Thom said ruefully, reaching for the last piece of currant bread.

'Like me, with the needle, you can see what you want to see, Thom Kelly – like a pretty girl.'

'Now, Cora, I never even winked at the Orla girls.'

'And mind you behave yourself when young Molly arrives!' his wife retorted. 'Anyway, Rory will no doubt see you toe the line. He thinks we don't know why he's so keen for Molly to join the Kellys. It's not exactly usual to take on someone so inexperienced, eh?' she added slyly and passed the letter back to him. 'It'll do!'

'She made it clear,' Rory said, 'that we were just friends, and not to expect more. So did Mrs Nagel. I made her a promise.'

'You shouldn't make promises you might not be able to keep,' Cora told him shrewdly. 'I might tease my old Thom, but I know he made his mind up when he first saw me that he'd stick by me for ever.'

'And I have! But I can't help the occasional twinkle in my eye, Cora, you know that, too.' He gave his wife's topknot an affectionate tweak.

92

They know I've fallen for Molly Sparkes, Rory thought wryly. Well, I'll stick by her, just like Thom with Cora. But I'll keep my word, if I can.

Molly hugged Nancy. 'Oh, you look so smart, Nancy! I've missed you. We've got lots of giggling to catch up on! I wish we were actually working together, too, only Alexa says my sewing'd never come up to scratch so I'm to be dogsbody in the office. But I don't mind, I'm determined to earn the money I need for the winter with the Kellys!'

They were in Molly's room on Sunday evening. On Monday morning they would report for duties at the House of Leather. Nancy was showing off her new working outfit, dark suit and smart white blouse, to Molly. Arms round each other's shoulders, they smiled happily at their reflection in the cheval mirror.

'I felt all grown up until you came home, Molly!' Nancy said. She patted her unswept hair ruefully. 'This took me ages to do! Alexa made me rub in almost a whole bottle of almond oil before I washed it.'

'Well, it was worth it,' Molly observed. 'It looks all soft and honey-coloured. You'll have lots of young men buzzing round you like bees, I reckon.'

Alexa, coming to see if Molly was unpacked, heard them laughing, and smiled herself. Lucy would have been pleased to know that she had not one, but two young protégées, she knew.

Chapter Two

The long table down the centre of the workroom was heaped with remnants of leather, suede, and smooth, soft doeskins, some pale, some dyed; then there were punches and hammers, the cutting boards and knives. Two women sat there, absorbed in their work: one painstakingly hand-sewing a loop of fringing on a pouched bag, the other repairing a strap to a travelling bag which had come unfastened. A man treadled a sewing machine in an alcove, framed by a tower of drawers on either side; a small, grilled window, above his bent head afforded a glimpse of the busy street below, with those hurrying to work holding on to hats in a sudden gusty shower of rain. It was still too early in the day for customers seeking to buy a handsome Gladstone bag, a valise or even a saddle. The gas lamps flared from the domed ceiling for it was a dreary, dark morning. There was a definite smell of new leather, not unpleasant but very different from the odour of soaped, sweat-stained and worn leather saddles, boots and chaps to which Nancy was so accustomed back home in Australia. When the door closed she felt immediate unease, a prickling sensation, as if she was cornered unlikely to escape. Another familiar feeling, disturbing in this instance.

She moved forward uncertainly with Mr Loom the manager – somewhat intimidating with his frock coat, bristling black eyebrows and side-whiskers accentuating his high forehead and jutting chin – looming, she thought, beside her. He spoke in a hushed, dry voice, as if whispering in chapel. 'This is Miss Nancy Atkins – Mr Walter?' The treadle ceased its momentum. 'I leave her in your capable charge.' He turned to Nancy and surprised her with a sympathetic smile and remark. 'No need to be nervous, Miss Atkins. We were all beginners once. I will talk to you later.'

He went out through the stockroom and they heard his footsteps echoing on the stairs as he descended to the offices on the first floor. The showroom took up the entire ground floor of this tall building, and the one next door, too. The workroom was in stark contrast to that.

Nancy was starting work a full hour before Molly, although this first morning she and Mrs Nagel had kindly accompanied her on the bus from Whitechapel to the heart of the City between the Bank of England and Liverpool Street Station. The shop was in Wormword Street, a narrow road off Old Broad Street; on the way they'd passed a nice old church with a pleasant garden and a Turkish Baths with striking minarets. She'd tried to memorise the journey, for she would be travelling home on her own tonight. She was so intent on this that she walked by the other businesses without a second glance, did not even notice the steps being scrubbed and whitened, the brass plates on solicitors' doors being energetically huffed on and rubbed by an anonymous band of pale-faced cleaning women in drab clothes. Finally they'd arrived at Mrs Nagel's House of Leather. Above, to the right of the double-fronted building, were rooms rented to a brace of bespoke tailors; to the left all was Nagel's. Nancy drifted dreamily through the showroom displays – she was getting as bad as Molly, she thought ruefully. Now, she faced reality.

Mr Walter's handshake was limp, his fingers cold, white at the tips. 'Poor circulation,' he told her, with a little sigh. He obviously suffered from bad feet, too, Nancy saw as he shuffled forward to introduce her to the sewing ladies who at last looked up and stopped working for a moment. 'Nancy – this is my sister, Agnes, and this is our youngest sister, Minnie, Mrs Gage. We are a family concern here, you might say.'

'But welcome anyway! We can do with another pair of hands. Some of this latest consignment of goods from abroad needs more than a stitch or two before it can go on display,' Agnes said bluntly. She patted a chair beside her. 'Throw you in at the deep end, shall we? See what you can do? No repairs for you today – that's skilled work; we repair anything the customer brings us, however worn. We're supposed to fill idle moments ... that's a laugh, ain't it, Minnie?' Her sister's sour expression belied this, as Agnes continued '... by making small items from the scraps of new leather – Mr Loom won't have no waste – bookmarks, pencil cases, spectacle and comb cases, and that. Madam's always pleased – as if we done it from the goodness of our hearts. Here, choose from this lot, and I'll show you how to go about it.'

'Give her an apron first, Aggie,' Minnie said quickly. 'She won't want to spoil them smart clothes.' Her tone was unmistakably malicious. We don't really need anyone else up here, you've been thrust on us, was unsaid but instantly interpreted by Nancy, who flushed miserably and obediently donned the coarse apron with deep pockets. Wearing this brought her down to earth. She wasn't a young lady at all, in clothes which were more suited to an office position, but an ignorant working girl – one step up from a nursemaid, perhaps. Or was she even that? No smart uniform came with this job.

Lanky, lean people, Walt, Agnes and Minnie, no longer young, Nancy thought, but it was hard to guess their ages. All three had wiry black hair peppered with grey, but the women obviously had better circulation than their brother, judging by their florid complexions. They mopped their damp foreheads occasionally with a man's large handkerchief which they passed from hand to hand. 'Get proper steamed up, we do, it's our time of life,' as Agnes soon confided. Unlike her sister, she seemed both kind and helpful, and slowly Nancy began to relax.

'What d'you know about leather?' Walt asked when, later, they sipped at chipped mugs of scalding tea brought to them by a whistling lad with a pencil stuck behind his ear and a pocketful of twine. Agnes unwrapped slabs of bread and cheese which she generously shared with the newcomer, despite Minnie's frowns. 'Second breakfast, eh?'

'Skins,' Nancy ventured. 'Tanned, ain't they?'

'Cleaned first, of course, steeped in lime water then scraped. Tanning used to take more'n a year – sometimes three or four. They used to lay the skins in a pit and cover 'em with tan, that's oak bark, then fill the pit with water and leave it. Nowadays, they use a concentrated solution of bark and it don't take long. Then they're greased, waxed, dyed; treated with vegetable extracts, so the hides won't rot when they get wet. Heard of skiver?' Nancy shook her head. 'That's the stuff for linings. Know what yufts are?' His eager look told her he guessed she wouldn't, so he could tell her.

'No.' The cheese was hard – leather-like, she thought, as she swallowed a lump, so as not to hurt their feelings. A bit of butter on the bread would've helped, she thought. Getting used to little luxuries, wasn't she? She'd never tasted butter until she went to work for Mrs Nagel, looking after Fay, back home in Australia. These people must be poor, too. But respectable, not like her family ... More thieving and drinking her dad and the boys did than honest toil. Being the only daughter was no privilege. And her ma – poor Ma – how was she getting on without Nancy? She blinked rapidly as she took in what Walt was saying.

'Russian leather, oxhides, tough stuff. Here, feel this ...' Walt was obviously knowledgeable and enthusiastic about his trade. She cautiously rolled the piece between finger and thumb. That seemed to be the procedure. He nodded approvingly.

Skiver and yufts – yufts and skiver, Nancy repeated to herself. She had a feeling Mr Loom was going to ask her a few questions later on!

'That's a piece of Moroccan you're working on,' Agnes told her.

Nancy was actually enjoying all this background information. She'd always had an insatiable thirst for knowledge. She already had sore fingers from pushing her needle through the material, but this made it seem worthwhile. 'From Morocco, I s'pose?' she asked pertly. Some of Molly's self-confidence was gradually rubbing off on her, but she'd always been determined, in her quiet way, to rise above whatever fate threw at her. She got that from Ma.

'Invented there, Nancy, but this was made in Clerkenwell. Goatskins take the dye better and produce much brighter colours . . .'

'Where's Morocco?' Nancy wondered.

'Barbary,' Walt told her.

'Is that where the barbarians come from?'

'Shouldn't be surprised. Northern coast of Africa, I believe. Now back to the grindstone, I reckon.' He returned to his treadling and the women picked up their work.

Nancy stabbed her finger with the needle. 'Ouch!' She sucked the puncture mark hard.

Minnie cleared her throat, gave her a sly, sharp dig in the ribs, which made Nancy flinch. 'Don't get that good strip spotted. You'll need to rub some lard on your fingertips tonight.'

'Your hands'll soon get hardened to the work,' her sister added comfortingly.

Just got 'em softened up, as a lady of leisure over here, and now I'm about to ruin 'em again, Nancy thought with a rueful smile, surreptitiously rubbing her sore side. Wonder how Molly's getting on?

Molly did not need to cover up her costume, or to worry

98

about her hands, in the cubby-hole in the office where the invoices were sorted and filed. She, too, worked hard, but her morning tea was served in a china cup and saucer, with two Osborne biscuits on a matching plate. Once Mr Loom had shown her the ropes, she was on her own, although there was a young man busily rattling away on a typewriter at a nearby desk who appeared oblivious of her presence. The lad with the pencil dashed in and out at intervals, requiring paperwork for goods packed ready for despatch, but Alexa had soon left Molly for the showroom and her own office downstairs, where she dealt with monies received, drafted letters for the typist, and supervised the sales staff.

Seven-and-six a week! Molly had been secretly dismayed to realise how little she was to earn, but Alexa was, after all, a businesswoman and had told her this was an excellent wage for a mere beginner. 'And you will be able to call it all your own, spend it as you wish, Molly. Thanks to your father you will not have to pay board and lodging as most working girls have to do . . .'

She's teaching me a valuable lesson, Molly realised. She wants me to be aware what lies ahead, when I'm out in the world on my own. I'll have to eat humble pie and accept gratefully the allowance Father insists on paying into a bank account for me until I'm able to stand on my own two feet, because I'll certainly need quite a bit of it when I join the Kellys in October. I thought it would be so easy to save £25! Nancy thinks I'm lucky, anyway. She's only getting five shillings plus her keep . . .

The young man suddenly ripped a sheet of paper from his machine, startling her; turning, he crumpled the paper into a ball and aimed it at the wastepaper basket. 'Time to down tools, Miss Sparkes. We close between one and two. I usually go out for a bite of lunch. Care to accompany me?'

'Thank you, Mr Gray. I'll fetch my hat,' Molly said demurely. Despite his slicked-back hair and moustache, she realised with some relief that they were of an age. I'll make sure to pay for my own lunch, she thought, keep things on a proper footing. Still, it's kind of him to look out for me on my first day. Belatedly, she remembered Nancy. 'Oh, my friend, upstairs . . .'

'*They* only get half-an-hour off, I'm afraid. You need the full hour for where I'm taking you today. Doesn't seem fair, eh? Pity, because I'd like to be properly introduced to your Miss Atkins . . . she'll find it best to bring a packed lunch, or buy a sandwich and eat it out in the fresh air as I usually do. I keep wondering about the Turkish Baths, but I haven't plucked up the courage to go there yet. And if you're wondering, and she didn't say – our esteemed Mrs Nagel usually lunches with Mr Loom. Well, I'll see you outside the shop shortly, shall I?' he added tactfully, for it had been a long morning without a visit to the cloakroom.

He's put two and two together, guessed Alexa and I are connected in some way, Molly thought, plonking her unsuitable hat firmly on her head and peering into the small mirror hung on the cloakroom wall. Really, I'd have thought Alexa would have advised me not to buy this; it's far too big and blooming for a mere dogsbody, with all these silly silk cabbage roses! Oh, and I must remember to buy Nancy a bun and tell her to pack some food for tomorrow. Alexa never said. I didn't realise we'd be, well, separated like this. Alexa believes she's liberal in her views, but *I'm* in the office, and *Nancy's* in the workroom . . .

Molly almost skipped along to keep up with Arthur Gray. 'We mustn't dawdle, it's a fair way,' he told her, 'and Mr Loom's a stickler for time . . . Call me Art, out of the office – and I'll call you Molly.'

From the outside the eating establishment looked a gloomy place; all peeling brown paint and windows almost obscured by trade advertisements, faded by the light. One wall was tiled in blue and white, which made Molly smile for they were identical to the tiles in the shop WC. There were high-backed settles facing narrow tables, the wood more scarred than polished; on the other side, a long counter with brass scales, a huge, crumbed ham with a lethal-looking knife to one side, yellow slab cake under a glass dome. The shelves behind were crammed with packets of tea, sugar, biscuits, jars of preserves and tins. The two men serving wore long white aprons and had rolled up their shirt sleeves displaying hairy arms and hands that were big and red like the ham they carved for almost every customer.

There was a wonderful smell coming from a room off the shop, and when the door opened it was intensified in a cloud of steam. The place was crowded: the menu always the same, the tables served in turn, Art told Molly. A little woman, almost tripping over her apron, carried forth a heavy tray on which stood a basin tied with a cloth turban, a tureen of floury boiled potatoes, a dish of mushy peas and four large white plates. She untied the pudding, cut into the suet crust and ladled out the portions of steak and kidney and thick gravy. The patrons waited in respectful silence as their plates were heaped with vegetables. Then they passed the cruet, dobbing on freshly made mustard, elbows well in, for space was limited. Just one last thing to make the meal perfect: a glass of beer, stout, or still lemonade.

When Molly had eaten as much as she could, she wondered how on earth she would be able to work through the afternoon, for she already felt sleepy; let alone skip, or more like stagger, back to Nagel's. All this for sixpence! Delicious but too filling for her small frame.

'It's very nice, but I don't think I could eat here every day!' she murmured faintly.

Art downed the last of his beer. There was froth on his moustache. He winked. 'Special treat – one to make you remember your first day at work, Molly. Tomorrow, if you like, I'll show you a few of the sights of London here-abouts, and we'll eat sandwiches in the churchyard. Don't worry, you can hang on to my arm on the way back.'

She remembered to buy a piece of the cake for Nancy, and she did take his arm; she already knew she liked young Art and that, along with the steak and kidney pud, he would be part of her memories of this day. She just wished Nancy could have been with them. Art obviously thought so, too, for he said casually at one point: 'Got a young man, has she, your friend? Must have, I suppose, she's got such a pretty face. Oh, and all that lovely fair hair . . . she must have brightened up the old workroom no end.'

'No, she's not spoken for,' Molly said, hoping she'd used the right expression. 'Like me to introduce you, when we get the chance?'

'*Rather!*' he said.

Nancy's day had been long and claustrophobic, closeted for ten hours in that top room. The cake Molly had sent up by the lad, with a scribbled note, had helped, but now she felt hungry and hoped that Mrs Nagel had something special in mind for their evening meal. 'See you tomorrow,' Walt said cheerfully, when they downed tools at last. She wondered where they lived; together, probably, she conjectured. She knew nothing about their lives outside the workroom after this first day, and they seemed incurious about hers. They hadn't even remarked on her accent.

As she hurried to catch her bus, she became aware of footsteps quickening behind her. She turned her head and with relief realised it was only Mr Loom. He caught her up. 'I go your way, I actually live just around the corner from you with my mother. We might travel together, eh?'

She took a deep breath, worries about the journey evaporating. 'Oh, yes, please, Mr Loom!' she said.

He, too, offered his arm, and Nancy took it, feeling happy again. He was a real gent, and not so old as she'd thought.

'I'm sure you're feeling tired after all your hard work,' he said kindly. 'Mr Walter tells me you are going to be a real asset to the workroom. Well done, Miss Atkins.'

'Thank you,' she said, all aglow.

The others had been home an hour before Nancy was delivered to her door. There was no tantalising smell of cooking, though. A letter had been waiting on the mat, from Australia. Shocking news from Elfie: Frank had died unexpectedly, following a fall from his horse. The farm would have to be sold up – wasn't it fortunate she had dear Ernst to help her with all this?

And all Molly could think was: Henny won't be able to get in touch with me now that link is gone.

Chapter Three

'I knew my luck was in,' Art said, 'when two pretty girls arrived at Nagel's on the same day! Glad you sneaked out to join us in the churchyard, Nancy. I'll make sure you get back in good time, don't worry. Did I tell you I was thinking of emigrating to Australia?'

'Don't believe a word he says, Nancy,' Molly advised her.

'Well, it could be true – who knows? I'm getting nowhere fast in leather goods. The only step up is into old Loom's shoes, and he's not going anywhere; he had his moment of glory being in charge while Madam was away, he's accepted his life sentence.'

'Now, Art, he's a nice chap. He's been particularly kind to you, hasn't he, Nancy?'

She nodded in agreement. She had needed a bit of persuading by Molly when they met up in the cloakroom at lunchtime, to come out here with her sandwiches. Art's evident interest in her was rather disconcerting, but she had to agree with Molly: he was jolly good company, and one of nature's gentlemen. Clever, too, he'd let slip that he made good use of the public library.

'I wonder why?' Art brushed the crumbs from his waistcoat and trousers. He looked at his watch. 'Two more minutes.' He struck a match to light a crumpled half of a cigarette, in what was obviously a familiar routine – half before lunch, the remainder after. Despite his superficial smartness, Art must have to juggle with his wages, too, Nancy thought. And what had he told them of his life outside the office? Nothing at all. She hoped he wasn't going to be too curious about her background before London. This was a challenging new start: she was determined to succeed and to rise above the trials of the workroom.

The wind ruffled the grass, and the pigeons rose in a flapping flurry as the heavy door of the church swung open and a woman in black came out, startling the three of them.

'We don't know what you mean with regard to Mr Loom,' Molly said, giving her skirts a twitch as she rose reluctantly from the bench by the wall. 'Up you get, Nancy, time we were walking you back.'

'He ain't past looking, as they say. Work it out for yourselves . . . Darn! Singed me 'tash!' he said ruefully, as the match flared. He gave up and ground the stub under his heel. 'All right, let's go!' He caught Nancy up, whispered in her ear: 'You'll come here again with us, won't you? And maybe next time you'll *talk* to me, not just nod your head . . .'

Mr Loom always asked: 'D'you mind if I glance at my paper?' when he and Nancy sat side by side, but with a definite space between them, on the journey home on the jolting horse-bus at the end of each working day. She nodded, and looked out of the window at the passing scene; the noise and bustle of London life no longer made her flinch. In the beginning, when the first excitement wore off, she had fought to conceal her almost overwhelming homesickness. She was so grateful to have left the harshness of her family life, but – home was still home, she thought . . . She didn't even confide in Molly. She was used to keeping secrets.

It was now almost the end of September. Soon, Molly would be leaving London and embarking on the rigorous training for her thrilling new life ... Nancy's work was exacting, too, but hardly exciting. Oh, she had swiftly become adept and both Walt and Mr Loom were generous with their praise and encouragement, but she found Minnie's covert dislike, spiteful nudges and pinching hard to bear. It puzzled and hurt her when she tried so hard to please. She did not suspect that Minnie was jealous of the attention paid to her by the manager.

Mr Loom waited at the gate to see Nancy enter the house, then he replaced his hat and set off briskly down the road. Gladstone bag in hand, furled umbrella under his arm. There was something about young Nancy, he thought, a hint of vulnerability, which prompted him to ensure that he accompanied her home from work now the nights were drawing in. She'd laugh, he smiled wryly to himself, if she knew that she was the first young woman he'd had on his arm. Yes, Nancy Atkins was someone to respect, despite her odd, sometimes slipshod speech; he actually found her accent appealing. Not that she would ever look at an old buffer like himself in a romantic light – and, anyway, Mrs Nagel was hardly likely to approve if he pursued this tenuous friendship, was she?

He lived in the top half of a house which was similar to Mrs Nagel's but not as well-kept. The properties in his road were all rented out, and mostly divided into flats. He had never been inside his employer's house; would not dream of inviting her into his own home. Mrs Nagel had a daily help to do the housework while she was away at her business; Mr Loom, so smart during the day, now donned an apron very similar to that worn by the siblings in the workroom, and by Nancy. Every evening he tidied up the living room, remade his mother's bed, helped her into a clean flannel nightgown, listened patiently to her grumbling, which he knew she could not help, being disabled and confined up here all day on her own. Then, while he cooked supper, he set the wax cylinder of his beloved

106

phonograph in motion, and the deep, almost masculine voice of Clara Butt, that statuesque singer, soothed them both with the soulful 'Abide With Me'. Later, he might play his violin, if Mother asked.

'Len!' came the querulous call as soon as his key turned in the lock. 'Is that you?'

'Yes, Mother, it's me,' he answered as he unloaded the shopping: the lamb chops, well wrapped in newspaper; the crusty bread, bought that lunchtime in Leadenhall market, from the smart leather bag, so essential for the businessman. Purchased at staff discount, of course.

Nancy and Molly sneaked a few moments together in the cloakroom: after lunch. Nancy had eaten in the workroom today.

Molly whispered, with one eye on the door: 'Art wants to take us out on the town one evening before I leave.'

Nancy winced as she dried her sore hands on the towel. 'Mrs Nagel wouldn't agree!'

'Nonsense, of course she would. He's a perfectly respectable young man, and we could, well, chaperone each other. Though that's ridiculous now we're both working girls and entitled to decide for ourselves who we go out with and where we go . . . I told him I'd love to go to a music hall – how about you? Just to get an idea of what it might have been like when my mother trod the boards, eh?'

Minnie came in just then, gave Nancy a meaningful glare but said nothing. She entered the cubicle and shot the bolt.

Nancy grimaced at Molly and whispered, 'She's checking up on me: that's the signal for me to get back to the workbench. Count me in! 'Bye!'

'I shall come with you,' Alexa decided. 'It will be my treat – I insist – I can't have that young man taking you girls up into the gallery. Or the Gods, I believe they call it. If you must go to the music hall rather than the new Gaiety Theatre in the Aldwych, where they put on some very good musical shows, I shall select the place and book four seats in the stalls.'

Molly tried not to show her disappointment at being cheated of sitting up aloft, which sounded much more fun as she said to Nancy later.

'*Very posh!*' Art exclaimed as he and Molly shivered a bit in the churchyard. Eating out at lunchtimes was obviously not going to last much longer. Today, Molly reflected, was much more steak-and-kidney pud weather, but that was the treat she had in mind for Art, and hopefully Nancy, before she went away. 'I wanted us to sit in style anyway,' he added gallantly, drawing on his squashed Richmond Gem fag-end.

'We're going for a bite to eat afterwards to make a real evening of it, so I'm not sure what time we'll roll back.'

'Oh, I imagine you young Cinderellas will have to be back before midnight!' he joked. 'I've got my own key to the door since I turned twenty-one.' He paused. 'The only thing is, Molly, I do feel . . . well, I would have liked to pay for all this myself. I'd been saving towards it.' Art's pride had taken a knock; he sounded wistful.

She squeezed his hand. 'I know, and I'm sorry, Art. But Alexa – Mrs Nagel – means well. And you'll get the chance to sit next to Nancy, I'll make sure of that. I'm glad to know she's got a friend her own age, being so far from home, when I'm away.'

'Can you keep a secret? I've always put on a bit of an act where girls are concerned . . . didn't want them thinking I was getting serious too soon, I suppose. Nancy's different, Molly. She hasn't given me any encouragement but I think she's warming to me, and that makes me happy as a lark. Think you could put in a good word for me, eh, without letting on I told you I was smitten with her?'

''Course I could!' Molly told him. 'I've had a taste of romance myself, Art, only I've given it up to further my career – oh, dear, that sounds old-fashioned, doesn't it?

You and Nancy, you're very different. Good luck, because I believe you were made for each other!'

The stalls were filling fast and the air was hazily blue with cigar smoke. The cacophony from the Gods was ear-splitting. Behind them, for they were in the second row, were the family parties, all most respectable, and in the back rows the sweethearts giggled and snatched kisses. Girls who by day were prim little shop assistants or seamstresses were wearing fashionable clothes stitched by themselves, for they pored earnestly over the latest fashions in the papers and magazines, adapting them to their purse with surprising success. Their young men, with their oiled hair, yellow waistcoats and shiny patent shoes, seized their chance while the lights were lowered. Of course, they were hardly alone, but here they could relax and enjoy each other's company to the full.

Nancy, sitting between Molly and Art, who was at the end of the row after he had gallantly ushered them through, caught his glance and returned it with one of her little half-smiles. She thought how presentable he looked in his best grey lounge suit, with his narrow, sharply creased trousers which she rightly guessed he had pressed himself while his mother's iron was still hot, and the tall white linen collar, dazzling in its newness, so different from the carefully sponged celluloid collar he wore every day. She was aware, of course, that Molly had stage-managed the seating arrangements. Dear Molly, Nancy thought, always the romantic. I'm very drawn to him, I can't help myself, but I can't quite quell those niggling little fears . . . Will I ever be able to put the past behind me?

He gave her a nudge. 'You look very pretty tonight, Nancy,' he said, for her ears only.

It was true, she did look attractive, if demure, in a dove-grey dress with creamy lace jabot plus a shoulder cape and hat in navy blue; an outfit she had proudly purchased herself from her saved-up wages. Hardly the outfit to fire a young man's passion, though.

Navy blue was certainly appropriate tonight: The Best Juveniles were very popular with the audience and responded accordingly – they really were excellent acrobatic dancers. 'Reminds me of the circus, does it you?' as Molly whispered excitedly to Nancy. The three girls wore spanking clean sailor suits. Their singing was feeble but as everyone joined in with the choruses of the sea-shanties, this didn't seem to matter one bit. They pulled on the ropes with gusto and back-flipped all round the stage to rousing cheers.

Then came Arthur Prince, the ventriloquist, dressed as a naval officer, and his dummy, Jim, a cheeky rating. The audience's sympathies were, of course, with the animated Jim, not his long-suffering superior whose lips hardly twitched, thus fostering the illusion.

'Wonder how he does it?' Art muttered through his own teeth.

Alexa wore a scarlet ruched cape, more in keeping with the opera, but the great Lottie Collins, one of the main attractions of the evening, was in red, too: a daringly short frock bunched out by layers of pretty petticoats. Incongruously, she wore a Gainsborough hat, secured firmly to her bouncing curls. Art, like the rest of the males present, wore a foolish grin.

The audience rose as one, even Alexa after a prod from an over-enthusiastic Molly, to sing along with Lottie until they were hoarse, many adding their own risque words. Nancy blushed like mad when she got the gist of these, especially as Art was gripping her hand. It didn't matter; Lottie Collins, despite the fact that she was pushing forty, could pirouette and kick like a lithe young girl. They could not bear to let her go and she did not let them down.

It was a wonderful, sparkling evening's entertainment. The party were still humming the finale song, that favourite of the troops in the recent Boer War, the evocative 'Goodbye, Dolly Gray'. They were about to round the evening off with something to eat and, more importantly, drink, for they were all husky from singing and laughing.

110

Art quoted from the programme, smoothing it out on the restaurant table. By unspoken consent they had gone to the nearest refreshment place; excitement was exhausting, after all. '"Goodbye Dolly" was first performed in 1900 by Hamilton Hill – he was an Australian singer, Nancy.'

'Fancy that!' She reached out and tapped Molly's hand. 'I bet *you* can kick just as high as Lottie Collins, Molly.'

'But not reveal as much, I hope,' Alexa put in, with a mere twitch of her own mouth, hiding her surprise at Nancy's bold words.

Art speared a large wedge of hot pie onto his plate, with his fork. 'Go on,' he challenged the girls, 'how about letting me into the secret, then? What's this celebration *really* about, eh? I know Molly's going away but . . .'

He'd quite forgotten that he was sitting down to supper with his boss, until she said drily: 'You might as well enlighten him Molly, but I don't suppose he'll be as surprised as you might imagine . . . And don't be too long about it as I anticipate an awful night with indigestion after eating all this rich food so late.'

'*I mean ter say* . . .' Art murmured, after the telling. He tried to jiggle his eyebrows as George Robey had done earlier when he intoned this familiar catchphrase, but it didn't have the same effect without the incongruous school cap and the jaunty pipe.

Alexa surprised them all – proved that she'd really enjoyed the entertainment too. She lifted her hand in a Robeyish salute and told Art: 'Desist! Time to go home. You may escort us to the tram, Arthur.'

'Art's really nice, isn't he, Nancy?' Molly hinted as they sat chatting on the edge of her bed. Alexa had taken a dose of bicarb and gone straight upstairs on their return. The girls weren't tired at all. Anyway, it was Sunday tomorrow, a day of rest. On Monday Alexa would see Molly off on the train, and Nancy would go to work as usual, but not in the workroom – to her surprise Alexa had informed her, just before they went out tonight, that she was to replace Molly in the office. She had actually enjoyed the sewing and learning about leather, but she was secretly relieved to be leaving Minnie who was right when she said they didn't need her there. A little thrill bubbled up inside her at the realisation that she would be working with Art from now on. She hoped he would be as pleased as she was.

'Mmm. He is,' Nancy agreed.

'He really fancies you, you know.'

'I *do* know . . .'

'I didn't get the chance to take you two to the pud shop after all – now you can go by yourselves, but I want it still to be my treat. You're to write often and tell me how the romance is progressing. Don't protest, Nancy, I shan't believe you . . . Oh, I'll miss you.'

'And I'll miss you, Molly Sparkes.'

'That you, Art?' his mother called out when he crept past her towards the winding narrow stairs which led to the little box room where he was privileged to sleep alone, being the only son. 'Have a good time?'

He poked his head round the door. She was reading the newspaper he always brought home for her on Saturday afternoons after his morning's work. He saw her by the light of the candle, as she smoothed the paper and folded it neatly. 'Finished with it, dearie. You want it?'

He shook his head. 'No, thanks. Looked through the news, when I was on the bus . . .'

His dad stirred a bit then gave vent to an ear-splitting snore which shook the bed.

'Don't know how you can put up with that racket,' Art told her. 'Had a good time, you asked. The *best*, I'd say . . .'

'A pretty girl have anything to do with that?'

'Two pretty girls. Remember, I told you? And the fierce Mrs Nagel, only she was quite different tonight. But *one* who was special—'

'Sweet dreams, then, son. And long may they last.' Another rasping snore from the sleeper beside her. She sighed. 'Just think, he was my big romance, twenty years ago.'

They followed the porter briskly bowling Molly's luggage along the platform to the waiting train. Liverpool Street Station on a Monday morning in mid-October, mid-morning: they had purposely evaded the early rush and crush.

The carriage door was open. Suddenly they were clutching each other tightly and Molly became aware that Alexa's eyes were full of unshed tears. Instantly she felt like crying herself, even though she had scarcely slept all night in delightful anticipation of being reunited with her friends from the circus.

Alexa actually sniffed: 'I'll miss you Molly. Now, promise me you'll send a telegram to let us know you have arrived safely, won't you?'

'Oh, Alexa, you've reminded me of that at least a dozen times, but of course I will – and I'll write to you and Nancy regularly – and I'll miss you too, you know ...'

A flash of the old Alexa then. 'Oh, you'll be far too busy enjoying yourself!' Another hug, then she straightened Molly's hat for her, with a little shake of her head, and stepped back, as Molly stepped aboard.

'Look after Nancy,' she called as the engine gathered steam. 'And give my love to Fay when you see her next weekend. Oh, and say hello to Matthew for me, won't you?'

'I will!'

Mr Loom took Nancy into the office, and she enjoyed the startled expression which came over Art's face.

'You'll look after Miss Atkins, I'm sure, Mr Gray – show her the ropes as you did Miss Sparkes? There's plenty of filing for you to do this morning, Miss Atkins, the usual task for one new to office work. It's simple but tedious, I'm afraid,' he added apologetically. 'I must go now – Mr Walter to advise of the change. Plenty to do before Mrs Nagel comes in this afternoon.'

'This is a bit of all right,' Art said when Mr Loom had gone. 'You didn't say—'

'I didn't know myself until Saturday, Art.'

'Wonder what old Minnie'll think?'

'She'll be pleased. But I must say, I'll miss Walt and Aggie, they've both been very kind to me.'

'Well, I thought I was going to be lonely today. I was wondering who they might employ in Molly's place.'

'I feel rather nervous,' Nancy confessed, seating herself at the desk and looking at the pile of invoices she was to shuffle.

Unexpectedly, Art ruffled her hair from behind, making her jump and her heart thump. 'Not of me, I hope. I promise you I'll be completely businesslike while we're together in this room. I hope that doesn't disappoint you?'

'*Art!*' she exclaimed.

'Out of work, mind,' he continued, 'it will be *very* different, that's another promise!'

Chapter Four

It was good to breathe country air again, Molly thought, after the fug and fogs of London, as she and Rory bowled along the winding lane from the station in the governess cart.

They passed clusters of cottages clinging together against the winds which blasted across the North Sea from Russia. Minuscule front gardens were crammed with hardy plants: tree lupins, curly kale, periwinkle, swaying ferny tamarisk.

The Kellys' winter quarters were in a dilapidated farmhouse built on a rise, looking down on the village below. The land surrounding it, long sold, was newly ploughed and richly brown after more rain. It had been an indifferent summer leading into autumn. Molly couldn't help contrasting this with Frank's spread in Australia. Here there were small fields, sheltered by traditionally layered hedges of hornbeam, hazel, ash, sloe, and shored by stout oaks; not vast areas wired or fenced on the perimeters.

Molly received a warm hug from Cora. 'Here you are at long last, then!' It was the welcome she had been half-expecting from Rory when she'd alighted from the train, but his greeting had been more restrained. He merely took her hands in his and said: 'I'm glad to see you are still wearing Mum's ring.'

'*Thom!*' Cora called. 'He's busy setting up in the barn. You'll be limbering up there tomorrow,' she told Molly.

It was Suffolk dumplings in thick stew for lunch; just when Molly was thinking she'd have to excuse herself and sleep away an hour or two on her bed, Rory insisted that they go for a walk across the fields to the sea.

The heather seemed to stretch endlessly towards the cliff edge. 'We've missed the glorious purple,' Rory regretted. 'It's all scrubby and grey now.' Both the sky and the sea were uncompromisingly grey, too. This stretch of soft sand and the crumbling cliffs above, not many feet high but hazardous to descend, was yet to be discovered by summer visitors.

They stood shivering on the beach, whipped by the wind, with the water lapping ever nearer their feet.

'It's beautiful,' Molly said sincerely.

'But chilly, eh?' His arm went round her shoulders.

'Oh, I love to feel the wind in my hair ...' She looked up at the dark clouds massing in the sky.

'All wild and flowing, your locks,' he said softly, his gaze suddenly intense. He drew her closer, and she knew he was going to kiss her. His lips were warm and moist. 'There! You don't mind, do you? Just to show you I'm really pleased to see you again.'

'The feeling is mutual.' A friendly kiss, she told herself. No more. But it made her feel warm, all the same, despite the cold.

'I don't like doing it,' Cora said, tackling the tangles in Molly's hair with a wide-toothed comb when they were relaxing by a welcome fire in the living room after supper. 'You won't be getting it all sea-sticky like this every day, after all.'

'I made my mind up before I came, Cora. Please chop my hair really short, and then I'll wash it and dry it by the fire before I go to bed. When Rory wrote telling me all about the new act he and Thom have dreamed up, I thought, if I'm to be convincing, appearing as a *boy*, not a girl, well, long hair would give the game away – don't you agree, Rory?' she appealed to him.

'Molly's right,' he confirmed. 'You've had plenty of practise Cora, trimming the poodles; a nice boyish bob, mind, not too masculine . . . Got the scissors?'

Cora nodded. 'What d'you think, Thom?'

'What I think, and what you'll do, are two different things,' he said enigmatically. 'As long as you don't leave a poodle-topknot.'

'Now, there's an idea!' Molly laughed.

As the scissors snipped, she stared entranced into the leaping flame: Monty, that's a good name, she thought. Like Molly, it goes with Sparkes. Then, just as the poodles did after a trimming, she shook her shorn head with pleasure.

Forward rolls, handstands, cartwheels, on the sawdust-strewn floor of the barn; Molly, in practice tights and loose top, punishing her aching limbs, sweating from her exertions and glad not to have masses of hair clinging damply to her neck.

Thom was an exacting tutor: *No stalling or missing a trick. Get back on the bouncing rope – balance and timing, remember, young Mont? Stretch, stretch, now relax. Practise juggling with those balls whenever you've a spare moment. Don't rush it – slowly does it. Rope burns on your hands? You'll learn to ignore 'em. If you don't feel pain, you're not giving of your best.*

'Maybe I'm too old to learn all this,' Molly said disconsolately after a particularly gruelling session. 'Fay could do better than me!' She drooped against Rory as they squatted on bales of straw, drinking hot chocolate brought to them by a sympathetic Cora.

He cuddled her close, dropped a light kiss on her forehead. 'Come the spring, the crowd will be cheering the Kellys and Monty will be a star, I promise you . . .'

'Think yourself someone, I s'pose,' Minnie said sarcastically when she encountered Nancy in the cloakroom.

'Anyway you'd never have made good in the workroom.'
No, you'd have made sure of that, Nancy thought miserably. But I can't answer back. She hurriedly tidied her hair, replaced a pin more securely. She and Art were going to the steak and kidney pud shop this lunchtime. She didn't want to quarrel with Minnie, was just thankful she didn't have to work with her any more.

Minnie caught at her arm to detain her. 'Another thing. Don't think I haven't noticed you making up to Mr Loom. I wonder what Madam would say if she cottoned on to that? Don't imagine anything'll come of it – he had a soft spot for me after I lost my husband. I didn't encourage him, of course, but it wouldn't have taken much. You're not good enough for him. Not his sort, I tell you.'

'I never imagined I was,' Nancy managed, shocked by the tirade. 'Please let me go, Minnie.'

'Oh, your other beau's waiting, is he? Go on then!' Minnie gave her a shove, so that she caught her elbow on the door handle.

Funny-bone indeed! Nancy clutched her arm in agony, feeling quite dizzy, but she went downstairs and didn't look back. The pain was such that she didn't see Mr Loom standing at the bottom of the stairs, outside his office, until she cannoned into him. He held her steady, full of concern. 'Are you all right, Miss Atkins?'

'Ye-es . . . Just knocked my elbow.' She managed a weak smile.

He opened his door. 'Come and sit down for a minute until it wears off,' he suggested kindly.

You're not his sort. The unkind words echoed in her head. But they were true, she thought. He wouldn't be so nice if he suspected what her early life had been.

'No, thanks!' Nancy blurted out, 'Arthur – Mr Gray – is waiting for me.' And she scuttled off and left him standing there.

Mr Loom caught a later bus home that evening. He'd been

118

in danger of making a fool of himself, he realised. Nancy must have misinterpreted his concern. Perhaps it was just as well. She was better off with a younger admirer – he'd noted the interest shown in her by young Art since she had taken Molly's place in the office.

He opened his paper, but didn't read it. Mother would be wondering where he was. He'd bought ham for tea; seen them both, in that popular shop, sitting at a table together, digging into their steaming meat pudding. But they were too absorbed in each other to notice him. They'd looked right together; of an age.

Mother did not call out as usual. She must have become tired of waiting; probably dozing, he thought. He unloaded the shopping before going into her room.

She wasn't in her bed. She lay, in a heap of soiled bedclothes, on the floor. She must have been trying to crawl to the door when she'd died.

'Just going to post a letter to Molly,' Nancy called to Alexa soon after she arrived home that evening. 'Shan't be long.'

She'd upset Mr Loom, she was convinced of it. Travelling home alone for once had given her an unsettled feeling. She was determined to apologise, even though she wasn't sure for what. Hopefully, he had caught the bus after their usual one. She knew where he lived.

A woman answered the door, pointed up the stairs. 'Top floor, love. Heard him come in a few minutes ago.'

As Nancy raised her hand to knock tentatively on the door it was flung open and she saw Mr Loom, his face so drained of colour that it was as white as his apron, standing there, obviously in shock.

'What's wrong?' she asked urgently. When he didn't reply, she pushed past him and went to see for herself.

Mr Loom sat, straight-backed, in the sitting room of Alexa's house. He was still in a state of profound disbelief. It was Nancy who had shut the door on that awful sight, who had alerted the woman downstairs to the tragedy while she ran home to ask Alexa to make the urgent telephone calls for assistance. It was Nancy who'd returned to comfort him, to prompt him gently for details, who had spoken on his behalf, who made strong, sugary tea and guided his trembling hands to his mouth when he attempted to drink from the cup. When the questioning was over and his mother was gone, Nancy took him by the hand and led him away.

The whole nightmare seemed to go round and round in his head. Natural Causes, the doctor said, but there would have to be a post-mortem. Is there anyone we should call? No, he said. I am the only one left now.

'Will you stay the night here, Leonard?' Alexa asked, using his given name for the first time. She had been sitting opposite him, looking at him with concern, for some time.

He shook his head, looked round for Nancy. 'I – thank you, Mrs Nagel – I appreciate – but—'

'Nancy went back to your flat. She's tidying up.'

'She's a wonderful young lady,' he said slowly.

'Yes, she is. We are very lucky to have her,' Alexa said, clearing her throat.

We? Mr Loom thought. Mrs Nagel perhaps didn't mean it quite like that, but – yes, we are fortunate indeed . . .

Half-a-dozen hothouse roses, velvety dark red, wrapped in cellophane, lay on Nancy's desk when she returned from lunch.

'What's this?' Art teased as she bent over them. 'You didn't tell me you had a secret admirer!'

Nancy didn't answer. She took the small card from the envelope. WITH GRATEFUL THANKS FOR ALL YOUR KINDNESS. L. LOOM. She tucked it in her pocket, unwrapped the roses and looked round for a suitable container.

'Like me to fetch a vase from the showroom?' Art offered.

'Please, Art.'

Mr Loom was back at work today after yesterday's funeral. He had declined further help from Nancy and Alexa after that traumatic evening, saying it would be best if he kept busy. This was the first time they had seen him since then. Nancy had actually felt a little hurt, but Alexa said it was the reaction she would expect from one as private as Mr Loom – they must respect his wishes.

He had wished the staff good morning, as if nothing had happened, and retired to his sanctum to catch up on outstanding tasks. The roses were a complete surprise. Nancy really didn't know what to say. Should she, in turn, thank Mr Loom for his kindness?

She took the vase and the roses to the cloakroom. She was just adding water when she was startled by the clang of the chain, the noisy flushing of the cistern, then the door of the WC opened and Minnie emerged. She seems to know when she can catch me unawares on my own, Nancy thought, flustered.

Minnie actually smiled. 'He can please himself now, eh?'

'Why don't you say what you really mean, Minnie?' Nancy surprised herself with the retort.

'Heard you discovered the body – gave *comfort* to Mr Loom?'

'How dare you!' Nancy picked up the vase with trembling hands, dislodging a stray rose which fell in the basin.

'How d'you dare, more like,' was the taunt as she walked away.

Minnie retrieved the rose, snapped off the stalk, and pushed it through her buttonhole. She'd make sure Mr Loom saw her wearing it later: he could draw his own conclusions, as she had . . .

Cora was dyeing her hair at the kitchen sink when Molly sought her out for a chat and a five-minute breather from the punishing routine in the barn. Still, it was worth it: the act was slowly taking shape.

121

'I didn't realise it was so cold out, we were getting all steamed up in there.' She held her hands out to the stove, rubbing her blanched fingers.

'You mean, old Thom's a real martinet, my dear. You must remember to slip your coat on when you come to and fro – it's November after all. And it's not as cold as it will be shortly.' Cora's voice was muffled as she squeezed the black liquid from her hair. She groped for her towel on the draining board; wound it round her head. 'There, now you know my secret – but no need to tell my husband!'

She confided further, towelling her hair vigorously: 'Heard from my cousin's daughter this morning, Molly. They've decided to sell the house. We're welcome to stay here until spring, as planned, but this news made me think. I've been away from my real homeland too long, Molly, I don't belong here any more. I miss the warmth – the breadth, I suppose – of my adopted country. I must talk it over with Thom and Rory first, of course, but I'd like to return to Australia some time after Christmas. There's often a white spell here in January. We might settle down near Serena, it's what she's hoping for. We've got a bit put by, with no young ones to spend it on. The only worry, as I see it, is what about you and Rory?'

'We should be ready by then, I hope, with a double act. Thom could make sure of it!'

'It's not quite as simple as that. You two working together without me and Thom to back you up ... but not married, for one thing. You'll feel lonely, I imagine. Unless ...' Cora looked at Molly speculatively.

'No,' she said positively. 'I'm really fond of Rory but I don't want to marry him or anyone else at the moment, Cora. I've no intention of giving up after all this hard work – you don't know how much I'm looking forward to the challenge and excitement of performing in the ring, and travelling all over Europe with the circus. We'll find a solution, though Rory, of course, intends to go home, too, in a year or so. Then, I just know that one day I'll visit Australia and see you all again . . .'

'It would be so much easier if we got married,' Rory said persuasively. They were sitting on the sofa together after Cora and Thom had said goodnight.

'But I don't want a marriage of convenience, Rory.'

'Why would it have to be that?'

'Because it would,' she said firmly. Molly uncurled her legs from under her, stretched, and then bent to put on her slippers. His lips were warm on the boyish, bare nape of her neck. She sat up abruptly, ruffled, because he had caught her unawares. Hands firmly on her shoulders, he turned her to face him. 'I don't love you in *that* way,' she insisted. His grip intensified. Those strong hands and arms in which she put her trust so often while she and Rory worked out. 'You're hurting me . . .' she reminded him now. He released her immediately.

'Sorry! But your father might insist you give up your circus career before you even begin it.'

'I'll be twenty soon – that's ridiculous. I'd rather go back to Alexa and Nancy, work in the House of Leather. But it won't come to that, Rory. I want to be your partner. It means a great deal to me, being your friend – don't spoil it. You'll go back home sooner or later. Cora said once that you've never been short of lady friends . . .'

He silenced her with a lingering kiss; his clasp light this time. 'You can't say you didn't respond to that, now can you?' he challenged. 'You didn't push me away.' His face was much too close to hers.

'Oh, you wouldn't understand, if I tried to explain . . .' I'm obviously ready for a loving relationship, she thought, so why do I feel so confused?

'Think about it,' he told her as he got to his feet. 'I won't rush you into anything, and anyway I made a promise—'

'Who to?' she asked sharply.

'Mrs Nagel. I said I wouldn't compromise you.'

'And you haven't,' she insisted.

'Ah, but I *wanted* to.'

In the end, Nancy said nothing about the roses. The evening ritual, the travelling together, was not resumed. Mr Loom stayed on later at work. He had nothing to go home for now. Nancy's friendship with Art, by contrast, flourished. Alexa appeared to think him a suitable escort. Most Saturday evenings they went out to one of the many music halls, most within a tuppenny tram or bus ride of Whitechapel; to the new picture shows; for a simple meal; sometimes just a bag of hot chestnuts from one of the glowing braziers to be found on street corners. He never presumed to kiss her or put his arm around her in the gallery, but they held hands unselfconsciously as they strolled along past the brightly lit shop displays, marvelling at what they could never afford to buy, and he made Nancy laugh and feel like the nineteen year old she was, instead of the wan waif she had been in New South Wales. Nancy was in love, and it was wonderful. Except . . . She wished that Molly was around, so that she could share her happiness with her. Nancy wasn't sure whether Mrs Nagel would approve if she realised how fast things were developing. Didn't want to let her down: she was so grateful for all the kindness she had been shown. She guessed, rightly, that Mrs Nagel relied increasingly on her companionship now that Molly had gone away, and, surprising as it might seem, had come to regard her almost as an adopted daughter.

She's ambitious for me, Nancy thought ruefully. She wants me to make a success of my life. I can't tell her that I actually enjoyed the sewing and repairing in the workroom much more than I do the endless filing in the office, the stamping of receipts, the sometimes puzzling paperwork . . . If it hadn't been for Minnie, I might have asked to stay on in that room upstairs. But I do have the lunch-hours with

Art, and the pleasure of being with him all day, even if we're too busy to talk much then!

She realised that he was getting really serious when he said one Friday evening as they were about to go home from work: 'Would you care to have tea at my place to-morrow afternoon, Nancy? Mum is looking forward to meeting you, she says.' He made a little joke when he saw her startled expression. 'I can show you off now I've fattened you up with all those meat puds, eh?' For the first time he daringly put his arm round her, squeezed her still-slender waist.

Her instinct was to pull away, to stiffen, but that would hurt him, maybe involve explanations ... She said, breath-lessly: 'Thank your mother for asking me, Art. I'd be very pleased to come. Now, don't want to miss my bus.'

Instantly, he let her go, gave her a teasing push towards the door where she came face to face with Mr Loom. He must have heard and seen all that, she thought, blushing deeply.

'Good evening, Miss Atkins,' he said politely. 'Excuse me, I'd just like a quick word with Mr Gray before he leaves ...'

Chapter Five

It was high tea in the Grays' third-floor flat over a green-grocer's in Shoreditch: liver, bacon, mounds of onions and a great pile of mashed potato. Nancy worried that she might drip gravy down her front, like Art sometimes did on his tie in the pud shop. It would have been easier to deal with little cakes and biscuits, she thought. The family grouped tightly round the table, watched her every mouthful, smiling encouragement. There was Art's mum and his dad, who said very little, and his three younger sisters, Bet, Josie and Ann.

It was obvious that they were proud of Art who had stayed on at school to the grand old age of sixteen: 'the first office worker in the family.' Mrs Gray beamed.

As I am, in mine, Nancy mused ruefully. When she put her knife and fork together on the plate, the rest clattered theirs down in unison.

'Tea, Nancy?' Mrs Gray asked quickly. Her eyes were all twinkly like her son's.

'Yes, please.' Nancy's fears had been realised but even as she glanced down helplessly at the brown spots on her cream blouse, Mrs Gray was dabbing at them with a spittle-wetted corner of her own handkerchief. 'There! They should wash out all right, dearie.' Her head, wound round with thick brown hair like Art's, was very close to Nancy's bosom, her thumping heart. Now she knows how nervous I am, the girl thought.

*

'Your mother's nice – they all are,' she said to Art on her doorstep later.

'They like you, too,' he said happily. The street light illuminated her face, gave her a little halo, as he dared to lean towards her and tentatively kiss her. She pressed her back against the door, shut her eyes.

If he was disappointed at her compressed lips, her passive acceptance, he did not show it. He followed the kiss with a quick hug. 'There! Now I guess, we're *really* walking out together, Nancy.' He stepped aside, gave her a little salute. 'Goodnight, sweet dreams!'

Alexa opened the door even as Nancy fished for her key in her bag. 'Is everything all right?' she asked perceptively. Then put her arms around her as the girl began to sob. 'Want to tell me about it? I've put the kettle on,' she added.

Nancy pulled herself together, managed a smile. 'I'm not sure I could drink another cup of tea – Art's mum kept on filling up my cup! And goodness knows where the WC was!'

Rory wasn't giving up. When he caught Molly after one of her daring acrobatic tumbles he held her longer than necessary before he set her down, hands still spanning her slight body. She broke away, stuck out her tongue at him. 'Stop teasing, Rory!'

Thom cleared his throat, aware of the tension between them. 'In the *trinka*, boy, get those feet rolling the balls. You should practise your juggling, Molly, on the bouncing rope.'

'I still need the balancing pole,' she reminded him.

'You'll give that up before Christmas, if I have anything to do with it.'

'I'm tired – I can't wait to go back to London for Christmas, even if you're only giving me a few days off – and my back aches,' she sighed.

'Try the splits, that'll soon ease it,' he replied unfeelingly.

However, later, she overheard him telling Cora: 'The girl's doing well, she's a natural. Kelly and Sparkes, that's the new act. Shame we're not going to stay around to see the first performance.'

'You'll see it in your mind's eye,' Cora said, 'having rehearsed them in every single move so many times, Thom.'

Nancy and Alexa overwhelmed Molly with their welcome, even though Alexa scolded her a bit about her hair: she was pleased to hear that Fay and her father were joining them that evening and staying until Boxing Day which meant that she and Nancy were sharing a room and there would be plenty of opportunity for sharing delicious secrets.

Fay wound her arms tightly round Molly's neck and whispered in her ear: 'Me and Matthew have made you some fudge for Christmas!' He looked down at Molly from his great height and said he was glad to see her again, and thanks for the cards she'd sent them with all her news.

'She's grown – I can hardly believe how much!' Molly exclaimed. 'It's obvious, Matthew, that you are really happy together.'

'Just one thing missing,' he said quietly. 'But you're right, and I'm glad I took up the challenge of bringing her up on my own.'

It was Christmas Eve, and like Fay the girls hung up their pillowcases, but talked so long into the night that it was a rather grumpy Alexa who eventually deposited their gifts. 'Get to sleep now!' she admonished, just as if they were children. When she had departed, they continued their chattering.

'He keeps asking me to marry him, and I really don't understand myself why I keep saying no, Nancy.'

'You can't forget Henny, I reckon,' she said wisely.

'But I've *got* to! I'll never see him again. I know that. Dear Nancy, what about you? You and Art were made for each other.'

'No, I'm not the girl for him; or for anyone. It wouldn't be right. But I can't help thinking that maybe, if I wasn't actually in love with someone . . .'

'Whatever d'you mean?' Molly was obviously baffled by this.

'Oh, I can't explain. All I'm sure of is, I can't marry Art,' Nancy insisted.

'Just as I know that I'll never be Mrs Rory Kelly!'

'Well, I reckon there's another as has his eye on you.' Nancy seized the chance to change the direction of their conversation.

'Whoever do you mean?' Molly demanded.

'Shush! *Matthew*. Every time we visit them he asks about you, you know, and your postcards to Fay are lined up along the mantelpiece.'

'Oh, I hope Matthew and I will always be good pals, because of Fay, but he made it plain when I stayed with them in Kent that week that he has no intention of marrying again . . .' Molly dismissed the very idea, adding positively: 'No one can ever live up to Lucy in his eyes.'

Easter Monday, 1908, and Jangles circus was on the road, stopping for a week in Great Yarmouth, that busy seaside town with its soft golden sands, recuperative air, flourishing fishing industry, new public recreation grounds – ideal for the circus and summer fairs – and Missions for Seamen. It was an easy transition for Molly and Rory, after wintering in Suffolk, to cross the border to Norfolk, but they were both eager to go much further afield.

They travelled and lived together in one caravan on their new employers' rather disinterested assumption, for there was a big turnover in acts each season, that they were two young men from the same family, despite their differing accents and surnames.

It was Molly's idea, of course, to act as Monty out of the ring as well as in. She was as glad to be rid of the newly fashionable hobble skirts – as she said, just try to do a high

129

kick in *them* – as she was to keep her hair short. At Cora's suggestion she frequently rinsed it with an infusion of camomile flowers to gently lift the colour so it matched Rory's sand-gold mop and their heads gleamed the same colour under the bright lights. The slight curves of her body were easily concealed beneath baggy shirts and trousers suspended from gaudy, eye-catching braces. She had to hide something else: the flashing opal ring was now threaded on a silver chain round her neck, and tucked away under her shirt. She fitted easily into the persona of the young lad she purported to be in the act, with her light voice and smooth face, although her real age was no secret from the Jangles. Odd characters were part and parcel of circus life. It made sense for Rory and her to share their accommodation, but their sleeping quarters were strictly segregated.

Thom had arranged their first employment as Kelly and Sparkes with his old friends, the Jangles, who provided the caravan and horse. This would enable Molly and Rory to venture on to Europe unencumbered, and easily arrange lodgings. Some of the big circuses were now on permanent sites.

Rory protected her unobtrusively. When there was hard work to be done on arrival at the site, he was ready and willing. When youngsters on the tober asked Molly to join in with their impromptu games of football, she agreed enthusiastically. 'You don't have to talk,' as she told Rory later with a grin. 'Just yell – and score a goal now and then through the tent poles, then run like mad!' However, after the evening performance they kept themselves to themselves. He was the better cook, but they didn't manage many hot suppers. 'If only Cora was here,' Molly mused.

The audience were noisy, cheerful, expectant. The antics of the clowns really stirred them up. When Rory staggered into the spotlight in the ring, put down his swag and rested against a gum tree to eat his tucker, they were instantly transported to the back of beyond. Many round here had relatives down under. Some never heard from again, most would never return. 'Waltzing Matilda' died away and was replaced by a slow, muffled drum beat. A disembodied voice began to proclaim:

'Not yet a year ago, in Australia in 1907, Cooktown, already a ghost town, was flattened by a cyclone. When this young toe-ragger, this tramp, passed through, he gained an unexpected companion . . . *Watch the bluey!*'

The focus was now on the tramp's bundle, the bulging blue and grey striped blanket, his swag. Slowly, the bluey began to roll away from its owner, then, gathering momentum, it gyrated and shook alarmingly all round the ring, finally coming to a halt back by the tree. The audience sucked in their breath as the knot on the blanket twisted this way and that, and finally unravelled. More gasps as first one small bare foot and then another emerged. Two slender legs waved in the air, the blanket fell away, and a young boy with floppy golden hair waltzed away from it on his hands as the music began again; then he flipped over and over in blurring swift succession before taking a bow to thunderous applause.

His companion scratched his head, yawned and rubbed his eyes. Then he rose, caught hold of the boy and tossed him in the air. Curled like a ball, the boy bounced back into his outstretched hands; another swift movement, and he was balancing on the other's shoulders. No amount of hand-springs could dislodge him: they were in tandem.

The older youth untied a rope from round his waist, still with his burden on his back. He wound it round the tree trunk, walked away and fastened the other end to a convenient pole; bending over, he tested the rope for bounce with his hands then decanted the boy, with a determined jerk, on to the rope. He swayed alarmingly – would he fall?

He straightened up, found is balance, and began to juggle

with items thrown to him by his irate partner: half a loaf of bread, a wedge of cheese, a folded jack-knife, a cap. The small feet clung like limpets, shifting with the rhythm of the juggling; the boy grinned widely, and the crowd cheered as he chucked it all back to his companion.

The tramp, he of the holey socks and disreputable boots, slumped back against the tree, tore a lump from the bread, cut the cheese with his knife, stuck the cap on his head. He did not appear to notice as the little juggler wriggled his way back into the bluey and tied the knot. A sigh of '*A-ah* . . .' rippled through the crowd.

They made way for the stately camels, about to parade round the ring, as they slipped through the back flap. The white-faced Auguste clown patted Molly on the head: 'Well done, boy! Got 'em eating out of your hand, you have . . .'

'Well done,' Rory repeated in her ear. 'I wish I could kiss you, but I daren't. Thom and Cora would have been very proud of you if they had seen your performance tonight, your best yet.'

'I couldn't do it without your support, bless you, Rory,' she said. 'Quick, pass me the rest of that grub, will you? I've expended all my energy!' Food somehow tasted really good, she thought, even plain old bread and cheese, sweating a bit, when eaten among the powerful mingled odours of the circus.

There was a package waiting for Molly, addressed merely to M Sparkes, as she had requested, at the main post office – she had promised Alexa and Nancy to keep them as up-to-date as possible regarding her whereabouts.

'Nothing from my lot yet.' Rory was disappointed.

'Be patient! It'll be another week or so before they're back in Melbourne.'

They sat on a seat on the front, looking out to sea, watching the family parties, still well wrapped up against the bracing wind, and Molly unwrapped her parcel, exclaiming: 'Oh, look, Rory – isn't this *wonderful*?'

Protected by cardboard was a sepia-coloured photograph, postcard-sized: a picture of a laughing girl in a daringly brief costume, sparkling with sequins and revealing shapely legs, her hair piled high in carefully arranged curls. Molly spotted a ring on her engagement finger. She put her hand involuntarily to her neck, to be sure her own ring was safe.

'It could be you, Molly,' Rory exclaimed, disregarding the Norfolk jacket and knee breeches she wore this morning. They still smelt musty: they had discovered boys' clothes in a chest of drawers at the farmhouse and Molly had pounced gleefully on them for future use.

'Don't you see, Rory – it's my mother, Florence Almond? Look, on the back: DARLING EDWARD FROM FLORENCE WITH LOVE, 1886.

There was a brief accompanying note, in her father's handwriting.

Dear Molly,

I know you have a photograph of your mother, but this one seems very appropriate.

She gave it to me when we became engaged.

I think you look like her now: she was about your age when it was taken. Keep it, with my love, my dear.

Your affectionate father,
Edward Sparkes

Rory had noticed the ring, too. 'I wish you would wear Mum's ring for me, Florence Almond's daughter. And I wish you would put on a dress when we go out together and stop pretending that you are not very feminine under your disguise – cause I know better! You can't deny that, can you?'

'Well, look, I'm having fun being Monty right now, but I'll have to be Molly once we're travelling abroad, of course. You won't have to endure the smell of mothballs for much longer anyway, I reckon these hairy tweed

133

knickerbockers will be far too hot when the sun shines! As for any other commitment, let's carry on as we are. Isn't it enough that our names go together, Kelly and Sparkes?'

'I'd like it to be Kelly and Kelly ...'

On the same day in August that Molly, pretty and cool in a summery dress sprigged with tiny rosebuds, steamed across the channel with Rory towards Europe, Nancy moved up another notch in Nagel's, becoming a junior sales assistant in the showroom.

This brought her into closer contact with Mr Loom, but she admitted to herself that she was relieved not to be closeted with Art all day. She was painfully aware that she had disappointed him, hurt his feelings, by the invisible barriers she had instinctively raised between them as their relationship became more intense. It couldn't lead anywhere, she thought sadly. A decent young chap like Art deserved a girl without a past. She made excuses not to go out with him on a Saturday night, and after some time he stopped asking her. He sloped off at lunchtimes by himself; Nancy stayed in the sales ladies' restroom, picking at a packed lunch and writing letters to Molly even though she really had nothing to say.

Mr Loom watched her unobtrusively, wistfully. Once she had conquered her initial uncertainty, she fitted in well. She looked quite the young lady in her long, narrow skirt and neat tucked blouses with a black velvet bow at her throat. Her freckles were fading in the English climate, her hair had deepened to golden brown and her hands were no longer rough. Customers liked her willingness to help, her knowledge of leather. They remarked on her accent and asked about Australia. She was a real asset to the company.

'You never brought that nice girl home no more,' Art's mum observed as her son applied a pin to the winkles on his plate. Nothing like a dish of sea food for Friday supper, as she often said. 'Flash in the pan, your friendship, was it?'

'Suppose so,' Art took a large bite of bread and butter. He couldn't talk with his mouth full. Mum made them all mind their manners. He was going to make an announcement in a short while, though, but he was still mulling over what to say.

When he did speak up, Mum spilt tea on the tablecloth in her agitation, and then there was panic, with the girls running for a cloth and mopping up to try to prevent a strain. Darns was one thing, as Mum said, they showed you cared for your nice linen – tea stains was hard to shift. Sign of a slovenly housewife.

'I said,' he tried again, 'I've given it a good go at Nagel's but it's time to move on now I've plenty of experience ... There's a job going in a stockbroker's in the city; lot of running here and there to start with, but good prospects, I hear.' Less pay, and back really to being an office boy, but he wouldn't let on. That would really upset Mum. Dad, of course, just grunted. A labourer, his father. Mum was the one with the ambition. The girls weren't going into service when their turn came. Oh, no.

'Might have asked our advice,' she said at last, giving up on the tablecloth. That stain would always remind her of the day Art had sprung this news. She suspected that Nancy had something to do with it. Lovesick, her poor boy. She added: 'Mrs Nagel'll be sorry to see you go, I'm sure – told her yet?'

He swallowed hard. 'I left today. Start the new job on Monday.' He'd said goodbye to Nancy, shaken her hand. She'd looked upset, but was too late to change his mind. Best not to see her again, even though she'd said: 'Keep in touch, will you, Art?' There was an envelope in his pocket, given to him by Mr Loom with Mrs Nagel's handwriting on the front: MR GRAY, IN APPRECIATION OF ALL YOUR HARD WORK. He knew it contained money. Mum could have it. He'd lost Nancy, and he didn't understand why.

'I thought you was settled at Nagel's?' Mum sighed now.

'I was, but—'

But you can't bear seeing her every day, his mum realised. 'Well, perhaps it's for the best, boy,' she said slowly.

'I'll buy you a new cloth,' he said, then got up from the table without an excuse-me and went out of the room.

Chapter Six

They'd made it! Kelly and Sparkes were low down on the bill, it's true, but they were with one of the big circuses, and in Paris. There was one evening off, per week for exploring and going to a spectacular show where the dancers had longer legs than Molly and much more voluptuous figures. The plush seats, the thrills, the glasses of wine: she snuggled closer to Rory and did not demur when his arm went round her and his fingers lightly caressed her waist, then daringly inched higher, through the silken folds of her gown. She seemed powerless to stop him; she didn't *want* to . . .

They stayed overnight in a small boarding house, in an unfashionable back street. Their rooms were cramped, not too clean, over-furnished and the sash on the windows was broken, but it didn't dispel the magic.

She knew very well what would happen if she was foolish enough to invite him into her room. However, she returned his ardent kisses; permitted him to hold her close outside the firmly closed door. His voice was muffled as his lips moved against her bare throat: 'Oh, Molly, Molly, you're making it hard for me, you know . . .'

Why? she asked herself later, as she let her clothes drop in a heap on the floor. I could marry him, then I wouldn't have to fend off illicit passion; I admit he knows exactly how to rouse my emotions, but I'm still chasing that elusive dream . . . Henny, where are you? D'you ever think of me? Don't they say, the first love is the best love?

Molly's diary, neglected since her return from Australia, was now filling up rapidly: there was so much to write about, so much she wished to record and not forget as they moved on constantly, into the autumn, in warmer climes. In Madrid Molly met Hanna, a Danish trapeze artiste, and toyed with the idea of adding new skills to her acrobatics; however, Rory dampened her enthusiasm when he told her he had no head for real heights. He was becoming rather possessive, she thought, seemingly unaware of her need for other friends, particularly a girl friend. She had not had a confidante since Nancy.

She watched Hanna at practise one day, marvelling at her agility, her confidence, as she hurtled through the air and was caught by her brother. This was yet another family act, one much higher in the billing than their own. 'Hello, Molly!' Hanna called cheerily as she came swinging down to the ground on the rope. Rory was right, in this respect. It was good to be Molly again, and to save Monty for the performance.

'I brought you a mug of tea,' Molly said. 'It's still hot.' They sat in ringside seats and observed Rory in the *trinka*, and the elephants obediently following their trainer through their familiar routine. She seized her chance with Rory otherwise occupied. 'Can I ask you something in private?'

'You don't wish to make him jealous, eh?' Hanna had deep dimples which transformed her chubby face. She was a stocky, muscular young woman, but under the bright lights she appeared beautiful, in shimmering silver.

'How did you guess? It's just that when I was in Australia I knew someone else who came from Denmark – he went back there before I left.'

'Where? Denmark consists of a series of islands – Faroes, Jutland. You have an address?'

'No ... But his name is Rasmussen, Henning Rasmussen.'

'I have to tell you, Molly, that Rasmussen is a name like – like Smith, in your country ... We come from Copenhagen, we are cosmopolitan. Your friend?'

'He was – I believe still is – a farmer in a small way. Dairy cows, I think. I don't know.' She added inconsequentially: 'He carved me a little horse from wood—'

'Did he ever say *huus* or *sted*?' Hanna speculated. 'That is a cottage farm – a bigger place is a *gaard*. A *bondergaarde* is a peasant farm, likely freehold. But, as in your country, lately, there has been a depression in agriculture. Our farmers are anxious, there is very little money to be made. Maybe that is why he went to Australia, though most emigrate to the United States or Canada. But in Jutland, we hear from family there, is nowadays much planting of pine trees on the heathland. This may help the economy. Does this help your thoughts or does it confuse you?'

'You've made me realise that it is probably impossible to find him,' Molly said disconsolately. Her hands suddenly trembled, her cup rattled. Why was she always so naive? she wondered. She should have known it was unlikely that Hanna and Henning would be acquainted.

'Then you must hope that one day he will come looking for you.'

Rory had finished his juggling. He stood up, looking round for Molly. When he spotted them, he waved a hand.

'Rory adores you, I think,' Hanna said perceptively.

'And I am very fond of him.' Molly sounded defensive.

'You are lovers?' her friend asked bluntly.

Molly was shocked. 'No!' She blushed deeply.

'He would like this, so?' Hanna's dimples flashed. 'That I can see ...'

'He wants to marry me,' Molly told her, cheeks aglow. Scandinavians, she had discovered, were very direct while she had not yet thrown off all the strictures of her upbringing at the convent school. Rory was beckoning her to join him. She pretended not to see him. 'But—'

'But you love another. This Rasmussen?'

'I can't be sure. It didn't last long. It would be easy for me to settle for Rory: I know his family, we all get on so well. He and I – well, if I put my heart and soul into it, we could be happy, I think. But doesn't everyone hanker for something more, Hanna?'

'He is coming ... Me, I aspire to the double somersault on the trapeze! So few artistes can do this. And they say Alfredo Cordona, the Mexican, is determined he will one day do the triple. Can you imagine it? To fly through the air is my great love in life. But I would not do it without the safety net. Maybe Rory Kelly is *your* net ...'

Back in Bodenflower, the pastor's wife was handed a letter by her Ernst. 'Mrs Mac diverted it, as it was addressed to Frank.'

Unfamiliar writing, an indistinct postmark, but obviously a missive from overseas: Elfie tentatively tore open the envelope. She read aloud:

Dear Mr Wills,

About eighteen months ago, I wrote to Miss Molly Sparkes care of your address. I was not fortunate to receive her reply before I returned to Denmark.

By now she will, I presume, be back in England. May I respectfully enquire from you her address? Or, if you prefer, would your sister be kind enough to let Miss Sparkes have mine, so that if she wishes, she may contact me? My grateful thanks in any case.

I hope all is well with you and Miss Wills.

Most sincerely,

H Rasmussen (former stockman on the farm)

Elfie was already flustered. 'What shall I do, Ernst? Goodness knows where Molly is at present with that circus.'

140

Sitting opposite her at the table, he tapped the teapot meaningfully. 'A cup of tea will help you decide but my advice is, it is best to write to her care of Alexa. She would forward the letter or keep it for Molly's return, whichever is best. Then Molly must make her own mind up whether to respond . . . May I have one of these small cakes or are they intended for the sewing party this afternoon?'

She pushed the plate towards him, smiling fondly. She had been shocked and saddened, even felt a little guilty having left him in the lurch, of course, when Frank died so suddenly and unfortunately in his prime, but she thanked God every day for giving her Ernst. His demands were few, both in and out of the bedroom, but his kindly presence was both a comfort and a pleasure. Coming to Australia as she had, full of fears and narrow prejudices, had so unexpectedly turned her life around for the best.

She thought now much more tolerantly of Molly, who had so irritated her on the journey out; she acknowledged to herself that she had been envious of Molly's youth and high spirits then, her magnetism for the opposite sex. She had observed the spark, the physical chemistry (although she did not think of it as that) between Molly and Henning Rasmussen, with disapproval at the time. Since her marriage, she was inclined to think that Molly may have really been in love with Henning. All the signs had been there.

'I shall write to Molly,' she announced. 'And to Alexa, too, of course. She sent such kind letters after I lost Frank. It was remiss of me not to reply sooner.'

'I believe they will be glad to hear from you, Elfie, particularly Molly; you will be love's messenger,' he said, old romantic that he was.

She surprised herself: 'I wish that everyone could be as happy as we are. Be with the one they love . . . Another cup of tea, Ernst dear?'

The circus performers were kept on their toes; there were

141

no less than fourteen theatres and a rival circus in Madrid, besides the Royal Opera House and the theatre in the Retiro Gardens, which was a great tourist attraction in the summer.

There was not too much time off for exploring the Spanish capital, but Molly's main impression was of a city of towering statues of kings and eminent soldiers of the War of Independence; great writers like Cervantes and Calderon.

Many fine new houses had been built recently in the suburbs, and impressive buildings transformed the centre of the city. The railway stations had all been refurbished to resemble the elegant façades of the ones they had travelled from in Paris. She did not wish to visit the Bull Ring built in 1874, although Rory had been quite keen to witness the spectacle, which could accommodate 16,000 eager spectators. Instead, she enjoyed visiting the shops crammed with souvenirs: beautiful shawls, mantillas, mandolins and lace. Quality leather goods, she was interested to discover, were made locally in one of the huge modern factories, despite being misleadingly gold-stamped Paris, London and Vienna: she fingered elegant cigar and card cases, purses and pocket books, wondering if similar items would also sell in the House of Leather back in London. She must write Alexa of her finds.

Madrid was certainly nothing like London. There was the definite presence of the unsmiling Civil Guards besides the *guardias urbanos*, the police. Rory, who was fairly fluent in Spanish, attempted to read the local papers, informing her that there was still much unrest in the country, and frequent strikes organised by the many socialists among the workers. 'One day it will all erupt again,' he said. 'Maybe it will spread round the world.' Meanwhile, they enjoyed the colour, the excitement, the seething warmth of the place.

The terrible accident, then the letter from Australia, cut short their stay.

The climax of the trapeze act, on the high wire, was always suspenseful. The whole audience gasped then fell silent; sat motionless, necks craned, staring upwards.

Hanna's father and brothers formed a human pyramid: she and her sister Birgit took it in turns to balance in top position. This night, it was Hanna who confidently took her place, hoisted by Birgit, even as the wire buckled and the performers swayed in what seemed to be an eternity of slow motion, then plummeted helplessly downwards. Father and sons bounced in the net; one of the young men struck the side; the girls landed in the ring outside its confines, lying crumpled and still.

The silence was unbroken for a few seconds, then there was uproar among the audience. The ringmaster appealed valiantly for calm, the band began to play, the clowns rushed on while the sisters were tended by circus staff, trained for just such an emergency, mercifully rare. The injured brother, helped to his feet, stood, dazed and bleeding from a cut to his head, one arm hanging limply at his side. 'Tell them to go home!' he moaned, in his own language.

Hanna had probably broken her pelvis and both legs; that was the conjecture of the doctor who had dashed to their aid from the stalls. He turned to examine her sister while Molly knelt beside her friend, trying to offer comfort. As usual, she had been peeping through the back flap of the canvas so as not to miss the most exciting moments of the show. Rory tried to restrain her, but she broke free and ran into the ring.

The girls lay still on the sawdust, swathed in blankets, for the doctor insisted they must not be moved until the hospital services arrived. The Big Top was slowly emptying all this time.

'I did not break my neck, I think, Molly ...' Hanna murmured faintly. 'I still breathe – I can move my arm, see – it does not hurt ...' There was a puzzled look on her face.

'Keep her quiet,' the doctor told Molly, 'the pain will overwhelm her all too soon; there may be internal injuries, also.'

Miraculously, as they would learn much later, neither of the sisters had broken her back, but Hanna's shattered pelvis needed urgent surgery. She drifted in and out of consciousness, now unable to speak.

Molly's pleas to accompany her friends to the hospital had gone unheeded.

'You can do nothing,' Hanna's father said, not meaning to sound harsh. 'This is family business. Rory should take you away now, I think.'

Late that night, Molly lay sobbing on her bed in the boarding house, glad of the semi-darkness, with just a candle puddling in a saucer on the washstand. She was still in the white tights and spangles which she wore for the finale. The magic of the circus was for her cruelly dispelled. Her friends would be months in hospital; it was doubtful if they would ever fully recover or perform again. Hanna's dreams of the double somersault would never be realised.

Rory tapped on her door, did not wait for a reply but came in, whey-faced and shocked to the core himself. He gripped a crumpled sheet of paper in one hand. 'Molly – this letter – waiting for me on my table,' he gabbled.

She sat up, rubbing her eyes fiercely on the sheet. 'What is it, Rory? Not *more* bad news?' Fear rose like gall in her throat.

He nodded. 'I'll have to go home – to Melbourne, just as soon as it can be arranged ... We'll have to abandon the act. I'm sorry, Molly, but—' He sat down abruptly on her bedside chair, crushing the day clothes strewn on it; facing her.

'What is it? Tell me? I don't care about the act! At this moment, I don't think I could ever go in the ring again.'

'It's my mother, she's had a stroke. The letter is from Thom and Cora. It's bad, Molly, very bad. The rest of the

144

family are there. She could be – gone – before I get there, but I *must* try . . .'

'Of course you must!' Molly cried. She subsided against her damp pillow, held out her arms instinctively, felt the weight of him as he almost fell on her; she cradled him close, despite the discomfort, hardly aware of his quickened breath. They could at least comfort one another, she thought, as friends should; it needn't lead to anything more. She wanted him to mop her tears, to reassure her that the injured trapeze artistes would certainly recover; in return she would listen while he talked out his fears about his mother.

She realised belatedly how Rory had interpreted that impulsive hug, when he began to kiss her passionately, to fumble with the silver buttons on her jacket with trembling hands. She was confused but, suddenly, to her own surprise, unafraid. What would it do to him if she rejected him now? In the morning, she thought, we can pretend it was all just another dream.

'Nip the candle out,' she whispered. It had to be dark, in that shabby airless room, so that they could forget the time and place, the reason *why*.

'Oh, Molly, I love you so much.' His voice was thick with longing.

'I know you do.'

'Are you sure?'

'*I'm sure.*'

Ten days later she was back in London. Alexa hurried down the steps from the house to pay the cabbie. It was months since they had met. Molly saw Alexa's eyebrows arch as she took in her careless appearance, her pallor. Would she have welcomed her back if she knew her guilty secret? she wondered.

'It's very good to have you home,' Alexa said. She had taken the day off work.

Molly was shivering despite her warm costume. She had

145

packed her thinner clothes on top of her spangled outfits in the big trunk. She didn't suppose she would wear those again. Was her career in the circus really over so soon?

'I hope you haven't caught a chill, my dear.' Alexa sounded concerned. 'I'll put a match to the fire in the sitting room. Nancy will be home in a couple of hours. She was so excited, I doubt she has been much use in the showroom today ... Sit down, and I'll ask Mrs Moore to bring us tea – hot buttered crumpets sound good to you?'

'Very good, thank you, Alexa.'

'Just say, are you back for a brief visit or—'

'If you'll have me, I'm here to stay. I'm hoping you'll take me back at Nagel's. Any job will do, but I must earn my own living! I had to help Rory out with his fare, you see.'

'Of course you did. We'll talk it all over when you feel like it. But I guess Nancy will be the one you really want to confide in.'

Molly leaned back in the chair and closed her eyes. Rory had begged her to go with him, in view of what had happened that night.

'No, Rory,' she'd insisted. 'Maybe one day we'll meet again. It would only complicate matters right now. I do love you, and I don't regret anything, honestly – I won't forget you, I promise, and I know you won't forget me.'

'How could I, after that?' he said, and she was aware that she had hurt him.

'Give Serena my love, and say to get well soon – and my best to Thom and Cora, too. There'll be a nice Australian girl for you one day, with an Irish name, no doubt, and you'll know I was right to say goodbye to you when I did, dear Rory Kelly.'

Chapter Seven

'It doesn't seem right, Molly, me being, well, superior to you,' Nancy worried on Molly's first day back at the shop.

'I'm not bothered and nor should you be,' she returned, smiling, as they stood for a moment together in the showroom, before Molly went upstairs to the office she had once shared with Art, and her old job. Fortunately, Alexa had prepared her for what would otherwise have been quite a shock: Minnie had requested a transfer to the accounts department as assistant clerk following Art's departure and the engaging of his successor, an educated but nervous lady who had not lasted long. 'Probably because of her,' Nancy whispered in Molly's ear. Minnie, working very hard on her own for several weeks, had earned the right to her promotion, recommended by Mr Loom. Since knowing Nancy, Alexa was much more open-minded regarding the aspirations of other members of her staff.

Molly certainly did not relish being under Minnie's thumb, recalling her treatment of Nancy in the workroom in the early days, but she told herself sternly that she was lucky to have a job to go to at all and that she would just have to develop a thick skin against Minnie's acid jibes.

Minnie, naturally, was already at her desk. Now she was no longer shrouded in a serviceable apron, her spare figure was better served by a long black shiny skirt, a severe white blouse with full sleeves and a cameo brooch at the throat. She had even toned down her high colour with face powder, Molly suspected, being herself now au fait with the art of makeup. Seeing her own pale reflection in the mirror first thing, she had rubbed a little rouge on her cheeks.

'Good morning, Miss Sparkes,' Minnie said, with a tight little smile. 'I have left some work ready for you on your desk. Please deal immediately with those accounts marked URGENT.' She had added her signature, M Gage (Mrs), so that Molly would realise how she expected to be addressed from now on. Then she stabbed away energetically at her typewriter keys, to prove that she had been practising assiduously, could use all her fingers and strike the correct letters.

Bet she gave up a good many lunch hours to achieve that standard, Molly thought ruefully. No visits to the pud shop for old Minnie; no yawning all afternoon. Art, where are you? Do you remember how you jerked me back into action when you took aim with a paper dart? How many hours before lunch when Nancy and I can enjoy a good old giggle together while we stroll along doing a spot of window-shopping? What really went wrong between you and Nancy, I wonder . . .

'Urgent, I said, remember,' Minnie chided, without turning round or pausing in her tapping.

'Yes, Mrs Gage.' Having to concentrate on all this paperwork would stop her thinking, well, the unthinkable . . .

'I hadn't realised you had got so thin, Molly,' Nancy exclaimed, when she clutched at her friend's arm to prevent her from stepping out absentmindedly in front of one of the new motor buses along New Broad Street.

'All that exercise. I suppose,' Molly said lightly, snapping to attention. 'Want to feel my muscles?' she joked.

'Molly, I keep waiting for you to tell me what's up when we're on our own. I just know there's something troubling you, but—'

'Well, I can't help worrying and wondering about Hanna and her sister – the girls on the trapeze who had that terrible accident. And how Rory won't yet have arrived in Australia, and what he might find there,' Molly gabbled.

'It's something else as well, isn't it?' Nancy insisted, linking her arm firmly in Molly's, steering her past a little group of people, standing chatting on the pavement, which was dark and slippery due to recent rain. There was the ever-present threat of fog by going-home time: that acrid tinge to the air they breathed.

'Nancy dear, I will talk to you, and soon ...' I have to tell someone, she thought, and Nancy can keep a secret. 'What a lark,' she added lightly, 'old Minnie and Loom going out to lunch together. She's definitely out to catch him, I think.'

Nancy surprised her with a vehement reply. 'Oh, no, he's far too nice for her! He was obviously ruled by his mother, he doesn't want another—'

'Martinet?'

'If that means what I want to say – yes! He doesn't deserve another of those in his life.'

'Why, Nancy, I do believe you've got a soft spot for him!'

She quickened her step, urging Molly to do the same.

'We'll be late back if we don't hurry – and that wouldn't do on your first day, would it? I've got real respect for Mr Loom, that's all. Don't you dare start making more of that, Molly Sparkes!'

It was the beginning of December, the House of Leather was enjoying a seasonal rush, and Molly had been back in the old routine for what seemed like forever, but was really only six weeks. Alexa had gone to the theatre this Saturday evening but the girls had opted to stay at home, to have their baths and wash their hair then toast their toes by the fire, as Molly said.

She rubbed Nancy's long locks for her, as her friend, on

149

the footstool, leaned back against her knees. Molly's own short mop was already dry. They were cosy and comfortable in warm nightgowns, loose wrappers and slippers. Now's my chance, Molly thought. Best to come straight out with it; shades of the old, impulsive, honest Molly.

'Nancy, I think I'm pregnant . . .'

She flicked back her damp hair and swivelled round to look at her friend, shocked. This was obviously not what she had expected to hear. '*Oh, Molly*! Are you sure? Did you—'

'Yes, I did. Only once but I didn't think that—'

'Once is enough,' Nancy stated simply. 'It was Rory, of course?' She hoped fervently that this was the case. He was in love with Molly, he wouldn't hurt her, force her against her will. The trouble was, he was in Australia now and Molly was here.

'Don't blame him. He kept asking me to marry him, and he didn't – start it. We were just, well, holding on to each other after the shocking events that night in the circus, and the sad news of Serena – it just happened, Nancy. I'm not ashamed, strangely enough. It seemed so natural – inevitable, I suppose.' The relief of telling Nancy caused the tears to flow, and Nancy knelt up on the stool and enfolded her in her arms, rocking her soothingly just as she had Fay when she was in pain, cutting teeth.

'There, Molly. Let it all out. You'll feel better for it. It's not the end of the world.'

'Isn't it?' Molly managed a wry smile. 'What am I going to do?'

'You must tell Alexa, tonight. She'll advise you.'

'She'll be disappointed in me, angry with Rory.'

'Wait and see. She learned a lot, too late, she says; she's still sad that she didn't listen to her daughter. She'll want to take care of you, help you, for Lucy's sake, I think.'

Alexa was certainly upset, but not with Molly. 'He promised me . . . how *could* he? Does he know?'

150

'I'm not going to tell him, Alexa, and nor are you! Anyway, he's not here. He's got enough trouble to deal with, I won't add to it. I don't want him to come back for me, to do the decent thing! I do care for him, else I wouldn't have done what I did, but I'm not ready for marriage – I'm not ready to be a mother either, but I can't help that – and I won't listen if you try to persuade me otherwise.

'In a way, it's a relief that we are so far apart, it makes it easier. He already knows I don't want to carry on with the circus. I was thinking of trying my luck as a dancer on the halls, like my mother, but I can't do that now, I suppose . . . I'll be twenty-one and responsible for my own actions in May before – before – it arrives. I can manage, I know I can.' Was she making sense, babbling away?

'Not without us, I hope?' Alexa said. She sat back in her chair, unhooked her evening cape, eased her feet out of her smart shoes. 'I brought up a child on my own, remember. But I didn't have to work while I was pregnant. I presume you haven't told your father yet? You must face up to that soon. He'll be shocked and disappointed, of course, but like all parents he will appreciate the truth from you, however unpalatable . . .

'You must decide for yourself, of course, but, and I know Nancy will agree, I really hope you will want to stay here with us. We would endeavour to support you in every way.'

Nancy came in with cups of hot chocolate. It was almost midnight. She looked searchingly from one to the other. 'Is everything all right?' she asked hesitantly.

Molly jumped to her feet. 'Put that tray down! I'm going to hug you both. I don't have to think about it, Alexa, I want to go on living here, working at Nagel's as long as I can, however embarrassing that becomes! And I just want to say thank you for understanding, that's all.'

'No high kicks, mind,' Alexa warned, but she smiled despite still reeling mentally from the shock. 'Fetch me a

tot of whisky will you, Nancy, please? I feel I've earned it
tonight.'

Nancy couldn't get to sleep. Would it have helped if I had
told Molly what I went through in the past? she wondered.
But that was – dirty. What happened with her and Rory was
very different; it just went further than they expected ...
She's brave, my dear friend Molly Sparkes. It's not going
to be easy for her, but I'll do everything I can to help. I
wish I hadn't pushed Art away. I hurt him, badly, I know
it. If it was me, carrying Art's baby, I couldn't keep it
secret from him ... I'd want to get married, to be with
him. Girls like me don't often get a second chance but Mrs
Nagel gave me that. I owe it to her to get on at Nagels, not
cry about what can't be.

Alexa lay wakeful, too. She had looked in briefly at Molly
when she made a trip to the bathroom. Molly, having told
them all, slept like a baby herself.

Make the most of the next few weeks, Alexa thought. It
won't be easy, the letter to your father, but I'm positive he
won't reject you because I'll write to him, too ... People
will talk, they always do. Will that bright spark of yours
enable you to come through? You're so young to be
embarking on motherhood, alone. But if you look after
your baby as you did my granddaughter, you'll be a lovely,
caring mother. I shouldn't help you too much materially
because you must learn to cope, as I did. Is Nancy lying
sleepless – has it brought back all the terrors for her?

She pushed back the covers, padded silently in her slippers along the landing to the girl's room.

'Nancy,' she said softly, 'I thought you might want to
talk ... I certainly do.'

'Oh, Mrs Nagel,' Nancy sniffed, 'I'm so glad you're
here.'

'It's time you called me Alexa, I think,' she said.

*

When her pregnancy had been confirmed, Molly duly wrote to her father. She made several false starts, but then decided to get the shock over at the beginning.

Dear Father,
I have something important to tell you.
Please forgive me for hurting you, but now I am getting used to the idea, I am actually glad. I am expecting a baby next summer. I must be honest with you; I am not marrying the baby's father. He has not abandoned me, because he has no idea of my condition.
If you wish to cut off my allowance, I shall not blame you one bit. I shall work, and save, as long as I can. Alexa has invited me to stay on here with her and Nancy, and I am very grateful for her kindness.
I have seen Alexa's doctor, and all is well so far. He says I must really hope for a small baby as I don't possess child-bearing hips! But I'm not going to worry for the next seven months about a forceps delivery! And nor should you. If little Florence Almond could manage, then so can I. Please don't worry about me.
My love to you.
Your daughter, Molly

The letter from Australia arrived before her father's reply. Alexa had made Molly take time off work. Morning sickness was now a real nightmare. 'At least,' she joked weakly, 'Minnie won't put two and two together about my straining waistband – I've actually lost weight with all that throwing up!'

'That's just why you're going to take it easy for the rest of the week,' Alexa said sternly. 'Put your feet up, as the doctor ordered.'

So Molly was at home when the morning post arrived and was presented to her by Mrs Moore the help who Molly guessed probably knew what was up, but could be counted on to be discreet.

She read it through several times in disbelief. Henning had been trying to contact her! She had an address at last for him, but she couldn't respond – how could she? Not now, *not ever*.

'Whatever's wrong, duck?' Mrs Moore asked, finding her in a real state. 'Here, back to bed with you, and you just stay there while I take my chance with that telephone and call the doctor . . .'

'Please, I'm not ill, just—'

'Then I'll telephone the Missus,' Mrs Moore said firmly. 'Something's upset you, ain't that right? She'll have to deal with it.'

She can't put the clock back, and nor can I, Molly thought as she obediently undressed and slipped under the bedcovers, clutching a flannel-wrapped hot water bottle. She was aware that the curtains were being briskly pulled to, that an extra quilt was being added to her bed.

'You're shivering, poor soul,' said Mrs Moore, adding, proving she did know although she hadn't been told: 'Hope you ain't goin' to lose it, duck.'

It was another ten days before the doctor allowed Molly to return to work. Christmas would be here before they knew it. By then, she had suddenly begun to 'show' as Nancy put it. Practical Nancy set to in the evenings, sewing elastic inserts into the waists of Molly's office skirts.

The only one who appeared not to observe the slight change in Molly's shape, to guess the reason for her absence, was Mr Loom.

'I shall have to tell him in due course,' Alexa said. 'But as you are sedentary in your work, not required to lift anything heavy, there should be no problems. Especially since the sickness has eased and you are eating properly again.'

'More than that.' Molly sighed ruefully. 'I seem to be making up for what I couldn't eat these last few weeks!'

On pay-day, Friday, she had an overwhelming desire for

something really filling. 'Let's go to the pud shop, Nancy, for lunch!'

'Fish tonight for dinner, you know,' her friend reminded her as they emerged from the shop and set off up the road.

'Precisely! Not much substance in that, 'specially steamed which Alexa says is best for one in my condition . . .'

'Shush!' Nancy warned, for Mr Loom and Minnie were just a few yards behind, obviously going out to eat themselves.

'Minnie knows,' Molly hissed. 'She told me to take care not to strain myself when stretching up to the top shelf in the stationery cupboard . . .'

'That was nice of her.'

'Oh, Nancy! You, of all people, know her better than that!'

'I said,' repeated Minnie to Mr Loom, who was looking rather bemused, 'd'you fancy a proper meal today, seeing's it's so cold?' She tapped her bag. 'My sandwiches'll keep for later. We could go to that place where they serve up a very good meat pudding. It's a fair way to go, but worth it, they say. Art used to go there regular, I believe.'

'Mmm?' Mr Loom murmured. 'Meat pudding? Sounds tempting, Mrs Gage. I know the shop: Mother liked the ham from there . . .'

'Minnie,' she reminded him archly.

'I must just stop off and buy a paper, Minnie, I didn't get a chance this morning. I do like something to read on the way home.'

His calling at the newsagent's meant that Molly and Nancy were soon well ahead, and settled in the pudding shop before the others arrived there.

I seem to be trapped into lunchtimes spent in the company of Mrs Minnie Gage, Mr Loom thought, as he rolled the paper and carried it under his arm. Where have the young ladies vanished to? I wonder. I'm not sure it's such a good thing, my being so involved with Nancy at work since her promotion to the showroom. That's all it is, of course, just our mutual interest in selling quality leather goods ... I threw away my chance with her when I drew back, as it were, leaving the field clear for Art. That came to nothing. But I'm too old for her, too staid and set in my ways. I always was. At twenty years old, Nancy can take her pick. I can't expect to be part of the selection.

Minnie poked him in the back. He'd been striding ahead, deep in thought, as usual. 'Here we are, Mr Loom – there's a table for two by the window. Hurry up before someone beats us to it!'

She felt thoroughly fed up. She'd splashed out on a nice new winter coat, navy with a velvet collar; she wore shoes instead of boots, but he never seemed to notice. She was climbing the ladder at work, not stuck in the mud like Walt and Aggie. Gage had passed away four years ago, a loss she'd quickly got over. She'd always had to work because the late unlamented was one for the gee-gees. The future Mrs Loom, if old Loom ever got round to asking her – and she was certainly working on it – would be treated like a lady, expected to stay at home, seeing to her husband's needs. He wouldn't be bothersome in bed, like the inebriated Gage, but would appreciate everything she did for him, she fancied. She said, as they duly claimed the table, sitting opposite, knee-to-knee, because of the cramped space: 'My late husband said I made a wonderful meat pudding myself. I hope it comes up to my standard!' She moved ever so slightly forward so that the pressure of her bony knees was intensified.

'Keep your head down, Molly, look who's just come in,' Nancy advised. Unfortunately, although they were some way down the shop, she caught Mr Loom's eye. He wore a pained, almost pleading expression. She turned her head, embarrassed; wondering.

None of them saw Art, but he saw them all. He sat among strangers, looking dejected, at a table near the rear

156

of the shop. He had been watching out, waiting and hoping. If Nancy had arrived on her own – well, he might have approached her, but perhaps it was too late for that.

Chapter Eight

Christmas Eve 1908: they would be closing the shop at noon.

It's not going to be easy for Molly, Nancy thought, as she wrapped gifts in tissue then strong brown paper and tied them neatly with string. She really has no idea, bless her, how tongues will wag when that little curve becomes a great big bulge ... She'll find out how cruel folk can be to a young mother without a man to support her and her baby. She'll feel cheated of all the excitement of working at what she really loves; she won't be poor of course, and desperate, like I would've been if it had happened to me back in Australia, but some of the sparkle will go from her, that's a sure thing ... I can't forget how she tore up that letter with Henning's address on it, saying she couldn't get in touch with him, not now.

'Nancy,' Mr Loom said, clearing his throat, suddenly standing beside her, 'Mrs Nagel has unexpectedly, very kindly, asked me to join you both for Christmas dinner tomorrow. Would – would *you* mind if I said yes?'

'Oh, of course you must come to us! I'm so glad Mrs Nagel thought of it. No one should be on their own on Christmas Day.'

Nancy was quite unaware of how attractive she looked, with her flushed face, shining eyes and spontaneous smile. It was a chance for them to become more relaxed with each

other again, which would be nice. She did like Mr Loom
... It might brighten the day up for them, having company:
Matthew would not be visiting them until the New Year,
because his parents were home on extended leave, and
naturally staying with their son and granddaughter at
Wren's Nest, so there would be no small girl to keep them
entertained this year.

Nancy and Mr Loom were washing up the many dishes in
the kitchen, while Alexa relaxed in the sitting room and
shut her eyes for what she warned them would certainly be:
'More than five minutes, more like an hour or two after
that Christmas pudding! Really, I think it is one of the
Army and Navy Stores best ... You two young people can
indulge in a parlour game or two no doubt, after you've put
away all those plates ... I wouldn't mind a cup of coffee,
say, at three-thirty?'

Molly had taken herself off, too, immediately after
lunch, declaring that she was going to her room for a
proper sleep. She had closed the door very firmly as
Nancy, worrying whether all was well, began to follow her
up but hesitated on the stairs. She quietly retreated at the
unexpected rebuff.

'*Young people* ...' Mr Loom said ruefully, putting his
hands in the hot soda-laced water and feeling for the dish-
cloth. 'I'm nearer Mrs Nagel's age than yours, Nancy.
Shall I let the plates drain in this wooden contraption?'

'Mmm,' she agreed. She'd had a go with Molly's
camomile solution, for her hair had darkened somewhat in
the gloomy London weather. It was constant sunlight which
had kept it childishly fair. She wore it tied back from her
face, hanging down her back, all ringletty due to her dili-
gence with the curling rags last night, with a moiré ribbon
which went very well with the new dress, her Christmas
present from Mrs Nagel. It was soft claret-coloured velvet,
which Nancy couldn't resist stroking from time to time. She
was glad Mr Loom had decided on the soapy side of the

159

job; she didn't want to cover up her lovely dress with an apron.

She looked sideways at him as she carefully dried the silver cutlery and placed it on a tray ready to return to the presentation box lined with blue which was kept in the oak sideboard in the dining room. Yes, that quizzical expression quite transformed his face, she thought. He wasn't to be feared at all, as she had imagined on meeting him that first day at work. They were certainly at ease with each other today.

She drew in her breath when his damp hand suddenly touched her shoulder. 'Nancy, I can't help it, I *must* say something. Not the right time, perhaps, but—'

'Whatever is it, Mr Loom?' she asked in some alarm. She realised that she was holding a knife towards his chest, and put it down with a clatter. Should she add: 'Sorry'? But he obviously hadn't noticed.

'I – I have a deep regard for you. Well, I believe it to be more than that – ridiculous, I know, in one my age, nearly forty, and I can't expect my feelings to be returned, of course, but—' he floundered. He removed his hand and stood there, his head bowed.

I mustn't hurt him, he doesn't deserve it, poor chap, flashed through Nancy's mind. He's so different from those others; even from Art who gave me just an inkling of what love could be like before I panicked and made him think I didn't really care ... I'd feel safe with undemanding Mr Loom.

'Leonard,' she said softly, 'the difference in our ages doesn't matter to me. Was – was there something more you wanted to say?'

He took both her hands in his, his face suddenly alight with hope. He made no attempt to draw her closer. 'Dear Nancy, will you do me the very great honour of becoming my wife? You don't have to say anything now ...'

'Oh, but *I will*! I will marry you, thank you for asking me,' she added childishly.

160

'I expect to wait, of course, we will need your father's permission—'

'That won't be a problem.' He'll sign me away like a shot, she thought. Knows I don't ever want to go back home to him, even though I miss Australia more than I can say. 'In the spring?' she suggested.

'My dear! That would be *wonderful!*'

'D'you want to kiss me?' she asked hesitantly, bracing herself just a fraction. She moved closer to him.

She was aware that he closed his eyes as their lips met in a brief, chaste kiss. She couldn't bring herself to put her arms around him but he smelled nice: of shaving soap, bay rum hair spirit and toothpowder, she mentally added up. Then he turned his attention to the washing up. 'We must finish this off before we celebrate! Whatever will the others say?' he wondered happily.

We'll be married before Molly has her baby, she thought. When she wants to pick up her career again, I'll be there, a respectable married woman with time to spare for looking after her baby, for it seems doubtful I'll fall myself as I never did before. And anyway, will Mr Loom expect more of me than affection? I can't imagine it . . .

Matthew and Fay arrived on the afternoon of New Year's Eve. Molly kept out of the way while the greetings went on in the hall. She wasn't sure if Alexa had told him about her condition. Fay, of course, was too young to notice.

She was curled up in an armchair near the fire when the visitors came into the drawing room. Fay dashed over and leapt on her, smothering her face with wet kisses: '*I love you, Molly!*' she shouted.

'Careful, don't be so rough,' her father admonished her.

So, he knows, Molly thought. Above Fay's mass of black curls, she looked at Matthew. There was something different about him; his own hair was slightly longer, she realised. It made him look younger, not like a soldier. He sat himself down in the chair opposite. 'It's good to see you again,' he said. 'But we miss all your cards from exciting places ...'

'I've nothing much to write about at the moment,' she said ruefully. Don't say you're sorry for me, she pleaded silently.

'You must come and see us – we're really settled. I cook more scrambled eggs and soft roes on toast – nursery food – than steak nowadays, and I know at least twenty nursery rhymes off by heart. Why not come back with us for a few days? Fay missed you a lot while you were away – despite teaching games, I can't walk on my hands or demonstrate back flips like the amazing Molly ...' He broke off, suddenly embarrassed.

'I'd like to, but I have to work, Matthew. No school holidays for me!'

'Well, Fay, we must make the most of Molly while we're here, I suppose, eh? I can hear Granny calling you. Go and find out what she wants, there's a good girl.'

Fay slid down from Molly's lap and went off obediently.

'Did you hear the news?' she asked quickly.

'About Nancy, you mean? Alexa approves, obviously; it was an opportune time for you to return, it seems. She is very fond of you both. She confided in me that she was loath to part with Nancy though.'

'She confided something else, didn't she?' Molly challenged him.

Matthew looked surprised. 'No. But she's aware that I know. Your father wrote to me, Molly.'

'He hasn't answered *my* letter yet!' she cried childishly. 'What did he say?'

'He suggested a solution, for both of us. He thought I should ask you to marry me—'

'How *dare* he? I turned down an offer of what I thought at the time was a marriage of convenience – from *him*.' She pointed defiantly at her stomach so that he couldn't miss the now unmistakable signs of her pregnancy. 'I don't feel guilty, you know. I'm not going to be a burden on you or anyone else – I mean it.'

'I guessed that was how you would react,' he said quietly. 'All right, take it that I have asked and you have refused. But you know that I really like you and consider myself to be your friend: that I appreciate all you have done for Fay in the past. I just want to repeat what I told you that night after dinner at Wren's Nest – was it really about eighteen months ago? You can always talk to me, Molly. I intend to be around if and when you need me.' He rose, held out his hand. 'Come on, let's shake on it!'

She stretched up, dabbed a kiss on his cheek. 'I'm sorry, Matthew. I always jump to conclusions.'

'Cool down,' he advised. 'Wait to hear from Colonel Sparkes. You may well be surprised at his reaction.'

'I will,' she promised. 'Now let's go and find out why they are so long in bringing in tea!'

'Molly?'

'Yes?' She turned at the door.

'I never saw Lucy, you know, like *that*. It's yet another regret for me. You look so young – but womanly, beautiful, at the same time. Don't forget, if I can help in any way, please say.'

'Thank you, Matthew,' she said. 'I'm glad I'll be seeing the New Year in with you.'

'Go and ask Walt how much longer he's going to be with mending the lining of that portmanteau,' Minnie said to Molly. No grudging pleases or thank yous from her: merely a challenge. She knew very well that Molly got all out of breath climbing those steep stairs now she was almost six months pregnant but wasn't going to make concessions for her. She couldn't get at Nancy, what with her about to wed Mr Loom. Minnie smouldered inwardly whenever she saw them together. But Molly, despite being a favourite of Mrs Nagel who seemingly had overlooked her rash behaviour, was vulnerable of course.

'Sit down, dearie, while you're waiting.' Aggie told her with real concern. She didn't stop sewing, nor did Walt, but he was on the last lap of his task.

Molly was all out front with the baby. The only comfortable way to sit was with her knees well apart, but she couldn't do that in mixed company. So she sat upright on the bench, biting her lip as her insides were butted and kicked by the baby, hoping that all this movement was cloaked by her skirt. She thought: Oh, it must be a boy, a tumbler and a juggler like the father who doesn't know of his existence ... Rory's written three times now, despite my brief replies: I was really happy to hear that dear Serena is slowly improving in health, and that he plans to join his brother for a while in mining for gemstones, but it was quite a shock to learn that he's taken me at my word and is getting to know his mother's young nurse rather well ... Sarah Riley – didn't I say he'd meet a nice Irish girl? Molly twisted the opal ring on her finger; she would have to take it off soon, wear it once more on the chain round her neck; it was becoming too tight. Anyway, it reminded her too much of the past.

'I said,' Aggie repeated, 'we was very pleased to get an invitation to the wedding next week and Walt was certainly surprised when the bride – such a lovely, natural girl, Nancy – said, "I wonder if you'd give me away?" which he's proud to do, not being a father himself so no chance otherwise. Of course she'd have asked Mr Loom, wouldn't she, if he, well ... Mr Loom seems over the moon.' She was overcome with one of her hectic flushes, having said more than she should.

'You sound quite the poet, old girl,' Walt observed, coming to her rescue. 'There! Check that for me, will you? Then Miss Sparkes can take it to Minnie. Bit of a slavedriver, our sister, eh, I imagine?'

Molly appreciated the sympathetic smile. 'A bit,' she agreed.

'Don't let her get you down,' Aggie advised. 'She's

jealous, poor thing. She was angling for Mr Loom herself, we could tell. She had a raw deal with that husband of hers.'

'Her bark's worse than her bite. She was a clever child, always got impatient with us, said we was too slow and not ambitious enough,' Walt said, opening the door for her and ushering Molly out. 'Not too heavy for you to carry, is it?' He indicated the portmanteau.

'I can manage, Walt, thank you. It's empty after all.'

'Oh, by the way,' he suddenly recalled, 'I met up with young Art by chance. Evening before last, wasn't it, Ag? I told him all the latest going on here, and I believe he thought I was joking at first when I said about Nancy getting married – 'specially who to, like . . . Then he come out with a bit of news himself. You know he always used to say he was going to emigrate to Australia? Well, he is! Made his mind up all of a sudden, apparently.'

'Oh!' Molly exclaimed. She wished Walt hadn't told her that. She suspected Nancy still had a soft spot for Art. Too late now in any case. Best say nothing, she decided. 'Cheerio!'

'Take care, my dear, God bless,' Aggie called after her.

'Poor soul,' she said to Walt, when Molly was out of earshot. 'She really don't know what she's in for before too long. Not everyone'll turn a blind eye like we do . . .'

April showers outside which made Alexa anxious, but, resolutely, no tears were shed by Nancy on her wedding day.

Alexa ordered: 'Arms out, let me ease the dress over your head, Nancy – mustn't spoil your coiffure, it took me long enough to arrange . . .' Pity the girl looked so pale and had refused the offer of powder and paint. The freckles were prominent today.

Nancy stood there obediently as the silk dress fell in sensuous folds over her new but simple underwear, for she had resisted all attempts by Alexa to buy her an expensive

165

trousseau, insisting that she wouldn't feel right in frilly fripperies. Molly was resting on her bed, by order of the other two, having still to change into her own special outfit. 'Everything flowing!' as she said ruefully. So it was the older woman who had the dual role of dresser to the bride and chief confidante.

Alexa buttoned the tight cuffs: it wasn't a wedding dress as such, Nancy hadn't wanted that, either, but Alexa had got her way with the colour, pastel rather than dark blue. 'There, you look very elegant. Let's pray it doesn't rain while you walk in and out of the church,' she pronounced, stepping back to appraise the effect. 'Shoes comfortable? You can manage the gloves yourself.' She opened the hat box, removed the layers of tissue and lifted out Nancy's hat. 'How d'you like my surprise? As worn by the Princess of Wales ...'

Nancy thought privately that the hat looked rather like a table decoration on a dinner plate, festooned with blue silk roses and ferns to tone with the dress. However would it stay on her head? And the Princess, still thought of as plain Mary of Teck by many, wasn't nearly as stylish as her mother-in-law, Queen Alexandra – even Nancy, a Colonial, knew that!

'It goes with the gloves and the parasol beautifully. Thank you very much, Mrs Nagel, you're very kind,' she managed. Then she observed that Alexa's eyes were suspiciously bright, and Nancy guessed intuitively that she was thinking of her only daughter's wedding and how she had refused to attend that ceremony. She took a few careful steps forward – ooh, the shoes really pinched her toes, she wasn't used to heels, and the skirt was so narrow, no wonder they called it a hobble – stretched up and kissed Alexa on her cheek. 'I'll never forget what you've done for me, I won't, I promise! And I'm not going far away, you know, and I'll still be working at Nagel's, even though Leonard thinks he should support me, and – I'd like to say, Mrs Nagel, I look up to you,

more'n anyone else, and – I'm really fond of you, you
know, just like I am of Molly ...'

'It's a silly hat but right for a wedding so bear with me,
dear Nancy, and wear it.' Alexa's voice sounded strange.
She cleared her throat fiercely. 'I should have adopted you,
Nancy. Too late now, of course, but to me, you and Molly
are my family since I lost Lucy.'

Nancy was hugging her now. She whispered: 'I love you
...' I don't want to leave you, she added silently, or this
house, because it's become home to me; but I can't let poor
Leonard down, not now.

'Lucky I'm not the bride,' Molly said ruefully, 'I'd need a
huge bouquet to cover this lot.' She patted the bulge. 'And
forgive me for not wearing a hat. They don't go with short
hair, and anyway, I don't want anyone looking at me, do
I?'

'You look very nice, Molly,' Nancy reassured her. They
were riding in an open carriage, more traditional than the
motor car, Alexa had insisted; not travelling far it's true,
just down the road and round the corner to the nearest
church, but as Alexa said, they must do things properly. A
rather watery sun shone down obligingly on the three of
them. Alexa wore a shantung costume with the splendid
feathers on her hat waving in the breeze, just like the
plumes on the grey horses' nodding heads.

I'm Mrs Loom, Nancy realised when they emerged from
the shadowy porch after a ceremony which had seemed
unreal and even dreamlike to her.

'Miss your dad, I expect,' Walt had whispered to her as
they prepared to make their entrance to the pealing organ.
He gave her hand a little squeeze of sympathy before offering her his arm.

Nancy didn't want to think of her father, not then. But
for the first time really since she'd left Australia, she
thought of her mother: Ma had suffered with her, but been

too afraid, too cowed, to stick up for her. 'I miss my mum,' she whispered back.

'She's with you in spirit,' Walt said.

He may be right, Nancy thought, as they walked down the aisle, but anyway, she'll be glad I got away from all that, and am marrying a decent sort . . .

Now, they were being showered with rice, and there was actually a photographer, which was another surprise arranged by Mrs Nagel, and Leonard was looking at her with beaming pride, and her friends were calling encouragingly: 'Smile, Nancy!'

It was as she was being assisted into the carriage, with her new husband at her side this time, that she suddenly spotted a lone figure standing opposite the church. It was Art, she was sure of it, even as he turned and walked briskly away. She gave an involuntary gasp, and Leonard looked at her with concern.

'Ready to go, dear? Take a deep breath, it's been quite a day, hasn't it?'

Chapter Nine

Just a small reception as they'd requested: wedding cake and a nice cup of tea, back at Alexa's house. Mrs Moore had actually prepared rather more than that, on her employer's secret instructions, but after two hours, the conversation was trailing off, Molly was looking tired, and Nancy couldn't say, of course, but her feet were really paining her in the pinching shoes.

Walt solemnly presented the newly-weds with a bottle of port. 'A bit of dutch courage,' he intimated to Leonard, who reverted to being Mr Loom and said politely: 'Thank you very much, this is most kind of you.'

Aggie and Minnie had clubbed together to buy a teapot. 'We know what store Nancy sets by a cup of tea,' Aggie said, adding archly: 'Only one of you should pour at a time, remember—'

'– or you'll have ginger twins!' Minnie finished, staring openly at Molly, not Nancy.

'I'm sorry you've decided against going away, Nancy,' Alexa said, as she waited in the hall while the bride put on her wrap.

'Well, we're having a few days off, aren't we? It will give us the chance to sort out a few things at – our place,' Nancy told her.

Alexa glanced round quickly to make sure Leonard was still talking to the guests in the drawing room. 'You mean, throw out a few things, eh? All still just as it was when his mother was alive? Oh, you must make changes to suit yourself, Nancy. I shouldn't say this, not today, but I do hope you've made the right choice – he's a splendid chap, of course, but not one to see the lighter side of life, though perhaps you might say the same of me ... But where's the romance, Nancy?'

'I don't want none of *that*' she said, lapsing grammatically, which didn't happen so much nowadays. 'I just want, well, respect, and to feel comfortable with my husband.'

There was no space for Nancy's clothes, which for now would have to remain in her trunk. The chest of drawers and wardrobe were chock-full of old-fashioned garments which, if she didn't just chuck 'em all out, Nancy decided, needed a jolly good washing and airing.

'It is very remiss of me,' Leonard apologised. 'I couldn't bring myself to sort out Mother's things.'

'There's plenty of folk'll be glad of them,' she said. 'Don't worry about it now. You sit down and I'll get changed, then I'll make us some supper.'

'I can do that,' he offered.

'No, it's my job now!'

She took her time in the bedroom, kicking off the shoes and thankfully putting on her slippers. She looked with fast-beating heart over at the double bed. Lucky she had changed the linen after the funeral, she thought. Let's hope it'd not got all damp in the meantime. It was a narrow double bed, and Mr Loom – *Leonard*! was a big man so they'd be well and truly lying side by side ...

In the living room, he uncorked the port, poured out a generous tumblerful. Old Walt had actually been right. Dutch courage was just what he needed.

There was not yet any sign or smell of cooking. In the kitchen, Nancy leaned against the sink for support, wearing Mr Loom's apron over the silk dress – it had seemed rather late in the day to change into something simpler. It was almost eight-thirty. She wasn't hungry anyway.

He took her by surprise, tickling the back of her neck. She flew round to face him. 'Sorry, I–' she faltered. 'I gather you're not in the mood for eating either?' His voice sounded teasing. He had a fatuous smile on his face. She suddenly realised there was alcohol on his breath. This was totally out of character. She remembered how Mrs Nagel had almost forced the brandy on him, the night his mother died. Leonard was no drinker . . .

He wrapped his arms round her, pulling her with him, towards his mother's room. They literally fell together onto the bed. 'Two innocents, you and me, Nancy,' he mumbled, allowing one hand to slide down and convulsively cup a firm young breast. 'We've both got so much to learn . . .' He let her go and stood up, rocking on his heels. 'Get undressed quickly, there's a good girl, we might as well go straight to bed . . .'

Obediently, shocked at the unexpectedness of it all, Nancy slowly unbuttoned the lovely silk dress and let it slip in a shivering heap to the floor. She sat there on the edge of the hard bed, with her head bent, rolling down her stockings mechanically as he set the phonograph in motion and the room throbbed to the notes of 'Abide With Me'.

In the light of early morning, they lay side by side, just as she had pictured it. Mr Loom – she couldn't think of him as Leonard just at this moment – slept deeply, his hairy chest rising and falling rhythmically. She reached down and stealthily pulled the eiderdown up under his chin. She had opened the window in the middle of the night; she didn't want him to catch cold.

It struck her that she could easily have pressed that eiderdown over his face, but she instantly dismissed the idea, with real horror.

She glanced down at her shoulders, which were still marked from his excited grip; but, after all, it had not been the ordeal she'd feared because he was inept and inebriated.

Nothing had really happened except that he'd mumbled over and over that he loved her so much, kissing her compressed lips and nuzzling her neck like a sleepy child. Which made her feel sad because she was now aware that she could never love him like that. Had Art lain awake too last night? Did he feel sad – and bitter? Why had he come to gaze at her after the wedding?

She must have slept at last because she woke to the sound of a rattling tea tray and opened her eyes to see Mr Loom, fully dressed, washed and shaved, immaculate as always, obviously apprehensive as he offered her the cup and saucer. 'Nancy, my dear, I must apologise for my unseemly behaviour last night. Whatever must you think of me?'

She took a sip of the tea. 'You've nothing to be sorry about, Leonard – but I'm going to hide that port away.' She managed a smile. 'Thank you for the tea.'

'Would you like a little music?' he asked.

She hoped he did not see her flinch. 'Not this morning ... Perhaps we could choose some new tunes together – something not so solemn. And, Leonard ...'

'Yes, dear?'

'Can we afford to change a few things – move out some of this heavy furniture?' Begin as you mean to go on, she told herself. He's already afraid of losing you. Thinks he overstepped the mark last night ...

'I understand. Of course we can. You don't want to be reminded of my mother at every turn, I should have realised that.'

It was going to be much easier than she had imagined, she thought with relief, and pushed back the bedclothes. 'Aren't we lucky? Living in the top half of the house means we have the bathroom! I must get washed and dressed now, Leonard.'

'I hung up your dress in the wardrobe,' he told her. Then she suddenly noticed the heap of clothes piled in the corner. He must have emptied it out for her earlier!

'Thank you, Leonard, that was very kind of you, but I won't be wearing that today,' she said demurely.

Molly had seen the onlooker at the wedding, too. She had escaped the group photograph and made her way down to the church gates, to ensure that she was close by to see the bride and groom drive off.

On the Sunday morning after the wedding, she stayed obediently in bed as Alexa decreed: 'We don't want that baby coming before time, now do we, Molly? You just rest up today – and give some serious thought to what I said last night, that you should finish work very soon. I shall advertise for a new clerk next week. I'm thankful that Nancy has decided to stay on for the time being, I must say.'

Molly couldn't help wondering if her friend's wedding night had gone smoothly; it was difficult – impossible, really – for her to imagine Mr Loom in the role of ardent lover ... She couldn't stop herself thinking sometimes of what had happened between herself and Rory; in different circumstances it could have been the commitment to what might well have proved to be a love story. How could she be sure now? If only Nancy had married Art, she thought.

On impulse, she reached into her bedside cabinet for her writing case. Pencil would have to do. The ink bottle was in the desk in the sitting room.

Dear Art,
I heard on the House of Leather grapevine you really are going to Australia! I expect Nancy told you how we two met there, so I know what a big adventure this will be for you – I hope you enjoy your travels as much as I did. Good luck!

Art, please don't think I am prying, but I saw you outside the church yesterday. I hope I can still count myself as one of your friends – I shall always remember you taking me to the pud shop, and all the fun we had working together ... Anyway, what's done is done, and

Nancy has chosen her future, surprising as it is. I'm sure you are doing the right thing in going away. I understand, because I had to make a decision rather like that myself.

Of course, I don't know where you are aiming to be in Australia, but if ever you are near this part of NSW, do call on the pastor, who is married to Mrs Nagel's cousin. They would make you very welcome, I'm sure, and offer help if ever you needed it. I'll enclose details . . .

'What are you up to?' Alexa asked, coming in to make sure she was still under the covers. But Molly knew of old that she didn't need to explain.

She placed the letter in the leather writing case. 'Nothing strenuous,' she grinned.

'You haven't been chewing that pencil, I hope?'

'Not much . . . Sometimes you sound like just Sister Margaret Mary, Alexa,' Molly said wryly.

'More like a mother hen, I hope,' she said unexpectedly. 'Now, what d'you fancy for breakfast?'

'I know – prunes are good for me, and it, and a poached egg,' Molly mused. She would have to look up Art's address at work, and post the letter off tomorrow.

'Molly's twenty-first on Friday,' Nancy reminded Mr Loom. She had a printed card on her desk in the showroom now: MRS N LOOM, SENIOR SALES ASSISTANT. Regular clients asked for her by name. She knew that her new husband was proud of her progress. He'd soon accepted the fact that she wished to go on working. 'We're invited for dinner,' she added.

He was just 'passing through' as he put it: in a way he was reassuring himself that she was still there, because she had made such a difference to his way of life. They made a good team at work, too, and it was a relief to him that Minnie's attention was now focused on her new assistant, an earnest middle-aged widower.

'Friday – mmm . . .' It sounded as if he was considering whether this would be convenient.

Nancy looked demure though she wanted to giggle. She was not yet wholly Mrs Loom. She knew very well that he considered their Friday nights together sacrosanct. It was bath-night, early-to-bed night . . . Married life really wasn't so bad now they'd got into this routine, and she was greatly relieved to discover that, without the port wine, Leonard was considerate and, Friday by Friday, becoming a more competent lover. Besides, there was their lovely new bed, generously sized and with a feather mattress which was a joy to sink into. He had dug deep into his savings to please her. She must be generous in return, and once a week was all he expected. Maybe it was easier to live with a man you liked and respected than to be consumed with passion, she thought, though now she'd never find out for sure, of course . . . Also, Leonard was willing to let her take the lead in household matters. He only needed a hint or two.

'There's always Saturday,' she said softly, for his ears only. Those large appendages were now scarlet with embarrassment.

Molly had just six more weeks to go before the baby, and had reluctantly given up work only last week. She'd imagined herself having a big party on her special birthday, with friends both old and new. She'd pictured herself in a beautiful dress, her shoulders bare, her waist a mere handspan, flowers in her long, loose hair and silver dancing shoes on her feet; reality was an intimate dinner for four at Alexa's, a voluminous garment which skimmed her swollen shape, and carpet slippers because her feet and ankles were too puffed up to fit into shoes. She had to keep her hair cropped now because it would be too much of an effort to brush and comb flowing tresses.

The dress, yet another gift from Alexa, would have to be a pink shiny satin; she sighed, thinking she must look rather like a stout little pig!

175

So the arrival of an unexpected guest during the afternoon was hardly a cause for celebration, even though he came in a shiny new motor car, laden with parcels.

It took her a while to reach the door. The others weren't due for another two hours. The food should arrive, piping hot, from a nearby restaurant an hour after that. 'Just dress yourself up in good time, and then rest 'til six o'clock,' were Alexa's instructions. Molly had barely put her feet up on the sofa and closed her eyes when the door knocker resounded.

'Matthew!' she exclaimed. Then: 'Where's Fay?'

'She stayed at home with my parents, I thought she might be too much for you right now ... she sends her love, though, and she's made you a very colourful card.'

He put down the packages in the hallway and squeezed both her hands warmly in his, not attempting to kiss her.

'I'm playing truant this afternoon, as you see,' he told her. 'Happy birthday.'

'I'm so glad you came, I need my friends more than ever right now ...' She sounded really doleful.

'Come and sit beside me on the sofa and open your presents, that'll cheer you up!'

She leaned against him and rested her head against his shoulder. It was broad and comfortable.

'Aren't you going to kiss me then?' she asked, adding: 'If you can get near enough to me, with all this between us, eh? I suppose a twenty-first birthday *is* the time for kisses.'

It was a satisfying kiss, and good to be cuddled, Molly decided. But it was down to earth with a bump when she opened a large, interesting-looking box and discovered it to be full of baby clothes, some of which she recognised from Fay-days.

'Sorry,' he said, seeing her face. 'My mother's suggestion.'

'No, it's nice of you,' she said ruefully. 'I've been putting off acquiring all this, which worries Alexa, but now I see my future laid out before me: tiny nightgowns,

pilches, bibs and bootees, mitts and matinee jackets ...'
She held a hand-smocked frock against her face, its faint
elusive scent instantly conjuring up a picture of Fay when
she'd dressed her in this as a baby on the boat. She guessed
that Lucy had chosen or made many of the smallest
garments before her baby was born, and that was why both
Alexa and then Matthew had hung on to them.

'Open this next, it's my choice,' he said softly, placing a
small square package in her lap.

His gift was sapphire earrings, as blue as the sea in
Sydney Harbour.

'They're beautiful! Oh, thank you!' Molly exclaimed.
'How did you know I had my ears pierced?'

'I've made it my business to learn a great deal about you,
Molly. Can't you guess why?'

'You like to make me smile, be happy, that's why ...
Will you put them on for me?'

As she leaned forward the opal ring was revealed, falling
free from the cleft between her breasts, and he touched the
stone briefly. 'I wondered where your ring had gone ...
It's warm and glowing from being against your skin. Who
gave you this? The baby's father?'

'No,' she said truthfully. 'It means a lot to me, though,
and these earrings will always be special, too, I can
promise you that, Matthew.'

'Marry me, little Molly Sparkes. Fay adores you and
would be thrilled with the baby, and I do believe we'd
make a good family, the four of us together.'

'I can't,' she said, beginning to cry. '*I can't* ...'

'It's still Friday – just,' Leonard murmured, as they lay
side by side. He stroked Nancy's hair, hooking a strand
carefully back behind her ear so he could kiss her cheek.

'It was a lovely dinner,' she said dreamily. 'Wouldn't it
be wonderful if Molly decided to marry Matthew? Did you
remember to mix yourself up some bi-carb?'

'Sometimes I think it would be nice if we had a baby, but

then I remember my advancing years and I know it wouldn't be fair on you if you were left with a child to bring up on your own.'

Nancy suddenly turned to him. She'd felt, well, funny tonight. Could it possibly be a touch of wistfulness? When Molly had showed her the baby clothes, she'd recognised some of them, too. 'You're not as old as all that, Leonard,' she said softly, invitingly.

Alexa tidied up the presents, piled them on the table. Molly was still an untidy young lady, she thought, whereas Nancy perfectly fitted the role of houseproud new wife ... Matthew had been the last to leave, they'd had a nightcap together after Molly had trailed wearily upstairs to bed. She'd seen the way he looked at Molly, realised exactly why he had come today. It was a solution which Molly ought seriously to reconsider. Alexa would hate to lose her, of course, especially now Nancy was married, but it probably wouldn't come to that, she sighed to herself. After all, Molly had been so stubborn regarding Rory, who, to his credit, had also wanted to marry her.

There was a sudden thumping on the floor from immediately above: Molly's bedroom! Alexa was instantly alert. She forced herself not to rush but to climb the stairs at her usual pace.

Molly was in her nightgown, but not in bed. She clutched at her swollen stomach. 'Alexa, something's wrong – I had a terrible pain ...'

Alexa helped her to lie on her side on top of the bedclothes. 'Draw your knees up slightly, it might help. Just try to relax and breathe deeply if the pain comes again, Molly, I'm going downstairs to telephone the doctor. Now, don't worry, it's probably just a warning sign that you've been overdoing things, been too excited today, but we can't ignore it. I'll be back as quickly as I can.'

'It's coming, I know it is,' Molly managed, as the pain consumed her again. 'Hurry, Alexa ... *oh, please hurry!*'

Chapter Ten

The double doors at the rear of the motor ambulance swung open and Molly was carried up the ramp on a stretcher. In her dazed state, it seemed to her that she was enclosed in a dimly lit square box. A nurse sat beside her on the jolting journey to the hospital, finger on her pulse, murmuring reassuringly. The box reeked of carbolic, the blankets were coarse – she wanted desperately to throw them off, to escape, but it was as if any such movements were beyond her. Not knowing that Alexa was travelling in front with the driver, she felt she had been abandoned to her fate . . .

Mercifully, it was a short journey: there were welcome lights illuminating the hospital windows, long corridors where the wheels of the bed-chair squealed protestingly; coifed night nurses glancing up from their stations where they studied their paperwork. Unseen patients sighed and turned on rubber-covered mattresses in the wards. Gas lamps hissed and flared.

She was in a small room, lying on a hard couch, uncovered now, with firm, cool hands probing her abdomen – hands which stilled whenever the pains gripped her. The sister held her limp hand while a more intimate examination was carried out by the doctor. Molly, past embarrassment, closed her eyes, determined not to cry out and disgrace herself.

She became aware of a muted discussion taking place but

she heard only: 'Lying in the transverse position . . . Matter of urgency . . .' Then the blankets were replaced; a chill, wet cloth was placed comfortingly on her forehead. If her eyes remained shut, if she could not see, she told herself in the confusion and fear the pain induced, then nothing could happen – could it?

Another room, much larger, with a bright overhead lamp. She couldn't help herself. Her eyes flickered open and focused on what looked like a fish kettle, steaming steadily. There was more than one doctor now, and several nurses. None of them spoke directly to her. There was the sharp prick of a needle in her arm, she saw the lid of the fish kettle lifted and a perforated metal tray was removed, revealing the glint of sterilised instruments. Something covered her face but she was unable to struggle, to scream out that she was being stifled, then she was oblivious.

The agony was still there, every time she shifted slightly, but it was a different pain: it didn't come in relentless waves, she was suffering but no longer in labour, she knew intuitively. The sunlight streaming through the windows of her room made her blink. She turned her head cautiously on the pillow. Beside her on the locker top she saw her treasures: the framed photograph of her mother, the little wooden horse, the earring box which had been under her pillow – she put a hand up to her throat and found the chain and the opal ring back in place. Alexa had snatched all these up when they'd left home.

She was startled when Alexa spoke. Had been unaware that she was sitting on a chair on the other side of the bed. 'Molly dear, thank God, you're back with us at last . . . They are bringing the baby to you in a moment. They think it best she should be baptised now, Molly.'

'It's alive then – my baby?' Relief washed over Molly: she was suddenly wide awake. It must be morning, she realised. Where had the night gone to? She swallowed

180

convulsively, her mouth was so dry. She longed for a long, cool draught of water.

'You have a daughter, Molly, too tiny even to weigh or to bathe. It was a caesarean birth: don't struggle to sit up, you will be sore for some time until the stitches are removed . . .'

Molly felt herself gingerly. The stitches – the wound – were concealed beneath firm bandaging. But it must be true, the baby must be born because she was flat at the front once more, she realised. 'Was she born on my birthday?' she wanted to know.

'Just. Molly, I have to tell you, she has survived the night, which the doctors hardly expected, but—'

'She's *alive*,' Molly stated firmly, and looked into the smiling face of her mother in the photograph.

'A name,' Alexa was saying. 'Can you think of a name for her?'

'Florence Almond,' Molly said. 'I want to call her Almond.' The chaplain's fingers dipped in holy water; Molly, propped up by pillows in her bed, held her baby for the anointing for what seemed like seconds only. This little scrap was nothing like she had imagined. The baby didn't open her screwed-up eyes or cry. She looked very old and wise with that wrinkled face and sparse hair, Molly thought, not newborn at all. The nurse had placed the tiny bundle against Molly's breast. There seemed no weight at all to it, just faint warmth seeping through the layers of flannel: the baby's wrappings and her own hospital gown. She discerned a feeble twitching of the baby's swaddled limbs, in sharp contrast to the energetic movements she had felt in the womb, then she linked her hands gently round Almond to keep her safe.

There were muted prayers, then Molly's baby was taken from her. 'Please can I have a drink?' she asked.

Alexa gently mopped the tears coursing down Molly's cheeks. She was suddenly very weary indeed. She had stayed at Molly's side ever since she was brought to this room after the operation. A nurse had been there too for some hours; it was touch and go for Molly as well as her baby during that long night, and there was the endless business of transfusing Molly with cooled, boiled saline water to alleviate the shock. At least it now looked as if she would recover, even if the same could not be said of her baby.

'You must get more sleep,' Alexa said, smoothing the covers. 'And I must go home and cable your father to let him know what has happened.'

'Nancy – you'll call and tell her, won't you?'

'Of course I will! I imagine you'll be overflowing with flowers and visitors shortly.'

'Alexa—'

'Yes?'

'Thank you for everything. I don't know how I can ever pay you back–'

'Don't worry about that. Just get well quickly. I'll be in to see you later today.'

Matthew was sitting in his car outside the house. He climbed out stiffly as Alexa's cab drove off. She stood at the gate, swaying slightly from sheer fatigue; waiting for him to join her. Instantly his hand supported her elbow and he guided her up the steps. She passed him the key.

As he inserted it in the lock, he said: 'I had a feeling – I was halfway home when I decided to return here to see if Molly was all right. The ambulance passed me as I waited to turn into your road.'

'You spent the rest of the night out here?' she asked.

'That doesn't matter! Tell me, please?' he said urgently.

'Molly had a baby daughter last night. There were complications. The doctor said she must go to hospital. Matthew, they had to operate—'

'Molly?'

'All stitched up, but she really will be all right in a

182

month or two ... The baby, well, that's a different matter, I'm afraid. She will need very special care, being premature. Would you like a cup of tea – anything to eat?'

'Sit down, I'll take care of it,' he said. There was real concern on his face. He was a nice man, she thought.

When he had made and poured them both a cup of tea Alexa decided to speak openly to him.

'Matthew, I must say this – Molly is obviously fond of you, and you have Fay in common, of course, but I don't think she'll change her mind about marrying you, even though her father, and Nancy and I think it would be, well, a truly happy ending.'

'No, I don't believe she will,' he said slowly, and drained his cup. 'I'm glad, though, that you would have been pleased if Molly had consented. It worried me that you might think me disloyal to Lucy's memory.'

'She's been gone three years, Matthew. To be blunt, you hardly had any time together.'

'But what we did have was very precious, Alexa. I hope it doesn't shock you when I describe those three months as ecstatic. I'm not sure I can ever attain that state of euphoria again: I don't really know if I want to. If Lucy were still alive I'm positive I would never have looked at another woman, but ...'

'You're a man, Matthew, with normal desires. I take it as a compliment that you feel you could love another who is also dear to me. Your coming together would make the bonds between us all even stronger.'

'I'm afraid it's not to be,' he said. Then, 'Don't tell Molly how I returned here, will you? She wants me in her life as her friend, that's what matters.'

Molly didn't like Nurse Mercy much. Her name didn't fit, she thought ruefully, as she bit her lip to stop herself from exclaiming 'Ouch!'

Mercy squeezed and pummelled at Molly's swollen breasts, red-marked from her efforts. 'Every little drop is precious to your baby,' she reproved her patient as she flinched.

'Why can't I nurse her myself?' Molly asked desperately. Surely that would bring her relief.

'You know why. Baby is small and frail. She doesn't have the right reflexes yet.'

'She's three days old now.'

'She should still be in the womb, Mother. Don't make such a fuss. You must learn to do this yourself. In a week or two . . .'

'I can't wait that long!' Molly cried.

'Don't be silly. You'll be leaving hospital without Almond, you know that. Mother's milk is vital to her wellbeing . . . There, cover yourself up. I will be back in two hours. Nurse Daniel will change your dressings, to make sure the stitches aren't suppurating . . .'

Molly turned her face to the pillow. Was there no end to the pain, the indignity? Her voice was muffled. 'I haven't seen her . . . Almond, since she was baptised – that's the only time I have held her. How can I get to know her . . .?'

She didn't see the sudden look of sympathy on Mercy's face. She said nothing more but went out with her tray of covered dishes, her retreat marked by the squeaking of her sensible shoes.

'Healing nicely. Lucky you're not allergic to catgut, my dear,' Nurse Daniel said cheerfully. She wrung out a piece of gauze in the antiseptic solution. 'There, that'll ward off any–'

'Suppuration?' Molly supplied.

'Now, whoever suggested that to you?' Nurse Daniel asked. Then she grinned. 'I can guess, of course!' She wound fresh bandage in place. 'Comfortable? Good. Stay sitting up, I've a surprise for you. Close your eyes for a minute . . .'

Shortly after that Molly brushed the baby's face with her lips. '*Almond*! You're still here.'

'Of course she is. She's a fighter, is our Almond Sparkes. Mercy and I had a little chat. Would you like to try to give her a little feed? Just a minute, each side. It might help both of you feel stronger. Don't be disappointed if you can't manage it this time, but it's a little step in the right direction.'

Nurse was right to have warned her. It was far from easy. The baby was too drowsy and disinclined to suck; but it was a step forward, because Molly was bonding with her daughter. Almond Sparkes, she mused to herself, Molly and Almond Sparkes ... I can just picture that on a billboard! At this moment I don't believe I shall ever do another high kick, but at least we've got each other, and *I love you*, I really do.

Nancy came with flowers, and letters from home. 'Oh, Molly, the nurse let me peep through the nursery window, and she held the baby up, and even though she's so tiny, I think she's beautiful!' She hoped she didn't sound wistful. No luck this month for the Looms, she thought. Perhaps it was just as well, as they were really busy at work with Alexa leaving more and more of the day-to-day running of the business to Leonard. Nancy suspected that Mrs Nagel might be considering handing over control to her husband, as she'd done while she was in Australia: she'd already told them she would be taking time off to look after Molly when she came home from hospital.

She scanned the letter from Wren's Nest. Warm congratulations were expressed and hopes of seeing her and the baby soon. Meanwhile, she should expect flowers shortly, despatched with love from Fay and Matthew. Enclosed was more of Fay's artwork, a crumpled picture of the new baby. There was a big crooked smile on the round pencilled face.

'You've missed one,' Nancy told her, picking up the letter with the Australian stamp.

Molly recognised the writing, of course. She opened it slowly.

Dear Molly,

This is to wish you a very happy birthday – you see, I did not forget! All of us here send our love and good wishes.

Well, Molly, you were right, and I know I will have your blessing. Sarah and I will be married by the time you receive this. She knows all about you and understands that you will always have a very special place in my heart. But she is here – and you are so far away. She has been so good to my mother, and will continue to care for her, whenever I am gem-seeking.

I miss the circus – I don't think it will be too long before I get back to that life, but if I do, I shall stick to touring in this country . . .

I hope that one day we will meet again. Meanwhile that you, too, will find the one who will be your soulmate – I have accepted that it would never have been me. Remember me to Mrs Nagel and Nancy. I shall understand if you decide that you will no longer keep in touch, but I shall never forget you.

Love from Rory

Molly pushed the letter back into the envelope. Then she swung her legs slowly over the side of the bed, feeling for the floor with her bare toes.

'Molly!' Nancy exclaimed, alarmed. 'Whatever are you doing?'

'It's all right, Nancy. Nurse Daniel has been helping me to walk round the bed two or three times a day. The other nurse doesn't really approve, but Nurse D says that patients must start getting back on their feet as soon as they can after an operation, or there's a danger of clots in the leg . . .'

'Doesn't it hurt?' Nancy worried, slipping an arm round Molly's waist as she stood up slowly.

'Oh, it does, but it'll be much easier when the stitches come out. You see, they won't let me out of this place until I'm fit, so—'

186

She suddenly longed to be home, to prepare for the baby to join her as soon as possible. Maybe she would have weakened, contacted Rory, left it to him to decide what to do about her and the child. That wouldn't happen now, after this letter. She had her good friends, including Matthew, but really it was just the two of them, herself and Almond, wasn't it?

Matthew drove up from Kent the following Sunday afternoon to fetch Molly home from hospital. He waited outside the nursery while she went to see Almond. The nurse allowed her to hold her for a brief moment.

'I told her Mummy would see her soon – you don't think I'm abandoning her, do you?' she appealed to Matthew. 'I know Alexa would think me indelicate saying such a thing to you, but Almond will still be having my milk – I'll be spending my days trying to express that for her, after all.'

'Nothing you say surprises me,' he told her, 'but I wouldn't advise you to broadcast the information! Get in the chair, Molly. I'm told I have to push you off the premises, or Nurse Mercy will report me to Matron. Of course you're not abandoning your baby: you'll feel much better when you're back in your own bed.'

'Don't you tell me what to do, Matthew Dunn! I don't intend to go to bed until my legs buckle, which I suspect they will, tonight. Alexa says Fay is bursting to see me, and is very disgruntled they wouldn't allow her anywhere near the hospital!'

'There's quite a party waiting for you, don't worry,' he said as they approached reception. 'Nancy and Leonard will be there, too. Try not to shock the dignified Mr Loom, eh?'

'Take care of yourself, Mrs Sparkes,' the nurse on duty, new to Molly, advised with a bright smile. Molly knew, of course, of the deception: Alexa had perpetuated it on the night of her arrival. 'It seemed the best thing to do at the time,' she'd confessed next day to Molly, who had then had to go along with it.

Now the nurse added: 'I'm glad your husband is home at last. Have you seen the baby? So tiny, but doing really well – let's hope you will be reunited in a couple of weeks.'

Matthew must have been surprised, but he did not correct her. 'Yes, she's a girl with spirit, Almond.'

'I'll escort you to the motor,' the nurse insisted. 'And then I'll wheel the chair back here. You've made arrangements about the milk supply, of course?'

'Yes. We will send it to the hospital every afternoon, by cab,' Molly promised.

'Goodbye then – and good luck to you both!'

Tucked up in the car with a warm rug, despite the summery weather, Molly wondered what to say to Matthew, but he put her at ease as usual.

'It was a natural mistake, Molly. Forget it, won't you?'

'Where's the baby?' Fay cried, disappointed, wriggling out of Nancy's restraining grasp.

'She can't come home just yet, I told you,' her grandmother reminded her.

Molly looked at all the smiling faces and suddenly dissolved into tears. It was all too much. She clutched Matthew's arm. 'Help me upstairs,' she gulped. 'I'm so sorry, I was so happy to come home and now—'

'Now you need to rest for half an hour,' Alexa said quickly. 'Just have Nancy with you, eh, until you feel like coming down to tea.'

She shooed Fay and Leonard into the sitting room and shut the door.

Matthew lifted her as if she weighed no more than his daughter, despite her feeble protests, and carried her up to her room; Nancy following close behind. He deposited her gently on her bed, then turned immediately to go. 'See you both later.'

'Oh, Nancy, give me a hug – but not too tight because it still hurts!' Molly wept. 'How will I cope with it all?'

'Where's your sparkle, Molly dear? You'll manage, I know you will . . .'

Chapter Eleven

The Pastor's wife was more wary of strangers than her husband. She tried to follow his example, but his flock at the nearby settlement seemed to accept that Mrs Hind was the one they could go to for practical help whereas the pastor would comfort, listen and offer spiritual guidance. In fact, they complemented each other very well. For the first time in her life. Elfie felt that she was really needed, appreciated, and, surprising as it still seemed to her but most important, that she was well liked.

So when she opened her door to a caller one day she did not immediately say 'Come in' but waited to hear why he had come. He had obviously been brought here by the carrier's cart which was now wheeling round in a flurry of dust outside the little house attached to the mission, before rumbling along to Mrs Mac's at the Indispensable Stores.

The young man had an English accent; from London she surmised. He wore a somewhat travel-stained suit, an outfit unusual in this farming area. He stood, hat in hand, bags at his feet on the step, a tentative smile lighting his handsome face.

'Mrs Hind? I am Arthur Gray, a friend of Molly Sparkes and formerly employed by your relative, Mrs Nagel. I have a letter of introduction from Molly.' He pulled a crumpled envelope from his pocket. Elfie accepted it rather reluctantly. To read this immediately would imply that she was suspicious of his intentions. The mention of Alexa was reassurance enough.

'I have just received some—' Elfie swallowed hard, it would not be charitable to say 'shocking' she realised '– surprising news from my cousin regarding Molly ... Have you travelled far today, Mr Gray? You are welcome to join my husband and me for supper. He should be home very shortly.' It would be up to Ernst to ask the young man if he required a bed for the night, she thought. Though where would he go otherwise? There was no hotel and, being midwinter here, there was not much travelling done after dark.

'Thank you,' Art said gratefully. 'May I leave my baggage in the hall?'

'You are seeking work in these parts?' Ernst asked him as they chatted over the meal.

'I'm not sure ... Somehow I don't think I'm up to farming on such a large scale – or hard physical work at all,' Art said ruefully, looking at his penpusher's soft hands. 'I will probably look for a desk job, perhaps back in Melbourne. Maybe I'll explore more of the country first, 'til my savings run out ...'

It was Ernst who told Art that Molly's baby had been born. 'Poor girl,' he said compassionately. 'To go through all this without a husband.'

'She was always impetuous,' Elfie had to say it, 'but she has generous support from Mrs Nagel, of course. More cheese, Mr Gray? I'm sorry this is all I can offer. We eat simply, you see. I have plenty more jars of my chutney in the store so don't hesitate to help yourself: it helps to make the bread more palatable. I used to make a batch of loaves every Friday back home, and it never seemed to get stale, but here ...' She sighed; here the flour sacks heaved with weevils.

'I can't quite picture Molly with a baby,' Art said, digging out the brown pickle obediently. It was too vinegary for his taste. Nothing like his mum's pickled onions,

191

as big as giant marbles. He smiled at the memory of the time he and his sisters had used some of those monsters for just that purpose. His mother's hand had caught each backside unawares in swift succession as they were kneeling, absorbed in their game.

'Still, at least she has had experience of caring for a young infant. She accompanied us out here to Australia three years ago, as nursemaid to Mrs Nagel's little granddaughter.'

'She handed over that task when they were staying here, to Nancy,' Ernst reminded his wife.

'Nancy? Nancy Atkins? Oh, so *that* is how they met . . .' Art exclaimed.

'You know Nancy? Oh, of course you do, if you worked at Mrs Nagel's, too,' Ernst realised. 'We were happy to hear of her recent marriage. It was well that Mrs Nagel took her to England. Her life here was – not good. Not good at all. She was one of my brightest pupils at the mission school. In fact, I recommended her to Mrs Nagel.'

'A terrible family . . . how that poor young girl must have suffered,' Elfie said. She had been aghast when Ernst had confided in her his suspicions regarding their brutality to Nancy.

Art sat looking from one to the other, wondering if they would enlighten him any further. 'She married a kind man,' he said at last. 'But rather too old for her. Nancy is a – wonderful girl. She never spoke of her life here to me.' His desolation was plain on his face.

'Let us go into the sitting room,' Ernst said compassionately. 'You will stay the night or a few days, of course? Elfie, my dear, will you prepare a room? I think our guest would like to talk, and I am here to listen and to help him understand . . .'

Molly's father had already been generous with financial help. Home on leave in August, he and Madelaine, his second wife, were seriously househunting in the West

192

Country because they would return for good the following year. He came almost immediately on his own to Alexa's house, with the obvious intention of trying to persuade his daughter to live with him and Madelaine when the time came. In the meantime, he intimated, when a suitable house was found Molly and the baby would be welcome to live there in comfort, all expenses paid.

He was polite but distant with Alexa, prompting her to make her excuses and leave them together in Molly's room, which she shared with Almond at her own insistence. 'I want us to be close. I missed her every day she was in the hospital ...'

Molly's favourite things were placed for the baby to see when she was awake. They caught her grandfather's eye immediately. He sat awkwardly in the wicker armchair, facing the portrait of Florence. 'It's definite, is it, her name?' he asked, gesturing to the sleeping baby and not lowering the military pitch of his voice.

'Yes, Florence Almond. For my mother,' she returned. She imagined that he must disapprove of her cropped hair, her loose smock top sewn by dear Nancy, front-buttoned which made it so much easier to accommodate the baby's frequent needs. It also concealed the fact that she wasn't wearing a corset: even so soon after her confinement she still had no need of that tortuous garment, anyway the area where she had been stitched was still very tender.

'Ah,' he said, clearing his throat noisily. 'But you really never knew your mother, my dear.'

'I knew enough to want to follow her footsteps and go on the stage.'

'Hardly the stage, I think – *the circus*,' he pronounced pedantically.

'Well, I believe Florence Almond would have approved! And I know I would have loved her,' Molly flashed.

Her father might have discarded his uniform but he was still an authoritative figure; fiercely moustached, tall and ramrod-straight like Matthew. She must make him aware that while she was grateful for what he had done so far, in future she wanted to resume running her own life. She didn't wish to remove herself so far from her friends. She was startled when she observed him flinching at her reply.

'Yes, you would. You remind me so much of her . . .' He was actually almost whispering now, still regarding the image of his late wife, avoiding Molly's gaze. 'Molly, will you allow me to take care of you – both of you? Isn't that what she would have wanted?' he pleaded. 'Paying your bills isn't the answer. It doesn't make up for all the years I had to be away.'

'I wasn't deprived, Father. You chose a good place for me to be; many whose parents have to leave them are not so fortunate. The Army was your career, I accepted that, and I'm glad that you've found someone else at last. Her children will be the family you never really had. It's too late for *me* to be part of that.'

'She's a fine woman, Molly. Her children appear willing to accept me. However, I imagine she will never quite live up to the memory of Florence. To others we may have appeared ill-matched, but there was—'

'A *spark* between you? I know, I really do. And I'm sorry to disappoint you but I've decided to stay with Alexa for the time being, not because I feel I owe it to her but because she needs me. We have things in common, like losing the most important person in our lives.'

'Your baby's father?' He looked keenly at her now as she sat on the low nursing chair beside the crib, allowing little Almond to grasp one finger of her outstretched hand in her tiny fist.

Molly gave a silent shake of her head. 'Maybe – I'm not sure anymore, since the baby was born – she's going to look like him, I think. He did love me at the time, that's important, and Matthew would marry me now. I'm aware that would please you, because you know him well, but it's someone else I dream of, you see . . .'

Almond stirred, opened her mouth, then her eyes.

Molly scooped her up in her arms gladly. 'Anyway, don't think I'm sad, will you, because this little one is the love of my life, and she's all I need right now.' Her hand hesitated over the buttons on her smock.

Her father rose instantly. 'Mess-time, eh?' he boomed. 'Well, I'll go downstairs and tell your self-appointed guardian that she isn't going to lose you after all!'

He turned at the door: 'Molly, thank you for her name, my dear. It means a great deal to me.'

'You don't mind if I go out for a bit, do you?' Nancy asked Leonard. She knew he liked a nap after Sunday lunch, so he wouldn't be deprived of her company.

'Of course not, my dear. Calling for Molly, I expect?'

'Mmm. It'll be nice in the park, all the flowers out and we can enjoy wheeling the baby round all the paths and seeing folk out and about.'

'Don't talk to any strange young men. You look very fetching today.'

'I'm not a flirt, you know that, Leonard!' she reproved him mildly.

Unexpectedly he caught at her sleeve as she rustled past, in crisp yellow cotton, as sunny as the day. All her spare time was spent at her sewing machine, she did not demand the latest fashions but set to and made them for herself. She was a thrifty young wife. He was very fortunate. 'Kiss me goodbye?' he asked.

'Oh, Leonard, anyone would think I was going away for ages, not just an hour or two!' Nancy bent over him as he lay back in the reclining leather chair she had insisted he buy from the shop because Alexa offered them such a generous discount. She had her soft bed, now he had his chair ... She kissed his forehead obediently. He looked off-colour, she thought, feeling a trifle worried but not enough for her to change her mind about going out. 'Still got that horrid headache? Never mind, a nice sleep'll cure that.' He was over-conscientious with the shop bookwork, to the extent of bringing it home with him at weekends.

He gave her a sudden fierce hug, actually making her catch her breath for a moment. 'I'm the luckiest chap in the world to have you,' he told her. 'You must get tired of hearing me say it, but I *adore you*, Nancy.'

Two pretty girls paused by the boating lake, then settled on a seat to watch the punters and rowers, to enjoy the splashes and the excited laughter from the couples out on the bright water.

Little Almond Sparkes, three months old now, slept peacefully in the fresh air, in the perambulator bought for her by her doting honorary grandmother, Alexa. She was growing fast, filling out, a fuzz of sand-gold hair just showing round her organdie bonnet. The worries over her early arrival were almost forgotten.

'She's a real Kelly,' Nancy observed, then wished she hadn't said that. 'Sorry, I didn't mean—'

'No, you're right, she is,' Molly said cheerfully. 'Sometimes I think how Serena and Cora would have loved her, but I guess Rory and his new wife will have a family one day and it's best this way, especially with that great distance between us, isn't it?'

'Rory would love her too – you're so lucky to have her, Molly, even though some folk wouldn't agree.'

'I know. What about you, Nancy? Are you considering starting a family?'

'Molly Sparkes, you know how to make me blush! We haven't been married more than a few months yet, remember. Not that I wouldn't love to be at home with a baby to care for like you, but I'm enjoying my work.'

'Alexa says she doesn't know what she'd do without the wonderful Mr and Mrs Loom! I suspect she secretly misses all the bustle and smells of the business but she adores the baby. I have to watch out that she doesn't take Almond over. Mind you, she looked rather relieved when I said I was going out this afternoon.'

'She's enjoying a sleep after a heavy roast lunch, like Leonard, I expect,' Nancy said.

'I still intend to return to the world of work myself, when the right opportunity comes up,' Molly confided. 'Having had a taste of independence, I dearly want to pay my own way in life. Don't worry, I'd never neglect my baby, she's far too precious, and I couldn't bear to farm her out, but there must be a way I can combine being a mother and – and —'

'A bright spark?' Nancy suggested wryly.

'That's it! I'd hate to think I'd lost my sparkle!'

'I'm back,' Nancy called out as she took off her straw boater and laid it on the hall table.

Leonard was obviously awake for she could hear music, a recording on the old phonograph he hadn't played since their wedding day. It must have gathered dust, for the words were being repeated over and over, *Abide with me . . . Abide, abide, abide . . .*

'*Leonard*!' she screamed, crouching over the body sprawled on the floor. It was no use: like his mother before him, Leonard Loom was beyond help. His pale face, with its look of surprise, glistened with Nancy's tears as she cradled his head against the sunshine yellow of her dress.

'I never told you what you wanted so much to hear,' she wept. 'I couldn't lie to you – but, Leonard, I felt safe with you, I really did . . .'

Two weeks after losing her husband, Nancy was back in the showroom. She had already, at Alexa's urging, paid a month's rent in lieu of notice and moved back in with Alexa, Molly and the baby. She brought with her only the bed, the chair, her sewing machine, new clothes and wedding photograph.

Alexa had swiftly resumed control of the business, but

her faithful long-standing employee would be sorely missed. 'You didn't need to come here yet,' she said, concerned. 'Minnie was only too pleased to stand in for you – she really has the makings of a good saleslady. When your finances are sorted ... the insurance and the lump sum I intend to pay you in lieu of the pension Leonard would have received ... well, I imagine there will really be no need for you to work at all. Molly might well be glad of your help with the baby, eh?'

It was all Nancy could think of. It gave her the strength to keep going, especially when she overheard Minnie talking to the new accounts clerk when she was about to enter the office one day. 'There'll never be another Mr Loom, in Mrs Nagel's opinion. What a pity he wore himself out trying to please a young wife. Died of over-excitement, I reckon ...'

When Molly was ready to return to work, Nancy would be there for Almond.

In 1909, the King's horse Minoru won the Derby at Epsom but it was to be the last popular royal racing win for in May 1910 the King died. The Edwardian age was not yet over, although his second son was pronounced George V. The following year the *Terra Nova* set sail for the Antarctic wastes with Captain Scott and his companions; it was the year the White Star liner *Olympic* was launched, whose sister ship would be the *Titanic*; it was the year Mrs Lambert Chambers won her first singles title at Wimbledon; it was also the year when a new name appeared in small print on the bills posted outside the provincial music halls: SPARKES – COMIC MIME AND DANCE

Nancy left it to the last minute to put on Almond's best dress. It didn't matter that the baby would not be on show; she must look her best for her mother's second debut, Nancy determined. Perhaps it was fitting that this should be in a seaside music hall not many miles from where Molly's circus career had first commenced, in Great Yarmouth.

The dressing room of the Hippodrome was bustling; artistes came in and out. Almond was having great fun toddling between the ladies making costume changes and those applying greasepaint. As Molly's newly self-appointed dresser, constant companion and child-minder, Nancy was kept busy herself. She was happy; some of the excitement and glamour rubbed off on her. She was aware, too, that Molly couldn't have managed to come this far without her.

They had left Alexa's house a few days ago and were touring, staying in not always salubrious lodgings – Molly had warned Nancy of that – the months of planning and meticulous rehearsing about to come to fruition.

She knew that Alexa would miss them a great deal, and hoped that she did not feel that Nancy had let her down, leaving the House of Leather soon after Alexa had decided to appoint her for a trial period to Leonard's old job.

'Remember, you are welcome back here at times when things are slack,' she'd told them both. 'You must have somewhere to call home.'

'When I get a London booking, don't worry, we'll take you at your word!' Molly said.

'I'll take great care of them both,' Nancy promised her mentor.

Against the backdrop of a shabby city street, pictured at night, a lad leaned against a make-believe lamp. As the music began, in the spotlight, the mop-haired urchin performed amazing, seemingly effortless acrobatic contortions, to enthusiastic applause. The expressions on his face made the audience crease up with laughing. They loved his patched breeks, his big boots, the shadows he cast on the wall.

In the stalls that first time, Alexa, dressed up to the nines and accompanied by Matthew, who had driven them here this morning, found herself silently weeping but fiercely proud; in the wings, Nancy held up flouncy-frocked Almond in her arms and breathed excitedly: 'That's your mum, Florence Almond, that is: *Sparkes!*'

When Molly cartwheeled off the stage, she returned with Almond and showed her daughter to the audience. 'One day, darling Almond,' she whispered, 'you'll really be centre stage with me.'

Part Three

Chapter One

1911

'If you're good, Florence Almond, when Matthew and Fay come this afternoon, we might take you along to Buckingham Palace to see that grand new statue of Queen Victoria – fancy, in real life she was short, just like me, but I hope I don't grow as wide one day, eh? Anyway, everyone looks up to her now she's thirteen feet tall!'

Molly, having stopped Leonard's phonograph, on which she had been playing her own choice of records, was now inelegantly sprawled out in his leather chair in Nancy's room at Alexa's house. Her lively daughter, unflagging, was still dancing about. Molly mopped the sweat off her own forehead. She wore her usual morning limbering-up clothes, chemise top and old tights.

'I can see your toes, Mummy!' Two-year-old Almond poked her finger through the holes with a sly grin.

'When you get changed, pass those stockings to me to mend,' Nancy said, bringing in refreshments. She'd timed her entrance for when the thumping overhead ceased, after she'd hung Almond's washing on the line.

'Oh, I can afford some new ones, surely, 'Molly said airily, sitting up then draining her glass of lemonade gratefully. 'Even if I'm out of work at present. Strange how my ventures never last long, though they start so well. Mind you, they say the music hall is competing – and losing –

against the cinematograph now, don't they? Who wants to see Molly Sparkes when they can watch Charlie Chaplin? Same size, same boots . . .

'Still, there's plenty going on in dear old London, and I'm always happy when May comes along! 'Specially now Almond and I share a birthday. Can you believe she's two and I'm twenty-three?' Nancy shook her head, mockingly. 'And there's the Coronation to look forward to, at the end of June . . . I was just telling Almond about the old Queen's statue, and how I hope *I* never become as round as she was.'

'Not much danger of that,' Nancy said drily. 'The way you carry on – how much longer are you going to lark about on stage being a lad, Molly?' Age didn't have much to do with it, she thought, you were either realistic, as she was, or not – like Molly . . . She really believed she was independent, but relied heavily on the moral support of her friends.

'Well, I've got enough sense to realise that I'm not cut out to be an adult male impersonator: I'm no Ella Shields – I was all goose-pimply waiting in the wings when she had the audience roaring and on their feet with "Burlington Bertie" . . . All those rousing songs they sing, too – jingoistic, Alexa says – and dashing uniforms accentuating bosoms and bottoms – which in my case wouldn't be much use, would it? Nothing like real soldiers or sailors at all, but what the audience calls for nowadays with all this talk of war. I haven't got a strong enough voice for a start, and my legs just aren't long enough . . . Got any ideas?'

'As I said, give me your tights to darn – and, by the way, Mrs Moore mentioned you made all the ornaments rattle downstairs when you were leaping about up here earlier! Just as well Alexa went into work today, though I keep telling her she ought to have Saturdays off now Minnie's well and truly in charge.' Nancy was still a bit self-conscious when using Alexa's christian name.

'Perhaps it was a mistake coming back here?'

'We can't afford anywhere else at the moment,' Nancy told her bluntly. 'And she was so pleased to see us.'

'It all started off so well,' Molly sighed, ''til I ran out of fresh ideas for the act. Variety is what you need nowadays. Rory planned everything when we were together – he learned a lot from Thom, of course, but he was born to that sort of life, which I certainly wasn't. I probably took it up when I was too old. Well, you know what I mean. Sometimes I wish I could go back to the circus, but it wouldn't be fair on you, living in a tent or caravan, looking after Almond while I indulged myself—'

'I wouldn't mind,' Nancy said loyally. 'So long as you were both happy ... That awful accident – your poor Danish friend – doesn't haunt you any more then?'

'Not once I heard that Hanna was recovering well after she finally went home to Copenhagen. Oh, Nancy,' she exclaimed, 'I haven't had a chance to pass on some exciting news which came by first post – you're always dashing about here and there! Hanna is now back in Madrid and she's about to marry the circus manager! Apparently, Miguel visited her faithfully in hospital there all those months, and has kept in touch with her ever since. She wants me to go over for the wedding, and to stay on a few days afterwards if I'd like to, but it's the week after next, so I couldn't possibly ...'

'Of course you could! Especially if you go on your own. Almond and me can stay on here with Alexa.'

'Nancy Loom, you're the most unselfish person I know!'

The door handle rattled and Matthew's voice called: 'Anyone at home? I know we're early, but I thought I might take you all out to lunch. Mrs Moore let me in as she was leaving.' He stood in the doorway, while Fay dashed into the room.

'Fay!' Almond shouted in excitement, turning a wobbly head-over-heels just as Fay had done at that age. '*Fay's here!*'

'And Matthew,' Nancy reminded her.

'*Downstairs*! And take Almond with you, eh?' Molly ordered. 'Avert your eyes, Matthew. I'm in no fit state to be seen: my daughter has already pointed out the state of my tights!'

'You look much the same as usual to me,' he said mildly. But he shooed the girls down the stairs, and closed the door after them.

Molly wriggled out of the offending garment and tossed it over to Nancy. 'You can have your heart's desire and darn away, my dear friend, because now I have to save our pennies for another voyage of discovery!'

And who knew what that might lead to? Nancy thought wryly. Didn't Molly even wonder why Matthew visited so frequently now they were back in London? They would make a lovely family, the four of them, if only Molly's head wasn't still in the clouds.

It pained Molly to see her friend still using crutches, but Hanna's bright welcoming smile reassured her: although she would never now realise her lofty dreams, she would shortly be back in the circus, the environment she loved, in a different capacity, as Miguel's wife and assistant.

Molly thought it best to enlighten Hanna straight away regarding her own changed status: 'I didn't tell you when I wrote because I wasn't sure if you were in touch with Rory – I'll explain all *that* later – but I have a little girl, named for my mother, Florence Almond, only I call her Almond, and she . . .' I should have brought her with me, she thought, only she's such a rascal. *Two weeks*! What will she get up to? How can I be parted from her that long?

'She is just like you, dear Molly, eh?' Hanna looked bemused. Her fiance had tactfully left them to talk over old times when he'd brought Molly back to the spacious house he and Hanna were already renting. Her own family were due to arrive shortly, so for propriety's sake she was sharing her large room on the ground floor with her friend until after the wedding. The shutters were down, it was

206

time for siesta, but the young women had so much to talk about. They lay on the big double bed, in their petticoats, having shed dresses, stockings and shoes. Hanna had actually let down her long hair, and figuratively Molly was doing the same.

'She looks like her father – those brilliant blue eyes and floppy gold hair. Rory would know at once if he saw her though she's small-boned and, they say, fearless, like me!' Molly suddenly vividly pictured that stuffy room, so different from this lofty, cool one, where she and Rory had turned to each other in almost feverish passion to assuage their distress that disastrous night. But she couldn't tell Hanna that. 'He doesn't know about Almond; he married someone else in Australia,' she added. It gave her a jolt to realise she regretted this.

'I don't think he would have done that if you had said you were carrying his baby,' Hanna said frankly. 'He loved you, for sure.'

'But I didn't love him – well, not enough.'

'How can you know? He was jealous, yes, but of your dream. Did you ever find Rasmussen?'

'It's nearly five years now since we parted though finally he did write again, in a roundabout way because he didn't know my address in England. But I never wrote back because by then there was the baby ... So I imagine he believes I never really cared. Maybe those feelings are at last fading, Hanna. I was only eighteen when I fell headlong in love with Henny, you see. I'm a mother now. The only ring I wear is the one Rory's mother gave me. I do have a handsome man in my life but we're just good friends. We are both bringing children up on our own, have that in common. Romance has probably passed me by,' she ended ruefully.

'I thought that when it seemed I would never get back on my feet again,' Hanna said softly, 'but I was wrong. I never really got to know Miguel when I was well and strong. He was not born to the circus, was never in the ring like me. If you had asked me then if he would be the one I would marry, I would have said, 'Oh, no!' But he showed me just how he felt for me all those months I was so alone, so in pain. Romantic he is not; loving and steadfast, oh, yes, he is, even though he knows we cannot have children because of my accident. Rest now, close your eyes, before he returns to take us out for dinner, to remind you again how this city lives by night ...'

Molly was much too excited to sleep. It had been a family evening of vibrant Spanish guitars, rich food, wine and laughter. A pre-nuptial celebration. She wore an oyster pink silk gown, with a full, draped skirt and plunging neckline which shimmered in the candlelight. It was a beautiful, expensive dress which she would probably never have the chance to wear again. Nancy had actually urged her to buy it. 'We'll share it,' Molly cried at the trying on. 'It'll be our special dress, and it'll look even better on you because you've got a splendid cleavage.'

Nancy ignored that bit, but murmured: 'I wish Matthew could see you at this moment.'

'Matthew?' Molly sounded surprised. 'I don't need to dress up to impress *him* ...'

'Are you awake?' she whispered tentatively now, knowing that she really ought not to disturb tomorrow's bride.

'Yes?' Hanna's voice was thick with drowsiness.

'I never expected them to clap like that, to shout for more, when I danced for them, Hanna, it was *wonderful!*' Molly exulted.

'It wasn't just the dancing, Molly, the menfolk were applauding with such excitement, such – vigour,' Hanna said drily. 'It was all those backflips, and your dinner dress round your ears. You didn't remember you were wearing stockings and frilly underthings, not tights, did you?'

'Oh, no! I disgraced myself, then, even though I only drank water?' Molly was instantly full of contrition. She had learned long ago that she didn't need alcohol to be uninhibited.

'No, you were yourself as always – Molly Sparkes who cannot resist a chance to entertain.' Hanna raised herself on one elbow, reluctantly awake. 'You would like me to say the truth?'

'Yes, please ...' Not really, she thought, her high spirits by now thoroughly deflated.

'It is easy to love you, your spirit, you make your friends happy, you make them laugh. Always you are indulged still as a child. We all love to spoil you. Me, I was always big and strong, my family expect me to be responsible at an early age ... Tonight you embarrass me, dear Molly. You take the spotlight from me—'

'Hanna, I'm so sorry, I really am!'

'You say you are grown-up now? But, my dear friend, you have yet to prove it.'

It's true, Molly thought, in a sudden wash of misery at her own thoughtlessness. I've always been cherished and petted. I imagined I was caring properly for my child, but I have denied her a father, his loving family ... I'm still protected from the worst things in life. I thought I was standing firmly on my own two feet, but tonight I was flirting outrageously and getting away with it. I wouldn't marry Matthew but I like to think he's always there and, I must admit, if he did find a wife, I'd be a little jealous ... I daydream about someone I hardly knew. I probably expect too much of Nancy because she is so willing to help. *Things have got to change, Molly Sparkes, they really have ...*

'I didn't mean to make you cry, dear Molly,' Hanna exclaimed contritely. 'I just wanted to make you think.'

'And you have. I shall always be grateful to you for that, Hanna,' Molly said softly, mopping her eyes with the sheet. 'Let's get to sleep. It's your big day tomorrow.'

What should have been a happy, relaxed weekend at Wren's Nest for Alexa and Almond turned into a

209

nightmare. It had been Nancy's idea that they should go – she would go to the House of Leather in Alexa's stead this Saturday, she'd insisted. Alexa was not looking at all well, in Nancy's opinion, though she kept that to herself. Matthew would entertain the two little girls, that was no problem.

He met them at the station as pre-arranged, looking rather distracted.

'It was too late to telephone you before you left, I'm afraid, but Fay was unwell during the night. However, she is bright enough this morning.'

'A summer cold, I expect,' Alexa told him. Fay looked a little pale and heavy-eyed, but she was chatting away nineteen to the dozen in the back of the motor with Almond.

'Children are so up and down. I remember how I used to fuss over Lucy . . .'

Fay seemed to have grown an inch or two taller every time her grandmother saw her. Today she looked quite the schoolgirl, Alexa thought, with braided hair which curled irrepressibly below the ribbons. She was wearing a sensible green cotton smock which made Alexa recall the ridiculous rompers Elfie had sewn when they were in Australia and Fay was a toddler.

Tugging imperiously at Almond's hand the minute they arrived at the house, Fay insisted: 'Let's go and play – *now!*'

'All right,' Matthew agreed. 'But remember she's younger than you, so keep an eye on her. I'll take Granny to her room and then we'll come along to the playroom to see what mischief you're getting up to, eh?'

'We'll be good,' Fay promised.

'You look tired,' Matthew observed as he carried Alexa's luggage into the bedroom, seeing how she sat down immediately on the side of the bed. They were now old friends. He could speak frankly without making her bridle. 'Are you sure that Molly is not, well, being rather selfish in blithely expecting so much of you?'

210

'I am tired, yes,' she admitted, 'but I'm pleased to have the girls back with me for a while. Life seems very dull without them, you know. Molly and I may seem like chalk and cheese, but we really have quite a lot in common. However, I'm often sharply reminded of our differences when I see what fun she has with her daughter. I was too intent on providing for Lucy materially. Life for me as a young mother was always a serious business . . .'

'She appreciated all that, Alexa. She adored you—'

'But I didn't allow her to show that, Matthew. I won't make the same mistake with Fay.'

'You should see the doctor.' He was obviously concerned.

'I will, when I can find the time. I expect I'll be told I am at a certain age and must expect changes. That I might perhaps benefit from a bottle or two of his most unpleasant – and expensive – iron tonic.'

'See him anyway. Ready to see what mischief the children are cooking up?'

'I am,' Alexa said. She gave herself a mental shake. Stop thinking you feel faint and in need of a rest; go and enjoy the children at play.

When Fay suddenly threw up after lunch, they were glad that they were eating out on the terrace and not indoors.

'Scrubbing carpets is not my forte,' Alexa said wryly, but she did her best with the sponging down and changing of clothes. Almond watched, solemn-faced, sucking her thumb.

Fay, who had been so full of energy half an hour ago, now looked very wan and sorry for herself. She touched her head. '*Hurts*, Granny . . .'

'Lie down, put your head on a cushion,' Alexa suggested. Matthew had carried his daughter indoors to the sofa. He was now calling the doctor on the telephone. 'Almond,' Alexa continued, 'you take the dollies out on the lawn, eh, and play with them there – leave the door open, then we can see each other.' She indicated some yards away. 'There, look.' Please God, don't let Almond catch whatever it is, she prayed silently to herself, Molly being so far away and Nancy in London.

For once Almond obeyed her unquestioningly, and Alexa turned her attention to Fay who lay drowsily, eyes flickering shut. She touched the child's abdomen fearfully; it was as tight as a drum. Her face was now flushed and she obviously had a high fever. Alexa had been an avid reader of medical books when Lucy was a child, always fearing the worst. *Oh, God*, she prayed again, for what else could she do? Don't let it be meningitis ... If only the doctor would come!

Nancy opened the door before Alexa could put the key in the lock. 'Whatever ...?' she exclaimed, as she took in the stricken expression. Then she shepherded Alexa and Almond into the hall, took the travelling bag from the cabbie after ascertaining that he had been paid. He was well pleased, having driven his fares all the way from Kent.

It was nearly seven in the evening and Nancy had been thinking of cooking up a favourite snack, cheese on toast, and enjoying it while relaxing in Leonard's chair and listening to the phonograph. She liked to think of him then. She sometimes felt guilty that she had so quickly replaced him in her life, but after all things were always changing and she believed that her kindly Mr Loom would have been pleased that she was happy. She had not expected Alexa to telephone, let alone return here so unexpectedly. Now she coped as she always did, seeing to Almond's needs first before the explanations. She knew that something serious had occurred.

'Mummy,' Almond wailed, clinging fiercely to Nancy. 'I want Mummy!'

'Mummy will be here soon ...' she promised. But Molly was not due home for several days.

*

Molly had packed her case. She plonked it down in the hall. She was the last of the wedding guests to leave. Hanna had urged her to stay on longer, but Molly was adamant. 'Not on your honeymoon!' she'd told them.

'But we are not going away, we are here for a week until Miguel returns to work.' Hanna glanced appealingly at her new husband. He looked awkward, and Molly knew she was right. She was *de trop*.

'Exactly! And don't say you have the rest of your lives to be together – you don't want to share this very special time with anyone else, you know. Don't give that up for me . . . Anyway, I didn't realise just how much I would miss Almond, Hanna.'

'Then go, dear Molly, with our blessing,' she said softly, dimples appearing and transforming her face, as always, when she squeezed her husband's hand. 'You really need to see your baby, don't you?'

'I do!' Molly agreed. But she also admitted to herself that she was missing what dear Hanna so patently had: a lover at her side.

Chapter Two

Alexa refused to go up to bed. She sat almost rigidly upright on an overstuffed chair by the telephone in the hall. When at last it rang, she snatched at the receiver: 'Hello! Yes?'

Nancy was beside her, a comforting hand on her shoulder. She could hear a man's voice crackling along the line. During the long evening she had gradually coaxed the full story from Alexa. Fay's condition was rapidly deteriorating by the time the doctor arrived; she was in the throes of a terrifying convulsion, which Matthew was forced to deal with by himself as Alexa attempted to shield Almond from the sight and sound of this trauma. It was imperative, the doctor told her father when the patient subsided, flaccid but still feebly twitching in Matthew's arms, that Fay be taken immediately to the cottage hospital where she could be kept under observation. He advised Alexa to return home and to watch Almond vigilantly for any suspicious symptoms which might develop.

What was it Alexa was so afraid of? Nancy remembered her fearful whisper: *inflammation of the brain* ... It sounded awful. But Alexa was sobbing in obvious relief as she replaced the telephone on its rest.

'Not what you thought, then?' Nancy managed.

'My dear, no. It's puzzling the doctors: they can't yet say what it is apart from conjecturing that Fay could be sickening for a bad attack of measles, which can itself be a serious illness, of course. The hospital has treated two similar cases recently and that proved the outcome. However, they are optimistic that Fay will be back home within a few days.'

'Come to bed now, Alexa. Don't worry, I'll sleep beside Almond each night until we know for sure.'

'How good you are to us, Nancy.'

'How good you always are to me!' She gently urged her forward, up the stairs. If anything should happen to Almond while Molly was away . . . But it didn't bear thinking about.

Nancy awoke with a start early in the morning. She had forgotten to pull the curtains to, and the room was flooded with pale light. She had been dreaming: she was cradling a baby in her arms, looking up and smiling at the baby's father. It was not the face of her late husband she saw, but the boyish grin of Art.

'Oh, Leonard, I'm sorry . . .' she said aloud. She stroked Almond's hair, spread on the pillow beside her, for she had put her there, rather than in the little bed in the corner. The child stirred, turned and sighed. Nancy felt her forehead, it was reassuringly cool.

'Mummy . . .' Almond yawned, eyes still closed.

If only, Nancy thought, gathering her close.

Molly alighted from the boat train with no hat and no gloves. She was wearing a trim blue linen costume, with tight frogged-fastening jacket, exactly matching Matthew's sapphire earrings winking in the sunlight. Alexa had insisted on treating her to this outfit to wear at the wedding. Nowadays, the allowance from her father was paid into a trust account for Almond's future education. She was well aware that she looked attractive and very feminine. She determined to be so from now on. No more Monty. When – if – she returned to the stage, it would be as herself.

*

'It's Mummy!' Almond cried joyfully when Nancy opened the door and they saw who was standing on the step. The telegram had only just preceded her arrival.

'Gran Lexa and me went to see Fay,' Almond told her mother before she'd even stepped over the threshold. 'Fay had to go to hospital, 'cos she was sick, and Gran Lexa and me comed home—'

'What is it? What's wrong, Nancy?' Molly demanded in a panic. 'Is – is it something catching? Will Almond be all right?'

'Oh, Almond's in the pink, aren't you, dearie? You'll smother the poor child if you carry on hugging her like that!' Nancy reproved Molly, shooing her down the hall so that she could close the front door. She added: 'Now don't get all alarmed again, but it's Alexa who isn't too well.'

'Where is she?' Molly demanded.

'Don't shout! In the sitting room, with her feet up – I said she should have a nap before you burst in to stir us all up!'

'Sorry . . .' Molly apologised, because Nancy's supposition had been accurate, but she hung on to Almond as if she couldn't bear to let her go, until the child wriggled in protest. 'Let me down, Mummy!'

'There's a lot to tell you, but it can wait. It's not as bad as it seemed in the beginning.' Nancy opened the door on her left and peeped in. 'She's back, Alexa!'

'I couldn't fail to be aware of that,' Alexa said drily. It was her turn to be embraced, and she couldn't resist, stretched out as Nancy had insisted on Leonard's leather chair which Nancy and Mrs Moore had lugged downstairs, knocking the banisters in the process and making Alexa wince. Her quiet ordered life was well and truly in the past.

'To think I was at a wedding while all this drama was taking place,' Molly said, when the tale was told.

'You mustn't feel bad about that; you are entitled to enjoy yourself now and then or motherhood would drain you,' Alexa observed frankly. 'I can recall one childish crisis after another . . .'

'This one has bowled you over, hasn't it?'

'It hasn't helped. I have to admit to feeling rather out of sorts.'

'What does the doctor say? You called him in, Nancy, didn't you?' Molly asked anxiously.

Nancy had poured tea and was now endeavouring to tie a napkin round Almond's neck before allowing her to take a piece of chocolate cake.

'Of course I did – although Alexa told me it wasn't necessary. Nervous strain and a touch of anaemia, he said, didn't he? She has to rest at home for a while. Now you're back Molly, and can look after Almond yourself, I will be able to go into the office and help out there, so Alexa won't have to worry about that.' Nancy had been rehearsing this little speech all day. She was springing a surprise on Alexa, too.

'I can speak for myself, you know,' she told her with a touch of asperity, but for once she didn't protest that Almond needed Nancy's help more than she did. 'Fetch the dustpan, Molly, your child has dropped crumbs all over the carpet . . .'

'Didn't expect to see *you* here again,' Minnie said ungraciously. She had opened the door of Alexa's office after a perfunctory tap, bearing the morning's post which she had already opened and sorted as Mr Loom had done in the past. Officially now Senior Saleslady, unofficially she regarded herself as in charge overall.

'Mrs Nagel asked me to stand in for her while she is unwell,' Nancy replied demurely. 'Don't let her get the better of you,' Alexa had warned. However, being kind, Nancy added a little white lie of her own. 'She appreciates how busy you always are without taking on extra work . . . Anything urgent in this lot?'

'Nothing I can't deal with – Mrs Loom.' Minnie refused to be mollified.

'Oh, come on, Minnie, you must know I prefer you to call me by my first name. That's how we started off, eh?' When you tried to undermine my confidence, thought Nancy. If it hadn't been for dear Walt and Aggie ...

Minnie had the last word as she turned to go. 'There is something in that pile which'll interest you. I'll be in Accounts if you need me.'

Orders for a special saddle, requests for catalogues, a letter of appreciation, several cheques settling outstanding accounts – then Nancy uncovered the postcard from Australia, boldly and inaccurately hand-coloured. She recognised the scene immediately. The mission chapel back home! She slowly turned it over. The address was almost obliterated by the postmark, but the simple message was clearly written.

Dear Mrs Nagel,
I am still with Mr and Mrs Hind.
    Unexpectedly, I have found my vocation! Working with them is a wonderful, humbling experience.
    Kind regards to all my friends in the House of Leather.
    Yours,
    Arthur Gray

Nancy fingered the card absently, lost in thought. It was difficult to take in that now she was here and he was there. It might have been so very different. She was free, surely he was aware of that? She was no longer afraid of giving and receiving love, but it was too late. She wondered if Art had learned of her troubled past: if so, at least he would understand why she had rejected him. Could he almost glimpse the pale, determined girl who had been hungry not only for food but for learning? They had both come from impoverished backgrounds, but Art's home had obviously been rich in love and laughter. She'd really liked his family but supposed that she was unlikely to meet them again.

The telephone on the desk rang, making her start. 'Mrs Nagel's House of Leather,' she said, as if she'd never been away.

It wasn't easy being a full-time mother, Molly discovered, especially when your child was ill and there was a chance she would normally have jumped at: to appear in a musical play in the West End. A bit part of course, but it could have been a diverting step forward in her career.

Fay had indeed succumbed to measles: she was now recovering at home, and Matthew telephoned them most evenings to report on her progress and to ask anxiously after Almond.

A week or so after her return, Molly became aware that her daughter was obviously sickening for the same complaint. She had a heavy cold, a runny nose which had to be constantly wiped, making her fractious, she was feverish and demanding, and in a way it was a relief when the telltale rash appeared on her face and behind her ears then rapidly spread all over her body and limbs. Molly sat by her bed, trying to amuse her, but Almond cried constantly. She rubbed at her sore eyes in the darkened room, and complained of earache.

Molly gently wiped her eyes with a weak solution of boracic acid, and treated her troublesome cough with a few drops of ipecacuanha wine as the doctor prescribed. He was reassuring: the illness was running its course; the cough must be watched, of course, in case the child developed bronchitis; the absence of a discharge from the ears was a good sign. As the fever ebbed, and the need for sponging down was no longer necessary, Almond was able to sit up and to take a spoonful or two of bread and milk, sprinkled with demerara sugar. She constantly grizzled to be allowed out of bed, to empty the toy cupboard. It was Molly who longed to slide under the covers and sleep the day away.

After nearly two weeks, the rash faded to a mere speckling of brown. Almond was on the mend.

Molly had been so busy and concerned with her that she realised with compunction she had hardly seen Alexa for days.

Now that Almond was officially no longer infectious, Molly was able to give her a quick refreshing bath, to get her dressed and to take her downstairs to see her fellow invalid, who had been cared for by the invaluable Mrs Moore while Nancy was at work.

Alexa too was dressed and sitting by the window, looking out at the small garden full of summer blooms, including full-blown roses. A newspaper lay untouched in her lap. She was obviously pleased to see Almond up and about.

'Here you are then! Up to all your pranks again?'

'Not exactly – I really wish she was,' Molly said ruefully.

'Can I go outside?' Almond asked hopefully.

'Not today, dearie, in a day or two. When that nasty cough's completely disappeared, eh? Sit down and look at your story book, there's a good girl. Well, how are you, Alexa?'

'Not much improved, which riles me,' she said frankly. 'I spoke to Matthew earlier. Now the quarantine is over, they intend to visit us this Saturday, just for the day he says. They go back to their respective schools next Monday. He was glad to hear that Almond, too, is better, and asked me to pass on his love to you both.'

'Thank you,' Molly said demurely.

'I have an appointment to see a specialist next Wednesday – Harley Street no less. Doctor Foster must think I'm made of money.'

'Doctor Foster – in a shower of rain, right up to his *muddle*!' Fay declaimed excitedly, having turned to that page in her nursery rhyme book.

'It's me in one of life's puddles, I'm afraid,' Alexa said wryly.

Don't let there be anything really wrong with Alexa,

Molly prayed silently. Though even I can tell it's more than the doctor has diagnosed so far . . .

Molly and Matthew, at Alexa's urging and Nancy's willingness to babysit the two small girls, had been out for the evening, for a meal followed by a visit to the Gaiety Theatre. 'Don't think of driving back to Kent tonight,' Alexa insisted. 'I'm afraid we haven't had a chance to make your usual room ready, but Fay can share with Nancy, and there's the long sofa in the living room. We have plenty of blankets.'

'Thank you, that would be fine,' Matthew agreed. 'We mustn't be late leaving tomorrow, though, as I have things to make ready for Monday.'

'You need a helpmate, Matthew, a wife.'

'I wouldn't disagree with that,' he said quietly. 'I found it a huge responsibility on my own when Fay was so ill. I longed for someone to be with me, to share my fears.'

'I understand.'

'I know you do, bless you.'

The house was quiet when they let themselves in. 'Take your shoes off,' Molly whispered. 'We don't want to wake anyone up – particularly Almond . . . She takes so long to settle down again. You can use the cloakroom off the hall. I'll make us a nightcap – don't get too excited – something milky and malty!'

'I don't know if I care for whisky and milk mixed,' Matthew said with a grin.

'You know very well what I mean! No alcohol after midnight in this house, all right?'

'All right. As long as you stay down here with me while you're sipping the righteous cup. Why not seize the moment to tell me if you've changed your mind about marrying me?' He almost sounded as if he were joking.

'Have I got to?' She didn't sound worried at the prospect.

'You have!'

221

Molly leaned against the pile of blankets which Nancy had placed at the end of the sofa.

'Why don't you lean on me instead?' Matthew invited.

'I don't want to be distracted while I say what I want to say,' Molly told him. 'Remember I did hold your hand when the lights went down in the theatre, and I got all excited, knowing exactly how the artistes were feeling. Wasn't that enough?' she teased.

'No. I was bewitched by your beautiful dress, Molly. It made me look at you in a different way, I suppose.'

'Silk purses and sow's ears, eh?' she quipped. Perhaps she shouldn't have worn the oyster silk, she thought, recalling how it had inflamed male passions at the party in Madrid ... 'Don't worry, I'm not about to cartwheel round the room,' she said mystifyingly.

Matthew looked puzzled. 'I should hope not,' he told her. Then: 'Let me start, eh? I know you don't love me—'

'You don't know anything of the sort! You're like the brother I never had—'

'Allow me to finish, girl! I know there is no great romance between us – maybe neither of us needs that now, with our children to think of – but we get on so well, we know each other through and through. We've both made mistakes. I shall always regret that I didn't leave the Army, come home to care for Fay nearly soon enough—'

'And I had a baby. Not *your* baby,' she stated baldly.

'But she could be, if you decide to marry me.'

'Well, I just *might*, Matthew – don't look so amazed! I thought things over, you see, while I was away. But, please, can we continue as we are – say nothing at present – until Alexa feels herself again? If I do marry you, and at this moment I almost believe I will, I'd even be prepared to give up cavorting on stage and to be a good schoolmaster's wife.'

'Are you sure?' he asked, just as Rory had, what seemed a long time ago.

'Put down your cup,' she said. 'And I'll show you how

sure I am.' She leaned dangerously close, completely disregarding her provocative neckline.

She's sure I won't take advantage, he thought. She has no idea how it was between me and Lucy . . .

In darkened rooms above both Nancy and Alexa lay awake, waiting for Molly to come up. More than an hour must have passed since they'd heard the couple come in.

Nancy hoped fervently that Molly would not be led astray, as she thought of it. There had been that look of sparkling anticipation about her when she'd turned to wave to Almond, in Nancy's arms, watching from the bedroom window, Fay at her side, holding the net curtain back. Perhaps she shouldn't have worn that gorgeous gown, Nancy thought. Still, she reassured herself, Matthew is always the gentleman, and it would be perfect if . . .

Alexa, reaching for the carafe of water on her bedside table, sighed. Well, it looks as if I was wrong when I told Matthew that time that I didn't think she'd ever commit herself to him: something, or someone, has changed her mind. Don't go too far, dear impulsive Molly, not tonight . . .

They would have smiled if they had seen the reality: Molly, curled up contentedly, head on Matthew's shoulder, having surrendered to sleep after that long, tender, but chaste embrace which put the seal on their tentative new relationship.

Matthew gazed down pensively at her. He made no attempt to adjust the table lamp. He was all too aware of disturbing feelings which had lain dormant within him since he'd lost his young wife. He was, despite his best intentions, hopelessly in love with Molly: hopeless because of the qualifications she had stipulated, which really meant that she was still unsure, despite her assurances when they embraced. Then he rested his face against her soft hair and closed his eyes.

*

223

Molly awoke before dawn. She stretched and yawned, suddenly aware of their compromising situation. Gently she removed herself from his clasp, scrabbled on the floor for her shoes, then pulled the blankets up over him and crept away.

She hesitated outside Nancy's door, but there was no indication that her friend was awake. She went into her own room, slipped out of the seductive dress and into bed, warmed by the presence of her little daughter. It was hard to break her of the habit of sharing her bed since she had been ill.

'I can't remember whether I actually committed myself to marrying Matthew or not,' she whispered to the sleeping child, tucking her hair behind her ears. 'But I don't need to worry about that yet, you see, because we're going to carry on as usual until ...' She sighed, and cuddled Almond to her. 'All I want is what's best for you, my love.'

Chapter Three

Alexa grimaced with disgust. 'Raw chopped liver – whoever decided this was the treatment for pernicious anaemia?'

Almond, mimicking her expression exactly, added: 'Nasty, Gran Lexa!'

'What, me? Or the contents of this sandwich your mother has just forced on me, Miss Sparkes?'

'Liver!' Almond reassured her, thumb in mouth because she wasn't too sure if this daily sparring was funny or not.

'Do you two have to watch every mouthful?' Alexa said plaintively.

Molly, switching to her other role as nurse, with her lengthening hair escaping the confining pins and one of Mrs Moore's baggy aprons tied twice around her waist, reproved her: 'Now you know the doctor said we must make sure you actually eat it.'

'Well, kindly pass me that vulgar stout with which I must wash it down, then.'

The sodden leaves on the lawn just visible through the long, misted windows were raked into tidy piles: Nancy's doing. She was still working in the House of Leather, despite Minnie's barely veiled animosity, while Molly, staunchly supported by Mrs Moore, coped here at home.

Alexa was really no better, which was worrying, but Molly was fiercely committed to caring for her. Since the shocking news in July – it was now November – Alexa no longer sighed that she really should return to her business, that Molly must take up any offers of theatrical work which might be offered.

It was fortuitous after all, she thought, that she and Matthew had not been alone together or spoken since of the half-decision they had come to that night they shared the sofa. She was sometimes aware that he was looking at her questioningly, but certainly not reproachfully, when he brought Fay to visit her sick grandmother. When Almond hugged him, Molly hung back. The old friendship was dissolving, but she was uncomfortably aware she was not permitting something more to take its place.

She confided eventually to Nancy: 'It's not as if we can't bear to be apart but we both hoped – believed – it could work out. Though this is not the moment, of course. It would be selfish of me to consider leaving Alexa now.'

'You should tell him that,' Nancy said solemnly. 'Be fair to him, Molly.'

'You can leave me to rest now,' Alexa's voice cut into Molly's reverie. 'Not that I do anything else these days . . .' She lay back limply on Leonard's chair, slipping her chilly, white hands under the rug which covered her. Even that small effort appeared to exhaust her.

How pale she is, Molly worried. I admire her so much for her determination to get out of bed each morning; the way she dresses and does her hair. She's still got her spirit, that's vital to her recovery. She *must* get better! We can't lose her.

'Nancy will be in soon,' she said to Almond. 'Let's get the table laid for dinner, and put Mrs Moore's casserole in the oven . . .'

Alexa didn't open her eyes, but she was still awake. 'Make the fire up before you go, will you, please, Molly? I feel very cold this afternoon . . . Foggy out, is it?'

'Getting that way,' Molly agreed. She motioned Almond to stay back while she unfastened the fireguard and shovelled coal on to what was already a good fire. 'Shall I pull the curtains, switch the light on?'

'Yes, to the curtains, no to the electricity . . . I like the firelight. Molly – you still there?'

'Mmm.'

'Before Nancy takes me upstairs tonight, I want to talk to you both . . .'

More coal on the drawing-room fire, and their chairs drawn up to the blaze so they could bask in its glow.

Nancy smothered a yawn. It had been a long day with plenty of problems to solve. She had taken a later bus home. She still wore her sober office costume, but had replaced her shoes with slippers and had loosened her hair, as Leonard had always encouraged her to do.

Almond had taken quite a while to settle down. Molly read so many stories she developed a husky throat and was sipping hot lemon and honey to soothe it.

'Now . . .' Alexa said, asking for their attention. 'I think it's probably best to come straight out with it. Doctor Foster advised that I would benefit from a move to the country; too much fog, not enough fresh air in London, he says. This has coincided with an offer which I find heart-warming in the extreme: Matthew has invited me to live with them at Wren's Nest. He believes it would do me a power of good to be with Fay. I can't argue with that, can I? However, I have made it clear that I will only agree if I am allowed to pay for the conversion of the old stables there, so that we could be, well, separate, on occasion. I would also need to engage a companion – no, hear me out, both of you – I do not intend to impose further on either of you . . . I believe I could persuade my invaluable Mrs Moore to come with me. She knows all my idiosyncrasies; her family have moved away, she is on her own and can please herself these days.

'You must be wondering why I have not spoken of this before. I needed to discuss the practicalities with my solicitor first. As you know, Molly, Mr Amos called with his clerk earlier this week; it is true what I intimated to you then: I wished to rewrite my will. To realise capital, I must sell this house and my business. There is no need for alarm on your part because I intend to ensure you are both well provided for now, rather than later.

'I suspect that you, Molly, would have announced your engagement to Matthew some time ago if I had not been incapacitated. But we both know that you need to resolve *another* matter first, my dear, even though you must go a long way to find the truth. And I have a strong feeling that Nancy yearns to return to Australia, too, to see a certain young man ... Won't you travel there together, say next spring when everything should be settled, with my backing and blessing?'

'I don't know what to say.' Nancy looked bewildered.

'For once, neither do I!' Molly cleared her throat. But she knew that she would seize the chance even though she would find it hard to tell Matthew when the time came.

During the wakeful small hours she suddenly realised that Matthew had not confided in her his plans for Alexa. Did that mean something? Had he given up hope of marrying her?

She couldn't help feeling chagrin at the thought.

'See, I told you I knew how to drive,' Molly remarked cheerfully, as the Packard open-top motor car lurched alarmingly and swerved along the unmade track towards the grassy knoll they had once climbed together with Fay. 'I've watched you like a hawk every time we've been out.'

'I must be mad to let you take the wheel,' Matthew muttered grimly through gritted teeth. The Packard 1904 model was his pride and joy. Another jolt decided it. 'Let go of the wheel!' he shouted, unceremoniously shoving her aside. 'Get in the back – get out of the way – unless you want us to crash.'

It was obvious he meant what he said so Molly tumbled

over into the rear seat, banging her head on the folded-back hood. She wasn't going to say another word, she decided furiously, rubbing her temple, until he apologised. It was so unlike Matthew to be hot-tempered.

They scrambled up the springy turf in silence. A balmy April day, too sunny and peaceful to quarrel. This wasn't at all what she had had in mind when Matthew suggested that they go for a drive and she had intimated she had something important to impart. Nancy was looking after the children, knowing just what that was.

They had moved with Alexa into her new home, at the beginning of the month, on a temporary basis. 'You must tell him,' Nancy urged her. 'Don't spring it on him at the last minute, that's not right . . .' Matthew knew Nancy was going to Australia, that was no secret, but Molly had asked them to say nothing of her own plans until she was sure she wanted to make the trip, too.

She almost tripped up in her hurry to get to the familiar resting place. Here, she stretched out, crossed her ankles and closed her eyes. Beast, she thought, I'll show you. One day I might even pilot an aeroplane. They say that'll be the way folk will travel in a few years' time . . . Why do men always think they're superior? Especially where engines are concerned.

'Sulking? I can only put up with so much, you know,' Matthew said furiously, his breath tickling her neck. She put out her hand, and the next thing she knew, she was pinioned by the weight of his body. He was kissing her fiercely, so that she could hardly breathe and she knew he was mad at her and didn't care at this moment if he hurt her. She beat a tattoo on his back with her fists. He released her abruptly, but she was forced to cling to him as he sat up, the buttons on their jackets being entangled.

'You've made my lip bleed,' she said, in disbelief.

'Is that all?' he asked bitterly, but he sorted out the buttons and set her free. Then he moved away and sat with folded arms, looking at her. He was grim, unsmiling.

'Aren't you going to say you're sorry?' she cried.

'No. You're about to tell me it's all over, aren't you, that all the waiting has been for nothing? I thought, when Alexa was settled—' He broke off, looking at her searchingly. 'I wouldn't hurt you for the world, you must know that, Molly.'

'Oh, Matthew! Actually, you've made it easier for me to tell you—'

'That you're going away, too? I guessed,' he said.

'But I'll come back, I'll marry you—'

'No. Give me time, Molly, to get over you. That's all I ask.'

'I'll miss you.' She was crying now, but he did not lend his handkerchief, or gather her close as he had always done before.

He rose, brushed himself down. 'Let's go, there's no point in hanging around.'

'I'm *so* sorry Matthew, I really am,' she said, as she followed him back down to where they had left the motor car.

Nancy was back in Shoreditch; in the greengrocer's shop, buying oranges and apples and a small bunch of bloomy black grapes for Art's mother. Maybe she was just putting off the moment when she would tread those noisy iron stairs to knock on the door of the flat, she thought.

Mrs Gray opened the door, showing surprise when she saw who was waiting there. 'Why, Nancy, I never thought—'

'You'd see me again,' she said simply. 'Can I come in? These are for you. I hoped I might catch you on your own.'

'You have, dearie. Not that I'm dressed for visitors.' Mrs Gray plucked off her apron, then the scarf from her head. 'But I can soon rustle up a bun or two and the kettle's singin' . . . The fruit is lovely, thank you. We usually make do with the bruised and battered bits from the shop at the end of the day.' She paused, still flustered. 'Do sit down.

You know Art's in Australia, don't you?'

Nancy nodded. 'He sent a card to the House of Leather. I found it hard to believe he's staying in the very place I come from! I didn't want to lose touch,' the words were rushing out now, 'but, you see, I got married, and I know how much that hurt him, and there was nothing I could say then, that would make him understand why. Then Mr Loom, my husband, died quite suddenly, and of course I was sad about that because he was such a good, kind man, but later I began to hope . . .'

'You loved my boy, didn't you? I could tell, that day he brought you round to meet us all,' Mrs Gray observed. 'And he was head-over-heels in love with you, we knew that. What went wrong between you, Nancy? Won't you tell me? I promise it won't go no further.'

'I'm going out there to see him – with or without your blessing – and it might be you'd rather I didn't. If I say what really happened early in my life—'

'Try me, dearie. I got broad shoulders, I won't say a thing 'til you've spilled it all out . . .'

The kettle hissed clouds of steam on the stove, the tea leaves dried out in the warming pot as Nancy poured her heart out.

Matthew was back from seeing the girls off to Australia. 'They are really looking forward to the journey,' he told Alexa. Relations had naturally been strained between Molly and himself after the last time they went out alone together, but they had tried hard to conceal this from Alexa.

'Unchaperoned, eh?' she said drily. 'Well, I suppose Nancy, as a young matron, will keep both Molly and Almond in check.'

'They are counting on seeing you bright and well when they return, Alexa.'

'We both know, don't we, Matthew,' Alexa stated quietly, 'that can't be.'

'My dear—' Matthew's voice betrayed his distress.

'I'm glad I have settled all my affairs; happy to be here with you and Fay. I feel privileged to call you my family. I'm glad I encouraged Molly and Nancy to go away, not to wait with me for the inevitable ... I only hope that I am spared to hear good news from Australia.'

Matthew bent and kissed her. 'Don't give up, not yet,' he murmured softly. 'We need you, you see, just as much as you need us.'

'Thank you, Matthew, for that.'

He awoke suddenly to hear himself groaning. His hands strayed to the spare pillow. It was cold, unflattened. Lucy, the love of his life, had never slept here, in this bed with him. He tried to conjure up her face but instead he saw Molly as they had said goodbye this morning, blinking away the tears from hazel eyes which really were green at that moment, suddenly clutching at him and repeating over and over: 'Oh, Matthew, I'm sorry, *so sorry* ... Will you forgive me for hurting you?' She was wearing the earrings he had given her, but also the opal ring.

He wanted to say he loved her, that she mustn't leave him. Instead, he'd hugged her in return and wished her bon voyage.

'Look after Alexa,' she'd called yet again after him as he walked away. He'd turned to wave up at them as they leaned on the ship's rail; Nancy, looking anxious, holding tightly on to Almond's hand, and Molly clutching at her other arm.

'I will!' he'd answered, hoping she could hear. He'd felt an awful sense of despair, wondering if he would ever see her again.

It must have been the knocking on the inner hall door, which connected the annexe to the house, which had actually woken him.

Mrs Moore stood there, a coat over her nightclothes, hair in curling rags. 'It's Mrs Nagel, Mr Dunn. Oh, *come quick!*'

232

Alexa lay motionless in her bed. The supporting pillows had been removed at her request. She looked tranquil, at peace with herself, he thought.

'Forgive me, Matthew, for disturbing you at this hour,' Alexa said slowly, as if each word were an effort.

He knew instinctively that she was nearing the end.

'I'll call the doctor—'

'No point. Don't leave me ...'

He motioned to Mrs Moore, mouthed urgently, 'Use the telephone.' She understood and quietly left the room.

He stroked Alexa's hand gently and talked to her: told her how glad he was that they had forged a good relationship; that she was here now with him and Fay, much loved by them, by Nancy and Molly and her little daughter.

She did not speak again. Soon she would be reunited with Lucy. Matthew wanted so much to believe that.

Chapter Four

Melbourne, June 1912

The journey to Australia had been uneventful, very different from that of six years ago except for the dreaded seasickness early on. Molly actually wished that Elfie were there to share her pungent smelling salts. She missed Wally the original purser, no doubt retired, and the stewardess was also unfamiliar. Only the sick-pan lady with her mop and bucket was the same.

There was no giddy dancing, deck games or late nights. Molly and Nancy took turns at keeping a very necessary weather-eye on Almond, amusing her whenever she demanded attention. The one off-duty lounged gratefully on deck and read of romance, when she was not catching up on her sleep ...

So here they were back in Melbourne, in blustery winter weather. They were taken to lodgings by a rather recklessly driven motor cab; it was a case of 'Stop! This one will do!' Such cabs were, of course, a common sight back in dear old London, and the Melbourne ones had caused the same rumpus and resentment amid the older forms of transport. Rain and wind, the glistening roads and roof tops reminiscent of home in December but not so cold: they didn't mind the lack of sun for it was a time to take a deep breath in readiness for what lay ahead.

That first evening, in their shared room, which they had

decided to take by the night in case they came across anything more salubrious, Nancy looked searchingly at Molly. 'Tomorrow?' she queried. 'Don't put it off, Molly, will you? We won't be here long, unless—'

'Unless I decide to stay for a while, but I think that's unlikely, don't you? I must consider Rory's wife,' Molly said, sitting at the washstand with a mirror propped against the jug – no bathroom here – tidying her soft hair which dipped to her shoulders now. She tucked wayward strands behind her ears, displaying her earrings. She hoped that she had put things right between Matthew and herself when they'd said goodbye. Still, it seemed he had also said farewell to the idea of marrying her eventually. She couldn't expect him to wait around indefinitely.

She involuntarily twisted and touched the opal ring on her right hand, as if seeking reassurance. 'I can't help wondering, now we're actually here, if I should spring such a surprise on Serena without warning,' she added. They had mutually decided not to write ahead to Australia, but at the last minute Nancy had posted a letter to Elfie and Ernst, asking if they could stay. 'Cowardly,' she'd said ruefully. 'They can't write back and say, "Art doesn't want you to see you again . . .".'

'As *if* he would ever say that!' Molly had told her firmly.

Now, Nancy advised: 'Go on your own first, break the news gently. Almond and I can go shopping, ride on a tram, maybe go round the museum, I've heard it's wonderful – though I'm not sure if she's too boisterous for such a place, I hope everything's under glass.'

'Oh, Nancy, you're right! I'll go tomorrow afternoon. I'm hoping Thom and Cora will be there – it would be lovely to see them again, too, and it could make it easier for me . . .'

Molly's favourite blue costume which she had first worn at Hanna's wedding was protected by a waterproof cape, but she needed her umbrella up as she hurried along the path to Serena's front door. The house had obviously been recently painted, there were different curtains at the windows and the thought suddenly struck her that Serena might no longer live here – anything could have happened in the years since they had last been in touch. She hesitated a moment, then the drips from the spokes of the umbrella running down her neck made her seize the knocker.

Light footsteps came along the hall; the door swung open and a girl of her own age stood there. She had an unruly mass of wavy dark hair and striking blue eyes, black-lashed. She was hastily drying her hands on her white apron. She wore a serviceable grey frock, with misshapen linen buttons which had obviously been through the mangle, and a frayed collar; her sleeves were rolled well up, revealing muscular arms. She was full-bosomed, narrow-waisted with generous hips, an Irish beauty even in her working clothes.

Molly instantly felt small and insignificant; over-dressed, too as she realised that this must be Sarah, Rory's wife. She lowered the umbrella, shook it away from the step to play for time; then she seemed to hear her own voice coming from a distance: 'Good afternoon. I am Molly—'

'Oh, I guessed that. And I am Sarah. I knew we would meet eventually – although I had no idea it would be today. Do come in out of the wet,' Sarah said pleasantly, ushering her into the hall. Startled, Molly saw that there were now framed pictures along the whitewashed walls: Circus posters, studio portraits of Thom and Cora in costume, Cora with her dogs on parade, the Kellys and Orlas on the slack rope – and the laughing, grimy faces of Kelly and Sparkes as they leaned nonchalantly, Rory's arm affectionately around her shoulders, against the fake gum tree . . . Sarah must have recognised her from that amateur snapshot, taken by a fellow circus performer with Molly's camera.

'I thought it important that Rory should remember his roots,' Sarah observed. 'Serena is having her after-lunch nap. She has her bed in what was the dining room, her not being able to manage the stairs, though she can walk with my help. She'll be delighted to see you, I know, in a while. Here, let me take your cape, it's not too damp for the hall-stand; your umbrella kept off the worst of the rain. Rory isn't here, I'm afraid. Have you come to stay?' She looked round as if for luggage.

'Oh, no! Just the usual break,' Molly floundered, 'before we go on to Sydney ... I am – with someone, you see.'

'Ah, you are married?' Sarah led the way to the big kitchen where she had obviously been in the process of clearing the table.

'No. Nancy is another old friend,' Molly said. She must be wondering why on earth I am here, she thought. I imagine she's relieved that Rory is away. I hope she doesn't feel threatened by my coming, I certainly didn't intend that.

'Would you care for anything to eat?' Sarah was certainly hospitable. 'Or a cup of tea?' She was obviously a new Australian, her Irish lilt very strong.

'I have eaten, thank you,' Molly lied. She had been too churned up inside to worry about a midday meal. 'Tea would be good.'

They made polite conversation while they drank this, sitting at the table, with the remains of the recent meal pushed aside. The child's chair which Fay had used stood in a corner. No cushions; it appeared not to be in daily use. The meal that had been partaken of had obviously been simpler than Serena's generous pies and puddings, Molly mused. There were depleted bowls of fresh fruit, of salad; a loaf of bread, a dish of cottage cheese, and empty soup cups on the draining board. Young Mrs Kelly was obviously in charge of things now. Nice as she was, she was making it clear to her unexpected visitor that she was the hostess.

'Thom and Cora?' Molly enquired belatedly.

'They became tired of being retired, you could say: like-wise the dogs, they couldn't settle to the house. Cora is training a young poodle to join them. They jumped at an offer to tour again with the circus. They tried to persuade Rory to join them, but he is absorbed in his gem-hunting nowadays ... I expect they are resting up for the winter months right now, somewhere more sunny, I guess. They will be sorry to have missed you.' Sarah listened. 'Ah, Serena's awake – rattling her stick to say, who's come? and more than ready for a cup of tea, to be sure.'

'How is she, Sarah?'

'Ah, she's the easiest patient I've ever had – she makes the most of her life, and thanks God she's not so disabled as she was in the beginning. Will you excuse me while I go and prepare her for seeing you?'

Sarah's still the nurse here, then, Molly thought. Obviously no children – yet, anyway. She and Rory must have been married three years, because I heard from him that last time when Almond was born ... Will that make it easier, or harder, when they know about Rory's daughter?

It was a slimmer Serena, with a happy beam on her face, who came slowly into the room, supported by Sarah, and cried: 'I'm real pleased to see you, my darlin'! You don't look so different – yet there's something about you ... Come and give old Serena Kelly a hug and tell me all your news. I won't scold you for neglecting me so disgracefully all this time, for you must have had good reason.'

Molly, holding her close, couldn't stop herself from letting it all spill out: 'I did, Serena. Oh, *I did*. I haven't married, but I have a lovely little girl. She's called Almond, for my mother. I do so want you to meet her but I thought one surprise was enough for today, eh?' There, she'd said it, even if she had avoided the most important issue of all. It was obvious from her suddenly wary expression that Sarah had taken it all in.

'Nothing surprises me, darlin', not any more ... You'll come again, with your friend and the child. Stay a day or two, won't you? I'm sure Sarah won't mind, for doesn't she see to the paying guests now? It's still our bread and butter, you see. Molly, our little Molly, with a baby – that's hard to believe, but I'd so love to cuddle her up—'

'Sit down in your chair, Serena. And you, Molly, where you were,' Sarah said calmly. 'Yes, we would be pleased to have you here. It would be no trouble to me at all. Why not come tomorrow? The rooms are always ready. Just the three of you, is it?'

'Yes. You're very kind.' Has she guessed? Molly wondered. I know I'm about to cause her pain. But I have to go through with it now: I must. Rory and Almond each has the right to know of the other's existence. Staying here, well, it could help, but I hadn't thought Rory might not be around . . .

'Rory should be back late tonight, isn't that lucky?' Sarah told her, as if she knew what she was thinking. 'Now, a cot or a bed for the child?'

'Almond's three years old, she sleeps in a bed: she and Nancy can share with me. One room will do . . . Serena, you remember my friend from the last time we stayed here?' As she nodded, Molly's fingers strayed again to the opal ring. She was aware that Sarah's gaze was intent upon her. She's working it out, Molly thought. How long since Rory and I parted?

'You still wear my opal ring!' Serena said, pleased. 'I told you it would bring you good fortune . . .'

'I thought you were keeping that outfit for when we arrive at the mission,' Nancy observed.

'I don't want to upstage Sarah when Rory's around,' Molly replied. Her clothes were not as plain as all that; the red silk blouse, which she had packed on impulse, was old but still striking, and went well with the good black skirt which she had worn when she worked at the House of Leather. Their country clothes, which included Molly's shabby jodhpurs for she planned to take a ride or two for old time's sake, were in the big trunk they had left on the boat. But she had dressed Almond in her best velvet frock, smart plaid wool cape and matching bonnet.

Not being overburdened with baggage, they were able to travel by tram as Almond excitedly demanded. She knelt up on the hard seat and pointed out the exciting things she could see going on through the window. 'Fire engine, Mummy, look!' It was not the most comfortable of rides. 'There's our driver waving at us!' when the cab drew alongside the tram.

Nancy gave Molly a gentle push. 'You go first and knock. Almond, stand back while I lift the cases on to the top step.'

Molly thought, in sudden panic: I hope Sarah answers the door . . .

'Hello, Molly,' Rory said evenly, looking at her searchingly for a long moment. He made no attempt to hug her as he always had done in the past. Sarah was not with him. 'Come in, I will see to the cases in a moment; take them straight upstairs.' He looked older, she saw, more serious, but then she supposed she did, too. He had attempted to smooth his hair back with oil but he wore a hand-embroidered waistcoat, which was familiar to Molly as her blouse must be to him. Cora had sewn it for him that winter Molly was training for her circus role.

Almond, blithely unaware of the tension, pulled away from Nancy's restraining clasp and almost bounced into the hall.

'Hello, I'm Almond Sparkes, I'm three and my mummy says I'm to call you Rory.'

'Why not? It's nice to see you again, Nancy. Hang your coats up,' he invited. He bent to untie the little girl's bonnet strings, revealing her tell-tale mop of hair. He touched it for a brief second, his face averted from the others, then took Almond's eagerly proffered hand and led the way into the comfortable sitting room. 'We have a good fire going in here today. Make yourselves comfortable, Molly, Nancy – will you come with me, Almond, I wonder?'

''Course I will!' Almond grinned.

240

'Mother and Sarah will be with you very shortly,' he said. 'Almond should meet them first, I think.'

Quarter of an hour passed, agonisingly slowly. Molly and Nancy sat there in silence waiting.

Then Almond burst into the room all excited, almost shouting the good news. 'Guess what, Mummy – I've got a *real* Grandma, not just Gran Lexa, and her name's S'rena and she gave me this bag of sweeties. And Sarah is my auntie but I can call her just Sarah, like I do Nancy, and *Rory is my daddy* – didn't you know?'

Rory swung her up in his arms as if he'd known her all her life, with a laughing, 'Hey, calm down!' but Molly recognised the look of challenge directed at her, over her daughter's head.

'Yes, I did know,' she managed to say.

Rory set Almond down between Molly and Nancy on the sofa. 'Hold on to her, Sarah's bringing the tea trolley and Mum's hanging on to the handle, too ... I'll be back shortly; must see to your luggage, as I said.'

'It's hard to take it all in,' Serena admitted as she sank into a chair and Sarah lifted her feet on to the footstool and plumped the feather cushions to support her back. 'Molly, dearie, how could you keep this from us all this time?'

Molly began to sob, she couldn't help herself. 'I'm sorry, so sorry, it just seemed the right thing at the time.'

'Don't alarm the child,' Sarah said briskly. 'Serena's had quite enough excitement for one day, too. I'll just fetch the teapot. We all know now, don't we? Explanations can come later ...'

'Sarah made all these lovely cakes, Mummy. Can I have one, please?' Almond asked eagerly. She was soon sticky with jam and cream. Mopping her up with her table napkin gave Molly a minute or two to compose herself before she began to talk over old times.

It took a long time for Molly and Nancy to persuade

Almond to settle in yet another strange bed and go to sleep. 'You go down, Nancy, and make my excuses,' Molly said finally. She and Rory had not yet addressed a single word directly to each other.

'But it's only just past eight o'clock.'

'Sarah is busy getting Serena to bed. I – I can't face Rory again tonight. The way he looked at me – oh, Nancy, he must *hate* me for all this . . .'

'I'll tell him you're tired, then,' she reluctantly agreed. 'Maybe he'll talk to me.'

'Maybe he won't. But will you try? I wanted to say I really kept silent because of Sarah . . . I wanted them to have a happy marriage, not spoil things for them, but now I have anyway.'

Molly gave her tear-stained face a perfunctory wash, peeped in at the sleeping child in the dressing room off the bedroom she was sharing with Nancy. This was the best bedroom in the house, it had been slept in by Serena and her husband in the old days. She wondered fleetingly why Rory and Sarah had not chosen it for themselves when they became a couple. She closed the door. Almond was a light sleeper, she didn't want to disturb her.

She turned the gas lamp low, looked for a book to read in bed. She was startled by a brief thump on the door. 'Nancy? I'm decent.' It occurred to her that Nancy might be carrying a tray of bedtime drinks. She reluctantly pushed back the covers, padded bare-foot to open the door.

Rory stood there, just as he had that night in Madrid. 'May I come in for a moment, Molly? There is something I must say to you . . . Please don't be nervous, it won't take long, I promise. Nancy knows – approves, I believe – that I am here.'

She moved back, allowing him to enter the room and close the door gently behind him. He was still fully dressed, of course; she wore her flannel nightgown, suitable attire for a mother likely to be called from her warm

242

bed by her child, the voluminous folds ideal for wrapping round her for a cuddle. She was thankful she was covered from neck to ankle, not in tights and cropped jacket as she had been the last time he came to her like this.

They sat opposite each other in the cane chairs and she was relieved that the light was not too bright because she did not want him to know that she had been crying again.

'I'm not mad at you any more, Molly,' he said at last. 'Nancy tried to tell me how it was – I appreciate that you have been brave and strong, particularly when Almond was born. When I saw my mother's face – the joy, when she realised this was my child – I knew I must swallow my pride, my resentment.'

'I was wrong. I had no right to keep the news from you. But you and Sarah—'

'We aren't married, Molly, didn't you realise? I wanted to go through with it, I felt we could be happy, but at the last minute she changed her mind. She said she'd thought she could live with the knowledge that I was in love with someone else, but when it came to it, she couldn't . . . She's a wonderful woman, Molly. Who else would have stayed on here, caring for my mother as she does, while I went gallivanting off, trying so hard to forget you?'

'Sarah still wants you, I can tell,' Molly said very softly.

He sighed. 'I know. And I know how special our daughter could become to me, to my family, if you will only allow it – oh, I realise that you'll go back home, but not too soon, I hope? I'm just asking you for this one chance, that's all, and for us always to keep in touch in the future . . .' He stood up, leaned over and kissed the top of her head. 'That's it, Molly. Goodnight.'

'Rory, don't go – not for a moment,' she said urgently. She was in such a hurry to get out of the chair she tripped over the hem of her nightgown and he instinctively caught hold of her.

'Oh, Molly, Molly . . .' His arms tightened round her. 'You look like a little cherub in that ridiculous flowing

243

gown.' She felt the warmth of his hands through the flannel.

'See, you haven't stopped loving me, have you?' she challenged him, moving closer.

'You aren't fair, Molly, you never were.' He put her from him firmly. 'This is how it has to be, unless *you* change your mind about me.'

Why? she asked herself as she pulled the bedcovers under her chin. Why am I trembling? Why couldn't I admit to him that I know my own mind at last – that the minute I saw him, I was sure of my feelings for him? But there's Sarah to consider now.

Chapter Five

Sarah stood at the stove, setting down the heavy kettle to boil. She was in her working clothes, with her unruly hair bundled up in a cotton piece. Her hands were grimy with coal dust for she had been fiercely riddling and making up the fire. It was just after six in the morning. Despite Molly's stealthy steps, for the rest of the household appeared still to be slumbering, Sarah was instantly aware that someone had come into the kitchen. She spun round, and Molly knew that her pallor and heavy-eyed appearance were due to lack of sleep, for didn't she look awful herself this morning?

'I was going to bring you tea in a while; you should have stayed in bed.' Sarah sounded rattled. 'I like to be undisturbed while I get things under way, before I have to see to Serena . . .'

'I'm sorry,' Molly said simply. 'But this might be the only chance we get to talk on our own.'

'I said, I'm busy.' She dabbled her hands in a bowl of cold water, wincing, then dried them on a rough towel.

'It won't take long. Please, Sarah.'

'You're not dressed,' the other girl reproved her.

'No, sorry. I'll go back to bed, stay out of the way, afterwards, I promise.'

Sarah sat down abruptly at the table, and Molly followed suit.

'I know he visited your room last night,' Sarah stated. 'He told you he still felt the same way about you, didn't he?'

'*No!*' Molly insisted. This was true, she thought guiltily. I was the one who challenged him with that, after all. He didn't actually admit it. 'I wasn't aware you and Rory were not married, Sarah. I am here for one reason only – to allow Rory and Almond to get to know each other. I couldn't bring myself to write to him about Almond because I knew you would be hurt, and I didn't want that. I was glad he had found someone with whom he could be happy. I would probably never have returned to Australia if the friend I travelled out here with the first time, who knows Rory, had not urged me to, and financed the trip. I had to convince myself that Almond's happiness must come first. Last night, Rory told me that I was – had been – unfair to him. This hurt me more than I can say . . .

'We both saw how Rory and Almond took to each other, and how delighted Serena is to have another granddaughter. I'm not here to take Rory away from you, Sarah. In fact, I think you should marry him and have a family of your own as soon as you can!

'We will be moving on very soon to stay with other friends many miles away. I should like to think we can return here in a few months' time to see you all before we go back to England. That's all, really it is.'

'Look me in the eye, Molly, and tell me you don't care for him?' Sarah pleaded.

'I *do* still care for him, I can't pretend differently. But nothing happened last night, Sarah. I hope we'll always think affectionately of one another, but the bond between us now must be Almond, nothing more.' Molly suddenly slid the opal ring from her finger. 'Give me your hand,' she ordered.

Mutely, Sarah obeyed. Molly placed the ring on her palm, closed her fingers round it.

'There, I've cut the ties . . . This is to prove you can trust me. You don't have to tell Rory any of this unless you want to, but anyway, leave it until we're gone. He didn't give me the ring, you know, Serena did.' She added softly: 'Beauty from the desert, a stone full of light and flickering flames – that's what I've always fancied.' Flickering flames die down eventually, she thought; smoulder and then disappear; ashes blow away in the wind.

'Molly,' Sarah said at last, sounding bemused, 'please take this back. Keep it for Almond to wear one day . . . I'm sorry I misjudged you.'

'Everything all right?' Nancy asked as Molly settled back into the adjacent bed. She did not ask where she had been.

'All right,' Molly repeated. The opal was cutting into her own palm now, she was clenching it so tightly, but Sarah was right: the ring should be for Almond, to remind her of the exotic country of her father, with its extraordinary changing colours, strange intense light, searing summer heat and blazing bush fires. May she fall in love just once and forever, she wished, not fall in love with love too readily, like me . . .

Rory and Molly walked along, with Almond between them, clinging to their restraining hands. They weren't walking anywhere in particular, just round the houses, as Rory put it. Almond's non-stop chatter was entertainment enough. She found excitement in everything. 'See, Daddy!' She pointed out a thin black cat with a kinked tail walking delicately along the ridge of a roof; railings painted black with warning gold spikes; daring boys hurtling on the pavement towards them on roller skates, the latest craze, and swerving audaciously to miss them by inches; two women having an irate exchange, arms akimbo, over a prickly garden hedge while the scruffy dog belonging to one of them, the cause of the argument, sloped slyly off into the distance in search of more rubbish to rifle through.

This was their last day here before they moved on.

247

'I wish you weren't going – not yet,' Rory said suddenly. 'It's for the best,' Molly said evenly. 'I want to see a happy ending for dear Nancy when she and Art meet up again. I want to show Almond where I stayed when I first came to Australia—'

'Where you fell in love with your Dane . . .'

She looked at him, startled, as Almond prattled on happily.

'I'm not so sure it was *love* now. Certainly it seemed very real, painful at the time, but I was even younger than when I met you, Rory. Henning was so much older than me. He made sure I was aware of that. Didn't encourage my infatuation with him, but in the end he admitted he was also strongly attracted to me. He'd be over forty now . . . He did make an effort to get in touch with me, back home, but I didn't respond. Does first love endure anyway?'

'Sometimes I think it does. I was beginning to believe I was over you until—'

'*Stop talking! Listen to me!*' Almond cried imperiously, jumping up and down to remind them she was there, for they had slowed to a snail's pace. 'You said you'd buy me some barley sugar.'

'That was for the journey tomorrow,' Rory reminded her.

'But I don't want to go tomorrow! I want to go up the mountains – I want to play in the snow like you said we could. I want to stay here with you and Grandma a bit longer!'

He saw the hurt in Molly's eyes. 'There'll be another time – you'll see the Australian Alps one day, I promise – and I guess you've seen plenty of snow before in London. You'll love it where you're going 'specially when it's spring. The sun's much nicer than the snow. You'll sit on a horse and gee him up, you'll see lots of different animals and you'll forget all about me until you come back again . . .' he assured her.

'Lift me up, Daddy, I want to tell you something.'

Almond pulled away from Molly's hand. They came to a halt. He swung her up into his arms and bent his head to catch her whisper. 'I won't forget you – *never!*' And she hugged him tight.

'Molly . . .' Rory said, knowing she had heard, but she was now striding ahead, hands in her pockets. They looked so right together, those two.

Nancy was feeling both apprehensive and excited as they were about to board the boat. They had sent a telegram this time to Elfie and Ernst, for they would need to be met at their final destination, of course. She wondered if Art would be there, waiting at that lonely station.

Sarah had hugged her and wished her all the luck in the world, knowing something of events in London: they had talked that last afternoon, sitting in the kitchen while Molly and Rory were out with Almond, and Serena had her rest.

'I'm sure he'll be happy to see you, Nancy. It sounds as if you were meant for each other.' Sarah paused, sighed. 'Like Rory and Molly. They can't pretend they were never close, that nothing happened between them. Almond is the proof of that. He's asked me again to marry him. I still don't know if I should.'

'They've hardly said a word to each other,' Nancy observed. 'They seem to have made their minds up to go their separate ways.'

'Be honest, Nancy, you know Molly through and through. Does she still love him, d'you think?'

'I shouldn't interfere—'

'I'm asking you to.'

'She wasn't ready to commit herself to him then, but *now* she could except she believes it's too late . . .'

Rory handed Almond to Nancy. 'Watch out, she's wriggling like mad! No more kisses, darling, you've made my face all wet! Goodbye and good luck, Nancy!'

He turned to Molly who stood quietly as if in a dream,

the collar of her cape turned up, half-concealing her face. He held out his hand, then changed his mind. He hugged her to him, his lips just brushing her hair, ruffled by the wind. She stood there passively, arms at her sides.

What he whispered was not quite what she longed to hear. 'You're a woman now, Molly ...' Then he gave her a little push. 'You must go. Goodbye, have a good journey. Keep in touch.'

She still couldn't say anything. He was going to marry Sarah after all; Serena had confided to her this morning. 'Of course, I'm pleased, but now—'

'It's good news,' Molly reassured her. 'She's already one of your family, Serena.'

They waved. Rory was just a face in the crowd now.

'Back of the Beyond, Nancy. It hasn't changed, has it?' Molly observed, trying to smooth the creases from her skirt. 'Thank goodness Almond is beyond the push-chair stage, it would be one more thing to handle.'

Nancy, who was carrying the sleepy, grumpy child along the deserted platform, for they were the only passengers to alight here, gave a wry grin.

'Exactly the same as it was when we arrived here six years ago: no on waiting to greet us ... Hope they got our message, Nancy. Only one thing is certain, it won't be poor old Frank, will it?'

She plonked herself down on the big trunk, decanted from the baggage trolley. The steam, the sharp odour of the train, now almost out of sight, lingered in the growing dusk. The lone porter lit a lamp and hung it outside the ticket office so that they could see more clearly. 'Not much of a waiting room, but you're welcome—'

'Thanks, but here comes that same old conveyance by the look of it. Ernst must have sent someone from the farm to fetch us ...' Molly jumped up, waving wildly. 'We're here!' she shouted.

Nancy yawned. Her arms really ached. She wondered

whether she should wake Almond, who had now succumbed to sleep. If it was the farm cart it wouldn't be Art she thought. After all that travelling it was just as well. She hoped she'd get the chance to freshen up before they met. Suppose he was no longer at the mission? She hadn't thought of that, had she? Molly could get the driver to move their luggage, she'd stay put for once.

'Hello, Nancy, I came along for the ride. Couldn't wait to see you after all this time. Pass the little one to me – Elfie thought of cushions and rugs,' Art said. His happy smile told her so much more.

'*Oh, Art . . .*' was all she could say in return.

Molly was having a leg-up to the front seat. 'Hurry up!' she called to Nancy. 'Plenty of time for a reunion, you two. You can sit in the back with the luggage – and Almond!'

The driver hadn't had time to introduce himself; Molly had been too busy telling him where things should go. 'Hope Elfie sent some sandwiches – we're starving,' she said, settling herself on the hard seat.

He spread a rug over her knees. 'Don't you recognise me, Molly? I thought we'd be enjoying a reunion ourselves.'

She looked at him, startled, in the gloom.

'*Henning*! I don't believe it!'

'Nor did I. When I came back to Australia a couple of years ago now, I never dreamed I'd get my old job back, that I'd see you again – it must be meant to be, don't you think?'

'All I can say, 'cause it's quite taken my breath away, is – I'm really pleased to see you again!' Molly shook her head. 'Are you sure I'm not asleep and you're not really here at all?'

'You're here, and I'm here,' he assured her.

'I was languishing for love of you for years, you know,' she blurted out, and then wished she hadn't.

Henning smiled at her. The beam from the lantern,

illuminating the rough road ahead, gave his skin a yellow-ish tinge; she saw, with a start, that the thatch of hair was shorter, receding from his temples, greying rather than bleached by the sun. He looked older, but then, she realised, like with Rory, so must she.

'*Was* – not still, I think. You have a child to show that,' he observed. 'I wrote you a letter before I left for Denmark that time; I should not have done so, it was not right to ask you to abandon all at a tender age – I apologise for that, Molly.'

'I would have come, Henning, I really would,' she exclaimed, 'only by then we were in Brisbane and your letter was sent on, but it was too late by the time I received it.'

'I don't wish to hurt you, but I felt relief as well as great disappointment when I realised I would be travelling alone . . . I still had things to resolve at home. They say you can't go back, Molly, it will not be the same, however much you try, and they were right. Yet here I am, and here you are.'

'I didn't come to Australia thinking I would see you,' she said truthfully. 'When you last tried to contact me, I tore up your letter at once so I would not remember your address. Be tempted . . . I'm in love with someone else now, Henny. I have been for years but wouldn't acknowledge it, and now it's far too late. However, I am really pleased to see you and I hope we can resume our friendship,' she gabbled. She had to stop thinking about the mistakes she had made in her love life.

'Not where we left off, of course, but friends, yes, I hope we will be always that, Molly. You do not have to tell me your story: real friends can accept what is past, is gone; what we have is now.'

'Just how I feel – ooh, these ruts! I'd forgotten how boneshaking this journey was from the station!'

In the shadows, surrounded by baggage, with the sleeping child lying in a cosy cocoon beside them, Nancy and Art, braced against the back-boarding, sat close under the blanket, vibrantly aware of each other, oblivious to the two in the front.

'I first heard that you were coming two days ago,' he said softly. 'I knew you were widowed, of course, but I didn't think it was my place to write. I suppose I couldn't face rejection again, even though Ernst told me something of what you had endured in the past . . .' He raised a hand and gently traced her face with his fingers as if trying to erase bad thoughts.

'I was helping out at the House of Leather when I read a card you'd sent from Australia. I had a feeling that you must be where you were because of me,' she told him simply. 'When you said you had found your vocation and were staying on, I was glad for you, but sad for me, as at that time it seemed I would be in England for good. Molly needed me, you see, and last year Alexa – Mrs Nagel – became ill and I felt I couldn't leave her: she's been so good to me. Then she moved to live with her son-in-law in the country, which is lovely for her because she sees Fay all the time. It's thanks to Alexa's generosity that Molly and I have been able to come here again. I went to see your dear mum before we left; she listened and hugged me, and gave me her blessing . . . You know, I can't quite picture you as a preacher—'

He laughed, squeezing her hand. 'Nor can I! I'm *teaching* at the mission, Nancy. It's something I always really wanted to do, but college was out of the question when I left school. My parents had kept me there as long as they could. It wouldn't have been fair on the rest of the family. I'm studying hard to pass my examinations by correspondence course, alongside my practical training with Ernst. The local people even built a new schoolhouse for me last year; just two rooms really, with a kitchen and a wash-house – all a bachelor needs.'

'Oh.' She was glad that he wouldn't see her blushing in the waning light.

He continued: 'They said: you can always have rooms tacked on when you marry and take a wife ... Am I presuming far too much, too soon, Nancy – that this is why you've come all this way to see me? For us to marry as soon as we can arrange it? We had our courtship long ago, after all ... Your message ended: *Love to Art*.'

'I wanted to put, *Tell Art I love him* ...'

Then they were clinging to each other as if they could never let go and there was no need to say any more.

We're together at last, Nancy exulted to herself. We love each other, that's all that matters.

Chapter Six

Elfie had made a real effort with supper: roast lamb with all the trimmings. She had even opened a jar of her precious mint sauce. It smelled very appetising. Henning excused himself politely. He'd had his fill from the packed provisions, he said, thank you very much. Better get on back and 'hope to see you all soon'. He included Nancy and Almond, clinging to her mother tearfully, having woken in yet another strange place.

'Yes, we'll see you soon! Thanks for bringing us safely here,' Molly called after him from the doorway. She turned to Elfie. 'Don't worry, I could eat a horse.' Then, as she saw her hostess's pained expression, added: 'Not really, of course! I hope it hasn't been too much for you, having to make ready for us all in a rush?'

'Visitors are always welcome in our home,' Ernst put in. 'We have open house, don't we, Elfie?' He held out his arms invitingly, and Almond amazed her mother by going to him and nestling her tear-stained face against his baggy jumper.

'You know, I recognise that colour. Puce, don't you call it?' Molly said cheerfully. 'Isn't that the same wool you were knitting with on the journey out six years ago?'

'Plum,' Elfie said. 'Fancy you remembering it! I made a cardigan for myself, but I pulled it out recently and re-knitted the wool for Ernst.'

'I am not fussy,' he laughed. Elfie didn't bridle as she would have done in the old days. Ernst could say what he liked that was soon obvious.

'Everything is ready – have a quick wash and then come and eat,' she told them. 'There's just the gravy to make, and Ernst will start the carving.'

'I'll show them their room, shall I?' Art offered. He had kept his arm firmly round Nancy's waist.

'If you would Art, please. You're staying for the meal, of course?' Elfie asked. 'I don't suppose you eat properly, living by yourself.'

'Well, that will soon be remedied!' Art told them. He winked at Nancy. 'I shall have someone to look after me very shortly, I hope.'

'You haven't wasted any time, you two, have you?' Molly cried excitedly.

But it was Elfie who, unexpectedly, made the first move to embrace them each emotionally in turn. 'I'm so glad, *so glad* . . . I was praying all would go well,' she whispered to Art. And to Nancy: 'You're a very lucky girl!'

'I know,' she said softly.

The girls talked long into the night, too excited to sleep like Almond, cuddled between them in the big bed in the spare room. Which meant they eventually drifted off around dawn, and would wake late.

'Nancy – Ernst says do you feel like getting up right now and having your breakfast, then going along to the school in about half an hour, to spend the morning with him and Art?'

She sat bolt upright in bed. The other two remained doggo beneath the covers. She rubbed her eyes, focused on Elfie peeping round the bedroom door. 'I'd love to . . .' she yawned.

'Then I'll fetch you a can of hot water to wash.'

Nancy took a clean blue and white striped blouse from the trunk, gave it a shake. Pity there was no time to press out the creases, she thought. She washed and dressed quickly, unwound the rags from her hair, for she'd wanted to look her best for Art today; combed out the springy, corkscrew curls and tied them back with a blue satin bow, to match the one at the neck of the blouse. There! Did she look like a schoolmaster's future wife? Her reflection smiled back at her from the mirror. 'I've never been so happy before in all my life,' she mouthed to herself. She wished Alexa was here so that she could tell her that, right at this moment. 'Sleep on for a bit, you two,' she murmured to Molly and Almond before she left the room.

The children sat on benches at long tables, with slates and chalk, copying the words from the smeared, swinging blackboards beside the teachers' desks. Art was stationed at one side of the big room, Ernst with the older children on the other side. Nancy sat unobtrusively, she hoped, at the back of the class. Art knew she was there, but apart from a brief smile in her direction, he had continued with calling the register.

Earnest faces; lustrous, laughing dark brown eyes; paler faces with nordic blue eyes and flaxen hair, girls in simple loose calico dresses which they had painstakingly sewn, as Nancy had done, during her time at the school, under the instruction of the ladies' circle. Boys larked about as boys did at school the world over, the older ones with dirt under their finger nails for they had raked the path to the school as usual first thing between the vegetable plots they would sow in the spring. These children were already learning to help themselves and their families. There had been many more aboriginal children here fifty years ago; the majority had moved on long ago when the first squatters arrived. The Lutheran mission and its school were part of their lives, as with the poorer white immigrants. Like the young Nancy, some were without shoes, some had a long trek to their classroom, some attended only spasmodically, others never missed a lesson.

She looked down at her neat boots, thinking. Her feet were clean nowadays, of course, but they were broad and the toes rather splayed from the years she had walked without worrying about shoes for her soles then were leathery and hard.

It was like going back in time, listening to the pupils reciting as Art moved the pointer along the chalked words.

When the children went outside to play and to share lunch with those who had little or none, Art came over to her at last.

'You teach well,' she observed.

'Not yet as inspiring as I want to be, because I'm still learning myself, but I'm striving to get there,' he told her. 'Nancy, before you go back to Elfie's, would you like a quick look at the school house, I wonder?' As she nodded, he added: 'Not tidy enough by Elfie's standards, I'm afraid.'

'As if I care about that!' she said, glad to stretch her legs after sitting still for so long.

'Art,' she teased, as he wasted no time in hugging her when they stepped straight into the living room, closing the door firmly behind them, 'it was just an excuse, wasn't it, bringing me here.'

He silenced her with a long kiss. 'There, you can tell how hungry I am! You look beautiful today, Nancy, and you smell so nice—'

'I sprayed myself with Molly's best perfume!' she admitted. 'Well, aren't you going to show me the rest of the house, then? Not much to look at in here. Haven't you even got a comfortable chair to sit in, Art?' She thought of Leonard's reclining leather chair; that would have been perfect for him, but she had naturally insisted that Alexa keep it.

'I spend most of my evenings studying at that table with my books spread out. But we'll buy a sofa for you so that you can put up your feet!' He opened another door with a flourish. 'Bedroom!'

When she saw the narrow single bed, Nancy knew instantly what she would bring to her future home. A generous bedstead with a plump new feather mattress! She might have to send off for it from Lassetter's catalogue, though.

'You're blushing,' he said. 'I wonder why?'

'You always have that effect on me, Art Gray,' she told him.

Molly was a bit disconcerted to discover that Nancy had gone out without waking her to tell her where she was going.

'Rather late for breakfast,' Elfie told her, keeping an anxious eye on what Almond was up to, with the piano lid up and little fingers exploring the keys. She'd hoped the sitting room would be out of bounds to Almond during the day, but Molly had blithely opened the door and let her in.

'One of those little buns apiece will do us, they look good and I love them still hot – all right if I take a couple? Almond! Stop that thumping and come and eat in the kitchen!' she called.

The buns had been intended for tea. Elfie had the feeling she would find it hard to keep up with her visitors' appetites. She took small plates out of the cupboard. 'Just one then, Molly. Nancy and Ernst will be back in about ten minutes. Art looks after the children out in the school yard. Have you any plans for the afternoon?' she added hopefully.

'I thought we might take the sulky, if you don't mind, and go for a drive round – to the stores, of course, because we must contribute to the catering, that's only fair, Elfie. Let me know if there is anything in particular you require.'

'But you're guests here,' she began, flustered.

'Family, Elfie. Well, as good as, eh? You've been so kind to welcome us at such short notice, we mustn't take advantage of that . . .'

'You're a thoughtful girl, Molly. I'm sorry that I was a

259

little – stiff – with you in the old days. I suppose I felt life had passed me by then while you had everything to look forward to. It's a shame that things haven't gone as you might have hoped. Finding Ernst completely turned my own life around. I'd like you to be happy like that one day.'

'Oh, Elfie!' Molly was touched at this unexpected speech. 'I wouldn't part with my darling Almond for anything. I don't regret having her, you know ... Almond! Don't wipe your fingers on Elfie's tablecloth! I'm happy right now for Nancy and Art, like you are. Something'll turn up for me. It always does! Don't worry about Molly Sparkes, will you?'

There was a knock on the door of the school house. 'Ernst, I expect, come to escort you home for lunch ...' Art opened the door.

A woman stood there. A shabby woman with a shawl over her head and shoulders; a weary, seamed face with a fading bruise on one cheekbone.

She cleared her throat. 'The pastor said you got my Nancy here.'

'Hello, Ma,' Nancy said, looking over Art's shoulder. She swallowed hard. 'I know you've got to get back to the children, Art. Will you tell Ernst not to wait? I'll walk back on my own in a little while ...'

He stepped aside, inviting Nancy's mother to enter the house. 'Good to meet you at last, Mrs Atkins. Just close the door after you, Nancy, when you leave. I'll be round to see you this evening, if you like?'

'Yes, please,' she said. When he had gone, she asked her mother: 'Would you like to sit down?'

Mrs Atkins shook her head. 'I mustn't be long. *He'll* want to know why, if I am. I was in the store and Mrs Mac told me she'd heard you was back from the Pastor's wife. I thought you wouldn't want to come to me so—'

'You came to me. I'm glad.' Nancy finished. They stood facing each other, but not touching.

'I knew you got married, of course, but I didn't know 'til today you had lost your husband. Is that why you're back here? I never thought I'd see you again . . .'

'I never thought I'd ever be back either. Leonard died getting on for three years ago, Ma. I married him because he was kind and good, a real gentleman. He treated me as if I was someone special. I loved him, and respected him for that. He was as much a father as a husband to me, being older. I'm not sure if he guessed I was in love with Art before we were wed. My feelings were all mixed up then. Art went right out of my life: it was a long time before I discovered that he was actually living and working here!'

'The school teacher?' her mother asked.

'Yes. I can't quite believe it but he still wants me, still feels the same way, like I do. We only met again yesterday but we're not going to waste any more time. We'll get married as soon as we can. This little place will be my home, Ma. You'll be welcome to visit us whenever you like. I don't want to stir things up between you and Dad; you have to live with him. Fortunately I don't, not ever again . . . I'm free of all that, don't even feel bitter about it now. There's no need for that. I've got my heart's desire, and that's enough.'

She moved nearer, gently touched the mark on her mother's face. 'If only you were free, too . . .' Then she held her close for a long minute, comforting her as if their role were reversed and she was the mother. 'Be happy for us, Ma.'

'Oh, Nancy, I *am* happy for you. Look, I got to go—'

'You know where I am now, at the mission house.'

In the weeks that followed, Molly saw Henning only once; he was working, of course. On that occasion they met up by chance at the store. Almond soon became bored as they stood chatting by the oil drums, and the next thing Molly knew, she had climbed up on to the counter via some boxes and was sitting there, legs swinging over the edge, entertaining the customers with her chatter. The assistant hastily moved the heavy scales out of reach.

'Oh, dear,' Molly exclaimed, 'I'd better take her away, I suppose, before she does some damage. When are we going to meet up properly, Henning?'

'How about this Sunday – shall we go for a ride?' he asked. 'If Nancy and Art are willing to take the child off your hands ...'

She felt a slight unease. He obviously thinks my daughter is a handful, and she is, but we come as a pair most of the time; Matthew accepted that, and Rory, though that was different, because he is her father. 'That would be nice,' she said.

'You'd better grab her,' he said. 'She's disappeared over the other side of the counter and the assistant is signalling rather frantically to you!'

'Funny trousers, Mummy,' Almond giggled when Molly paraded in the old jodhpurs in their bedroom first thing that Sunday.

'I can understand now why Alexa thought they weren't for the well-endowed,' Molly remarked ruefully. 'They're definitely straining across my rear.'

'Don't be silly,' Nancy reproved her. 'I'm sure you don't weigh any more than you did when I first saw you.'

'I've got curves in places I didn't have then. I daren't do my daily limbering up here, which might even 'em out, it would upset Elfie – she's so house proud.'

'Maybe, but she's had a lot to put up with, Molly Sparkes, what with you *and* Almond, you know!'

'Both she and Ernst have been so patient with us,' Molly agreed. 'Still, I shall make tracks back to Melbourne soon after your wedding next weekend, then hope to book an earlier passage home. I do worry about Alexa – I know she'll be thrilled to bits about you and Art, but she'll no doubt be glad to see the two of us return! Also, I don't want to outstay our welcome here.'

'You haven't heard from Rory yet.'

'No. That's strange, because he promised to write, but I suppose he and Sarah have been busy with their own wedding plans . . .' Molly tried to sound casual, but she couldn't keep secrets from Nancy.

'Don't forget your hat, Molly. It may be only the start of spring, but the sun can beat down when you're out in the open. And don't go too far—'

'Promise I won't. In every sense, dear Nancy. Stop worrying about me!'

'Someone has to damp you down occasionally, Molly.'

'Talking of which – save your efforts for controlling my lively daughter in Chapel during the morning service! I wouldn't like her to embarrass Elfie!'

'We mustn't go too far this time, Molly – what are you laughing at?' Henning asked, puzzled. 'I am concerned you have not sat in the saddle since you and I were last together.'

'Not quite true,' she teased him. 'I tried to ride bareback on one of the circus ponies but I soon slithered off . . .'

'The circus?'

'Ah, it's a long story. I won't tell you today. Maybe I won't tell you at all. It doesn't concern you and me, you see.'

She wasn't riding old Rusty, the pony had been pensioned off, but another placid plodder, so it wasn't likely they'd cover a great distance anyway. Certainly not to the mysterious place she now and then still dreamed about. She always woke at the point where she and Toby splashed in the dawn-cold water. Henny hadn't even kissed her then, just held her hand for a while in the dark, un-fathomable night.

Mid-morning they dismounted under some trees by a water hole.

'Lunchtime, I think,' Molly said cheerfully, opening the canvas bag. 'What's in the sandwiches, I wonder – cheese or meat?'

263

'You haven't changed, Molly. Shall I boil a billy?'

'Mmm. Tea! You're wrong, Henny, I *have* changed, in many ways.'

'You're not making, for certain, moon-eyes do you say? at me. I miss that,' he teased her.

'Oh, isn't it nice to feel, well, comfortable with each other – over all that?' she asked. 'I'm glad we met so unexpectedly again because I suppose I might have continued thinking, if only I had received your letter, that first one, we would be together—'

'No, Molly. It wouldn't have lasted.'

'How do you know?'

'Because I know myself. I often thought of you, yes, regretted what might have been. Still, I did not remain celibate all this time. Yes, I found you desirable then, which was dangerous for you were young and innocent. It would have been easy for me to play on your infatuation. Let me be honest, those feelings could be revived . . .' He gave her a pretend cuff round the ear. 'None of that. I told you before, it cannot be the same, however much you try, when you go back.'

'Prove it. Kiss me,' she challenged.

He smiled. 'You trust me for that?'

'I trust you. And, more important, I trust myself,' she said.

It was a brief kiss, warm and friendly.

'There,' Molly told him. '*Now* I'm sure. Watch out, the billy's boiling over!'

I still have that little carved horse, she thought, to remind me of past passion, damped down now like the camp fire.

Chapter Seven

'I've got something for you,' Elfie told Nancy when they were on their own in the kitchen, preparing the meal. Art was amusing Almond out in the yard, showing her how to steer an orange box on wheels. Ernst was still talking to parishioners in the chapel porch; the others had come on ahead. 'When you said you weren't buying anything new for the wedding—'

'Well, we will be marrying on a shoestring, Elfie. Art's savings are long gone. I've got some money, praise be, which will help us out while he is studying which could be years, couldn't it? So it seems sensible not to spend unnecessarily. At least I brought all my decent clothes with me from England. I suppose I'd already made up my mind that I wouldn't be going back . . .'

'Don't worry, I didn't make this gift for you myself,' Elfie said wryly. She was well aware that homespun efforts were not always appreciated. 'I also sent an order to the Universal Providers – I thought of it when you ordered the mattress. Alexa once surprised me with a very pretty hat from the catalogue, I've still got it, in fact. I always thought it was that hat which turned Ernst's head.' She actually sounded arch. 'The package came yesterday. It's on top of my wardrobe. We've got ten minutes before we have to lay the table, so come with me and see what you think.'

Remembering the hat Alexa had bought her on that other wedding day, Nancy thought: Oh, please, let it be a garment I would have chosen myself, even though that's unlikely because Elfie obviously has no idea what young people like to wear. I could never hurt her feelings, of course ...

'Don't try it on now, just tell me if you approve.' Elfie sounded anxious as she laid the box on her bed and lifted the lid. 'Molly told me your size, in confidence. It's what they call Japanese crêpe. Nice for now, cool enough to wear through the summer. Do you like the checks? Latest London fashion, they say, but I'm not sure I believe all that.'

Nancy lifted the two pieces of the costume from the folds of tissue paper. The shadowy grey check on rose pink was very pretty. The bodice and hem of the gored skirt were cut on the bias. The outfit was elegant, looked good. It would suit her slender figure, accentuate her waist. Nancy absently counted the pearly buttons on the jacket. 'It's exactly right, Elfie, but it must have cost the earth.'

'A guinea well spent,' she said, pink-cheeked and pleased. 'You deserve it, Nancy. I didn't take the money out of the housekeeping, or the money Frank left me, that's our insurance for the future. My father gave me a little bag of sovereigns on my twenty-first birthday, a long time ago, and I thought it was about time I dipped into it ... Now, put this all away before Art comes to find us and catches sight of it, which wouldn't do!'

'Elfie—'

'Yes?'

'Thank you! I'm sure that Art will appreciate it as much as me. And, Elfie, won't you wear your special hat, the one you wore when Ernst fell for you – to our wedding?'

The chapel was fragrant with bright flowers arranged simply in jam jars on the windowsills. Beams of sunlight danced on the uneven whitewashed walls. Elfie and her loyal band of helpers had polished the furnishings and flooring to a special shine with beeswax, despite the scratches and scuffs of regular use.

Nancy and Art knelt at the altar rails. She carefully arranged her skirt for she didn't want to crease it or to catch the hem with her heels. She wore a chip hat, bought at the stores for a few shillings, but trimmed by herself with pink silk roses and ribbon to match the costume, which looked as if it had been tailor-made for her.

Art wore his only suit, the same one he'd had back in the days when they were walking out together in London, which Elfie had insisted on sponging and pressing, despite his mild protests that he was quite capable of doing this for himself – his mum had expected him to, he said with a grin.

Elfie wore her hat as Nancy had requested. As it was such a special occasion, she had pinned her hair-piece into place also. This had taken her some time as she had not touched it since her marriage. She silently dared anyone to comment.

Molly sported her best blue linen, complemented by Matthew's earrings of course, and Almond wore a new gingham dress, in blue and white, with a wide satin sash. She looked angelic, but Molly was keeping her fingers crossed and fruit-drops, thoughtfully donated by Mrs Mac, in her handbag.

It would have been perfect if Art's family could have been with them, and Alexa had been sitting next to Molly in the front pew, Nancy thought. But she was really happy when, as she entered the church on Art's arm for the simple wedding ceremony, she caught a glimpse of her mother sitting on her own, right at the back. She might be unable to stay for the whole of the service, Nancy rightly guessed, but she indicated to her mother, with a smile, the lace handkerchief just showing in her pocket. She had taken it from an envelope addressed simply TO NANCY, pushed through the mission letter box sometime during yesterday evening. No message, but Nancy knew who it was from ... Then she saw the sea of expectant faces as the children from the school turned to watch their progress. The harmonium, pumped with vigour, welcomed them with cheerful music that almost invited them to dance, and certainly quickened their step, and Almond's cheek bulged as she sucked blissfully on her boiled sweet.

They were on their own at last, in the schoolhouse. Nancy put her wedding posy in water, and gave a little sigh. Art took off his jacket and hung it on the back of a chair. The table was still littered with books.

'Elfie did us proud with the meal,' he observed. 'We won't want anything else tonight. Anyway, I don't want you busy in the kitchen on our wedding night . . . Come and sit down on the sofa.'

'Silly things you think of,' Nancy said, sinking down gratefully into the cushions. The sofa was second-hand, but very comfortable. The plaid shawl which covered the back displayed the sofa's origin: they had bought it from Mrs Mac. 'When we were enjoying those cold cuts and Elfie's best pickle, I suddenly had a yearning for meat pud.'

'Steaming under a turban in the old pudding shop, eh?'

'Yes. And you with a glass of beer and froth round your lips, and—'

'Ah, you were aware of my lips, were you?' he teased. 'Well, it was root ginger beer today, but I was so busy looking at you that it tasted like champagne.' He cuddled her close. 'I was so proud to be marrying you today, Nancy, especially as I never believed this day would come. Have I ever told you how much I love you?'

'You didn't have to: I knew.' She yawned this time.

'You're tired, you must be. It's a much more hectic day for a bride than a groom.' He looked at her so tenderly. For a moment she was reminded of Leonard and the way he had regarded her; it was hard to banish such thoughts from her head.

'I must say, I'm looking forward to trying out that lovely feather bed – oh!' she ended, when she realised what she had said, and was grateful that he didn't laugh at her confusion. She thought, I won't try to delay that moment as I did before . . . Art and I have wasted enough time when we might have been together.

'Shall we retire then?' he asked. 'I'm sorry I didn't tidy up the books, by the way. I certainly didn't intend to do any studying today.'

'I've been thinking about that, Art. Would you mind if I – well, began learning alongside you? I might not be up to it, of course, but I'd like to try to see if, one day, I could teach here, too – pass on some of the knowledge I've been so grateful for myself.'

He didn't answer at first, just looked at her, bemused.

'Of course, if you don't want me to, I'll understand,' she floundered.

'Of course I want you to! It's a *wonderful* idea. I'm just sorry I didn't think of it myself! Is tomorrow soon enough to start?' he joked.

'Let's go to bed,' she said softly.

They certainly didn't rise early the following morning. 'We ought to be getting ready for chapel,' Nancy said drowsily at last, making no move to disengage herself from his arms. The new bed took up most of the small room: they had thrown back the covers because it was so warm, and bright light flooded through the slats in the blinds which they had forgotten to close.

'I don't imagine they'll send out a search party . . .' he murmured. 'Don't go; don't spoil it.' His lips gently brushed her bare skin; her fingers tangled in his hair as he lowered his head.

'How can I?' she whispered after a while. 'Oh, Art, I love you so much.'

'You don't need to say it either – just show me.'

'Someone called after all.' Art opened the front door and discovered a huge bunch of flowers wrapped in newspaper on the step. There was a muffled burst of laughter, as he stood there, clad in his dressing gown at midday, but he did not catch sight of anyone. There was a note: TO THE BRIDE & GROOM. 'It's from my class,' he said, pleased.

'Oh . . .' Nancy said, in the kitchen. At least they didn't get a glimpse of *me*, she thought, in my nightie, frying this great panful of bacon and eggs. 'I don't even know if you like your egg served on top of the fried bread,' she told him wryly.

'Everything you do for me is perfection,' he teased her, catching hold of her waist from behind.

'Oh!' she exclaimed again. Then: 'Art! D'you want me to drop the lot?'

'Let's have breakfast in bed,' he said.

'Suppose – suppose we get more callers—'

'We'll pretend we don't hear 'em. Want some toast?'

'That'll take time. Bread and butter will do,' she said demurely.

They forgot about lunch, but at around nine in the evening Nancy moved the books on to the windowsill and spread a pretty new cloth, one of their wedding gifts, on the table in the living room. They pulled the curtains across; Art lit a fat candle to illuminate the plates of bread and cheese, and they toasted their first day of married life with tea poured into rose-patterned bone-china cups, gold-rimmed, which in future would be kept in the cabinet for special occasions only. Another unexpected present from Elfie and Ernst; Art was obviously held in high regard by them both.

'I wish Alexa could see us now . . .' she said dreamily, adding more hot water to the teapot. She had changed into the oyster silk dinner dress, the first wearing for her, but Molly had insisted. 'Just the dress for an intimate dinner for two . . .' Not at all the dress, she thought now, for such a simple meal, but *intimate*, none the less . . . She was rosily aware that Art could hardly take his eyes off her.

'I'm not so sure about that,' he teased.

'She'll be so pleased, I know, when she gets my letter . . . I wonder why we haven't heard from her yet? I thought we'd find a letter waiting for us here.'

Not just a childish thump on the front door this time, more an irate battering with fists, followed by kicking with heavy boots: they sat looking at each other in dismay for a long moment.

Then Art pushed back his chair. 'I'd better see who this is,' he said grimly.

Nancy caught at his sleeve. 'Art, I reckon it's my dad. He attacks the door like that when Ma locks him out and he gets real mad. Oh, Art, ignore it.'

The hammering intensified, and they now heard a hoarse bellow: 'Nancy! I know you're there. Let me in.'

'Stay where you are, Nancy, I'll deal with him,' Art told her.

'He'll be blind drunk—'

'Then he won't be able to aim straight . . .'

'He's much bigger than you,' she cried in terror.

Art opened the door, braced himself. 'What do you want?' he demanded of the burly figure swaying on the top step.

'You the school teacher?'

'Yes, I am.'

'Wed my Nancy, did you? *She* only told me this mornin' – said I'd've caused a commotion if I'd gone to the chapel—'

'I imagine you would. I'm afraid Nancy doesn't wish to speak to you.'

'Why's that?' her father asked belligerently.

'You *know* why.'

'I haven't seen her for years – heard she'd married another feller. What's she doin' back here with you?'

'She's my wife now, I'm proud to say. She's also over twenty-one and doesn't have to answer to you. If you have any decent feelings at all, you'll go away and leave her alone. I know exactly what you put her through, but she's suffered enough for it. I'm going to make sure she has a happy, secure life from now on. Hitting you would relieve my feelings, but I'm not going to upset her. She doesn't want any more violence. Just go. *Now.*'

He closed the door slowly and the other man lurched off down the path.

'Art – you stood up to him! He didn't take a swing at you.' Nancy was in a state of shock.

'I believe I've laid your final ghost, Nancy darling,' he said. He hoped fervently that she was unaware that he sat down so suddenly because his legs were buckling. 'I think I deserve another cup of tea, don't you?' He just about managed a smile. He'd never been one for fighting, not even at school being a natural swot, but had redeemed himself in the other boys' eyes by becoming rather a joker; they'd liked him for that. However, where Nancy was concerned, he'd protect her to the ends of the earth.

'You were wonderful!' she said softly.

'Nancy,' he murmured later, when they lay once more in the hollow in the middle of their feather-filled nest.

'Mmm?'

'I haven't, well, expected too much of you, too soon, I hope?'

'No, Art, you haven't ... What you said, after you saw Dad off, 'bout laying ghosts – well, you have. I should have known, when I let you go all those years ago that I was making a mistake.'

'We were both very young then, Nancy. I fancied myself as a bit of a lad, and you – you weren't ready for me, after all you'd been through. It's very different now, isn't it?'

'It's perfect, Art, perfect.'

Nancy's ma was waiting fearfully for her husband to return. He'd flung her across the room when he'd found out about Nancy and Art. She nursed her bruised arm, almost oblivious to the pain. Since the boys had left home, one after the other, she'd borne the brunt of his violence. Her own mother had warned her she shouldn't marry him, but by then she was heavily pregnant and had thought, in her naivety, that fatherhood would sober him up. His sons took after him – the only thing that kept her going was her little daughter, Nancy. Later had come the terrible realisation of what she seemed powerless to stop.

She hadn't bolted the door. What was the point? She had no illusions about what was coming – he'd been drinking all day. What had happened at the schoolhouse? He looked a gentle type, Nancy's new husband, while hers had been a pugilist in his youth. Were the two of them lying battered and beaten at this moment?

He came in at last; looked at her cowering in the corner of the room. 'Goin' to bed,' he muttered. He had a bottle in his hand.

She found her voice, some strength. 'You didn't dare – you – I'll *kill* you if you did!'

'I ain't touched 'em. Let 'em get on with it. Not worth getting fired up about . . . Get me some grub, woman.'

'Get it yourself!' she shouted, then pushed past him. 'And you can sleep down here, you drunken beast – you're not coming near me 'til you sober up! If you hurt me again, I'll have the law on you, and I won't stop at telling them what you've done to me, either. You'll rot in jail!' She'd always believed a wife couldn't give evidence against her husband, but by the open-mouthed alarm on his face she realised that he was unaware of that. There was one final thing she had to say: 'And I shall go and see Nancy whenever I want to, and *you're not going to stop me!*'

She went upstairs, head held high. He didn't follow. She fell on her knees beside the bed and prayed, then sat with tears of relief rolling down her cheeks, laughing helplessly at the way he'd looked when she'd stood up to him at last.

273

Chapter Eight

Molly was packing again. It was time to leave Nancy and Art; to free Nancy, she thought, of the responsibility, for she realised with a pang that was what it had become, of always being there for Almond and herself. She wanted, more than anything, for her friends to seize this second chance of happiness without worrying about anyone else.

She put a few things to one side which she would no longer need: Elfie might be glad of them for the mission box. She hesitated over the worn jodhpurs, then tucked them at the bottom of the trunk together with the pink tights with darned toes which she had foolishly packed for sentimental reasons, to remind her of the circus. She had pictured herself, before she left England, displaying these, with a flash of the old impish grin, to Rory. But, of course, that would not have done at all. Why was she always so naive?

Three lovers – well, perhaps only one could really be called that – had rejected her in swift succession. The one she had languished over for far too long, Henning, she thought ruefully, had been the most tactful, the least hurtful; Matthew had decided to draw an abrupt, firm line under their friendship; Rory – maybe she shouldn't have come back into *his* life at all . . . Almond at last knew her father, that was good, but she might never see him again after they returned home, which was surely wrong. And at

274

such a tender age, as she grew up it was likely she would retain few memories, if any, of him.

A tap on the door; a smiling Nancy. 'Need any help?'

'Nearly done, thanks,' Molly replied. 'What's Almond up to? I haven't seen her for at least ten minutes.' She suddenly panicked.

'Elfie's wrapped her in an enormous apron, letting her mix up some buns at the kitchen table – and before you say it, can you imagine Elfie not washing her hands for her before she began? Mind you, she's very good with Almond when you think how awkward she was with Fay.' Nancy looked closely at her friend. 'What's up, Molly? You're not crying surely?'

'Not really, just being rather pessimistic, I suppose.' As if she was Almond's age, Molly wiped her tears away on her sleeve, then rubbed at the glistening marks with a finger.

'I've got time to listen,' Nancy offered. 'Art's at school, and not being Elfie, I can finish my housework in half an hour – I don't dust Art's books, of course, what's the point? He's just as untidy as he was in Accounts when we first knew him – and just as clever! If I lost his place, he'd be cross.'

'He couldn't be cross with *you*, Nancy.'

'Not yet, maybe! Not while the wedding glow lasts, eh? Actually, it's lovely. We're right back to where we were before . . . He teases me and makes me laugh about the silliest things. Hey! You really are crying now. Come on, out with it?'

'Nothing goes right for me lately. I know it's my own fault, but I can't seem to change—'

'None of us wants you to, Molly dear. How many times do I have to tell you that? We love you just as you are. Look how my life has turned round: I can still hardly believe it! But even when I'm so happy, I still feel guilty for leaving Alexa when she was so low, even though she urged us to. And I keep worrying about you two travelling all that way without me, but—'

'Now you must put yourself first for once, Nancy Gray!'

'*Nancy Gray*. It sounds good, doesn't it?'

'It does; a new name, a new life – will it ever be like that for me?'

'Of course it will,' Nancy comforted her. 'When you're down, as they say, well, you can only go up – think of that, Molly Sparkes!'

'Sparkes, Sparkes, *Sparkes!*' Almond chanted, bursting in on them with hands all floury, and Elfie in hot pursuit. 'I'm Almond Sparkes *Kelly* – my daddy said so!'

Henning drove Molly and Almond to the station to commence the first stage of the long journey. Nancy and Elfie came along for the ride.

'Now you mind what I said,' Nancy told Almond as Molly began to hug them all in turn. 'Quiet as a mouse, all the way.'

'I hope we meet again one of these days,' Henning said gallantly. 'I don't forget you.' He kissed the top of her head in what Molly could only think of as an avuncular fashion.

She turned to Elfie. 'Thank you for putting up with my daughter, Elfie,' she said ruefully.

'I enjoyed it, Molly. I shall miss you both very much, and so will Ernst.' Elfie was obviously sincere. 'Still, I'll have Nancy close by; one of Alexa's girls, as I always think of you ...'

'Don't forget to read Alexa's letter on the train; we're saving ours for when we get back, to enjoy over a nice cup of coffee,' Nancy reminded her. 'We've waited long enough for news, haven't we?' The postman had delivered separate bulky letters to the three of them, Molly, Nancy and Elfie, as they were about to leave the mission, which was fortuitous otherwise Molly's letter would have had to be sent on to Melbourne.

'I won't. Nancy, suppose Rory isn't at home, hasn't had my letter? Suppose there's no one to meet me the other end?'

276

'Then just hail a cab and go to Serena's anyway! She'll be pleased to see you.' Nancy hugged her so tightly she almost squeezed the breath out of her. She whispered: 'Stop worrying, Molly. Remember how you were capable of taking just one painful step at a time when you struggled out of that hospital bed after Almond was born? You got there in the end, didn't you?' She kissed her warmly, then spoke up normally. 'Off you go, you two, with our love, Art's and mine – and don't forget to write!'

They had been travelling for more than two hours when Almond finally settled down with a picture book, leaning against her mother. Molly took the letter from her bag. Strange: the envelope looked as if it had been opened and re-sealed, she thought. Alexa must have thought of something else to say ... The writing was uncharacteristically uneven, as if the writer's hand was shaky. It was undated.

Dearest Molly,
This will, I believe, be the last letter I shall write to you. Please read on before you get too upset ...
    By now you will have met Rory again and I hope all went well. As for Nancy, I am looking forward to the news of her impending marriage to Arthur. I always thought very highly of that young man while he was in my employ. Then the first of my hopes for you girls would be fulfilled. I hope that, in due course, they will be blessed with a family; Nancy has cared for, so lovingly, first dear Fay, and lately little Almond. My only regret is that I will not be with her on her special day.
    Somehow, I don't think it will be long before you, too, are fulfilled in a happy partnership. I was sorry you decided against Matthew, but, as I told him some time ago, I thought you would not agree to marry him. I believe you are, though, ready to commit yourself to – forgive me for being, just once, sentimental! – true love.

And while I am feeling thus, I want to say that although you sometimes have me sighing over your impulsiveness, our friendship, and your staunch support have meant so very much to me and it was a real wrench to part with you when I despatched you to Australia. All right, I'll put it in writing ... Lucy was irreplaceable, but you and Nancy, nevertheless, became like daughters to me, too. Thank you for your generous gift of love, Molly. Always remember I loved you in return, you and my honorary granddaughter.

I enclose a copy of my will. As I told you before, Fay, Nancy and yourself are the main beneficiaries.

You will see that I have set aside an amount to help Elfie and Ernst in their good works. I provided for my loyal employees at the House of Leather when I sold the business; I stipulated that the new owners keep them on.

There is but one change: my accommodation here at Wren's Nest will, with the kind agreement of Matthew, always be available to you, for as long as you like, if ever you have need of it.

Try to smile, for Almond's sake, when the news is confirmed, won't you? But I know that, being Molly, you will shed tears for me anyway.

Time to say goodbye.

Fondest love,

Alexa

Slowly, Molly refolded the letter. She could not look at the enclosed document now. As she was about to insert the letter in the envelope, she noticed another sheet of paper, a second letter. It was dated the day after they had embarked for Australia. Why had these letters taken so long to reach them?

Dear Molly,

I am sorry to have to write with sad news. Alexa passed peacefully away last night. I was with her at the end. I discovered these letters awaiting posting on her bedside table, and took the liberty of opening, but not reading yours, in order to enclose this note.

You will forgive the brevity, I know, because this happened sooner than we thought it would although it was inevitable. I know that she kept the serious nature of her illness from you. She was so determined that you should go to Australia once more.

We will arrange flowers from you and Almond. Alexa will be laid to rest with Lucy.

With love and best wishes,
Matthew

Postscript: On reading the letter Alexa left for me, I have delayed relaying this sad news for a while. She wanted you to seek, and find, your happy ending first. Please let me know that, indeed, you did.

'Mummy, Mummy ...' Almond was plucking at her sleeve. 'Will you read to me?'

Alexa had urged her not to be sad. Resolutely, Molly put the letters back into her bag, and brought out another book. '*The Tailor of Gloucester* – you like that one, don't you?'

'No more twist,' Almond said cheerfully, as the mice said in Beatrix Potter's story.

No more Alexa, Molly thought; but I can't tell Almond that yet, or I really will cry and alarm the whole carriage.

She alighted from the final train, holding tightly on to her daughter, while a helpful man passed out her luggage to the porter. She stood there, blinking as if she had been asleep, praying someone would come. Nancy was right, it was difficult for her to cope on her own.

As she swayed on her feet, a steadying arm went round her shoulders and Rory said quietly: 'Come over here to this seat, you look all in ...'

'Daddy!' Almond squealed in delight.

'Hang on to my other arm,' he told her. 'We must see to your mummy before I give you a great big hug to show how pleased I am to see you. Both of you,' he added.

Molly sipped tea, brought by the porter; Almond raided Rory's pocket for sweets and was not disappointed.

'I'm sorry,' Molly said at last. 'You got my letter, then ...'

'I got all your letters, Molly. I'm sorry I couldn't bring myself to write back.'

'That's all right.'

'No, it isn't. But I had a lot to think about. Do you feel less wobbly? I'll ask the porter to call a cab, shall I?'

'Please.'

'I'm taking you to a hotel – I'll explain later. You'll see Mum very soon, I hope. She sent her love. So did Sarah.'

Oh, she thought. Sarah doesn't want me there, now they're married. I can understand that ...

In the cab, she closed her eyes, leaning away from him. Almond sat on his lap, talking nineteen to the dozen.

'When did you get married?' she heard herself say.

'I haven't, not yet. I've obtained a special licence, though.'

'This isn't a good time for me to come – be honest, Rory?'

'We'll see,' he said. 'Here we are, I hope this meets with your approval. Don't worry about the cost, I did a very good deal with my stones. I guess I'm wealthy for five minutes. Anyway, the Manager is a cousin of mine.'

Molly opened her eyes, allowed herself to be helped from the cab. She stood looking up a grand sweep of steps.

'This must be the best hotel in Melbourne!' she exclaimed.

Rory chuckled as he paid off the driver. 'Not quite, but I haven't stayed anywhere as grand as this before, either.'

'You're staying here, too? I don't understand.'

'I thought it would be nice to spend some time on my own with my daughter – you, too, of course. Can you manage the steps? Feeling better?'

280

'Feeling better . . .' she assured him.

They had connecting rooms. 'I hope you don't mind? This suite is for a family, I'm told,' he commented. 'You'll be sharing with Almond, of course, as there are two beds in this room and only a double in the other. But, look, there are dining facilities in my room, and space for Almond to play. You could have a nice rest before dinner while I amuse her, if you like. Are you sure you're all right?' He looked at her anxiously.

'Rory, I – I've had some bad news. From home. I don't want to talk about it, not now.' She gave a little nod at Almond. 'Where's the bathroom? We both need a good wash and brush up!'

They sat for a while in Rory's room, talking, after Almond was at last in bed and asleep. A firm tucking in by Rory seemed to do the trick.

Molly told him about the letter, and finally the tears gushed forth. He reached out across the table, at which she had elected to sit instead of the sofa, and clasped her hand.

'I'm here for you now, Molly,' was all he said.

When she had composed herself, she asked: 'Are you sure Sarah is happy about you being here with us?'

'No, she isn't happy – how could she be? But, actually, it was her idea . . .'

'I don't understand,' Molly faltered.

'Don't attempt to, not tonight. Why not go to bed now, get some sleep? We'll sort things out properly tomorrow.' He released her hand, stood up. 'Goodnight, Molly.'

She pushed back her chair. 'Goodnight, Rory. And thank you for all this.'

Surprisingly, she fell asleep almost immediately, but she awoke in the early hours when her mind began to work feverishly. Almond already loved her father; he would shortly be married to Sarah. Together, they could surely provide a good and stable background. Could she make the ultimate sacrifice: give her beloved little girl up, in order that she could have two parents?

'I can't,' she said aloud. '*I can't . . .*'

She found herself out of bed, feeling her way across the room to the connecting door. 'I'm here for you, now, Molly,' he'd said, just a few hours ago.

The handle turned, but the door would not open. Rory had locked it, on his side.

She dreamed that she was being kissed, lying back on her pillow; her face cupped by warm hands. She opened her eyes to blink at the brightness of late morning, catching her breath as she realised Rory was there, sitting on the edge of the bed. He leaned towards her, not touching, regarding her solemnly. His breath gently fanned her hair.

'Did you kiss me?' she asked. She pulled at the sheet, to cover her bare shoulders, her confusion. She had slid under the covers last night in her cotton petticoat, feeling too weary to rummage for her nightdress in the case.

He straightened up. 'Yes,' he said simply. Then: 'Almond woke much earlier. We had breakfast together, then my cousin's wife took her off to give her a bath – at Almond's insistence, by the way! You were really exhausted, weren't you, after all that travelling? Changing trains, and trying to be cheerful after the shocking news you'd received, for Almond's sake. You've had a good sleep?'

'Hardly. I was awake most of the night. I don't usually sleep through Almond's alarm call! Did she knock you up?'

'I heard movements from your room, so I opened my door to enquire if you were ready for breakfast when she burst in on me, all smiles, and said she was awfully hungry and Mummy wasn't taking any notice so . . .'

'You decided to let me sleep on . . . I wanted to talk to you in the early hours, Rory. I tried your door, but you'd locked it.' Whatever would he think of her now? she wondered.

'Only because I wasn't sure I could trust myself,' he admitted. 'I didn't want to jump the gun again. What about you?' he suddenly challenged her.

'Me?'

'When we last met, you told me you were sure I was still in love with you. Well, unless I read the signals wrongly, it's the same for you, isn't it?'

'Oh, Rory.' She sat up abruptly, revealing what had been concealed; the taut swell of her bosom visible through fine cotton, as she endeavoured to control her agitated breathing.

'I had it all planned. The licence for the wedding – our wedding, Molly, arranged for three days' time. Sarah told me plainly that was what I should do. Giving me up gracefully, she said, but she wasn't going to give up caring for my mother ... As for caring, she felt she must break Nancy's confidence, make me really aware of all you had to go through when Almond was born; how you were determined to make out on the stage by yourself and succeeded until you decided that Almond and Alexa needed you more ...

'This won't be a shot-gun affair as it would have been the last time I urged you to marry me – we were both too immature then, weren't we? It would never have worked. But after the shock of hearing about Alexa, well, naturally I'll understand if you want to wait a while ...'

'Alexa wouldn't agree, Rory. I'm sure this is what she was hoping for: that you would still be free to marry me; why she insisted I should return here. She'd tell me to stop prevaricating, if I loved you, and—'

'And?'

'I wasn't *sure*, you know, when I said I was, in Madrid, when we made love when we were both so upset ...'

'You are prevaricating!'

'Well, I *am* sure now. I love you, Rory Kelly, and I've been in turmoil ever since I realised that, believing it was too late. But now it's amazing – and three days will seem an eternity, so kiss me properly this time, even though I'm not decently clad, then I'll know I'm not dreaming.'

'Well, I suppose if it stops you babbling and getting all overexcited ...' he said firmly; proving the point in a most satisfactory manner.

'Jumping the gun,' she murmured at last, arms still tight around his neck. 'More like launching myself off a trapeze, whizzing through space and trusting you to catch me by my toes!'

'Strange you should say that – since you came back into my life again, I keep thinking constantly about the circus, remembering what a great time we had ...'

'I've still got my pink tights, holes and all,' she said.

Chapter Nine

'Telegraph came through for you,' Mrs Mac told Nancy. 'From your friend. Like you, my dear, she hasn't wasted any time since she came back here.'

Nancy, pale and puffy-eyed, having shed many tears for Alexa, read the message there and then, thinking wryly there wasn't much point in finding somewhere more private, if Mrs Mac already knew the content.

MR & MRS ARTHUR GRAY.
HAPPIER NEWS. MARRY RORY
THURSDAY.
LETTER FOLLOWS. LOVE WE THREE.
MOLLY.

'Don't forget your groceries,' Mrs Mac reminded her, as Nancy turned to go. The stores door had hardly closed behind her, when the shopkeeper confided in the next lady customer: 'And that won't be the last of the surprises, I reckon . . .'

Art popped in at the house each lunchtime, to make sure she was all right, following the distressing news from England. Nancy found him rummaging in the cupboard for something to eat.

'Sorry, Art,' she said breathlessly, 'but I remembered we had run out of sugar and were almost out of tea, so I ran down to the stores, and Mrs Mac had just received this along the wires – look!'

'*Now* you can manage a smile again, can't you?' he said. 'That's really good news.'

'Alexa would have been so pleased; I just feel, she knows . . .' said Nancy. 'And, Art, I'm almost sure – well, I *am* 'cause I've never been this late before – but I hope it's not too much of a shock, and I'm still going to study and be a teacher some day, I've made my mind up on that . . . *and we're going to have a baby, Art*. Isn't that the best news of all?' Wasn't that just what Alexa had hoped for her? And they wouldn't need to worry whether they could afford it, for she had made that possible, too, with her legacy. As one soul departs, a new one takes its place, Nancy thought . . .

Then he was whooping just like the old full-of-fun Art she'd fallen for in London; lifting her off her feet and whirling her round and kissing her all at the same time. 'Now, you'll have to make me a meat pud, to celebrate, eh?'

Molly couldn't help feeling nervous later that day as Rory opened the door of his mother's house and ushered them in. 'Sarah, we're here!' he called out.

She appeared instantly from the kitchen, and Molly's fears evaporated: Sarah's arms went round her and hugged her warmly. 'Molly dear – Almond – I'm so glad to see you both again; Serena is waiting in the sitting room, all dressed up for the occasion. Go straight in there! I'll bring the tea . . .'

She's keeping busy, Molly thought, her heart going out to her. She's determined not to show how she really feels. It's thanks to Sarah, her generous spirit, that Rory and Almond and I are about to become a real family.

'Here they are, Mum,' Rory said proudly.

'You've got the ring on the right finger at last,' Serena observed. 'It's all turned out for the best: you've got each other, and about time, too. And Sarah, dear girl, has promised not to desert me . . .'

Sitting beside Serena on the sofa, and squeezing her hand, Molly said quietly: 'We owe her a lot, Serena.'

'You do indeed. But I'm not averse to matchmaking, as you know. Remember I've another unmarried son, even if he's mostly burrowing into dark places searching for all that glitters – I tell myself Sam'll have to come up for air one day, eh? Now, Almond, are you going to sit without too much fidgetting on my lap? I wonder, I just might have a surprise for you, in my pocket . . .'

As they drank their tea and ate slices of soft lemon sponge oozing with sweet, buttery fresh-made curd, Sarah asked Molly: 'Will you allow us to have Almond for a couple of days – Thursday and Friday? I promise we'll take great care of her. She could sleep in my room with me. You'll want a little time to yourselves, that's for sure.'

Molly's eyes were misting again. What could she say except a heartfelt: 'Thank you, Sarah.'

It was a civil ceremony, but they both wanted a church blessing later. Molly wore her blue outfit, because Alexa had chosen it with her, and Almond was in the gingham she had worn for Nancy's wedding just a short while before. Sarah had washed and ironed both sets of clothes for them.

Sarah and Serena, who had been determined to make the effort to be there, despite her disabilities, were the witnesses.

Rory's hair was newly cut; he wore a smart, unfamiliar suit. The wedding ring he slid on Molly's finger was fashioned from Kimberley gold. There was no music, no singing, but plenty of flowers and smiling faces.

Back at the hotel, Rory's relatives laid on a special lunch of several courses but Molly couldn't have said afterwards what she had eaten, if anything, apart from a sweet meringue filled with fresh cream which she shared with

Almond. It all seemed surreal, as if she was drifting in one of her dreams.

She hugged and kissed her daughter and told her to be good for her grandma and Sarah. Almond was impatient to be gone now. She had been promised some surprises back at Serena's. She couldn't understand why her mother was blubbing when it was supposed to be a happy day.

''Bye, Mummy!' she said. 'See you Saturday!'

'It's all right, Molly, really it is,' Sarah whispered, for her ears only. 'Don't worry about Almond – we'll spoil her between us, of course.'

'Thank you, Sarah, for everything,' Molly whispered back.

'Serena's flagging a bit, bless her, better go,' the other girl said, and turned quickly before Molly could tell from her eyes how she really felt.

The maid had turned down the double bed. Molly undressed in the room she had shared with Almond, gave her hair a perfunctory brush, slipped into the exotically embroidered silk wrapper which was Rory's wedding gift to her.

She rattled the knob on the connecting door.

'It's open tonight!' he called.

'Do I meet with your approval? she asked, indicating the wrapper. 'It's lovely, Rory, you couldn't have chosen anything nicer.'

'I do approve – though I see you've had to roll the sleeves up. And I'm really pleased with my slippers, too.'

'I bought them at Alexa's shop, before it closed. I wondered why afterwards.' They were too small for Matthew, she thought, blushing, so I tucked them away, 'just in case' ... She concluded lamely: 'But I suppose I kept them for you. Rory—'

'Mmm?'

'Turn your back for a moment, will you? Don't ask why!'

'Can Molly Sparkes-as-was actually be feeling shy?' he mocked fondly, as she checked that the edges of the silk had not parted. But he turned tactfully as she requested. Quickly, she draped the silk wrapper over the back of a chair, then almost leapt into the high bed.

Rory regarded her; just her face visible over the fold of the linen sheet. 'You look as if you're ready to go to sleep,' he joked. 'Would you like me to turn out the light?' he added.

'Please,' she said demurely. Then she giggled. 'I didn't know you wore nightshirts – 'specially red and white stripes.'

'There's a great deal you'll find out shortly, no doubt.'

'Nothing to what you'll discover about me,' Molly said airily, anticipating his reaction, but wondering belatedly if she'd been too rash.

They were both under the covers now, the curtains at the window effectively shutting out any vestige of light.

Molly touched his shoulder. 'You're all trembly,' she said softly. 'But then, so am I . . . Put your arms round me, Rory, so I know I'm here, and you're here. Besides, I'm cold – I need warming up.'

'What are you wearing, Molly?' he asked as he obediently cuddled her close. She could picture his look of incredulity as the truth dawned.

'Not much,' she admitted. 'Well, actually, nothing at all. Sorry! As always I acted on impulse. I hope you don't mind, as you're covered in that thick flannel?'

'I didn't—'

'Want to jump the gun?'

'Want to take too much for granted. I suppose I didn't give you a chance to think twice about marrying me, after all.'

'You're not going to worry about that all night, are you, Rory Kelly? D'you want me as I am, or what?'

'As you are now,' he said simply.

*

289

'What fools we were, parting like that,' he said, next morning. He very gently traced the outline of the scar on her stomach. 'Remember what one night of passion can do.'

'I don't care, I love you! If it happens, well, it happens, Rory Kelly . . .'

'Sarah would advise you, I know. Not from experience, of course, but because she's a nurse . . . Will you talk to her, Molly?' he suggested diffidently.

'I might. Nothing – happened between you two, then? Oh, I wouldn't blame you, darling Rory, if it had. I've no right to do that.'

'Nothing happened. I'm not saying I wasn't tempted but I channelled all my energy into digging pits and gem-seeking,' he said ruefully. 'Which reminds me, I can't expect you and Almond to join me in that way of life. And I can't expect you to stay here, living with my mother and Sarah, waiting for me to come back, now and then; it just wouldn't be fair. This is one thing we haven't discussed, isn't it? Suppose you had been thinking I would come back with you to the old country—'

'Suppose I did want that: would you agree?'

'Yes, if it made you happy. That's all that matters to me now.'

'Well, I feel exactly the same. Being with you, sharing Almond with you, is all I want . . . Now that Alexa has gone, I am in no hurry to go back. Let's go and see Cora and Thom – find out if there is any possibility of us teaming up with them again.'

'What about Almond?' he reminded her.

'She'll take to it like a duck to water – look who her parents are!'

'Well, as long as you don't get pregnant again too quickly.'

'Rory, Alexa gave me a bit of advice after Almond, in case I ever, you know, needed it in the future. Not that I ever put it into practice; after what you said about you and

290

Sarah, I want you to know that – I wasn't going to say – but I *did* remember it last night . . .'

'Just one thing,' he said, lifting the strands of hair clinging round her neck. 'No short haircuts, *no more Monty.*'

'Just Kelly and Sparkes,' she said happily.

'I must write to Matthew,' she told Rory, before they left for Adelaide, to meet up with Thom and Cora. 'He must wonder why he hasn't heard from me, after all.'

He looked at her in a speculative way. 'I know you grew fond of him, having cared for his daughter – as I did of Sarah who cared for my mother. You had so much in common – did he hope for more, d'you think?'

'Yes, I know he did . . . Alexa would have liked that, too, but she also knew, better than I did, where I would eventually find fulfilment and contentment. He's so nice, Rory, I hope he doesn't feel I've let him down.'

'It seems to me from his letter that what he most wanted for you was your happiness, Molly. Yes, write to him, you owe him that. Do it now, while you think of it.'

'I'll show you the letter,' she offered.

'I trust you, Molly, no need for that,' he said. 'I'd better go and relieve poor Mother of entertaining our little Almond.'

Dear Matthew,

The news from you came as a great shock, as you can imagine. The letter from Alexa meant so much in those sad circumstances. I will never, ever forget her and all she did for me over the years. I was privileged to know her and will miss her so much.

Your letter, too, is one I shall always treasure. You and Fay are very special to me, and to Almond. I believe you will understand and be happy for us when you hear that Rory and I have married; I really know my own mind at long last.

We are staying out here in Australia: rejoining the

circus – it is all such a challenge, and so exciting. One day, dear Matthew, I know we will see each other again. Wherever I am, I promise I will always keep in touch – you will certainly add to your postcard collection!

I do care for you, you know – oh, not in the way you might have hoped, but I'm glad we met.

Much love from me and from Almond. Rory sends his best,

Your 'little sister',

Molly Kelly (Sparkes)

Then she dipped her pen again in the ink bottle to write to her father and Madelaine.

'Why are you looking sad, Daddy?' Fay asked her father. She squeezed his hand to comfort him. It was nearing the end of the summer holiday, and they were enjoying a lazy afternoon in the garden at Wren's Nest. The letter had come by the afternoon post. 'Are you missing Granny?' she added.

He nodded. 'That's it. Where's your tennis racquet? Shall we have a game?' She was getting long and leggy now she'd turned seven; she was athletic and had a good eye for aiming a ball. He was fortunate, he thought. Fay and he were good companions, despite the lack of a mother and wife in their life.

'That old net you found in the shed's got lots of holes in it,' she told him.

'You're supposed to lob the ball over the net, not through it.' He smiled.

'All right, I know! Daddy—'

'Yes?'

'I wish – I wish that Molly and Nancy and Almond hadn't gone away.'

'So do I, darling. So do I.'

'If it's a girl, Art, would you mind if we name her for Alexa?'

'I wouldn't mind at all,' he said. 'I was fond of her, too, you know – even if I was in awe of her when I worked for her! What if the baby's a boy?'

'Alec, I suppose. D'you like that?'

'Alec Arthur Gray – sound all right to you?'

'Yes – and Alexandra Nancy, I suppose . . .'

'What's your ma's christian name?' he asked.

'Rose, why?'

'Alexandra Nancy Rose, that's why!'

'Art, darling, Ma'd love that!'

'Lucky it's my mum's name, too.' He grinned. 'Have you told Elfie and Ernst yet?'

'Well, I thought you—'

'That's women's stuff. Put 'em all out of their suspense, Nancy. Despite your not showing yet, the settlement's full of speculation – I get my leg pulled when I go out for a beer, you know.'

'Molly's made her mind up not to follow my example. She wants to get back into training as soon as she can.'

'Well, they've got Almond, haven't they? She's quite a handful.'

'And I've got you, and I see quite a bit of Ma, and I never thought that'd happen, but I'm sorry, of course, we're so far from your dear mum – and a baby to come. I'm *so* happy, Art.'

'So am I – come here,' he said. One day, he determined, they'd visit his family again; maybe not until they had a sizeable family themselves, and Mum would be so proud and say she always knew he and Nancy would get together one of these days.

'I wonder what Molly's up to at this very moment . . .' Nancy said dreamily, before his kisses distracted her.

'Can't you guess?' he said, making her giggle when he raised his eyebrows just like George Robey had at the music hall years ago.

Rory massaged Molly's back with warm oil. His fingers

slid over her supple skin as he located the sore spots.

She lay on her front on the caravan bunk. 'Ooh, that's better, Rory – I thought I'd never stand up straight again after Thom's merciless cracking of the whip . . .' She rolled over on the towel. 'We've got half an hour before Cora brings Almond back,' she said invitingly.

He poured more oil into his palms, rubbed his hands together. 'You know what I love most about you, Molly Sparkes?'

'Molly Kelly – remember? What?'

'You always act on impulse,' he said. 'Roll back over. I haven't finished the massage yet . . . You always fended off my ardour in the early days – remember? You must be fresh and fit for tonight; our first appearance in the ring as a married couple, don't forget.'

'I'm sure it's something I'll never forget,' she said, softly.

The magic of the sawdust, the rosin, the ring, was still there. Sure-footed, Molly performed on the bouncing rope. She sparkled with spangles, sequins and rhinestones. She played to the audience, but most of all, to Almond, peeping round the flap of the canvas, holding on to the studded collar of one of the big black poodles, while Cora gamely held on to her.

She and Rory took their bows, glancing happily at each other.

'We're back, Rory,' Molly breathed, 'it's as if we were never away.'

Chapter Ten

1914

The circus was back in town: in the very place where Molly and Rory had met seven years before. It all seemed the same – the billowing canvas, flaring lights and steam; colours, music *con brio*; the clowns and acrobats; animals, great and small; the flying trapeze, the snaking ropes; the unpredictable and the expected: timeless. But of course it wasn't. The petrol engine was slowly superseding the horse. The circus even smelled different; there were tell-tale patches of oil on the grass when it moved on.

Rory and Thom were well aware of the need for fresh routines while retaining the highlights of the old, the thrills and near-misses which made the audience gasp or laugh. The practice sessions were as rigorous as ever; Thom still a demanding taskmaster.

Five year old Almond, bright and demanding, needed the discipline of school. They would soon have to send her away, let her board: her parents dreaded the thought. For now, while Molly was busy rehearsing and appearing with the Kellys, in her spangles and tights, the little girl stayed with Cora and the dogs. Three hours a day were set aside for elementary lessons; the hardest thing for Almond to learn was to sit still and concentrate, she was spilling over with energy and questions.

Molly smiled, recalling last night's surprise performance,

when Almond, wearing a sequinned costume sewn for her by doting Aun Cora, proudly led the performing poodles into the ring; waving regally to the audience and obviously loving the cheering and clapping. No wonder she was taking a pre-lunch nap today. Molly glanced over at the far bunk where her daughter had curled up, still in her circus outfit, for she had refused to take it off at bedtime yesterday. Fallen in action ... she thought.

Molly and Cora were in the older couple's caravan, relaxing over mugs of strong, sugared tea and succulent ham sandwiches. Rory and Thom were still checking the equipment for the first show of the day.

'Two years – I can hardly believe it's our anniversary coming up: July almost over, and it'll be August ... 1914 is slipping away fast,' Molly mused. She flipped her long plait over her shoulder, the end having dipped into her tea. Cora still darned her tights and Rory sewed on any loose buttons. They spoil me, she thought, revelling in it.

'No one would believe you were the mother of a growing daughter,' Cora mildly reproved her as a brown stain spread on the sleeve of her white blouse. She dabbed at it with a dampened end of a tea towel. Then added bluntly: 'When are you going to provide her with a little brother or sister, Molly? She could do with a bit of competition.'

Molly could still blush. 'Not yet, Cora. I'm enjoying being part of the act too much ...' She didn't usually confide intimately in Cora as she had in Nancy or Alexa in the past.

'Your friend Nancy's very contented with her two babies,' Cora reminded her slyly.

Molly, to her disappointment, hadn't yet seen Alec, already fifteen months old, or the new baby, Nancy Rose, whose arrival had just been announced. Maybe she was just a little jealous that Elfie and Ernst saw so much of them. 'Nancy's still determined to become a teacher despite the demands of motherhood,' she reminded Cora. 'You should understand, having always been a working woman.'

'Ah, but I wasn't a mother, was I? When I met Thom I was already in my late-thirties. We hoped, but it wasn't to be. My dogs are my family. I don't waste time on regrets. Thom and I are very close.'

'So are we – Rory and I are like bread and butter, you know that. Anyway, he says war is inevitable, after that dreadful business at Sarajevo in Serbia last June, when that Archduke and his wife were killed. Rory says . . .'

'What do I say?' he asked, stepping up into the caravan.

'You say Australia will be bound to get involved this time, with the Old Country threatened in Europe.'

'And like most other patriotic young chaps I'll be joining up to fight the minute we're called on, which I'm sure we will be. They're already rallying sportsmen, in the peak of fitness, so I reckon they'll welcome athletes like me, even if we were trained in the circus.'

'You didn't say that before.' Molly bit her lip, feeling suddenly anxious.

'Didn't I? We can't let 'em get away with it. We can't let the enemy on to British soil. And we won't,' he stated decisively.

'I only meant, well, it could turn everything upside down, a war, even if it isn't here, and – maybe, we should wait and see . . .' Molly floundered, giving a little warning shake of her head at Cora. Don't mention babies . . .

'No, it's not here – not now – but when it spreads to the East, we'll be more than ready.'

Grim talk: Molly hated it. 'Eat your sandwich, Rory, I'm going back to our 'van to wash my hair, it's sticky from the sugar in the tea,' she said. He raised his eyebrows but she didn't elucidate. 'All right if Almond stays with you, Cora, 'til she wakes up?'

'Of course. Like me to make a cake for your special day?'

'Oh, please! She means our anniversary, Rory.' She saw him visibly relax, smile at her.

'As if I could forget, with all your heavy hints,' he said

affectionately, as she squeezed past him to the door. 'I'll join you in a minute.' His hand lightly caressed her bare arm. He could still make her go all weak at the knees with his touch. She instantly got the message. We're still catching up, she thought; making up for all the time we've wasted, been apart.

'I'll make it a quick wash then,' she whispered in his ear.

By April 1915 Molly and Almond had been back some months with Serena and Sarah, now Mrs Sam Kelly, in the house in Melbourne. Almond was doing well at the local day school, after a rebellious start, and Sarah was newly, and euphorically, pregnant. She looked beautiful, shining, her hair was thick and glossy, she couldn't stop beaming. It was a pity Sam was not here to appreciate it. He'd always kept in the background when his brother was in the running to marry Sarah, but now he'd come into his own. Sam was older than Rory, somewhat phlegmatic, but you could tell he was Rory's brother, Molly thought: once he'd decided to marry Sarah he'd proved to her emphatically that he wasn't second-best ... He'd made her bloom, that was the only word for it.

Serena, of course, considered the marriage was all her doing, and that now Sarah really was part of her family as she had always hoped she would be. Sam and Sarah had been privileged to have what Serena called, with satisfaction, a proper wedding: nuptial mass, a white dress, veil, hot-house flowers and showerings of rose petals. Molly remembered wistfully how she and Rory had talked of a church blessing for themselves, but somehow never got around to it.

Molly was pregnant, too. Just three weeks off giving birth. She hadn't seen Rory since the end of last year. Longing for his presence, his support, for a comforting hand rubbing her aching back, caused her tearful nights, though she believed he would have a shock if he saw her like this. It was ironical that he should miss out on both her pregnancies. Mind you, he was much more excited about the new baby than she was, already mapping out a circus career for it – what else? They were set on a son this time and naming him Rory the second.

She was glad she hadn't brought that shiny pink maternity dress to Australia, she looked pasty-faced and unattractive enough as it was; lumbering not limbering nowadays, she lamented to herself. Despite the affection lavished on her by her new family, she wished Nancy was with her – she missed Alexa still . . .

She knew exactly when she had conceived, of course. The afternoon they'd talked of anniversary cake and war; when she'd felt so fearful that Rory would leave her and go off to fight a world away; when her hair had hung in a dripping wet curtain but not dampened their ardour; when she threw caution to the winds . . . There was always a price to pay for passion, for impetuosity. But it was a sublime coming together, a time she would never forget, even in old age.

It was small consolation to her to know that Nancy was second in the expectant mother stakes. Things always came in threes, Molly mused. Art had enlisted in the Australian Imperial Force soon after Rory, and now Sam was in the Army, too, with the second wave of older men.

Their Russian allies were in desperate straits due to Turkey entering the conflict; the naval attack on the Dardanelles had failed, and although they could not know that, the 'diggers' of Australia and New Zealand, the fearless Colonials, were about to be immortalised at Gallipoli . . .

Nancy, six months pregnant, was capably assisting Ernst at the school, firmly intending to do so until the first sign of labour, while Elfie, amazingly, coped with the little Grays one and two. She wheeled them along to the school yard each day at the noon break, and the schoolchildren crowded round the perambulator to amuse them. Sometimes,

Nancy's mother slipped away from home and came to the mission house to relieve Elfie for an hour.

In her latest letter to Molly, Nancy wrote: 'I'm a working mother, and I always will be – I love both parts of my life, but I do miss dearest Art more than I can say ...'

Every evening, when the little ones were in bed, she sat resolutely at the table, poring over his books.

She had produced the other babies remarkably easily; Art, despite the midwife's misgivings, had been with her throughout each labour. She could conjure up the soothing sensation, the reassurance transmitted as he stroked back her damp hair; his sharply drawn breath, then his shout of joy as their children emerged into the world. He wouldn't be with her this time, she thought, as the new baby kicked and protested when she bent over her studies; so weary that she found herself reading the same sentence over and over.

Tonight, hot tears welled in her eyes. She slumped, head in hands. How was Molly managing without her support? she wondered.

She'd left the door on the latch, in case Ma managed to come.

Her thin arm slid comfortingly round her daughter's shaking shoulders.

'Oh, Ma ...' she wept.

'Shush, dearie, you'll wake the little ones. Fancy a nice cup of tea? I'm staying with you, Nancy.'

'Dad—'

'I told him: "I'm leaving you. I oughter done it years ago. I'll look in on you now and again, to make sure you're all right. I didn't do right by Nancy all them years ago, and I'm going to make up for it now; she needs me, with her husband away." He took it meek, Nancy – he knows I mean what I say nowadays. You coming home when you did give me strength to stand against him, you see. Now close them books. Off to bed with you!'

'Oh, Ma, did I ever say I love you?'

'You didn't have to, dearie, I knew all right ...'

300

'Ma, I'll go to bed, but I must write to Art, I always do.'
'You do that, dearie. He's pure gold, your Art, and so are you.'

Molly kept her fears about the possibility of another caesarean to herself. Sarah reassured her that all seemed to be well this time. No danger signals indicating a premature birth.

'You're lucky, you've got your own private nurse, after all,' she joked, to keep Molly's spirits up, and unconsciously patted her own delicious secret, discreetly concealed by her apron.

'I know I won't hurt your feelings, Sarah, when I say this, but I wish Nancy was here.'

'She's got enough on her own plate, Molly. Three babies in as many years, eh? Not that I'd mind one bit if I followed her example!'

'*I* would,' Molly said with feeling. She quickly quashed the slight resentment at the thought that Rory was so excited about the new baby because he had no idea what she was about to go through.

On 25th April, the first landings were made on the peninsula. The troops were smartly deployed on the beach below the steep cliffs, immediately dubbed the Folkestone Leas, because of its strange resemblance to that very English resort in Kent before the growth of the town overlooking the sea. It was a place Art had never visited, but Molly, who had, would have thought the same.

The men were backed by the fiercely blazing guns of the warships from which they had disembarked; digging trenches, dressing stations; massing field guns, equipment, pack animals, and stockpiling provisions. A cheer went up when a plentiful supply of fresh water was discovered on the foreshore. When they were entrenched, the vital communication links would begin with the laying of wires. But all the while they were being bombarded by shells from the enemy above. Bullets hit and caused a continuous spray of water, soaking all in the vicinity. The noise was incredible, ear-splitting in intensity and ferocity.

Two days later, Privates Rory and Sam Kelly, along with other pioneers, scrabbled and scrambled heroically up the cliff-face finding footholds; clinging to scrub, hauling themselves to the ridges, giving priority to digging the essential bombproof shelters; marking out the first rudimentary roads, while the bullets whistled round their heads . . . Some, inevitably, found their mark.

Molly was at long last in the final stage of labour, after a pain-filled forty-eight-hour struggle. Sweat poured off her as she clung desperately to the knotted sheet dangling above her from the bedhead. She stifled her moans as best she could, not wanting Almond, downstairs with Serena, to hear was was going on.

'It's coming – not long now,' Sarah tried to comfort her, hoping that Molly could not see the fear in her own eyes. Should she have called the doctor before now – he was on his way – would all this effort and suffering be wasted? Would Molly have to be rushed to hospital as she had when Almond was born?

Molly was hallucinating: Rory was with her, supporting her. He was telling her to lean on him, to be brave, to give an almighty push when the next wave of pain intensified its grip. She tilted her chin, trying to see his face. '*Now!*' he shouted.

Where was that terrible groaning emanating from? '*Rory, help me!*' she screamed.

At the other end of the bed, Sarah caught the slithery little body as it was propelled forward, held the baby up and massaged it fiercely until it gave its first indignant cry.

Molly lay back, shaking so that the bed actually rocked, as Sarah snipped and tied the cord. Then, she laid the tiny bundle, wrapped in sheeting, on her breast, and placed her tired arms round it.

'Another little girl, Molly dear – well done! I'm so proud of you . . . What are you going to call her, I wonder?'

'Rory—' Molly said faintly, as the door opened and the doctor came in, taking in the situation at a glance.

'No, dearie, you know he'd be here if he could, but it's not possible. A name for the baby, I meant.'

'Rory.' Molly said, clearly this time. 'I know she's a girl, but it's what *he* wants me to call her . . .'

'Take the baby,' the doctor ordered Sarah. He rolled up his sleeves, soaped his hands in the water in the bowl she had put ready. 'I'll see to the rest. She's bleeding badly, and she'll need stitching. She's in shock: we're in danger of losing her. We'll need to get her to hospital as soon as we can.'

Sarah, shocked herself, went out on to the landing with the baby, cradled in her arms. She saw two anxious faces looking up at her from the foot of the stairs; young Almond supporting her grandmother, with her arm round her waist. It was a real effort for her to smile now. Almond looked so like Rory at this moment.

'You've got a little sister, Almond, you can both see her properly soon. She's got really red hair, bless her. And – her name is Rory . . .'

'He's gone,' Molly managed, as they wrapped her, much as Sarah had swaddled the baby, ready for the journey ahead. '*He's gone, Sarah.*'

Ma opened the door, in some trepidation, because it was well past midnight. She'd woken up when she heard the rumbling of the wheels outside. A solider on the cart jumped down and lugged over a heavy kitbag to the schoolhouse. 'It's a long way to Tipperary, mate – won't stop – all the best. You're out of it, now.'

'It's me, Ma,' Art said.

'Art, whatever are you doin' here?' she exclaimed. 'You been wounded?'

'I'd feel better about it if I had . . . Aren't you going to let me in, Ma?'

She turned up the lamp. 'I'll put the kettle on. Wake Nancy gently, mind. She don't want a fright in her condition.'

But Nancy had heard. She came out of the bedroom, supporting the small of her back with one hand, the other outstretched towards him.

'Yes, it's me, Nancy ... Don't I deserve a kiss?'

'I'm coming as quick as I can!' she said wryly.

'I got bad pains in my chest,' he told them as he held Nancy close to him on the sofa. 'They decreed I've got a weak heart – must be due to that rheumatic fever I had as a child. Why they never picked up on it when I had my medical, I'll never know ... They had me in hospital for several weeks, then I got my discharge.'

'And we thought you were out, you know, with our boys at Gallipoli ... Oh, I was so frightened, Art!'

'Well, I guess you can do with me at home, eh?' He gently patted her rounded belly. 'I'm proud of you for all you've done, with the children and the school while I've been away. But now I can make things easier for you.'

'Are you all right, Art?' she asked anxiously.

'They say I'm fit enough to teach, even if I'm not up to fighting; they even say it's the ideal occupation for me, so you don't need to worry, old girl.'

Nancy couldn't get to sleep again after they were in bed. Ma had promised to let Ernst know first thing that Art was back, but that neither of them would be in school next day – just one day off, Nancy insisted, for her.

She rested her head against his shoulder. Her prayers for his safety had been answered, she thought, if not in the way she had expected. But what of Molly, who must be about to give birth without Rory by her side?

Epilogue

1920

The school hall, with its rows of chairs, was already full of chattering parents and relatives when they arrived. The end of summer term concert was the highlight of the school year. They had hung on at home until the very last minute for Molly, then decided to go without her. He had scribbled a brief note: *See you there!* and hoped for the best.

The dusty orange velvet curtains masking the activity on stage twitched continually and now and then a beaming face was glimpsed through the centre gap. Three minutes to curtain call, to dimming the audience lights, to illuminating the stage, to striking up the opening music. Already, the girls in the school orchestra were making discordant noises with their instruments, as they tuned-up.

'Molly Sparkes!' Sister Margaret Mary exclaimed. 'Late as usual.' She ushered Molly through the door. 'Over there – that spare seat on the end of the row, see?'

'I see.' Molly smiled. She dared to give her favourite teacher a quick hug. 'Sorry about the last-minute arrival, but I had a flying lesson this afternoon and it took me hours longer than I expected to get home because I had to change a flat tyre ...' She held out her hands for inspection to prove she'd scrubbed them since. 'Remember your hands are always on show, Molly Sparkes – keep them clean.'

'Shush!' reproved a parent nearby. 'Curtain's just going up ...'

Sister Margaret Mary gave the oustretched hands a tap. She smiled at the elegant young woman in her short-skirted, sleeveless blue silk frock, with silver bangles on her tanned arms. Bobbed hair, tucked behind her ears, revealed sparkling sapphire studs. 'Tell me all in the interval,' Sister Margaret Mary whispered. 'Your girls are nervous but they'll do well, I'm sure,' she whispered.

Molly slipped into the seat next to her younger daughter Rory.

'We thought you weren't going to make it,' she hissed.

'Oh, Molly ...' he sighed, on Rory's other side.

'Wouldn't miss it,' Molly returned. The lights went down, the curtains swished, the overture commenced rather uncertainly, and she couldn't make head nor tail of the print on the folded sheet.

'Number six, Mummy,' Rory tugged at her arm. 'TWO BRIGHT SPARKS.'

'Oh do hush!' was the exasperated caution from behind.

It was a year since the Kellys had come home from Australia, to Alexa's converted cottage attached to Wren's Nest.

Despite the disparity in their ages: Fay was fifteen and Almond eleven, the older girls got on like a house on fire. They boarded at Molly's old school during the week and came home at weekends.

Molly didn't want to part with little Rory yet: perhaps next year, she thought, when she's six ... Almond seemed to have grown up, become independent so quickly; Rory was quieter, more clinging. She certainly did not live up to the promise of that flaming hair! She was very special to her mother because of the sad circumstances of her arrival.

For months after her birth Molly had been very low both physically and mentally. Looking back she wondered now how she had come through. But when Sarah had her own baby, a boy, she made a tremendous effort to get back to normal, to care properly for her daughters on her own. She told herself she must, for Sarah and Serena's sake. They had been so good to her and the girls. When the four years of war were over and Sam was home, she decided it was time to leave. Sam needed to get to know his own little son, not to have to take on responsibility for his brother's children as well, she told him firmly.

She hadn't seen her dear friend Nancy during the war, and couldn't go back to England without visiting her, Art and their family first. After two weeks, Nancy had bidden her an emotional farewell. 'We'll be back again one day, I promise!' Molly choked, but even as she said it, she wondered if she would ... Nancy had Art still, her life was good; Molly was glad for her. Their friendship would outlast any separation, she was positive.

Now, she was beginning to live her own life to the full again. It was as if she had woken up from a long, dreaming sleep. She bought new clothes, cut her long hair, drove her little car at speed. The flying lessons were Matthew's idea: her father paid for them as a birthday present. She didn't have to work, because of Alexa's bequest, but lately she had begun to make plans in that direction. The circus, the music hall, even the House of Leather, were all in the past – but there must be some sphere in which she could sparkle!

The spotlight followed the two girls, one tall, one small, in their comic routine. They had enjoyed expert tuition.

Spangles and tights, cartwheels and splits; Molly's eyes misted as she thought of the circus days and Rory. She had believed when she'd lost him that there would be no more men in her life.

The applause seemed to go on for ever, for the TWO BRIGHT SPARKS, then the lights snapped on for the interval.

'Please – can I go backstage and see the girls?' Rory begged.

'Go on, then,' Molly agreed. 'But come back in good time for the second half.'

She moved along into Rory's vacated seat. She noticed the man next to her looking at her with some concern. 'Molly, are you all right?' he asked. 'We were worried about you when you didn't arrive home in time, imagined all sorts of awful things – you're not crying, are you?'

'Just old memories, that's all . . .' she said softly.

When they'd met again, after all those years, they were immediately on the old friendly footing. She knew what he was hoping for, but she wasn't ready for that, quite yet. The children loved him, her father approved, of course, but for now, she was content with her lot. Or so she'd imagined.

'There's no one like you, there never will be for me,' he murmured, so that she had to strain her ears to hear.

She turned to smile at him. 'Dear Matthew, don't *ever* give up on me, will you?' she said.

Now he'd know he had a good chance . . .

'Do watch the children, Art,' Nancy requested.

'Shall I take them along for a game of deck quoits?' he asked. 'Then you can have a bit of peace and quiet, write your letters or have a snooze.'

They were on the way home to England at last. Maybe the thought that Molly was already there had prompted the decision; or the fact that Ernst had recently retired, and he and Elfie had moved away, 'to civilisation', as she put it. Then there was the young, enthusiastic new pastor, who was also headmaster of the mission school. They had lost Nancy's ma during the war; Nancy had been 'home for years – it's your turn, now,' she generously told her husband. 'We've got the nest-egg you always refuse to let me touch, to see us through. I think Alexa would be pleased if we used it in this way, don't you?'

'I won't write to Molly,' she said now. 'I want to surprise them . . .'

You'll do that, Art thought. The two girls were tussling over a balloon. 'Let it go, then maybe you'll be satisfied,' he admonished them, removing Mary Ellen, known as Molly, from Nancy Rose's grasp.

'Come on, Dad!' Alec cried impatiently.

'Look!' Art pointed.

The balloon hovered above them, as they watched, standing on the ship's deck; its string dancing in the current of air, then it wafted upwards.

'It might reach the stars,' little Molly imagined, entranced.

'You would think that,' Nancy Rose scoffed.

'Oh, it could,' Nancy reproved her. '*I know.*'